MISTRESS *of the*
ART *of* DEATH

ALSO BY ARIANA FRANKLIN

City of Shadows

MISTRESS *of the*

ART *of* DEATH

Ariana Franklin

G. P. Putnam's Sons
New York

G. P. PUTNAM'S SONS
Publishers Since 1838
Published by the Penguin Group
Penguin Group (USA) Inc., 375 Hudson Street, New York, New York 10014, USA ·
Penguin Group (Canada), 90 Eglinton Avenue East, Suite 700, Toronto, Ontario
M4P 2Y3, Canada (a division of Pearson Penguin Canada Inc.) · Penguin Books Ltd,
80 Strand, London WC2R 0RL, England · Penguin Ireland, 25 St Stephen's
Green, Dublin 2, Ireland (a division of Penguin Books Ltd) · Penguin Group
(Australia), 250 Camberwell Road, Camberwell, Victoria 3124, Australia
(a division of Pearson Australia Group Pty Ltd) · Penguin Books India Pvt Ltd,
11 Community Centre, Panchsheel Park, New Delhi—110 017, India · Penguin
Group (NZ), 67 Apollo Drive, Mairangi Bay, Auckland 1311,
New Zealand (a division of Pearson New Zealand Ltd.) · Penguin Books (South
Africa) (Pty) Ltd, 24 Sturdee Avenue, Rosebank, Johannesburg 2196, South Africa

Penguin Books Ltd, Registered Offices:
80 Strand, London WC2R 0RL, England

Copyright © 2007 by Ariana Franklin
All rights reserved. No part of this book may be reproduced, scanned, or distrib-
uted in any printed or electronic form without permission. Please do not partici-
pate in or encourage piracy of copyrighted materials in violation of the author's
rights. Purchase only authorized editions.
Published simultaneously in Canada

Library of Congress Cataloging-in-Publication Data

Franklin, Ariana.
Mistress of the art of death / Ariana Franklin.
p.   cm.
ISBN-13: 978-0-399-15414-0
ISBN-10: 0-399-15414-0
1. Historical fiction.   2. Suspense fiction.   I. Title.
PR6064.073M57   2007   2006024710
823'.92—dc22

Printed in the United States of America
1   3   5   7   9   10   8   6   4   2

BOOK DESIGN BY VICTORIA KUSKOWSKI

Frontmatter map by Red Lion

This is a work of fiction. Names, characters, places, and incidents either are the
product of the author's imagination or are used fictitiously, and any resemblance to
actual persons, living or dead, businesses, companies, events, or locales is entirely co-
incidental.

While the author has made every effort to provide accurate telephone numbers and
Internet addresses at the time of publication, neither the publisher nor the author
assumes any responsibility for errors, or for changes that occur after publication.
Further, the publisher does not have any control over and does not assume any responsibility for author or third-party websites or their content.

To Helen Heller,

Mistress of the art of thrillers

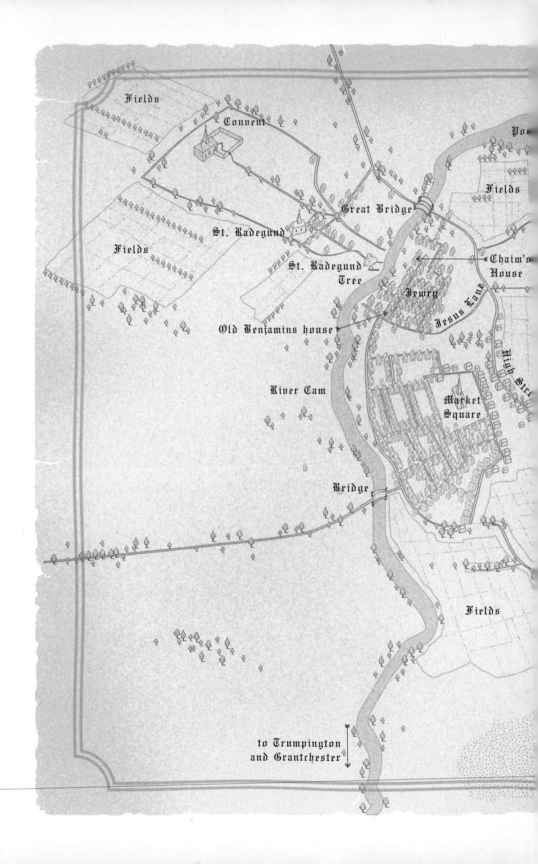

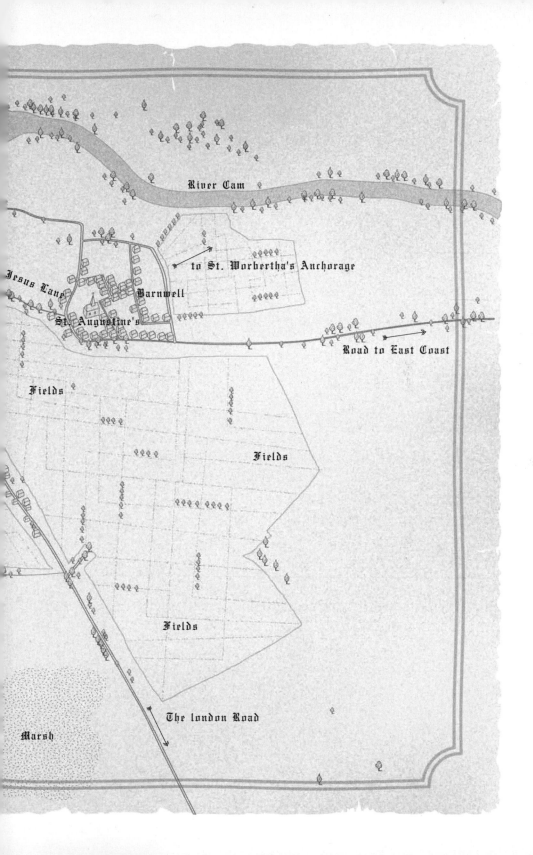

One

ENGLAND, 1171

Here they come. From down the road we can hear harnesses jingling and see dust rising into the warm spring sky.

Pilgrims returning after Easter in Canterbury. Tokens of the mitered, martyred Saint Thomas are pinned to cloaks and hats—the Canterbury monks must be raking it in.

They're a pleasant interruption in the traffic of carts whose drivers and oxen are surly with fatigue from plowing and sowing. These people are well fed, noisy, exultant with the grace their journey has gained them.

But one of them, as exuberant as the rest, is a murderer of children. God's grace will not extend to a child-killer.

The woman at the front of the procession—a big woman on a big roan mare—has a silver token pinned to her wimple. We know her. She's the prioress of Saint Radegund's nunnery in Cambridge. She's talking. Loudly. Her accompanying nun, on a docile palfrey, is silent and has been able to afford only Thomas à Becket in pewter.

The tall knight riding between them on a well-controlled charger—

he wears a tabard over his mail with a cross showing that he's been on crusade, and, like the prioress, he's laid out on silver—makes sotto voce commentaries on the prioress's pronouncements. The prioress doesn't hear them, but they cause the young nun to smile. Nervously.

Behind this group is a flat cart drawn by mules. The cart carries a single object; rectangular, somewhat small for the space it occupies—the knight and squire seem to be guarding it. It's covered by a cloth with armorial bearings. The jiggling of the cart is dislodging the cloth, revealing a corner of carved gold—either a large reliquary or a small coffin. The squire leans from his horse and pulls the cloth straight so that the object is hidden again.

And here's a king's officer. Jovial enough, large, overweight for his age, dressed like a civilian, but you can tell. For one thing, his servant is wearing the royal tabard embroidered with the Angevin leopards and, for another, poking out of his overloaded saddlebag is an abacus and the sharp end of a pair of money scales.

Apart from the servant, he rides alone. Nobody likes a tax gatherer.

Now then, here's a prior. We know him, too, from the violet rochet he wears, as do all canons of Saint Augustine.

Important. Prior Geoffrey of Saint Augustine's, Barnwell, the monastery that looks across the great bend of the River Cam opposite Saint Radegund's and dwarfs it. It is understood that he and the prioress don't get on. He has three monks in attendance, and also a knight—another crusader, judging from his tabard—and a squire.

Oh, he's ill. He should be at the procession's front, but it seems his guts—which are considerable—are giving him pain. He's groaning and ignoring a tonsured cleric who's trying to engage his attention. Poor man, there's no help for him on this stretch, not even an inn, until he reaches his own infirmary in the priory grounds.

A beef-faced citizen and his wife, both showing concern for the prior and giving advice to his monks. A minstrel, singing to a lute. Behind him there's a huntsman with spears and dogs—hounds colored like the English weather.

Here come the pack mules and the other servants. Usual riffraff.

Ah, now. At the extreme end of the procession. More riffraffish than the rest. A covered cart with colored cabalistic signs on its canvas. Two men on the driving bench, one big, one small, both dark-skinned, the larger with a Moor's headdress wound round his head and cheeks. Quack medicine peddlers, probably.

And sitting on the tailboard, beskirted legs dangling like a peasant, a woman. She's looking about her with a furious interest. Her eyes regard a tree, a patch of grass, with interrogation: What's your name? What are you good for? If not, why not? Like a magister in court. Or an idiot.

On the wide verge between us and all these people (even on the Great North Road, even in this year of 1171, no tree shall grow less than a bowshot's distance from the road, in case it give shelter to robbers) stands a small wayside shrine, the usual home-carpentered shelter for the Virgin.

Some of the riders prepare to pass by with a bow and a Hail Mary, but the prioress makes a show of calling for a groom to help her dismount. She lumbers over the grass to kneel and pray. Loudly.

One by one and somewhat reluctantly, all the others join her. Prior Geoffrey rolls his eyes and groans as he's assisted off his horse.

Even the three from the cart have dismounted and are on their knees, though, unseen at the back, the darker of the men seems to be directing his prayers toward the east. God help us all—Saracens and others of the ungodly are allowed to roam the highways of Henry II without sanction.

Lips mutter to the saint; hands weave an invisible cross. God is surely weeping, yet He allows the hands that have rent innocent flesh to remain unstained.

Mounted again, the cavalcade moves on, takes the turning to Cambridge, its diminishing chatter leaving us to the rumble of the harvest carts and the twitter of birdsong.

But we have a skein in our hands now, a thread that will lead us to that killer of children. To unravel it, though, we must first follow it backward in time by twelve months. . . .

. . . TO THE YEAR 1170. A screaming year. A king screamed to be rid of his archbishop. Monks of Canterbury screamed as knights spilled the brains of said archbishop onto the stones of his cathedral.

The Pope screamed for said king's penance. The English Church screamed in triumph—now it had said king where it wanted him.

And, far away in Cambridgeshire, a child screamed. A tiny, tinny sound, this one, but it would reach its place among the others.

At first the scream had hope in it. It's a come-and-get-me-I'm-frightened signal. Until now, adults had kept the child from danger, hoisted him away from beehives and bubbling pots and the blacksmith's fire. They *must* be at hand; they always have been.

At the sound, deer grazing on the moonlit grass lifted their heads and stared—but it was not one of their own young in fear; they went on grazing. A fox paused in its trot, one paw raised, to listen and judge the threat to itself.

The throat that issued the scream was too small and the place too deeply isolated to reach human help. The scream changed; it became unbelieving, so high on the scale of astonishment that it achieved the pitch of a huntsman's whistle directing his dogs.

The deer ran, scattering among the trees, their white scuts like dominoes tumbling into the darkness.

The scream was pleading now, perhaps to the torturer, perhaps to God, *please don't, please don't,* before crumbling into a monotone of agony and hopelessness.

The air was grateful when eventually the child fell silent and the usual night noises took over again; a breeze rustling through bushes, the grunt of a badger, the hundred screams of small mammals and birds as they died in the mouths of natural predators.

AT DOVER, an old man was being hurried through the castle at a rate not congenial to his rheumatism. It was a huge castle, very cold and echoing with furious noises. Despite the rate he had to go, the old man remained chilled—partly because he was frightened. The court sergeant was taking him to a man who frightened everybody.

They went along stone corridors, sometimes past open doors issuing light and warmth, chatter and the notes of a lyre, past others that were closed on what the old man imagined to be ungodly scenes.

Their progress sent castle servants cowering or flung them out of the way so that the two of them left behind them a trail of dropped trays, spattered piss pots, and bitten-off exclamations of hurt.

One final circular staircase and they were in a long gallery of which this end was taken up by desks lining the walls and a massive table with a top of green felt partitioned into squares. There were varying piles of counters on the squares. Thirty or so clerks filled the room with the scratch of quills on parchment. Colored balls flicked and clicked along the wires of their abaci so that it was like entering a field of industrious crickets.

In the whole place, the only human being at rest was a man sitting on one of the windowsills.

"Aaron of Lincoln, my lord," the sergeant announced.

Aaron of Lincoln went down on one painful knee and touched his forehead with the fingers of his right hand, then extended the palm in obeisance to the man on the windowsill.

"Do you know what that is?"

Aaron glanced awkwardly behind him at the vast table and didn't answer; he knew what it was, but Henry II's question had been rhetorical.

"It ain't for playing billiards, I'll tell you that," the king said. "It's my Exchequer. Those squares represent my English counties, and the counters on them show how much income from each is due to the Royal Treasury. Get up."

He seized the old man and took him to the table, pointing to one of the squares. "That's Cambridgeshire." He let Aaron go. "Using your considerable financial acumen, Aaron, how many counters do you reckon are on it?"

"Not enough, my lord?"

"Indeed," Henry said. "A profitable county, Cambridge—usually. Somewhat flat, but it produces a considerable amount of grain and cattle and fish, and pays the Treasury well—usually. Its sizable Jewish population also pays the Treasury well—usually. Would you say the number of counters on it at the moment do not present a true representation of its wealth?"

Again, the old man did not reply.

"And why is that?" Henry asked.

Aaron said wearily, "I imagine it's because of the children, my lord. The death of children is always to be lamented. . . ."

"Indeed it is." Henry hoisted himself up on the edge of the table, letting his legs dangle. "And when it becomes a matter of economics, it's disastrous. The peasants of Cambridge are in revolt and the Jews are . . . where are they?"

"Sheltering in its castle, my lord."

"What's left of it," Henry agreed. "They are indeed. *My* castle. Eating *my* food on *my* charity and shitting it out immediately because they're too scared to leave. All of which means they're not earning me any money, Aaron."

"No, my lord."

"And the revolting peasants have burned down its east tower, *which* contains all records of debts owed to the Jews, and therefore to *me*—to say nothing of the tax accounts—because they believe the Jews are torturing and killing their children."

For the first time, a whistle of hope sounded among the execution drums in the old man's head. "But you do not, my lord?"

"Do not what?"

"You do not believe Jews are killing these children?"

"I don't know, Aaron," the king said pleasantly. Without taking his eyes off the old man, he raised his hand. A clerk ran forward to put a piece of parchment in it. "This is an account by a certain Roger of Acton saying that such is your regular practice. According to the good Roger, Jews usually torture at least one Christian child to death at Easter by putting it in a hinged barrel inwardly pierced by nails. They always have, they always will."

He consulted the parchment. "'They do place the child into the barrel, then close the barrel so that the pins do enter his flesh. These fiends do then catch the blood as it seeps into their vessels to mix with their ritual pastries.'"

Henry II looked up: "Not pleasant, Aaron." He returned to the parchment. "Oh, and you laugh a lot while you're doing it."

"You know it is not true, my lord."

For all the notice the king took, the old man's interjection might have been another click on an abacus.

"But this Easter, Aaron, *this* Easter, you've started crucifying them. Certainly, our good Roger of Acton claims that the infant who's been found was crucified—what was the child's name?"

"Peter of Trumpington, my lord," supplied the attendant clerk.

"That Peter of Trumpington was crucified, and therefore the same fate may well overcome the other two children who are missing. Crucifixion, Aaron." The king spoke the mighty and terrible word softly, but it traveled along the cold gallery, accreting power as it went. "There's already agitation to make Little Peter a saint, as if we didn't have enough of them already. Two children missing and one bloodless mangled little body found in my fenland so far, Aaron. That's a lot of pastries."

Henry got down from the table and walked up the gallery, the old man following, leaving the field of crickets behind. The king dragged a stool from under a window and kicked another in Aaron's direction. "Sit down."

It was quieter at this end; damp, bitter air coming through the unglazed windows made the old man shake. Of the two, Aaron was the more richly clothed. Henry II dressed like a huntsman with careless habits; his queen's courtiers oiled their hair with unguents and were scented with attars, but Henry smelled of horses and sweat. His hands were leathery; his red hair was cropped close to a head as round as a cannonball. Yet nobody, Aaron thought, ever mistook him for other than what he was—the ruler of an empire stretching from the borders of Scotland to the Pyrenees.

Aaron could have loved him, almost did love him, if the man had not been so horrifyingly unpredictable. When this king was in a temper, he bit carpets and people died.

"God hates you Jews, Aaron," Henry said. "You killed His Son."

Aaron closed his eyes, waiting.

"And God hates me."

Aaron opened his eyes.

The king's voice rose in a wail that filled the gallery like a despairing trumpet. "Sweet God, forgive this unhappy and remorseful king. Thou knowest how Thomas à Becket did oppose me in all things so that in my rage I called for his death. *Peccavi, peccavi,* for certain knights did mistake my anger and ride to kill him, thinking to please me, for which abomination You in Your righteousness have turned Your face from me. I am a worm, mea culpa, mea culpa, mea culpa. I crawl beneath Your anger while Archbishop Thomas is received into Your

Glory and sitteth on the right hand of Your Gracious Son, Jesus Christ."

Faces turned. Quills were poised in mid-account, abaci stilled.

Henry stopped beating his breast. He said conversationally, "And if I am not mistaken, the Lord will find him as big a pain in the arse as I did." He leaned over, put a finger gently beneath Aaron of Lincoln's lower jaw, and raised it. "The moment that those bastards chopped Becket down, I became vulnerable. The Church seeks revenge, it wants my liver, hot and smoking, it wants recompense and must get it, and one of the things it wants, has always wanted, is the expulsion of you Jews from Christendom."

The clerks had returned to their work.

The king waved the document in his hand under the Jew's nose. "This is a petition, Aaron, demanding that all Jews be sent away from my realm. At this moment, a copy also penned by Master Acton, and may the hounds of hell chew his bollocks, is on its way to the Pope. The murdered child in Cambridge and the ones missing are to be the pretext for demanding your people's expulsion, and, with Becket dead, I shall be unable to refuse, because if I do, His Holiness will be persuaded to excommunicate me and put my whole kingdom under interdict. Does your mind encompass interdict? It is to be cast into darkness; babies to be refused baptisms, no ordained marriage, the dead to remain unburied without the blessing of the Church. And any upstart with shit on his trousers can challenge my right to rule."

Henry got up and paced, pausing to straighten the corner of an arras that the wind had disarranged. Over his shoulder, he said, "Am I not a good king, Aaron?"

"You are, my lord." The right answer. Also the truth.

"Am I not good to my Jews, Aaron?"

"You are, my lord. Indeed, you are." Again, the truth. Henry taxed his Jews like a farmer milked his cows, yet no other monarch in the world was fairer to them or kept such order in his tight little kingdom that Jews were safer in it than in almost any other country of the known world. From France, from Spain, from the crusade countries, from Russia, they came to enjoy the privileges and security to be found in this Plantagenet's England.

Where could we go? Aaron thought. *Lord, Lord, send us not back into the wilderness. If we can no longer have our Promised Land, let us live at least under this pharaoh, who keeps us safe.*

Henry nodded. "Usury is a sin, Aaron. The Church disapproves of it, doesn't let Christians sully their souls with it. Leaves it to you Jews, who haven't got any souls. It does not stop the Church borrowing from you, of course. How many of its cathedrals have been built on your personal loans?"

"Lincoln, my lord." Aaron began counting on his shaking, arthritic fingers. "Peterborough, Saint Albans, then there have been no less than nine Cistercian abbeys, then there's—"

"Yes, yes. The real point is that one seventh of my annual revenue comes from taxing you Jews. And the Church wants me to get rid of you." The king was on his feet, and once again harsh Angevin syllables blasted the gallery. "Do I not maintain peace in this kingdom such as it has never known? God's balls, *how do they think I do it?*"

Nervous clerks dropped their quills to nod. *Yes, my lord. You do, my lord.*

"You do, my lord," Aaron said.

"Not by prayer and fasting, I tell you that." Henry had calmed himself again. "I need money to equip my army, pay my judges, put down rebellion abroad, and keep my wife in her hellish expensive habits. Peace is money, Aaron, and money is peace." He grabbed the old man by the front of his cloak and dragged him close. "Who is killing those *children?*"

"Not us, my lord. My lord, we don't *know.*"

For one intimate moment, appalling blue eyes with their stubby, almost invisible eyelashes peered into Aaron's soul.

"We don't, do we?" the king said. The old man was released, steadied, his cloak patted back into shape, though the king's face was still close, his voice a tender whisper. "But I think we'd better find out, eh? *Quickly.*"

As the sergeant accompanied Aaron of Lincoln toward the staircase, Henry II called, "I'd miss you Jews, Aaron."

The old man turned round. The king was smiling, or, at least, his spaced, strong little teeth were bared in something like a smile. "But not near as much as you Jews would miss me," he said.

IN SOUTHERN ITALY several weeks later . . .

Gordinus the African blinked kindly at his visitor and wagged a finger. He knew the name; it had been announced with pomp: *"From Palermo, representing our most gracious king, his lordship Mordecai fil Berachyah."* He even knew the face, but Gordinus remembered people only by their diseases.

"Hemorrhoids," he said, triumphantly, at last, "you had piles. How are they?"

Mordecai fil Berachyah was not easily disconcerted; as personal secretary to the King of Sicily and keeper of the royal secrets, he couldn't afford to be. He was offended, of course—a man's hemorrhoids should not be bandied about in public—but his big face remained impassive, his voice cool. "I came to see whether Simon of Naples got off all right."

"Got off what?" Gordinus asked interestedly.

Genius, thought Mordecai, was always difficult to deal with and when, as here, it was beginning to decay, it was near impossible. He decided to use the weight of the royal "we."

"Got off to England, Gordinus. Simon Menahem of Naples. We were sending Simon of Naples to England to deal with a trouble the Jews are having there."

Gordinus's secretary came to their aid, walking to a wall covered by cubbyholes from which rolls of parchment stuck out like pipe ends. He spoke encouragingly, as to a child. "You remember, my lord, we had a royal letter . . . oh, gods, he's moved it."

This was going to take time. Lord Mordecai lumbered across the mosaic floor that depicted fishing cupids—Roman, at least a thousand years old. One of Hadrian's villas, this had been.

They did themselves well, these doctors. Mordecai ignored the fact that his own palazzo in Palermo was floored with marble and gold.

He sat himself down on the stone bench that ran round an open balustrade overlooking the town below and, beyond it, the turquoise Tyrrhenian Sea.

Gordinus, ever alert as a doctor if nothing else, said, "His lordship will require a cushion, Gaius."

A cushion was fetched. So were dates. And wine. Gaius asked nervously, "This is acceptable, my lord?" The king's entourage, like the kingdom of Sicily and southern Italy itself, consisted of so many faiths and races—Arabs, Lombards, Greeks, Normans, and, as in Mordecai's case, Jews—that an offer of refreshment could be an offense against some religious dietary law or another.

His lordship nodded; he felt better. The cushion was a comfort to his backside, the breeze from the sea cooled him, and the wine was good. He shouldn't be offended by an old man's directness; in fact, when his business was over, he would indeed bring up the subject of his piles; Gordinus had cured them last time. This was, after all, the town of healing, and if anyone could be described as the doyen of its great medical school, it was Gordinus the African.

He watched the old man forget that he had a guest and return to the manuscript he'd been reading, the drooping, brown skin of his arm stretching as his hand dipped a quill in ink to make an alteration. What was he? Tunisian? Moor?

On arrival at the villa, Mordecai had asked the majordomo if he should remove his shoes before entering, adding, "I have forgotten what your master's religion is."

"So has he, my lord."

Only in Salerno, Mordecai thought now, *do men forget their manners and their god in the greater worship of the sick.*

He wasn't sure he approved; very wonderful, no doubt, but eternal laws were broken, dead bodies dissected, women relieved of threatening fetuses, females allowed to practice, the flesh invaded by surgery.

They came in the hundreds: people who'd heard the name of Salerno and yet journeyed to it, sometimes on their own account, sometimes carrying their sick, blundering across deserts, steppes, marshes, and mountains, to be healed.

Looking down on a maze of roofs, spires, and cupolas, sipping his wine, Mordecai marveled, not for the first time, that this town of all towns—and not Rome, not Paris, not Constantinople, not Jerusalem—had developed a school of medicine that made it the world's doctor.

Just then the clang of the monastery bells sounding for nones clashed with the call to prayer from the muezzin of mosques and fought with the voice of synagogue cantors, all of them rising up the hill to assault the ears of the man on the balcony in an untidy blast of major and minor keys.

That was it, of course. The mix. The hard, greedy Norman adventurers who'd made a kingdom out of Sicily and southern Italy had been pragmatists, but far-seeing pragmatists. If a man suited their purpose, they didn't care which god he worshipped. If they were to establish peace—and therefore prosperity—there must be integration of the several peoples they'd conquered. There would be no second-class Sicilians. Arab, Greek, Latin, and French were to be the official languages. Advancement for any man of any faith, as long as he was able.

Nor should I complain, he thought. After all, he, a Jew, worked with

Greek Orthodox Christians along with popish Catholics for a Norman king. The galley he'd disembarked from was part of the Sicilian
royal navy in the charge of an Arab admiral.

In the streets below, the jellabah brushed against knightly mail, the
kaftan against monkish habit, their owners not only *not* spitting at one
another but exchanging greetings and news—and, above all, ideas.

"Here it is, my lord," Gaius said.

Gordinus took the letter. "Ah yes, of course. Now I remember. *'Simon
Menahem of Naples to set sail on a special mission . . .'* Nymm, nymmm. *'. . . the
Jews of England being in a predicament of some danger . . . native children are put to
torture and death . . .'* Oh, dear. *'. . . and blame falling on the Jews . . .'* Oh dear,
dear. *'You are commanded to discover and send with the aforementioned Simon a person versed in the causes of death, who speaks both English and Hebrew yet gossips in
neither.'"*

He smiled up at his secretary. "And I did, didn't I?"

Gaius shifted. "There was some question at the time, my lord. . . ."

"Of course I did, I remember perfectly. And not just an expert in
the morbid processes but a speaker of Latin, French, Greek, as well as
the languages specified. A fine student. I told Simon so because he
seemed a little concerned. 'You can't have anyone better,' I told him."

"Excellent." Mordecai rose. "Excellent."

"Yes." Gordinus was still triumphant. "I think we met the king's
specification exactly, didn't we, Gaius?"

"Up to a point, my lord."

There was something in the servant's manner—Mordecai was
trained to notice such things. And why, now that he came to think of
it, had Simon of Naples been concerned at the choice of the man who
was to accompany him?

"How is the king, by the way?" Gordinus asked. "That little trouble
clear up?"

Ignoring the king's little trouble, Mordecai spoke directly to Gaius:
"Who did he send?"

Gaius glanced toward his master, who'd resumed reading, and lowered his voice. "The choice of person in this case was unusual, and I did wonder . . ."

"Listen, man, this mission is extremely delicate. He didn't choose an Oriental, did he? Yellow? Stick out like a lemon in England?"

"No, I didn't." Gordinus's mind had rejoined them.

"Well, who did you send?"

Gordinus told him.

Incredulity made Mordecai ask again, "You sent . . . who?"

Gordinus told him again.

Mordecai's was another scream to rend that year of screams: *"You stupid, stupid old fool."*

Two

O ur prior is dying," the monk said. He was young and desperate. "Prior Geoffrey is dying and has nowhere to lay his head. Lend us your cart in the name of God."

The whole cavalcade had watched him quarreling with his brother monks over where their prior should spend his last earthly minutes, the other two preferring the prioress's open traveling catafalque, or even the ground, to the covered cart of heathenish-looking peddlers.

In fact, the press of black-clad people on the road attending to the prior so hemmed him in where he reeled in his pain, pecking at him with advice, that they might have been crows fluttering around carrion.

The prioress's little nun was urging some object on him. "The saint's very finger knuckle, my lord. But apply it again, I beg. This time, it's miraculous property . . ."

Her soft voice was almost drowned in the louder urgings of the clerk called Roger of Acton, he who had been importuning the poor prior for something ever since Canterbury. "The true knuckle of a true saint crucified. Only believe . . ."

Even the prioress was trumpeting concern of a sort. "But apply it to the afflicted part with stronger prayer, Prior Geoffrey, and Little Saint Peter shall do his bit."

The matter was settled by the prior himself, who, between bellows of profanity and pain, was understood to prefer anywhere, however heathenish, as long as it got him away from the prioress, the pestering damn cleric, and the rest of the gawking bastards who were standing around watching his death throes. He was not, he pointed out with some vigor, a bloody sideshow. (Some passing peasants had stopped to mingle with the cavalcade and were regarding the prior's gyrations with interest.)

The peddlers' cart it was. Thus, the young monk made his appeal to the cart's male occupants in Norman French and hoped they'd understand him—until now, they and their woman had been heard gabbing in a foreign tongue.

For a moment, they seemed at a loss. Then the woman, a dowdy little thing, said, "What is the matter with him?"

The monk waved her off. "Get away, girl, this is no matter for women."

The smaller of the two men watched her retreat with some concern but said, "Of course . . . um?"

"Brother Ninian," said Brother Ninian.

"I am Simon of Naples. This gentleman is Mansur. Of course, Brother Ninian, naturally our cart is at your service. What ails the poor holy man?"

Brother Ninian told them.

The Saracen's facial expression did not change, probably never did, but Simon of Naples was all sympathy; he could imagine nothing so bad. "It may be that we can be of even more assistance," he said. "My companion is from the school of medicine at Salerno . . ."

"A doctor? He's a doctor?" The monk was off and running toward his prior and the crowd, shouting as he went. "They're from Salerno. The brown one's a doctor. A doctor from Salerno."

The very name was a physic; everyone knew it. That the three came from Italy accounted for their oddity. Who knew what Italians looked like?

The woman rejoined her two men at the cart.

Mansur was regarding Simon with one of his looks, a slow form of ocular flaying. "Gabblemouth here said I was a doctor from Salerno."

"Did I say that? Did I say that?" Simon's arms were out. "I *said* my companion . . ."

Mansur turned his attention to the woman. "The unbeliever can't piss," he told her.

"Poor soul," said Simon. "Not for eleven hours. He exclaims he will burst. Can you conceive of it, Doctor? Drowning in one's own fluids?"

She could conceive of it; no wonder the man capered. And he would burst, or at least his bladder would. A masculine condition; she'd seen it on the dissecting table. Gordinus had performed a post-mortem on just such a case, but he had said that the patient could have been saved if . . . if . . . yes, that was it. And her stepfather had described seeing the same procedure in Egypt.

"*Hmmm,*" she said.

Simon was on it like a raptor. "He can be helped? Lord, if he might be healed, the advantage to our mission would be incalculable. This is a man of influence."

Be damned to influence; Adelia saw only a fellow creature that suffered—and, unless there was intervention, would continue to suffer until poisoned by his own urine. Yet if she were wrong in the diagnosis? There were other explanations for retention. If she fumbled?

"*Hmmm,*" she said again, but her tone had altered.

"Risky?" Simon's attitude had also altered. "He could die? Doctor, let us consider our position. . . ."

She ignored him. She almost turned and opened her mouth to ask Margaret's opinion before deadening loneliness overtook her. The space that had been occupied by the bulk of her childhood nurse was empty, would remain empty; Margaret had died at Ouistreham.

With desolation came guilt. Margaret should never have attempted the journey from Salerno, but she had insisted. Adelia, overfond, needing female companionship for propriety's sake, dreading any but this valued servant's, had acquiesced. Too hard. Near a thousand miles of sea voyaging, the Bay of Biscay at its worst, it had been too hard on an old woman. An apoplexy. The love sustaining Adelia for twenty-five years had withdrawn into a grave in a tiny cemetery on the banks of the Orne, leaving her to face the crossing to England alone, a Ruth among the alien corn.

What would that dear soul have said to this?

"I don't know why you'm asking, you never take no heed anyway. You'm going to take the chance with the poor gentleman, I know you, flower, so don't you bother with my opinion, the which you never do."

The which she never did.

Adelia's mouth became gentle as the remembered rich Devonian syllables sang in her head; Margaret had only ever been her sounding board. And her comfort.

"Perhaps we should leave well alone, Doctor," Simon said.

"The man is dying," she said. She was as aware as Simon of the danger to them if the operation failed; she had felt little but desolation in this unfamiliar country since they landed, its strangeness giving even the most jovial company a seeming of hostility. But in this matter, the possible threat was of as little account as the possible benefit to them if the prior could be mended. She was a doctor; the man was dying. There was no choice.

She looked around her. The road, probably Roman, ran straight as a pointing finger. To the west, on her left, was flatness, the beginning of the Cambridgeshire fens, darkening meadow and wetland meeting a linear sunset in vermilion and gold. On her right, the wooded side of a hill of no great height and a track leading up to it. Nothing habitable anywhere, not a house, not a cottage, not a shepherd's hut.

Her eyes rested on the ditch, almost a dike, that ran between the road and the rise of the hills; she'd been aware of what it contained for some time, as she was aware of all nature's goodies.

They'd need privacy. Light too. And some of the ditch's contents.

She gave her instructions.

The three monks approached, supporting their suffering prior. A protesting Roger of Acton trotted alongside, still urging the efficacy of the prioress's relic.

The oldest monk addressed Mansur and Simon: "Brother Ninian says you are doctors from Salerno." His face and nose could have sharpened flint.

Simon looked toward Mansur over the head of Adelia, who stood in the middle of them. With strict adherence to the truth, he said, "Between us, sir, we have considerable medical knowledge."

"Can you help me?" The prior yelled it at Simon, jerkily.

There was a nudge in Simon's ribs. Bravely, he said, "Yes."

Even so, Brother Gilbert hung on to the invalid's arm, reluctant to surrender his superior. "My lord, we do not know if these people are Christians. You need the solace of prayer; I shall stay with you."

Simon shook his head. "The mystery about to be performed must be performed in solitude. Privacy is a necessity between doctor and patient."

"For the sake of Christ, give me *relief*." Again, it was Prior Geoffrey solving the matter. Brother Gilbert and his Christian solace were knocked into the dust, the other two monks pushed aside and told to stay, his knight to stand guard. Flailing and staggering, the prior reached the cart's hanging tailboard and was heaved up it by Simon and Mansur.

Roger of Acton ran after the cart. "My lord, if you would but try the miraculous properties of Little Saint Peter's knuckle . . ."

There was a scream: "I tried it and I *still can't piss.*"

The cart rocked up the incline and disappeared among the trees. Adelia, having grubbed around in the ditch, followed it.

"I fear for him," Brother Gilbert said, though jealousy outweighed anxiety in his voice.

"Witchcraft." Roger of Acton could say nothing unless he shouted it. "Better death than revival at the hands of Belial."

Both would have followed the cart, but the prior's knight, Sir Gervase, always one to tease monks, was suddenly barring the way. "He said no."

Sir Joscelin, the prioress's knight, was equally firm. "I think we must leave him be, Brother."

The two stood together, chain-clad crusaders who had fought in the Holy Land, contemptuous of lesser, skirted men content to serve God in safe places.

The track led to a strange hill. The cart bumped up the rise that eventually led to a great, grassy ring standing above the trees, catching the last of the sun so it gleamed like a monstrous bald, green, flat-topped head.

It cast unease over the road at its foot, where the rest of the cavalcade had decided not to proceed now that its force was split but to camp on the verge within call of the knights.

"What is that place?" Brother Gilbert asked, staring after the cart even though he could not see it.

One of the squires paused in unsaddling his master's horse. "That up there's Wandlebury Ring, master. These are the Gog Magog hills."

Gog and Magog, British giants as pagan as their name. The Christian company huddled close around the fire—and closer yet as the voice of Sir Gervase came whoo-hooing across the road from the dark trees: "Bloo-oo-od sacrifice. The Wild Hunt is in cry up here, my masters. Oh, horrible."

Settling his hounds for the night, Prior Geoffrey's huntsman blew out his cheeks and nodded.

Mansur didn't like the place, either. He reined in about halfway up, where the cart could be on a wide level dug out of the slope. He unharnessed the mules—the moans of the prior inside the cart were making them restless—and tethered them so that they could graze, then set about building a fire.

A bowl was fetched, the last of the boiled water poured into it. Adelia put her collection from the ditch into the water and considered it.

"Reeds?" Simon said. "What for?"

She told him.

He turned pale. "He, you . . . He will not allow . . . He is a *monk*."

"He is a patient." She stirred the reed stems and selected two, shaking them free of water. "Get him ready."

"Ready? No man is ready for that. Doctor, my faith in you is absolute but . . . may I inquire . . . you have carried out the procedure before?"

"No. Where's my bag?"

He followed her across the grass. "At least you have seen it performed?"

"No. God's ribs, the light will be bad." She raised her voice. "Two lanterns, Mansur. Hang them inside from the canopy hoops. Now, where are those cloths?" She began delving in the goatskin bag that carried her equipment.

"Should we clarify this matter?" Simon asked, trying for calm. "You have not performed the operation yourself, nor have you seen it done."

"No, I told you." She looked up. "Gordinus mentioned it once. And

Gershom, my foster father, described the procedure to me after a visit to Egypt. He saw it depicted on some ancient tomb paintings."

"Ancient Egyptian tomb paintings." Simon gave each word equal weight. "In color, were they?"

"I see no reason why it should not work," she said. "With what I know of male anatomy, it is a logical step to take."

She set off across the grass. Simon threw himself forward and stopped her. "May we pursue this logic a little further, Doctor? You are about to perform an operation, it may be a *dangerous* operation . . ."

"Yes. Yes, I suppose it is."

". . . on a prelate of some importance. His friends await him there"—Simon of Naples pointed down the darkening hill—"not all of them rejoicing at our interference in this matter. We are strangers to them, we have no standing in their eyes." To continue, he had to dodge in front of her, for she would have gone on toward the cart. "It could, I'm not saying it will, but it *could* be that those friends have a logic of their own, and, should this prior die, they will hang the three of us like logical washing on a clothesline. I say again, should we not let nature take its course? I merely ask it."

"The man is *dying,* Master Simon."

Then the light of Mansur's lanterns fell on her face and he stood back, defeated. "Yes, my Becca would do the same." Rebecca was his wife, the standard by whom he judged human charity. "Proceed, Doctor."

"I shall need your assistance."

He raised his hands and then let them drop. "You have it." He went with her, sighing and muttering. "Would it be so bad if nature took its course, Lord? That's all I'm asking."

Mansur waited until the two had climbed into the cart, then settled his back against it, folded his arms, and kept watch.

The last ray from the dying sun went out, but no compensating moon had yet taken its place, leaving fen and hill in blackness.

DOWN ON THE ROADSIDE VERGE, a bulky figure detached itself from the companionship round the pilgrims' fire, as if to answer a call of nature. Unseen in the blackness, it crossed the road and, with an agility surprising in the weighty, leaped the ditch and disappeared into the bushes by the side of the track. Silently cursing the brambles that tore its cloak, it climbed toward the ledge on which the cart rested, sniffing to allow the stink of the mules to guide it, sometimes following a glimpse of light through the trees.

It paused to try and listen to the conversation of the two knights who stood like forbidding statuary on the track out of sight of the cart, the nosepieces of their helmets rendering the one indistinguishable from the other.

It heard one of them mention the Wild Hunt.

". . . the devil's hill, no doubt of it," the companion replied clearly. "No peasant comes near the place, and I could wish we hadn't. Give me the Saracens any day."

The listener crossed himself and climbed higher, picking his way with infinite care. Unseen, he passed the Arab, another piece of statuary in the moonlight. Finally he had reached a point from which to look down on the cart, its lanterns giving it the appearance of a glowing opal on black velvet.

He settled himself. Around him, the undergrowth rustled with the comings and goings of uncaring life on the woodland floor. Overhead, a barn owl shrieked as it hunted.

There was a sudden gabble from the cart. A light, clear voice: "Lie back; this shouldn't hurt. Master Simon, if you would lift up his skirts. . . ."

Prior Geoffrey was heard to say sharply, "What does she do down there? What's in her hand?"

And the man addressed as Master Simon: "Lie back, my lord. Close your eyes; be assured this lady knows what she's about."

And the prior, panicking: "Well, I don't. I am fallen to a witch. God have mercy on me, this female will snatch my soul through my pizzle."

And the lighter voice, sterner, concentrating: "Keep still, blast you. Do you want a burst bladder? Hold the penis up, Master Simon. *Up,* I need a smooth passageway."

There was a squeak from the prior.

"The bowl, Simon. The bowl, quick. Hold it there, *there.*"

And then a sound, like the splash of a waterfall into a basin, and a groan of satisfaction such as a man makes in the act of love, or when his bladder is relieved of a content that has been torturing it.

On the ledge above, the king's tax collector opened his eyes wide, pursed his lips in a moue of interest, nodded to himself, and began his descent.

He wondered if the knights had heard what he'd heard. *Probably not,* he thought; they were nearly out of earshot of the cart, and the coifs that cushioned their heads from the iron of their helmets deadened sound. Only he, then, apart from the cart's occupants and the Arab, was in possession of an intriguing piece of knowledge.

Returning the way he had come, he had to crouch in shadow several times; it was surprising, despite the darkness, how many pilgrims were venturing on the hill this night.

He saw Brother Gilbert, presumably attempting to find out what was going on in the cart. He saw Hugh, the prioress's huntsman, either on the same business or maybe investigating coverts, as a huntsman should. And was the indistinct shape slipping into the trees that of a female? The merchant's wife looking for somewhere in private in which to answer a call of nature? A nun on the same errand? Or a monk?

He couldn't tell.

Three

D awn lighted on the pilgrims by the side of the road and found them damp and irritable. The prioress railed at her knight in discontent when he came to ask how she had passed the night: "Where were you, Sir Joscelin?"

"Guarding the prior, madam. He was in the hands of foreigners and might have needed assistance."

The prioress didn't care. "Such was his choice. I could have proceeded last night if you had been with us for protection. It is only four miles more to Cambridge. Little Saint Peter is waiting for this reliquary in which to lodge his bones and has waited long enough."

"You should have brought the bones with you, madam."

The prioress's trip to Canterbury had been a pilgrimage not only of devotion but also to collect the reliquary that had been on order from Saint Thomas à Becket's goldsmiths for a twelvemonth. Once the skeleton of her convent's new saint, which was lying in an inferior box in Cambridge, was interred in it, she expected great things from it.

"I carried his holy knuckle," she snapped, "and if Prior Geoffrey possessed the faith he should, it would have been enough to mend him."

"Even so, Mother, we could not have left the poor prior to strangers in his predicament, could we?" the little nun asked gently.

The prioress certainly could have. She had no more liking for Prior Geoffrey than he had for her. "He has his own knight, does he not?"

"It takes two to stand guard all night, madam," Sir Gervase said. "One to watch while the other sleeps." He was short-tempered. Indeed, both knights were red-eyed, as if neither had rested.

"What sleep did I have? Such a disturbance there was with people coming and going all around. And why does *he* demand a double guard?"

Much of the ill feeling between Saint Radegund's convent and Saint Augustine's canonry of Barnwell was because Prioress Joan suspected jealousy on the prior's part for the miracles already wrought by Little Saint Peter's bones at the nunnery. Now, properly encased, their fame would spread, petitioners to them would swell her convent's income, and the miracles would increase. And so, without doubt, would Prior Geoffrey's envy. "Let us be on our way before he recovers." She looked around. "Where's that Hugh with my hounds? Oh, the devil, he's surely never taken them onto the hill."

Sir Joscelin was off after the recalcitrant huntsman on the instant. Sir Gervase, who had his own dogs among Hugh's pack, followed him.

THE PRIOR WAS REGAINING strength after a good night's sleep. He sat on a log, eating eggs from a pan over the Salernitans' fire, not knowing which question to ask first. "I am amazed, Master Simon," he said.

The little man opposite him nodded sympathetically. "I can understand, my lord. *'Certum est, quia impossibile.'*"

That a shabby peddler should quote Tertullian amazed the prior further. Who were these people? Nevertheless, the fellow had it exactly; the situation must be so because it was impossible. Well, first things first. "Where is she gone?"

"She likes to walk the hills, my lord, studying nature, gathering herbs."

"She should take care on this one; the local people give it a wide berth, leaving it to the sheep; they say Wandlebury Ring is the haunt of the Wild Hunt and witches."

"Mansur is always with her."

"The Saracen?" Prior Geoffrey regarded himself as a broad-minded man, also grateful, but he was disappointed. "Is she a witch, then?"

Simon winced. "My lord, I beg you. . . . If you could avoid mentioning the word in her presence. . . . She is a doctor, fully trained."

He paused, then added, "Of a sort." Again, he stuck to the literal truth. "The Medical School of Salerno allows women to practice."

"I had heard that it did," the prior said. "Salerno, eh? I did not believe it any more than I credited cows with the ability to fly. It appears that I must now look out for cows overhead."

"Always best, my lord."

The prior spooned some more eggs into his mouth and looked around him, appreciating the greenery of spring and the twitter of birdsong as he had not for some time. He was reassessing matters. While undoubtedly disreputable, this little company was also learned, in which case it was not at all what it seemed. "She saved me, Master Simon. Did she learn that particular operation in Salerno?"

"From the best Egyptian doctors, I believe."

"Extraordinary. Tell me her fee."

"She will accept no payment."

"Really?" This was becoming more extraordinary by the minute; neither this man nor the woman appeared to have a shilling to bless themselves with. "She swore at me, Master Simon."

"My lord, I apologize. I fear her skills do not include the bedside manner."

"No, they do not." Nor any womanly wiles, as far as the prior could see. "Forgive an old man's impertinence but, so that I may address her correctly, to which of you is she . . . attached?"

"Neither of us, my lord." The peddler was more amused than offended. "Mansur is her manservant, a eunuch—a misfortune that befell him. I myself am devoted to my wife and children in Naples. There is no attachment in that sense; we are merely allies through circumstance."

And the prior, though not a gullible man, believed him, which also increased his curiosity. What the devil were the three doing here?

"Nevertheless," he said out loud and sternly, "I must tell you that, whatever your purpose in Cambridge, it will be compromised by the peculiarity of your ménage. Mistress Doctor should have a female companion."

This time it was Simon who was surprised, and Prior Geoffrey saw that the man did indeed see the woman as merely a colleague. "I suppose she should," Simon said. "There was one in attendance when we started out on this mission, her childhood nurse, but the old woman died on the way."

"I advise you to find another." The prior paused, then asked, "You make mention of a mission. May I inquire what it is?"

Simon appeared to hesitate.

Prior Geoffrey said, "Master Simon, I presume that you have not traveled all the way from Salerno merely to sell nostrums. If your mission is delicate, you may tell me with impunity." When the man still hesitated, the prior clicked his tongue at having to point out the obvious. "Metaphorically, Master Simon, you have me by the balls. Can I betray your confidence when you are in a position to counter such betrayal merely by informing the town crier that I, a canon of Saint Augustine, a person of some consequence in Cambridge, and, I flatter myself, in the wider realm also, did not only place my most private member in the hands of a woman but had a plant shoved up it? How, to paraphrase the immortal Horace, would that play in Corinth?"

"Ah," Simon said.

"Indeed. Speak freely, Master Simon. Sate an old man's curiosity."

So Simon told him. They had come to discover who was murdering and abducting Cambridge's children, he said. It must not be thought, he said, that their mission was intended as a usurpation of local officials, "only that investigation by authority sometimes tends to close more mouths than it opens, whereas we, incognito and disregarded . . ." Being Simon, he stressed this at length. It was not interference. However, since discovery of the murderer was protracted—obviously a particularly cunning and devious killer—special measures might fit the case. . . .

"Our masters, those who sent us, appear to think that Mistress Doctor and I have the appropriate skills for such a matter. . . ."

Listening to the tale of the mission, Prior Geoffrey learned that Simon of Naples was a Jew. He felt an immediate surge of panic. As master of a great monastic foundation, he was responsible for the state of the world when it must be handed over to God on the Day of Judgment, which might be anytime soon. How to answer an Almighty who had commanded that the one true faith be established in it? How to explain at the throne of God the existence of an unconverted infection in what should be a whole and perfect body? About which he had done nothing?

Humanism fought the training of the seminary—and won. It was an old battle. What *could* he do? He was not one of those who countenanced extermination; he would not see souls, if Jews had souls, severed and sent into the pit. Not only did he countenance the Jews of Cambridge, he protected them, though he railed mightily against other churchmen for encouraging the sin of usury in borrowing from them.

Now he, too, was in debt to one such—for his life. And, indeed, if this man, Jew or not, could solve the mystery that was causing Cambridge's agony, then Prior Geoffrey was his to command. Why, though, had he brought a doctor, a *female* doctor, with him?

So Prior Geoffrey listened to Simon's story, and where he had been amazed before, he was now floundered, not least by the man's openness, a characteristic he had not come across in the race until now. Instead of canniness, even cunning, he was hearing the truth.

He thought, *Poor booby, he takes little persuasion to unload his secrets. He is too artless; he has no guile. Who has sent him, poor booby?*

There was silence when Simon had finished, except for a blackbird's song from a wild cherry tree.

"You have been sent by Jews to rescue the Jews?"

"Not at all, my lord. Really, no. The prime mover in this matter appears to be the King of Sicily—a Norman, as you know. I wondered at it myself; I cannot but feel that there are other influences at work; certainly our passports were not questioned at Dover, leaving me to opine that English officialdom is not unaware of what we are about. Be assured that, should the Jews of Cambridge prove guilty of this most dreadful crime, I shall willingly lay my hands to the rope that hangs them."

Good. The prior accepted that. "But why was it necessary for the enterprise to include this woman doctor, may I ask? Surely, such a rara avis, if she is discovered, will attract most unwelcome attention."

"I, too, had my doubts at first," Simon said.

Doubts? He'd been appalled. The sex of the doctor who was to accompany him had not been revealed to him until she and her entourage boarded the boat to take them all to England, by which time it was too late to protest, though he *had* protested—Gordinus the African, greatest of doctors and most naïve of men, taking his gesticulations as waves of farewell and *fondly waving back* as the gap between taffrail and quay took them away from each other.

"I had my doubts," he said again, "yet she has proved modest, capable, and a proficient speaker of English. Moreover"—Simon beamed, his creased face crinkling further in pleasure, taking the prior's attention away from a sensitive area; there would be time to reveal Adelia's particular skill, and it was not yet—"as my wife would say, the Lord has His own purposes. Why else should she have been on hand in your hour of greatest need?"

Prior Geoffrey nodded slowly. That was undoubted; he'd already been on his knees in thanks to Almighty God for putting her in his way.

"It would be helpful, before we arrive in the town," pursued Simon of Naples, gently, "to learn what we can of the killing of the murdered child and how it came about that two others are missing." He let the sentence hang in the air.

"The children," Prior Geoffrey said at last, heavily. "I have to tell you, Master Simon, that by the time we set off for Canterbury, the number of those missing was not two, as you have been told, but three. Indeed, had I not vowed to make this pilgrimage, I would not have left Canterbury for dread the number might rise again. God have mercy on their souls; we all fear the little ones have met the same fate as the first child, Peter. Crucified."

"Not at the hands of Jews, my lord. We do not crucify children."

You crucified the Son of God, the prior thought. *Poor booby. Admit to being a Jew where you are going and they will tear you to pieces. And your doctor with you.*

Damn it, he thought, *I shall have to take a hand in the business.*

He said, "I must tell you, Master Simon, that our people are much aroused against the Jews, they fear that other offspring may be taken."

"My lord, what inquiry has been made? What evidence that Jews are to blame?"

"The charge was made almost immediately," said Prior Geoffrey, "and, I am afraid, with reason . . ."

It was Simon Menahem of Naples's genius as agent, investigator, go-between, reconnoiterer, spy—he was used in all such capacities by such of the powerful as knew him well—that people took him to be what he seemed. They could not believe that this puny, nervous little man of such eagerness, even simplicity, who spilled information—all of it trustworthy—could outwit them. Only when, the deal fixed, the alliance sealed, the bottom of the business uncovered, did it occur to them that Simon had achieved exactly what his masters wanted. *But he is a booby,* they would tell themselves.

And it was to this booby, who had judged the prior's character and newfound indebtedness to the last jot and tittle, that a subtle prior found himself recounting everything the booby wished to know.

It had been just over a year ago. Passiontide Friday. Eight-year-old Peter, a child from Trumpington, a village on the southwest edge of Cambridge, was sent by his mother to gather pussy willow, "which, in England, replaces the palm in decoration for Palm Sunday."

Peter had shunned willows near his home and trotted north along the Cam to gather branches from the tree on the stretch of riverbank by Saint Radegund's convent, which was claimed to be especially holy, having been planted by Saint Radegund herself.

"As if," said the prior, bitterly interrupting his tale, "a female German saint of the Dark Ages would have tripped over to Cambridgeshire to plant a tree. But that harpy"—thus he referred to the prioress of Saint Radegund's—"will say anything."

It happened that, on the same day, Passiontide Friday, several of the richest and most important Jews in England had gathered in Cambridge at the house of Chaim Leonis for the marriage of Chaim's daughter. Peter had been able to view the celebrations from the other side of the river on his way to gather branches of willow.

He had not, therefore, returned home the same way but had taken the quicker route to Jewry by going over the bridge and passing through the town so that he could see the carriages and caparisoned horses of the visiting Jews in Chaim's stable.

"His uncle, Peter's uncle, was Chaim's stabler, you see."

"Are Christians allowed to work for Jews here?" Simon asked, as if he didn't know the answer already. "Great heavens."

"Oh, yes. The Jews are steady employers. And Peter was a regular visitor to the stables, even to the kitchens, where Chaim's cook—who *was* a Jew—sometimes gave him sweetmeats, a fact that was to count against the household later as enticement."

"Go on, my lord."

"Well. Peter's uncle, Godwin, was too busy with the unusual influx of horses to pay attention to the boy and told him to be off home, indeed thought he had. Not until late that night, when Peter's mother came inquiring to town, did anyone realize the child had disappeared. The watch was alerted, also the river bailiffs—it was likely the boy had fallen into the River Cam. The banks were searched at dawn. Nothing."

Nothing for more than a week. As townsfolk and villagers crawled on their knees to the Good Friday cross in the parish churches, prayers were addressed to Almighty God for the return of Peter of Trumpington.

On Easter Monday the prayer was granted. Hideously. Peter's body was discovered in the river near Chaim's house, snagged below its surface under a pier.

The prior shrugged. "Even then blame did not fall on the Jews. Children tumble, they fall into rivers, wells, ditches. No, we thought it an accident—until Martha the laundress came forward. Martha lives in Bridge Street and among her clients is Chaim Leonis. On the evening of Little Peter's disappearance, she said, she had delivered a basket of clean washing to Chaim's back door. Finding it open, she'd gone inside—"

"She delivered laundry so late in the day?" Simon expressed surprise.

Prior Geoffrey inclined his head. "I think we must accept that Martha was curious; she had never seen a Jewish wedding. Nor have any of us, of course. Anyway, she went inside. The back of the house was deserted, the celebrations having moved to the front garden. The door to a room off the hall was slightly open—"

"Another open door," Simon said, apparently surprised again.

The prior glanced at him. "Do I tell you something you already know?"

"I beg pardon, my lord. Continue, I beseech you."

"Very well. Martha looked into the room and saw—*says* she saw—a child hanging by his hands from a cross. She was given no chance to be other than terrified because, just then, Chaim's wife came down the passageway, cursed her, and she ran off."

"Without alerting the watch?" Simon asked.

The prior nodded. "Indeed, that is the weakness in her story. If, *if,* Martha saw the body when she says, she did *not* alert the watch. She alerted nobody until *after* Little Peter's corpse was discovered. Then, and only then, did she whisper what she had seen to a neighbor, who whispered it to another neighbor, who went to the castle and told the sheriff. After that, evidence came thick and fast. A branch of pussy willow was found dropped in the lane outside Chaim's house. A man delivering peat to the castle testified that from across the river on Passiontide Friday, he saw two men, one wearing the Jewish hat, toss a bundle from Great Bridge into the Cam. Others now said they had heard screams coming from Chaim's house. I myself viewed the corpse after it had been dragged from the river and saw the stigmata of crucifixion on it." He frowned. "The poor little body was horribly bloated, of course, but there were the marks on the wrists, and the belly had been split open, as if by a spear, and . . . there were other injuries."

There had been immediate uproar in the town. To save every man, woman, and child in Jewry from slaughter, they had been hurried to Cambridge Castle by the sheriff and his men, acting on behalf of the king, under whose protection the Jews were.

"Even so, on the way, Chaim was seized by those seeking vengeance and hanged from Saint Radegund's willow. They took his wife as she pleaded for him and tore her to pieces." Prior Geoffrey crossed himself. "The sheriff and myself did what we could, but we were outdone by the townsfolk's fury." He frowned; the memory pained him. "I saw decent men transform into hellhounds, matrons into maenads."

He lifted his cap and passed his hand over his balding head. "Even then, Master Simon, it might be that we could have contained the trouble. The sheriff managed to restore order, and it was hoped that, since Chaim was dead, the remaining Jews would be allowed to return to their homes. But no. Now onto the floor steps Roger of Acton, a cleric new to our town and one of our Canterbury pilgrims. Doubtless you noticed him, a lean-shanked, mean-featured, whey-faced, importunate fellow of dubious cleanliness. Master Roger happens"—the prior glared at Simon as if finding fault with him—"*happens* to be cousin to the prioress of Saint Radegund, a seeker after fame through the scribbling of religious tracts that reveal little but his ignorance."

The two men shook their heads. The blackbird went on singing.

Prior Geoffrey sighed. "Master Roger heard the dread word 'crucifixion' and snapped at it like a ferret. Here was something new. Not merely an accusation of torture such as Jews have ever inspired . . . I beg your pardon, Master Simon, but it has always been so."

"I fear it has, my lord. I fear it has."

"Here was a reenactment of Easter, a child found worthy to suffer the pains of the Son of God and, therefore, undoubtedly, both a saint and a miracle-giver. I would have buried the boy with decency but was denied by the hag in human form who poses as a nun of Saint Radegund."

The prior shook his fist toward the road. "She abducted the child's body, claiming it as hers by right merely because Peter's parents dwell on land belonging to Saint Radegund. *Mea culpa,* I fear we wrangled over the corpse. But that woman, Master Simon, that hellcat, sees not the body of a little boy deserving Christian burial but an acquisition to the den of succubae she calls a convent, a source of income from pilgrims and from the halt and the lame looking for cure. An *attraction,* Master Simon." He sat back. "And such it has become. Roger of Acton has spread the word. Our prioress was seen taking advice from the money changers of Canterbury on how to sell Little Saint Peter relics and tokens at the convent gate. *Quid non mortalia pectora cogis, auri sacra fames!* To what do you not drive human hearts, cursed craving for gold!"

"I am shocked, my lord," Simon said.

"You should be, Master Simon. She has a knuckle taken from the boy's hand that she and her cousin pressed on me in my travail, saying it would mend me in the instant. Roger of Acton, do you see, wishes to add me to the list of cures, that my name might be on the application to the Vatican for the official sainting of Little Saint Peter."

"I see."

"The knuckle, which, such was my pain, I did not scruple to touch, was ineffective. My deliverance was from a more unexpected source." The prior got up. "Which reminds me, I feel the urge to piss."

Simon put out a hand to detain him. "But what of the other children, my lord? The ones still missing?"

Prior Geoffrey stood for a moment, as if listening to the blackbird. "For a while, nothing," he said. "The town had sated itself on Chaim and Miriam. The Jews in the castle were preparing to leave it. But then another boy disappeared and we did not dare to move them."

The prior turned his face away so that Simon could not see it. "It was on All Souls' Night. He was a boy from my own school." Simon heard the break in the prior's voice. "Next, a little girl, a wildfowler's daughter. On Holy Innocents Day, God help us. Then, as recently as the Feast of Saint Edward, King and Martyr, another boy."

"But, my lord, who can accuse the Jews of these disappearances? Are they not still locked in the castle?"

"By now, Master Simon, Jews have been awarded the ability to fly over the castle crenels, snatching up the children and gnawing them before dropping their carcasses in the nearest mere. May I advise you not to reveal yourself. You see"—the prior paused—"there have been signs."

"Signs?"

"Found in the area where each child was last seen. Cabalistic weavings. The townsfolk say they resemble the Star of David. And now"—Prior Geoffrey was crossing his legs—"I *have* to piss. This is a matter of some moment."

Simon watched him hobble to the trees. "Good fortune, my lord."

I was right to tell him as much as I did, he thought. We have gained a valuable ally. For information, I traded information—though not all of it.

THE TRACK TOWARD the brow of Wandlebury Hill had been made by a landslip that breached part of the great ditches dug out by some ancient peoples to defend it. The passage of sheep had evened it out and Adelia, a basket on her arm, climbed to the summit in minutes without losing breath—to find herself alone on the hilltop, an immense circle of grass dotted currantlike with sheep droppings.

From a distance, it had appeared bald. Certainly the only high trees were down its side, with a clump along one easterly edge, and the rest was covered with shrubby hawthorn and juniper bushes. The flattish surface was pitted here and there with curious depressions, some of them two or three feet deep and at least six feet across. A good place to wrench your ankle.

To the east, where the sun was rising, the ground fell away gently; to the west, it dropped fast to the flat land.

She opened her cloak, clasped her hands behind her neck, stretching, letting the breeze pierce the despised tunic of harsh wool bought in Dover that Simon of Naples had begged her to wear.

"Our mission lies among the commoners of England, Doctor. If we are to mingle with them, learn what they know, we must appear as they do."

"Mansur looks every inch a Saxon villein, naturally," she'd said. "And what of our accents?"

But Simon had maintained it was a matter of degree that three foreign medicine peddlers, always popular with the herd, would hear more secrets than a thousand inquisitors. "We shall not be removed by class from those we question; it is the truth we want, not respect."

"In this thing," she'd said of the tunic, "respect will *not* be forthcoming." However, Simon, more experienced in deception than she, was the leader of this mission. Adelia had put on what was basically a tube, fastened at the shoulders with pins but retaining her silk undershift—though never one to swim in the stream of fashion, she'd be damned if, even for the King of Sicily, she tolerated sackcloth next to the skin.

She closed her eyes against the light, tired from a night spent watching her patient for signs of fever. At dawn the prior's skin had proved cool, his pulse steady; the procedure had been successful for the moment; it now remained to be seen whether he could urinate without help and without pain. So far so good, as Margaret used to say.

She started walking, her eyes searching for useful plants, noticing that her cheap boots—another blasted disguise—sent up sweet, unfamiliar scents at each step. There were goodies here among the grass, the early leaves of vervains, ale-hoof, catmint, bugle, *Clinopodium vulgare,* which the English called wild basil, though it neither resembled nor smelled like true basil. Once she had bought an old English herbal that the monks of Saint Lucia had acquired but couldn't read. She'd given it to Margaret as a reminder of home, only to reappropriate it to study for herself.

And here they were, its illustrations, growing in real life at her feet, as thrilling as if she'd encountered a famed face in the street.

The herbalist author, relying heavily on Galen, like most of his kind, had made the usual claims: laurel to protect from lightning, all-heal to ward off the plague, marjoram to secure the uterus—as if a woman's uterus floated up to the neck and down again like a cherry in a bottle. Why did they never *look?*

She began picking.

All at once she was uneasy. There was no reason for it; the great ring was as deserted as it had been. Clouds changed the light as their shadows chased one another briskly across the grass; a stunted hawthorn assumed the shape of a bent old woman; a sudden screech—a magpie—sent smaller birds flying.

Whatever it was, she had an apprehension that made her want to be less vertical in all this flatness. So foolish she'd been. Tempted by its plants and the apparent isolation of this place, tired of the chattering company she'd been surrounded with since Canterbury, she'd committed the error, the idiocy, of venturing out alone, telling Mansur to stay and care for the prior. A mistake. She had abrogated all right to immunity from predation. Indeed, without the company of Margaret and Mansur, and as far as men in the vicinity were concerned, she might as well be wearing a placard saying "Rape me." If the invitation were accepted, it would be regarded as her fault, not the rapist's.

Damn the prison in which men incarcerated women. She'd resented its invisible bars when Mansur had insisted on accompanying her along the long, dark corridors of the Salerno school, making her look overprivileged and ridiculous as she went from lecture to lecture, and marking her out. But she'd learned—oh, she'd learned—her lesson, that day when she'd avoided his chaperonage: the outrage, the desperation with which she'd had to scrabble against a male fellow student; the indignity of having to scream for help, which, thank God, had been answered; the subsequent lecture from her professors and, of course, Mansur and Margaret, on the sins of arrogance and carelessness of reputation.

Nobody had blamed the young man, although Mansur had afterward broken his nose by way of teaching him manners.

Being Adelia and still arrogant, she forced herself to walk a little farther, though in the direction of the trees, and pick a plant or two more before looking around.

Nothing. The flutter of hawthorn blossom on the breeze, another sudden dimming of light as a cloud chased across the sun.

A pheasant rose, clattering and shrieking. She turned.

It was as if he had sprung out of the ground. He was marching toward her, casting a long shadow. No pimply student this time. One of the pilgrimage's heavy and confident crusaders, the metal links of his mail hissing beneath the tabard, the mouth smiling but the eyes as hard as the iron encasing head and nose. "Well, well, now," he was saying with anticipation. "Well, well, now, mistress."

Adelia experienced a deep weariness—at her own stupidity, at what was to come. She had resources; one of them, a wicked little dagger, was tucked in her boot, given to her by her Sicilian foster mother, a straightforward woman with the advice to stick it in the assailant's eye. Her Jewish stepfather had suggested a more subtle defense: "Tell them you're a doctor and appear concerned by their appearance. Ask if they've been in contact with the plague. That'll lower any man's flag."

She doubted, though, whether either ploy would prevail against this advancing mailed mass. Nor, considering her mission, did she want to broadcast her profession.

She stood straight and tried loftiness while he was still a way off. "Yes?" she called sharply. Which might have been impressive had she been Vesuvia Adelia Rachel Ortese Aguilar in Salerno, but on this lonely hill, it did little for a poorly dressed foreign trull known to travel in a peddler's cart with two men.

"That's what I like," the man called back. "A woman who says yes."

He came on. No doubt about his intention now; she dropped, groping into her boot.

Then two things happened at once—from different directions.

Out of the clump of trees came the *whoom-whoom* sound of air being displaced by something whirling through it. A small ax buried its blade in the grass between Adelia and the knight.

The other was a yell from across the hill. "In the name of God, Gervase, call your bloody hounds and go down. The old girl's champing at her bit."

Adelia watched the knight's eyes change. She leaned forward and, with an effort, pulled the ax from the ground and stood up with it, smiling. "It must be magic," she said in English.

The other crusader was still shouting for his friend to find his dogs and go down to the road.

The discomfiture in this one's face changed to something like hatred, then, deliberately, to disinterest as he turned on his heel and strode away to join his fellow.

You've made no friend there, Adelia told herself. *God, how I loathe being afraid. Damn him, damn him. And damn this damned country; I didn't want to come in the first place.*

Ill-tempered because she was shaking, she walked toward a shadow under the trees. "I told you to stay with the cart," she said in Arabic.

"You did," Mansur agreed.

She gave him back his ax—he called it Parvaneh (butterfly). He tucked it into the side of his belt so as to be out of sight under his robe, leaving his traditional dagger in its beautiful scabbard on display at the front. The throwing ax as a weapon was rare among Arabs but not for the tribes, and Mansur's was one of them, whose ancestors had encountered the Vikings that had ventured into Arabia where, in exchange for its exotic goods, they had traded not only weapons but also the secret of how to make the superior steel of their blades.

Together, mistress and servant made their way down the hill through the trees, Adelia stumbling, Mansur striding as easily as on a road.

"Which of the goats' droppings was that?" he wanted to know.

"The one they call Gervase. The other's name is Joscelin, I think."

"Crusaders," he said, and spat.

Adelia, too, had little opinion of crusaders. Salerno was on one of the routes to the Holy Land and, whether going out or coming back, most soldiers of the crusading army had been insufferable. As pig-ignorant as they were enthusiastic for God's work, those going out had disrupted the harmony in which different creeds and races lived in Sicily's kingdom by protesting against the presence of Jews, Moors, and even Christians whose practices were different from their own, often attacking them. On the way back, they were usually embittered, diseased, and impoverished—only a few had been rewarded with the fortune or holy grace they'd expected—and, therefore, just as trouble-some.

She knew of some who'd not gone to Outremer at all, merely stay-ing in Salerno until they'd exhausted its bounty before returning home to gain the admiration of their town or village with a few tall tales and a crusading cloak they'd bought cheap in Salerno's market.

"Well, you scared that one," she said now. "It was a good throw."

"No," the Arab said, "I missed."

Adelia turned on him. "Mansur, you listen to me. We are not here to slaughter the populace. . . ."

She stopped. They had come to a track, and just below them was the other crusader, the one called Joscelin, protector of the prioress. He had found one of the hounds and was bending down, attaching a leash to its collar, berating the huntsman who was with him.

As they came up, he raised his head, smiling, nodded at Mansur, and wished Adelia good day. "I am glad to see you accompanied, mis-tress. This is no place for pretty ladies to wander alone, nor anyone else for that matter."

No reference to the incident on the top of the hill, but it was well done; an apology for his friend without directly apologizing, and a re-proof to her. Though why call her pretty when she was not, nor, in her present role, did she set out to be? Were men obliged to flirt? If so, she thought reluctantly, this one probably had more success than most.

He had taken off his helmet and coif, revealing thick, dark hair curled with sweat. His eyes were a startling blue. And, considering his status, he was showing courtesy to a woman who apparently had none.

The huntsman stood apart, unspeaking, sullenly watching them all.

Sir Joscelin inquired after the prior. She was careful to say, indicating Mansur, that the doctor believed his patient to be responding to treatment.

Sir Joscelin bowed to the Arab, and Adelia thought that, if nothing else, he'd learned manners on his crusade. "Ah, yes, Arab medicine," he said. "We gained a respect for it, those of us who went to the Holy Land."

"Did you and your friend go there together?" She was curious about this disparity between the two men.

"At separate times," he said. "Oddly enough, though both of us are Cambridge men, we did not meet up again until our return. A vast place, Outremer."

He had done well out of it, to judge from the quality of his boots and the heavy gold ring on his finger.

She nodded and walked on, remembering only after she and Mansur had passed that she ought to have curtsied to him. Then she forgot him, even forgot the brute who was his friend; she was a doctor, and her mind was directed to her patient.

When the prior came back in triumph to the camp, it was to find that the woman had returned and was sitting alone by the remains of the fire while the Saracen packed the cart and harnessed the mules.

He'd dreaded the moment. Distinguished as he was, he had lain, half-naked and puling with fear, before a woman, a *woman,* all restraint and dignity gone.

Only indebtedness, the knowledge that without her ministration he would have died, had stopped him from ignoring her or stealing away before they could meet again.

She looked up at his step. "Have you passed water?"

"Yes." Curtly.

"Without pain?"

"Yes."

"Good," she said.

It was . . . he remembered now. A vagabond woman had gone into a difficult labor at the priory gates, and Brother Theo, the priory infirmarian, had perforce attended her. Next morning, when he and Theo had visited mother and baby, he wondering which would be most ashamed by their encounter—the woman, who'd revealed her most intimate parts to a man during the birth, or the monk, who'd had to involve himself with them.

Neither. No embarrassment. They had looked on each other with pride.

So it was now. The bright brown eyes regarding him were briskly without sex, those of a comrade-in-arms; he was her fellow soldier, a junior one perhaps; they had fought against the enemy together and won.

He was as grateful to her for that as for his deliverance. He hurried forward and took her hand to his lips. *"Puella mirabile."*

Had Adelia been demonstrative, which she wasn't, she would have hugged the man. It had worked then. Not having practiced general medicine for so long, she had forgotten the incalculable pleasure of seeing a creature released from suffering. However, he had to be aware of the prognosis.

"Not as *mirabile* as all that," she told him. "It could happen again."

"Damn," the prior said, "damn, *damn* it." He recovered himself. "I beg your pardon, mistress."

She patted his hand and sat him down on the log, settling herself on the grass, her legs tucked beneath her. "Men have a gland that is accessory to the male generative organs," she said. "It surrounds the neck of the bladder and the commencement of the urethra. In your case, I believe it to be enlarged. Yesterday it pressed so hard that the bladder could not function."

"What am I to do?" he asked.

"You must learn to relieve the bladder, should the occasion arise, as I did—using a reed as a *catheter*."

"*Catheter?*" She'd used the Greek word for a tube.

"You should practice. I can show you."

Dear God, he thought, *she would.* Nor would it mean anything to her but a medical procedure. I am discussing these things with a woman; she is discussing them with me.

On the journey from Canterbury he'd barely noticed her, except as one of the ragtag—though, now that he came to think of it, during the overnight rests at the inns she had joined the nuns in the women's quarters rather than staying in the cart with her men. Last night, when she had frowned down on his privates, she might have been one of his scribes concentrating on a difficult manuscript. This morning, her professionalism sustained them both above the murky waters of gender.

Yet she *was* a woman and, poor thing, as plain as her talk. A woman to blend so well into a crowd as to disappear, a background woman, a mouse among mice. Since she was now in the forefront of his atten-tion, Prior Geoffrey felt an irritation that this should be so. There was no reason for such homeliness; the features were small and regular, as was what little he could see of her body beneath an enveloping cloak. The complexion was good, with the dusky, downy fairness to be found sometimes in northern Italy and Greece. Teeth white. Presumably there was hair beneath the cap with its rolled brim pulled down to her ears. How old was she? Still young.

The sun shone on a face that eschewed prettiness for intelligence, shrewdness taking away its femininity. No trace of artifice, she was clean, he gave her that, scrubbed like a washboard, but, while the prior was the first to condemn paint on women, this one's lack of artifice was very nearly an affront. A virgin still, he would swear to it.

Adelia saw a man overfed, as so many monastic superiors were, though in this case gluttony was not the result of an appetite for food compensating for the deprivation of sex; she felt safe in his company. Women were natural beings for him; she knew that in an instant because it was so rare, neither harpies nor temptresses. The desires of the flesh were there but not indulged, nor kept in check by the birch. The nice eyes spoke of someone at ease with himself, worldliness living cheek by jowl—too much jowl—with goodness, a man who tolerated petty sins, including his own. He found her curious, of course—everybody did once they'd noticed her.

Nice as he was, she was becoming irritated; she'd been up most of the night attending to him; the least he could do was attend to her advice now.

"Are you listening to me, my lord?"

"I beg pardon, mistress." He sat up straight.

"I *said* I can show you the use of a catheter. The procedure is not difficult when you know how to do it."

He said, "I think, madam, we will wait upon the necessity."

"Very well." It was up to him. "In the meantime, you carry too much weight. You must take more exercise and eat less."

Stung, he said, "I hunt every week."

"On horseback. Follow the hounds on foot instead."

Domineering, Prior Geoffrey thought. *And she comes from Sicily?* His experience of Sicilian women—it had been short but unforgettable—remembered the allures of Araby: dark eyes smiling at him above a veil, the touch of hennaed fingers, words as soft as the skin, the scent of . . .

God's bones, Adelia thought, *why do they attach such importance to frippery?* "I can't be bothered," she said snappily.

"Eh?"

She sighed with impatience. "I see you are regretting that the woman, like the doctor, is unadorned. It always happens." She glared at him. "You are getting the truth of both, Master Prior. If you want them bedecked, go elsewhere. Turn over that stone"—she pointed to a flint nearby—"and you will find a charlatan who will dazzle you with the favorable conjunction of Mercury and Venus, flatter your future, and sell you colored water for a gold piece. I can't be bothered with it. From me you get the actuality."

He was taken aback. Here was the confidence, even arrogance, of a skilled artisan. She might be a plumber he'd called in to mend a burst pipe.

Except, he remembered, that she'd stopped his particular pipe from bursting. However, even practicality could do with ornamentation. "Are you as direct with all your patients?" he asked.

"I don't have patients usually," she said.

"I'm not surprised."

And she laughed.

Entrancing, the prior thought. He remembered Horace: *Dulce ridentem Lalagen amabo.* I will love Lalage, who laughs so sweetly. Yet laughter in this young woman gave her instant vulnerability and innocence, being at such odds with the stern lecturing she'd assumed before, so that his sudden welling affection was not for a Lalage but for a daughter. *I must protect her,* he thought.

She was holding something out to him. "I have prescribed a diet for you."

"Paper, by the Lord," he said. "Where did you obtain paper?"

"The Arabs make it."

He glanced at the list; her writing was abominable, but he could just decipher it. "Water? Boiled water? Eight cups a day? Madam, would you kill me? The poet Horace tells us that nothing of worth can come from drinkers of water."

"Try Martial," she said. "He lived longer. *Non est vivere, sed valere vita est.* Life's not just being alive but being well."

He shook his head in wonder. Humbly, he said, "I beg you, tell me your name."

"Vesuvia Adelia Rachel Ortese Aguilar," Adelia said. "Or Dr. Trotula, if you prefer, which is a title conferred on women professors in the school."

He didn't prefer. "Vesuvia? A pretty name, most unusual."

"Adelia," she said, "I was merely found on Vesuvius." She was stretching out her hand as if to hold his. He held his breath.

Instead she took his wrist, her thumb on its top, the other fingers pressed into its soft underpart. Her fingernails were short and clean, like the rest of her. "I was exposed on the mountain as a baby. In a crock." She talked absently, and he saw that she was not really informing him, merely keeping him quiet while she sounded his pulse. "The two doctors who found and raised me thought it possible I was Greek, exposure having been a Greek custom with an unwanted daughter."

She let go of his wrist, shaking her head. "Too fast," she said. "Truly, you should lose weight." *He must be preserved,* she thought. He would be a loss.

Peculiarity after peculiarity was making the prior's head reel. And while the Lord might exalt those of low degree, there was no necessity for her to display her ignoble beginnings to all and sundry. Dear, dear. Away from her milieu, she would be as exposed as a snail without its shell. He asked, "You were raised by two men?"

She was affronted, as if he suggested her upbringing had been abnormal. "They were *married,*" she said, frowning. "My foster mother is also a Trotula. A Christian-born Salernitan."

"And your foster father?"

"A Jew."

Here it was again. Did these people blurt it to the fowls of the air? "So you were brought up in his faith?" It mattered to him; she was a brand, *his* brand, a most precious brand, to be saved from the burning.

She said, "I have no faith except in what can be proved."

The prior was appalled. "Do you not acknowledge the Creation? God's purpose?"

"There was creation, certainly. Whether there was purpose, I don't know."

My God, my God, he thought, *do not strike her down. I have need of her. She knows not what she says.*

She was standing up. Her eunuch had turned the cart ready for its descent to the road. Simon was walking toward them.

The prior said, because even apostates had to be paid, and he pitied this one with all his heart, "Mistress Adelia, I am in your debt and would weight my end of the scales. A boon and, with God's grace, I will grant it."

She turned and regarded him, considering. She saw the nice eyes, the clever mind, the goodness; she liked him. But the command of her profession was for his body—not yet, but one day. The gland that had restricted the bladder, weigh it, compare it . . .

Simon broke into a run; he'd seen that look of hers before. She had no judgment other than in medicine; she was about to ask the prior for his corpse when he died. "My lord, my lord." He was panting. "My lord, if you would grant a kindness, prevail upon the prioress to let Dr. Trotula view Little Saint Peter's remains. It may be that she can throw light on the manner of his passing."

"Indeed?" Prior Geoffrey looked at Vesuvia Adelia Rachel Ortese Aguilar. "And how may you do that?"

"I am a doctor to the dead," she said.

Four

As they approached the great gate of Barnwell Abbey, they could see Cambridge Castle in the distance on the only height for miles around, its outline made ragged and prickly by the remains of the tower that had been burned the year before and the scaffolding now surrounding it. A pygmy of a fortress compared with the great citadels hung upon the Appenines that Adelia knew, it nevertheless lent a burly charm to the view.

"Of Roman foundation," Prior Geoffrey said, "built to guard the river crossing, though, like many another, it failed to hold off either Viking or Dane—nor Duke William the Norman, come to that; having destroyed it, he had to build it up again."

The cavalcade was smaller now; the prioress had hastened ahead, taking her nun, her knight, and cousin Roger of Acton with her. The merchant and his wife had turned off toward Cherry Hinton.

Prior Geoffrey, once more horsed and resplendent at the head of the procession, was forced to lean down to address his saviors on the driving bench of the mule cart. His knight, Sir Gervase, brought up the rear, scowling.

"Cambridge will surprise you," the prior was saying. "We have a fine School of Pythagoras, to which students come from all over. Despite its inland position, it is a port, and a busy one, nearly as busy as Dover—though blessedly more free of the French. The waters of the Cam may be sluggish, but they are navigable to their conjunction with the River Ouse that, in turn, discharges into the North Sea. I think I may say that there are few countries of the world's East that do not come to our quays with goods that are then passed on by mule trains to all parts of England along the Roman roads that bisect the town."

"And what do you send back, my lord?" Simon asked.

"Wool. Fine East Anglian wool." Prior Geoffrey smirked with the satisfaction of a high prelate whose grazing provided a good proportion of it. "Smoked fish, eels, oysters. Oh, yes, Master Simon, you may mark Cambridge to be prosperous in trade and, dare I say it, cosmopolitan in outlook."

Dare he say it? His heart misgave as he regarded the three in the cart; even in a town accustomed to mustached Scandinavians, Low Countrymen in clogs, slit-eyed Russians, Templars, Hospitallers from the Holy Lands, curly-hatted Magyars, snake charmers, could this trio of oddities go unremarked? He looked around him, then leaned lower and hissed. "How do you intend to present yourselves?"

Simon said innocently, "Since our good Mansur has already been credited with your cure, my lord, I thought to continue the deception by setting him up as a medical man with Dr. Trotula and myself as his assistants. Perhaps the marketplace? Some center from which to pursue our inquiries . . ."

"In that damned cart?" The indignation Simon of Naples had courted was forthcoming. "Would you have the lady Adelia spat on by women traders? Importuned by passing vagabonds?" The prior calmed himself. "I see the need to disguise her profession, lady doctors being unknown in England. Certainly, she would be considered outlandish." *Even more outlandish than she is,* he thought. "We shall not have her degraded as some quacksalver's drab. We are a respectable town, Master Simon, we can do better for you than that."

"My lord." Simon's hand touched his forehead in gratitude. And to himself: *I thought you might.*

"Nor would it be wise for any of you to declare your faith—or lack of it," the prior continued. "Cambridge is a tightly wound crossbow, any abnormality may loose it again." *Especially*, he thought, *as these three particular abnormalities were determined on probing Cambridge's wounds.*

He paused. The tax collector had come up and reined his horse to the mule's amble, waving an obeisance to the prior, sending a nod to Simon and Mansur, and addressing Adelia: "Madam, we have been in convoy together, and yet we have not been introduced. Sir Rowley Picot at your service. May I congratulate you on effecting the good prior's recovery?"

Quickly, Simon leaned forward. "The congratulations belong to this gentleman, sir." He indicated Mansur, who was driving. "He is our doctor."

The tax collector was interested. "Indeed? One was informed that a female voice was heard directing the operation."

Was one, indeed? And by whom? Simon wondered. He nudged Mansur. "Say something," he told him in Arabic.

Mansur ignored him.

Surreptitiously, Simon kicked him on the ankle "*Speak* to him, you lump."

"What does the fat shit want me to say?"

"The doctor is pleased that he has been of service to my lord prior," Simon told the tax inspector. "He says he hopes he may administer as well to anyone in Cambridge who wishes to consult him."

"Does he?" Sir Rowley Picot said, neglecting to mention his own knowledge of Arabic. "He says it amazing high."

"*Exactly,* Sir Rowley," Simon said. "His voice can be mistaken for a woman's." He became confidential. "I should explain that the lord

Mansur was taken by monks while yet a child, and his singing voice was discovered to be so beautiful that they . . . er . . . ensured it would remain so."

"A castrato, by God," Sir Rowley said, staring.

"He devotes himself to medicine now, of course," Simon said, "but when he sings in praise of the Lord, the angels weep with envy."

Mansur had heard the word "castrato" and lapsed into cursing, causing more angels' tears by his strictures on Christians in general, and the unhealthy affection existing between camels and the mothers of the Byzantine monks who'd gelded him in particular—the sound issuing in an Arabic treble that rivaled birdsong and melted on the air like sweet icicles.

"You see, Sir Rowley?" Simon asked over it. "That was doubtless the voice heard."

Sir Rowley said, "It must have been." And again, smiling with apology, "It must have been."

He continued to try and engage Adelia in conversation, but her replies were short and sullen; she'd had her fill of importuning Englishmen. Her attention was on the countryside. Having lived among hills, she had expected to be repelled by flat land; she had not reckoned on such enormous skies, nor the significance they gave to a lonely tree, the crook of a rare chimney, a single church tower, outlined against them. The multiplicity of greenness suggested unknown herbs to be discovered, the strip fields made chessboards of emerald and black.

And willows. The landscape was full of them, lining streams, dikes, and lanes. Crack willow for stabilizing the banks, golden willow, white willow, gray willow, goat willow, willows for making bats, for growing osiers, bay willow, almond willow, beautiful with the sun dappling through their branches, and more beautiful still because, with a concoction of willow bark, you could relieve pain. . . .

She was jerked forward as Mansur pulled in the mules. The procession had come to an abrupt halt, for Prior Geoffrey had held up his hand and begun to pray. The men swept off their caps and held them to their breasts.

Entering the gate was a dray splashed with mud. A dirty piece of canvas laid on it showed the shape of three small bundles beneath. The drayman led his horses with his head bowed. A woman followed him, shrieking and tearing at her clothing.

The missing children had been found.

THE CHURCH of Saint Andrew the Less in the grounds of Saint Augustine's, Barnwell, was two hundred feet long, a carved and painted glory to God. But today the grisailled spring sunlight from the high windows ignored the glorious hammer roof, the faces of recumbent stone priors round the walls, the statue of Saint Augustine, the ornate pulpit, the glitter of altar and triptych.

Instead it fell in shafts on three small catafalques in the nave, each covered with a violet cloth, and on the heads of the kneeling men and women in working clothes gathered round them.

The remains of the children, all three, had been found on a sheep path near Fleam Dyke that morning. A shepherd had stumbled over them at dawn and was still shuddering. "Weren't there last night, I'll take my oath, Prior. Couldn't have been, could they? The foxes ain't been at them. Lying neat side by side they was, bless them. Or neat as they could be, considering . . ." He'd stopped to retch.

An object had been laid on each body, resembling those that had been left at the site of each child's disappearance. Made from rushes, they resembled the Star of David.

Prior Geoffrey had ordered the three bundles taken to the church, resisting one mother's desperate attempts to unwrap them. He had sent to the castle, warning the sheriff that it might be attacked again and requesting the sheriff's reeve in his capacity as coroner to view the remains immediately and order a public inquest. He'd imposed calm—though it rumbled with underlying heat.

Now, resonating with certainty, his voice stilled the mother's shrieks into a quiet sobbing as he read the assurance that death would be swallowed up in victory. "We shall not all sleep, but we shall all be changed in a moment, in the twinkling of an eye, at the last trump."

Almost, the scent issuing in from the bluebells outside the open doors and the lavished incense from within them covered the stench of decay.

Almost, the clear chant of the canons drowned out the buzz of trapped flies coming from under the violet mantles.

Saint Paul's words assuaged a little of the prior's grief as he envisaged the souls of the children romping in God's meadows, yet not his anger that they had been catapulted into them before their time. Two of the children he did not know, but one of the boys was Harold, the eel seller's son, who had been a pupil at Saint Augustine's own school. Six years old and a bright child, learning his letters once a week. Identified by his red hair. A right little Saxon, too—he'd scrumped apples from the priory orchard last autumn.

And I tanned his backside for him, the prior thought.

From the shadow of a rear pillar, Adelia watched some comfort seep into the faces round the catafalques. The closeness between priory and town was strange to her; in Salerno, monks, even monks who went out into the world to perform their duties, kept a distance between themselves and the laity.

"But we are not monks," Prior Geoffrey had told her, "we are canons." It seemed a slight dissimilarity: Both lived in community, both vowed celibacy, both served the Christian God, yet here in Cambridge the distinction made a difference. When the church bell had tolled the news that the children were found, people from the town had come running—to hug and to be hugged in commiseration.

"Our rule is less rigid than Benedictine or Cistercian," the prior had explained, "less time given to prayer and choral duty and more to education, relief of the poor and sick, hearing confession, and general parish work." He'd tried to smile. "You will approve, my dear Doctor. Moderation in all things."

Now she watched him come down from the choir after the dismissal and walk with the parents into the sunlight, promising to officiate at the funerals himself, "and discover the devil who has done this."

"We know who done it, Prior," one of the fathers said. Agreement echoed like the growl of dogs.

"It cannot be the Jews, my son. They are still secured in the castle."

"They're getting out someways."

The bodies, still under their violet cloths, were carried reverently on litters out a side door, accompanied by the sheriff's reeve, wearing his coroner's hat.

The church emptied. Simon and Mansur had wisely not attempted to come. A Jew and a Saracen among these sacred stones? At such a time?

With her goatskin carryall at her feet, Adelia waited in the shadow of one of the bays next to the tomb of Paulus, Prior Canon of Saint Augustine's, Barnwell, taken to God in the year of Our Lord 1151. She nerved herself for what was to come.

She had never yet shirked a postmortem examination; she would not shirk this one. It was why she was here. Gordinus had said, "I am sending you with Simon of Naples on this mission not just because you are the only doctor of the dead to speak English, but because you are the best."

"I know," she'd said, "but I do not want to go."

She'd had to. It had been ordered by the King of Sicily.

In the cool stone hall that the Medical School of Salerno devoted to dissection, she'd always had the proper equipment and Mansur to assist her, relying on her foster father, head of the department, to relay her findings to the authorities. For, though Adelia could read death better than her foster father, better than anybody, the fiction had to be maintained that the investigation of bodies sent by the *signoria* was the province of Dr. Gershom bin Aguilar. Even in Salerno, where female doctors were permitted to practice, the dissection that helped the dead to explain how they'd died—and, very often, at whose hands— was regarded with revulsion by the Church.

So far science had fought off religion; other doctors knew the use of Adelia's work, and it was an open secret among the lay authorities. But should an official complaint be made to the Pope, she'd be banned from the mortuary and, quite possibly, the school of medicine itself. So, though he writhed under the hypocrisy, Gershom took credit for achievements that were not his.

Which suited Adelia to her boots. Staying in the background was her forte: for one thing, it avoided the Church's eye; for another thing, she did not know how to converse on womanly subjects as she was ex- pected to, and did it badly because they bored her. Like a hedgehog blending into autumn leaves, she was prickly to those who tried to bring her into the light.

It was another matter if you were ill. Before she devoted herself to postmortem work, the sick had seen a side to Adelia that few others did, and still remembered her as an angel without wings. Recovering male patients had tended to fall in love with her, and it would have surprised the prior to learn that she'd received more requests for her hand in marriage than many a rich Salernitan beauty. All had been turned down. It was said in the school's mortuary that Adelia was in- terested in you only if you were dead.

Cadavers of every age came to that long marble table in the school from all over southern Italy and Sicily, sent by *signoria* and *praetori* who had reason to want to know how and why they'd died. Usually, she found out for them; corpses were her work, as normal to her as his last to a shoemaker. She approached the bodies of children in the same way, determined that the truth of their death should not be buried with them, but they distressed her, always pitiful and, in the case of those who had been murdered, always shocking. The three awaiting her now were likely to be as terrible as any she had seen. Not only that, but she must examine them in secrecy, without the equipment provided by the school, without Mansur to assist her, and, most of all, without her foster father's encouragement: "Adelia, you must not quail. You are confounding inhumanity."

He never told her she was confounding evil—at least, not Evil with a capital E, for Gershom bin Aguilar believed that Man provided his own evil and his own good, neither the devil nor God having anything to do with it. Only in the medical school of Salerno could he preach that doctrine, and even there not very loudly.

The concession to allow her to carry out this particular investigation, in a backward English town where she could be stoned for doing it, was a marvel in itself and one that Simon of Naples had fought hard to gain. The prior had been reluctant to give his permission, appalled that a woman was prepared to carry out such work and fearing what would happen if it were known that a foreigner had peered at and prodded the poor corpses: "Cambridge would regard it as desecration; I'm not sure it isn't."

Simon had said, "My lord, let us find out how the children died, for it is certain that incarcerated Jews could have had no hand in it; we are modern men, we know wings do not sprout from human shoulders. Somewhere, a murderer walks free. Allow those sad little bodies to tell us who he is. The dead speak to Dr. Trotula. It is her work. They will talk to her."

As far as Prior Geoffrey was concerned, talking dead were in the same category as winged humans: "It is against the teaching of Holy Mother Church to invade the sanctity of the body."

He gave way at last only on Simon's promise that there would be no dissection, only examination.

Simon suspected that the prior's compliance also arose less from belief that the corpses would speak than from the fear that, if she were refused, Adelia would return to the place from which she'd come, leaving him to face the next onslaught of his bladder without her.

So now, here, in a country she hadn't wanted to come to in the first place, she must confront the worst of all inhumanities alone.

But that, Vesuvia Adelia Rachel Ortese Aguilar, is your purpose, she told herself. In times of uncertainty, she liked to recount the names that had been lavished on her, along with education and their own extraordinary ideas, by the couple that had picked her up from her lava-strewn cradle on Vesuvius and taken her home. *Only you are fitted to do it, so do it.*

In her hand was one of the three objects that had been found on the bodies of the dead children. One had been already delivered to the sheriff, one torn to pieces by a rampaging father. The third had been saved by the prior, who had quietly passed it to her.

Carefully, so as not to attract attention, she held it up to catch a shaft of light. It was made of rushes, beautifully and with great intricacy woven into a quincunx. If it was meant to be a Star of David, the weaver had left out one of the points. A message? An attempt to incriminate the Jews by someone poorly acquainted with Judaism? A signature?

In Salerno, she thought, it would have been possible to locate the limited number of people with skill enough to make it, but in Cambridge, where rushes grew inexhaustibly by the rivers and streams, weaving them was a household activity; merely passing along the road to this great priory, she had seen women sitting in doorways, their hands engaged in making mats and baskets that were works of art, men thatching rush roofs into ornate sculptures.

No, there was nothing the star could tell her at this stage.

Prior Geoffrey came bustling back in. "The coroner has looked at the bodies and ordered a public inquest—"

"What did he have to say?"

"He pronounced them dead." At Adelia's blink, he said, "Yes, yes,

but it is his duty—coroners are not chosen for their medical knowledge. Now then, I've lodged the remains in Saint Werbertha's anchorage. It is quiet there, and cold, a little dark for your purposes, but I
have provided lamps. A vigil will be kept, of course, but it shall be delayed until you have made your examination. Officially, you are there
to do the laying out."

Again, a blink.

"Yes, yes, it will be regarded as strange, but I am the prior of this
foundation and my law is second only to Almighty God's." He bustled
her to the side door of the church and gave her directions. A novice
weeding the cloister garden looked up in curiosity, but a click of his
superior's fingers sent him back to work. "I would come with you, but
I must go to the castle and discuss eventualities with the sheriff. Between us, we have to prevent another riot."

Watching the small, brown-clad figure trudge off carrying its
goatskin bag, the prior prayed that in this case, his law and Almighty
God's coincided.

He turned round in order to snatch a minute in prayer at the altar,
but a large shadow detached itself from one of the nave's pillars, startling him and making him angry. It had a roll of vellum in its hand.

"What do you here, Sir Rowley?"

"I was about to plead for a private view of the bodies, my lord," the
tax collector said, "but it seems I have been preempted."

"That is the job of the coroner, and he's done it. There will be an
official inquest in a day or two."

Sir Rowley nodded toward the side door. "Yet I heard you instructing that lady to examine them further. Do you hope for her to
tell you more?"

Prior Geoffrey looked around for help and found none.

The tax collector asked with apparent genuine interest, "How
might she do that? Conjurement? Invocation? Is she a necromancer?
A witch?"

He'd gone too far. The prior said quietly, "Those children are sacred to me, my son, as is this church. You may leave."

"I apologize, my lord." The tax collector didn't look sorry. "But I
too have a concern in this matter, and I have here the king's warrant
whereby to pursue it." He waved a roll so that the royal seal swung.
"What is that woman?"

A king's warrant trumped the authority of a canonry prior, even
one whose word was next to God's. Sullenly, Prior Geoffrey said, "She
is a doctor versed in the morbid sciences."

"Of course. *Salerno.* I should have known." The tax collector whistled with satisfaction. "A woman doctor from the only place in Christendom where that is not a contradiction in terms."

"You know it?"

"Stopped there once."

"Sir Rowley." The prior raised his hand in admonition. "For the
safety of that young woman, for the peace of this community and
town, what I have told you must remain within these walls."

"*Vir sapit qui pauca loquitur,* my lord. First thing they teach a tax
collector."

Not so much wise as cunning, the prior decided, but probably able
to keep silent. What was the man's purpose? At a sudden thought, he
held out his hand. "Let me see that warrant." He examined it, then
handed it back. "This is merely the usual tax collector's warrant. Is the
king taxing the dead now?"

"Indeed not, my lord." Sir Rowley seemed affronted by the idea.
"Or not more than usual. But if the lady is to conduct an unofficial
inquest, it might subject both town and priory to punitive taxes—I
don't say it *will,* but the regular amercements, confiscation of goods, et
cetera, might apply." The plump cheeks bunched in an engaging smile.
"Unless, of course, I am present to see that all is correct."

The prior was beaten. So far Henry II had withheld his hand, but it was fairly certain that at the next assize, Cambridge would be fined, and fined heavily, for the death of one of the king's most profitable Jews.

Any infringement of his laws gave the king an opportunity to fill his coffers at the expense of the infringers. Henry listened to his tax collectors, the most dreaded of royal underlings; if this one should report to him an irregularity connected with the children's deaths, then the teeth of that rapacious Plantagenet leopard might tear the heart out of the town.

"What do you want of us, Sir Rowley?" Prior Geoffrey asked wearily.

"I want to see those bodies." The words were spoken quietly, but they flicked at the prior like a lash.

APART FROM THE FACT that its three-foot-thick walls kept it cool, and its situation in a glade at the far end of Barnwell's deer park was isolated, the cell in which the Saxon anchoress Saint Werbertha had passed her adult life—until, that is, it had been ended somewhat abruptly by invading Danes—was unsuitable for Adelia's purposes. For one thing, it was small. For another, despite the two lamps the prior had provided, it was dark. A slit of a window was shut by a wooden slide. Cow parsley frothed waist-high around a tiny door set in an arch.

Damn all this secrecy. She would have to keep the door open in order to have enough light—and the place was already beset by flies trying to get in. How did they expect her to work in these conditions?

Adelia put her goatskin bag on the grass outside, opened it to check its contents, checked them again—and knew she was putting off the moment when she would have to open the door.

This was ridiculous; she was not an amateur. Quickly, she knelt and

asked the dead beyond the door to forgive her for handling their remains. She asked to be reminded not to forget the respect owed to
them. "Permit your flesh and bone to tell me what your voices cannot."

She always did this; whether the dead heard her she was unsure,
but she was not the complete atheist her foster father was, though she
suspected that what lay ahead of her this afternoon might convert her
into one.

She rose, took her oilcloth apron from the bag, put it on, removed
her cap, tied the gauze helmet with its glazed eyepiece over her head,
and opened the cell door. . . .

Sir Rowley Picot enjoyed the walk, pleased with himself. It was going to be easier than he'd thought. A mad female, a mad *foreign* female,
was always going to be forced to succumb to his authority, but it was
unexpected bounty that someone of Prior Geoffrey's standing should
also be under his thumb through association with the same female.

Nearing the anchorage, he paused. It looked like an overgrown
beehive—*Lord, how the old hermits loved discomfort.* And there she was, a figure bending over something on a table just inside its open door.

To test her, he called out, "Doctor."

"Yes?"

Ah, hah, Sir Rowley thought. How easy. Like snatching a moth.

As she straightened and turned toward him, he began, "You remember me, madam? I am Sir Rowley Picot, whom the prior—"

"I don't care who you are," the moth snapped. "Come in here and
keep the flies off." She emerged, and he was presented with an
aproned human figure with the head of an insect. It tore a clump of
cow parsley from the ground and, at his approach, shoved the umbel-
lifers at him.

It wasn't what Sir Rowley had in mind, but he followed her,
squeezing through the door to the beehive with some difficulty.

And squeezing out again. "Oh my God."

"What's the *matter*?" She was cross, nervy.

He leaned against the arch of the doorway, breathing deeply. "Sweet Jesus, have mercy on us all." The stench was appalling. Even worse was what lay exposed on the table.

She tutted with irritation. "Stand in the doorway then. Can you write?"

With his eyes closed, Rowley nodded. "First thing they teach a tax collector."

She handed him a slate and chalk. "Put down what I tell you. In between times, keep fanning the flies away."

The anger went out of her voice, and she began speaking in monotone. "The remains of a young female. Some fair hair still attached to the skull. Therefore she is"—she broke off to consult a list she'd inked onto the back of her hand—"Mary. The wildfowler's daughter. Six years old. Disappeared Saint Ambrose, that is, what, a year ago? Are you writing?"

"Yes, ma'am." The chalk squeaked over the slate, but Sir Rowley kept his face to the open air.

"The bones are unclothed. Flesh almost entirely decomposed; what there is has been in contact with chalk. There is a dusting of what appears to be dried silt on the spine, also some lodged in the rear of the pelvis. Is there silt near here?"

"We're on the edge of the silt fens. They were found on the fen edge."

"Were the bodies lying faceup?"

"God, I don't know."

"Hmm, if so, it would account for the traces on the back. They are slight; she wasn't buried in silt, more likely chalk. Hands and feet tied by strips of black material." There was a pause. "There are tweezers in my bag. Give them to me."

He fumbled in the bag and passed on a pair of thin wooden tweezers, saw her use them to pick at a strip of something and hold it to the light.

"Mother of God." He returned to the doorway, his arm reaching inside to continue whisking the cow parsley about. From the woodland beyond came the call of the cuckoo, confirming the warmth of the day, and the smell of bluebells among the trees. *Welcome,* he thought, *oh God, welcome. You're late this year.*

"Fan harder," she snapped at him, then resumed her monotone. "These ties are strips of wool. *Mmm.* Pass me a vial. Here, *here.* Where are you, blast you?" He retrieved a vial from her bag, gave it to her, waited, and retook possession of it, now containing a dreadful strip. "There are crumbs of chalk in the hair. Also, an object adhering to it. *Hmm.* Lozenge-shaped, possibly a sticky sweetmeat of some kind that has now dried to the strands. It will need further examination. Hand me another vial."

He was instructed to seal both vials with red clay from the bag. "Red for Mary, a different color for each of the others. See to it, please."

"Yes, Doctor."

Usually Prior Geoffrey went in pomp to the castle, just as Sheriff Baldwin returned his visits with equal pomp; a town must always be aware of its two most important men. Today, however, it was a sign of how troubled the prior was that trumpeter and retinue had been left behind and he rode across Great Bridge to Castle Hill with only Brother Ninian in attendance.

Townspeople pursued him, hanging on to his stirrups. To all of them he replied in the negative. No, it wasn't the Jews. How could it have been? No, be calm. No, the fiend hadn't been caught yet, but he would be, God's grace he would be. No, leave the Jews be, they did not do this.

He worried for Jew and Gentile. Another riot would bring the king's anger down on the town.

And as if that wasn't enough, the prior thought savagely, *there was the tax collector, God punish him and all his breed.* Apart from the fact that Sir Rowley's probing fingers were now investigating a matter the prior would rather, much rather, they had not meddled with, he was concerned for Adelia—and for himself.

The upstart will tell the king, he thought. *Both she and I will be undone. He suspects necromancy; she will be hanged for it, while I . . . I shall be reported to the Pope and cast out. And why, if the taxman wished to see the bodies so much, did he not insist on being present when the coroner examined them? Why avoid officialdom when the man was, himself, official?*

Just as troubling was the familiarity of Sir Rowley's round face—*Sir* Rowley, indeed; since when did the king confer knighthood on tax collectors?—it had bothered him all the way from Canterbury.

As his horse began to labor up the steep road to the castle, the prior's mind's eye pictured the scene that had been played out on this very hill a year ago. Sheriff's men trying to hold off a maddened crowd from frightened Jews, himself and the sheriff bellowing uselessly for order.

Panic and loathing, ignorance and violence . . . the devil had been in Cambridge that day.

And so had the tax collector. A face glimpsed in the crowd and forgotten until now. Contorted like all the others as its owner struggled . . . struggled with whom? Against the sheriff's men? Or for them? In that hideous conglomeration of noise and limbs, it had been impossible to tell.

The prior clicked his horse to go on.

The man's presence on that day in this place was not necessarily sinister; sheriffs and taxmen went together. The sheriff collected the king's revenue; the king's collector ensured that the sheriff didn't keep too much of it.

The prior reined in. *But I saw him at Saint Radegund's fair much later. The man was applauding a stilt-walker. And that was when little Mary went missing. God save us.*

The prior dug his heels into the horse's side. Quickly now. More urgent than ever to talk to the sheriff.

"Mmm. The pelvis is chipped from below, possibly accidental damage postmortem but, since the slashes seem to have been inflicted with considerable force and the other bones show no damage, more probably caused by a instrument piercing upward in an attack on the vagina. . . ."

Rowley hated her, hated her equable, measured voice. She did violence to the feminine even by enunciating the words. It was not for her to open her woman's lips and give them shape, loosing foulness into the air. She had become spokesman for the deed and thereby complicit in its doing. A perpetrator, a hag. Her eyes should not look on what she saw without expelling blood.

Adelia was forcing herself to see a pig. Pigs were what she'd learned on. Pigs—the nearest approximation in the animal world to human flesh and bone. Up in the hills, behind a high wall, Gordinus had kept dead pigs for his students, some buried, some exposed to the air, some in a wooden hut, others in a stone byre.

Most of the students introduced to his death farm had been revolted by the flies and stench and had fallen away; only Adelia saw the wonder of the process that reduced a cadaver to nothing. "For even a skeleton is impermanent and, left to itself, will eventually crumble to dust," Gordinus had said. "What marvelous design it is, my dear, that we are not overwhelmed by a thousand years' worth of accumulated corpses."

It *was* marvelous, a mechanism that went into action as breath departed the body, releasing it to its own device. Decomposition fasci-

nated her because—and she still didn't understand how—it would occur even without the help of the flesh flies and blowflies, which, if the
corpse were accessible to them, came in next.

So, having achieved qualification as a doctor, she'd learned her new
trade on pigs. On pigs in spring, pigs in summer, pigs in autumn and
winter, each season with its own rate of decay. How they died. When.
Pigs set up, pigs with heads down, pigs lying, pigs slaughtered, pigs
dead from disease, pigs buried, pigs unburied, pigs kept in water, old
pigs, sows that had littered, boars, piglets.

The piglet. The moment of divide. Recently dead, only a few days
old. She'd carried it to Gordinus's house. "Something new," she'd said.
"This matter in its anus, I can't place it."

"Something old," he'd told her, "old as sin. It is human semen."

He'd guided her to his balcony overlooking the turquoise sea and
sat her down and fortified her with a glass of his best red wine and
asked her if she wanted to proceed or return to ordinary doctoring.
"Will you see the truth or avoid it?"

He'd read her Virgil, one of the Georgics, she couldn't remember
which, that took her into roadless, sun-soaked Tuscan hills, where
lambs, full of winey milk, leaped for the joy of leaping, tended by
shepherds swaying to the pipes of Pan.

"Any one of which may take a sheep, shove its back legs into his
boots and his organ into its back passage," Gordinus had said.

"No," she'd said.

"Or into a child."

"No."

"Or a baby."

"No."

"Oh, yes," he'd said, "I have seen it. Does that spoil the Georgics
for you?"

"It spoils everything." Then she'd said, "I cannot continue."

"Man hovers between Paradise and the Pit," Gordinus told her cheerfully. "Sometimes rising to one, sometimes swooping to the other. To ignore his capacity for evil is as obtuse as blinding oneself to the heights to which he can soar. It may be that it is all one to the sweep of the planets. You have seen Man's depths for yourself. I have just read you some lines of his upward flight. Go home, then, Doctor, and put on the blindfold, I do not blame you. But at the same time, plug your ears to the cries of the dead. The truth is not for you."

She *had* gone home, to the schools and hospitals to receive the plaudits of those she taught and to whom she administered, but her eyes were unbound now, and her ears unplugged, and she had become pestered by the cries of the dead, so she'd returned to the study of pigs and, when she was ready, to human corpses.

However, in cases like the one on the table before her now, she resumed a metaphorical blindfold so that she could still function, donning self-imposed blinkers to halt a descent into uselessness through despair, a necessary obscurity that permitted sight but allowed her to see not the torn, once immaculate body of a child but instead the familiar corpse of a pig.

The stabbing around the pelvis had left distinctive marks; she had seen knife wounds before, but none like these. The blade of the instrument that had caused them appeared to be much faceted. She would have liked to remove the pelvis for leisurely examination in better light, but she had promised Prior Geoffrey to do no dissection. She clicked her fingers for the man to pass her the slate and chalk.

He studied her while she drew. Slants of sunlight from between the bars of Saint Werbertha's tiny window fell on her as on a monstrous blowfly hovering over the thing on the table. The gauze smoothed the features of her face into something lepidopteral, pressing strands of hair against her head like flattened antennae. And *hmmm,* the thing buzzed with the insistence of the feeding, winging, clustering cloud that hovered with her.

She finished the diagram and held out the slate and chalk so that the man could receive them back. "Take them," she snapped. She was missing Mansur. When Sir Rowley didn't move, she turned and saw his look. She'd seen it on others. Wearily, she said, almost to herself, "Why do they always want to shoot the messenger?"

He stared back at her. Was that what his anger was?

She came outside, brushing away flies. "This child is telling me what happened to her. With luck, she may even tell me where. From that, with even more luck, we may be able to deduce who. If you do not wish to learn these things, then get to hell. But first, fetch me someone who does."

She lifted the helmet from her head, clawing her fingers through her hair, a glimpse of dark blond, turning her face to the sun.

It was the eyes, he thought. With her eyes closed, she reverted to her years, which, he saw, numbered a few less than his own, and to something approximating the feminine. Not for him; he preferred them sweeter. And plumper. The eyes, when open, aged her. Cold and dark like pebbles—and with as much emotion. Not surprising, when you considered what they looked on.

But if in truth she could work the oracle . . .

The eyes turned on him. "Well?"

He snatched the slate and chalk from her hand. "Your servant, mistress."

"There's more gauze in there," she said. "Cover your face, then come in and make yourself useful."

And manners, he thought, he liked them with manners. But as she retied her mask over her head, squared her skinny shoulders, and marched back into the charnel house, he recognized the gallantry of a tired soldier reentering battle.

The second bundle contained Harold, redheaded son of the eel seller, pupil at the priory school.

"The flesh is better preserved than Mary's, to the point of mummification. The eyelids have been cut away. Also the genitals."

Rowley put down the whisk to cross himself.

The slate became covered with unutterable words, except that she uttered them: binding cord. A sharp instrument. Anal insertion.

And, again, chalk.

That interested her. He could tell from the humming. "Chalkland."

"The Icknield Way is near here," he told her helpfully. "The Gog Magog hills, where we stopped for the prior, are of chalk."

"Both children have chalk in their hair. In Harold's case, some has been embedded in his heels."

"What does that say?"

"He was dragged through chalk."

The third bundle contained the remains of Ulric, eight years old, gone missing on Saint Edward's of this year and which, because his disappearance had taken place more recently than the others', brought forth frequent *hmm*s from the examiner—an alert to Rowley, who'd begun to recognize the signs that she had more and better material to investigate.

"No eyelids, no genitals. This one wasn't buried at all. What was the weather this March in this area?"

"I believe it to have been dry all over East Anglia, ma'am. There was general complaint that newly planted crops were withering. Cold but dry."

Cold but dry. Her memory, renowned in Salerno, searched the death farm and fell on early-spring pig number 78. About the same weight. That, too, had been dead just over a month in the cold and dry, and was of more advanced decomposition. She would have expected this one to be in an approximately similar state. "Were you kept alive after you went missing?" she asked the body, forgetting that a stranger, and not Mansur, was listening.

"Jesus God, why do you say that?"

She quoted Ecclesiastes as she did to her students: "*To everything there is a season . . . a time to be born and a time to die; a time to plant, a time to pluck up that which is planted.* Also a time to putrefy."

"So the devil kept him alive? How long?"

"I don't *know.*"

There were a thousand variations that could cause the difference between this corpse and pig 78. She was irritable because she was tired and distressed. Mansur wouldn't have asked, knowing better than to treat her observations as conversation. "I won't be drawn on it."

Ulric also had chalk embedded in his heels.

The sun was beginning to go down by the time each body had been wrapped up again, ready for encoffining. The woman went outside to take off her apron and helmet while Sir Rowley took down the lamps and put them out, leaving the cell and its contents in blessed darkness.

At the door, he knelt as he once had in front of the Holy Sepulchre in Jerusalem. That tiny chamber had been barely larger than the one now before him. The table on which the Cambridge children lay was about the same size as Christ's tomb. It had been dark there, too. Beyond and about had been the conglomeration of altars and chapels that made up the great basilica that the first crusaders had built over the holy places, echoing with the whispers of pilgrims and the chant of Greek Orthodox monks singing their unending hymns at the site of Golgotha.

Here there was only the buzz of flies.

He'd prayed for the souls of the departed then, and for help and forgiveness for himself.

He prayed for them now.

When he came out, the woman was washing herself, laving her face and hands from the bowl. After she had finished, he did the same— she'd lathered the water with soapwort. Crushing the stems, he washed his hands. He was tired; oh, Jesus, he was tired.

"Where are you staying, Doctor?" he asked her.

She looked at him as if she hadn't seen him before. "What did you say your name was?"

He tried not to be irritated; from the look of her, she was even more weary than he was. "Sir Roland Picot, ma'am. Rowley to my friends."

Of which, he saw, she was not likely to be one. She nodded. "Thank you for your assistance." She packed her bag, picked it up, and set off.

He hurried after her. "May I ask what conclusions you draw from your investigation?"

She didn't answer.

Damn the woman. He supposed that, since he'd written down her notes, she was leaving him to draw his own conclusions, but Rowley, who was not a humble man, was aware that he had encountered someone with knowledge he could not hope to attain. He tried again: "To whom will you report your findings, Doctor?"

No answer.

They were walking through the long shadows of the oaks that fell over the wall of the priory deer park. From the priory chapel came the clap of a bell sounding vespers, and ahead, where the bakery and brew house stood outlined against the dying sun, figures in violet rochets were spilling out of the buildings into the walkways like petals being blown in one direction.

"Shall we attend vespers?" If ever he'd needed the balm of the evening litany, Sir Rowley felt he needed it now.

She shook her head.

Angrily, he said, "Will you not pray for those children?"

She turned and he saw a face ghastly with fatigue and an anger that outmatched his. "I am not here to pray for them," she said. "I have come to speak for them."

Five

———

Returning from the castle that afternoon to the not inconsiderable house that had accommodated the succession of Saint Augustine's priors, Prior Geoffrey had yet more arrangements to make.

"She's waiting for you in your library," Brother Gilbert said curtly. He didn't approve of a tête-à-tête between his superior and a woman.

Prior Geoffrey went in and sat himself in the great chair behind his table desk. He didn't ask the woman to sit down because he knew she wouldn't; he didn't greet her, either—there was no need. He merely explained his responsibility for the Salernitans, his problem, and his proposed solution.

The woman listened. Though neither tall nor fat, in her eelskin boots, her muscled arms folded over her apron, gray hair escaping from the sweat-stained roll round her head, she had the massive, feminine barbarity of a sheela-na-gig that turned the prior's comfortable, book-lined room into a cave.

"Thus I have need of you, Gyltha," Prior Geoffrey said, finishing. "*They* have need of you."

There was a pause.

"Summer's a-coming in," Gyltha said in her deep voice. "Summer I'm busy with eels."

In late spring, Gyltha and her grandson emerged from the fens wheeling tanks full of squirming, silver eels and settled into their reed-thatched summer residence by the Cam. There, out of a wonderful steam, emerged eels pickled, eels salted, eels smoked, and eels jellied, all of them, thanks to recipes known only to Gyltha, superior to any other and bought up immediately by waiting and appreciative customers.

"I know you are," Prior Geoffrey said patiently. He sat back in his great chair and reverted to broad East Anglian. "But that's dang hard work, girl, and you're getting on."

"So're you, bor."

They knew each other well. Better than most. When a young Norman priest had arrived in Cambridge to take over its parish of Saint Mary's twenty-five years before, his house had been kept for him by a well-set-up young fenland woman. That they might have been more to each other than employer and employee had not raised an eyebrow, for England's attitude toward clerical celibacy was tolerant—or slack, depending on which way you looked at it—and Rome had not then begun to shake its fist at "priests' wives," as it did now.

Though young Father Geoffrey's waist had swelled on Gyltha's cooking, and young Gyltha's waist had swelled also, though whether from her cooking or something else, nobody knew the truth of it except those two. When Father Geoffrey was called by God to the canonry of Saint Augustine, Gyltha had disappeared into the fenland from which she had come, refusing the allowance offered to her.

"What iffen I throw in a skivvy or two," the prior said now, winningly. "Bit of cooking, bit of organizing, that's all."

"Foreigners," said Gyltha. "I don't hold with foreigners."

Looking at her, the prior was reminded of Guthlac's description of the fen folk in whom that worthy saint had tried to instill Christianity:

"Great heads, long necks, pale faces, and teeth like horses. Save us, from them, O Lord."
But they'd had the means and the independence to resist William the
Conqueror longer and more strongly than the rest of the English.

Nor was intelligence lacking among them. Gyltha had it; she was
the beau ideal as housekeeper for the ménage Prior Geoffrey had in
mind—outré enough, yet sufficiently well known and trusted by the
townsfolk of Cambridge to provide a bridge between it and them. If
she would agree . . .

"Weren't I a foreigner?" he said. "You took me on."

Gyltha smiled, and for a moment the surprising charm reminded
Prior Geoffrey of their years in the priest's little house next to Saint
Mary's church.

He pressed home his advantage. "Be good for young Ulf."

"That's doing well enough at school."

"When that do bother to come." Young Ulf's acceptance at the
priory school had been less to do with his cleverness, which was considerable if idiosyncratic, than to Prior Geoffrey's unconfirmed suspicion that the boy, being Gyltha's grandson, was also his own. "Sore
need of a bit of gentrifying, though, girl."

Gyltha leaned forward and put a scarred finger on the prior's writing desk. "What they doing here, bor? You going to tell me?"

"Took ill, didn't I? Saved my old life, she did."

"Her? I heard it was the blackie."

"Her. And not witchery, neither. Proper doctor she is, only best nobody don't know it."

There was no point in concealing it from Gyltha, who, if she took
on the Salernitans, would find out. In any case, this woman was as
close as the seaweeded oysters that she made him a present of every
year, of which a fine selection was at this moment in the priory's ice-
house.

"I don't be sure who sent they three," he went on, "but they do
mean to find out who's killing the children."

"Harold." Gyltha's face showed no emotion, but her voice was soft; she did business with Harold's father.

"Harold."

She nodded. "Weren't Jews, then?"

"No."

"Didn't reckon it was."

From across the cloisters connecting the prior's house with the church came the bell calling the brotherhood to vespers.

Gyltha sighed. "Skivvies as promised, and I only do the bloody cooking."

"Benigne. Deo gratias." The prior got up and accompanied Gyltha to the door. "Old Tubs still breeding they smelly dogs?"

"Smellier than ever."

"Bring un with you. Attach it to her, like. If her's asking questions, it'll maybe cause trouble. Her needs keeping an eye on. Oh, and they don't none of 'em eat pork. Or shellfish." He slapped Gyltha's rump to send her on her way, folded his arms beneath his apron, and went on his own toward the chapel for vespers.

ADELIA SAT ON A BENCH in the priory's paradise breathing in the scent of rosemary from the low hedging that bordered the flower bed at her feet and listened to the psalms of vespers filter out of cloister through the evening air across the walled vegetable garden and thence to the paradise with its darkening trees. She tried to empty her mind and let the masculine voices pour salve on the hurt caused by masculine abomination. *"Let my prayer be counted as incense before you,"* they chanted, *"and the lifting of my hands as an evening sacrifice."*

There would be supper at the priory guesthouse, where Prior Geoffrey had lodged her and Simon and Mansur for the night, but it would entail sitting round the table with other travelers, and she was not fit for petty conversation. The straps of her goatskin bag were buckled tight so that, for this little space, the information the dead children had given her was trapped within it, chalk words on a slate. Undo the straps, as she would tomorrow, and their voices would burst out, beseeching, filling her ears. But tonight even they must be muted; she could bear nothing but the stillness of the evening.

Not until it was almost too dark to see did she stand, pick up her bag, and walk along the path leading to the long shafts of candlelight that indicated the windows of the guesthouse.

It was a mistake to go to bed without food; she lay in a narrow cot in a narrow cell off the corridor devoted to women guests, resenting the fact that she was there at all, resenting the King of Sicily, this country, almost the dead children themselves for imposing the burden of their agony on her.

"I cannot possibly go," she'd told Gordinus when he'd first broached the subject. "I have my students, my work."

It was not a matter of choice, however. The command for an expert in death had come down from a king against whom, since he also ruled southern Italy, there was no appeal.

"Why do you choose me?"

"You meet the king's specifications," Gordinus had said. "I know of no one else who does. Master Simon will be fortunate to have you."

Simon had considered himself not so much fortunate as burdened; she'd seen that at once. Despite her credentials, the presence of a woman doctor, an attendant Arab, and a female companion—Margaret, *blessed* Margaret, had been alive then—had piled a Pelion of complication on the Ossa of an already difficult assignment.

But one of Adelia's skills, honed to perfection in the rough-and-tumble of the schools, was to make her femininity near invisible, to demand no concession, to blend in almost unnoticed among the largely male fraternity. Only when her professionalism had been called into question did her fellow students find that there was a very visible Adelia with a rough edge to her tongue—in listening to them, she had learned how to swear—and an even rougher edge to her temper.

There had been no need to display either to Simon; he had been courteous and, as the journey went on, relieved. He found her modest—a description, Adelia had long decided, that was applied to women who gave men no trouble. Apparently, Simon's wife was the acme of Jewish modesty, and he judged all other women by her. Mansur, Adelia's other accessory, proved to be his invaluable self and, until reaching the coast of France, where Margaret had died, they had traveled in sweet accord.

By now, it took the regularity of her periods for her to remember that she was not a neutered being. On reaching England, the trio's transfer to a cart and adoption of their roles as a traveling medicine troop had caused none of them little more than discomfort and amusement.

There remained the mystery of why the King of Sicily should involve Simon of Naples, one of his most capable investigators, let alone herself, in a predicament that the Jews of a wet, cold little island on the edge of the world had gotten themselves into. Simon had not known, nor had she. Their instructions were to see the Jews' name washed of the taint of murder, an aim to be accomplished only by discovering the identity of the true killer.

What she *had* known was that she would not like England—and she didn't. In Salerno, she was a respected member of a highly regarded medical school where nobody, except newcomers, expressed surprise on meeting a female practitioner. Here, they'd duck her in a pond. The bodies she'd just examined had darkened Cambridge for her; she'd seen the results of murder before but rarely any so terrible as these. Somewhere in this county a butcher of children walked and breathed.

Identifying him would be made harder by her unofficial position and the pretense that she wasn't doing it at all. In Salerno she worked, however unacknowledged, with the authorities; here she had only the prior on her side, and even he dare not declare the fact.

Still resentful, she went to sleep and dreamed dark dreams.

SHE SLEPT LATE, a concession not usually granted to other guests. "Prior said as you could forgo matins, you being so tired," Brother Swithin, the chubby little guest-master told her, "but I was to see you ate hearty when you woke."

She breakfasted in the kitchen on ham, a rare luxury for one who traveled with a Jew and a Moslem, cheese from the priory's sheep, bread fresh from the priory's bakery, new-churned butter and preserve of Brother Swithin's own pickling, a slice of eel pie, and milk warm from the cow.

"You was thrawn, maid," Brother Swithin said, ladling her more milk from the churn. "Better now?"

She smiled at him through a white mustache. "Much." She *had* been thrawn, whatever that was, but vigor had returned, resentment and self-pity gone. What did it matter that she must work in a foreign land? Children were universal; they inhabited a state superseding nationality with a right to protection by an eternal law. The savagery inflicted on Mary, Harold, and Ulric offended no less because they were not Salerno-born. They were everybody's children; they were hers.

Adelia felt a determination such as she had never known. The world had to be made cleaner by the removal of the killer. *"Whoso shall offend one of these little ones, it were better for him that a millstone were hanged about his neck. . . ."*

Now, round the neck of this offender, though he was as yet in ignorance of it, had been hung Adelia, Medica Trotula of Salerno, doctor to the dead, who would strive with all her knowledge and skill to bring him down.

She returned to her cell to transcribe her observations from slate to paper so that, on her return to Salerno, she might deliver a record of her findings—though what the King of Sicily wanted with it, she did not know.

It was terrible work, and slow; more than once she had to throw down her quill in order to cover her ears. The walls of the cell echoed with the children's screams. *Be quiet, oh, be quiet, so that I may track him down.* But they had not wanted to die and could not be hushed.

Simon and Mansur had already departed to take up residence in accommodation the prior had found for them in the town so that the mission might have privacy. It was gone noon before Adelia set off after them.

Believing it to be her business to investigate the murderer's territory and see something of the town, she was surprised, but not displeased, to find that Brother Swithin, busy with a new influx of travelers, was prepared to let her go without an escort and that in Cambridge's teeming streets, women of all castes bustled about their business unaccompanied and with faces unveiled.

This was a different world. Only the students from the School of Pythagoras, red-capped and noisy, were familiar to her; students were the same the world over.

In Salerno, thoroughfares were shadowed by upper walkways and overhangs built to keep out a barbarous sun. This town opened itself wide like a flat flower to catch what light the English sky gave it.

True, there were sinister side alleys with tweedy, reed-thatched houses crammed together like fungi, but Adelia kept to main roads, asking her way without fear for her reputation or purse as she would not have done at home.

Here it was water, not sun, that the town bowed to; it coursed in runnels down both sides of a street so that every dwelling, every shop, had a footbridge to it. Cisterns, troughs, ponds confused the sight into seeing double; a roadside pig was exactly reflected by the puddle it stood in. Swans apparently floated on themselves. Ducks on a pond swam over the arched, chevroned doorway of the church looming above it. Errant streams contained images of roofs and windows, and willow fronds appeared to grow upward from the rivulets that mirrored them.

Adelia was aware that Cambridge piped to her, but she would not dance. To her, the double reflection of everything was symptomatic of a deeper duplicity, two-faced, a Janus town, where a creature that killed children walked on two legs like any other man. Until it was discovered, all of Cambridge wore a mask that she could not look on without wondering if a wolf's muzzle lay beneath.

Inevitably, she lost her way.

"Can you direct me to Old Benjamin's house, if you please?"

"What you want with that, then, maid?"

This was the third person she'd stopped with a request for direction and the third to inquire why she wanted it. "I'm considering opening a bawdy house" was an answer that came to mind, but she'd already learned that Cambridge inquisitiveness needed no tweaking; she merely said, "I should like to know where it is."

"Up the road a ways, turn left onto Jesus Lane, corner facing the river."

Turning to the river, she found a small crowd had gathered in order to watch Mansur unpack the last contents of the cart, ready to carry them up a flight of steps to the front door.

Prior Geoffrey had considered it only just, since the three were here on the Jews' behalf, that the Salernitans should occupy one of Jewry's abandoned houses during their stay.

He'd considered that to move them into Chaim's rich mansion a little farther along the river would be ill-advised.

"But Old Benjamin has inspired less animosity in the town, for all he's a pawnbroker, than did poor Chaim with his riches," he'd said, "and he has a good view of the river."

That there was an area called Jewry, of which this place stood on the edge, brought home to Adelia how the Jews of Cambridge had been excluded from or had excluded themselves from the life of the town—as they had been from nearly all the English towns she'd passed through on the way.

However privileged, this was a ghetto, now deserted. Old Benjamin's house spoke of an incipient fear. It stood gable end on the alley to present as little of itself as possible to outside attack. It was built of stone rather than wattle and daub, with a door capable of withstanding a battering ram. The niche on one of the doorposts was empty, showing that the case holding the mezuzah had been torn out.

A woman had appeared at the top of the steps to help Mansur with their luggage. As Adelia approached, an onlooker called, "You doing for they now, then, Gyltha?"

"My bloody business," the woman on the steps called back. "You mind yours."

The crowd tittered but did not move away, discussing the situation in uninhibited East Anglian English. Already, something of what had happened to the prior on the road had become common currency.

"Not Jews, then. Our Gyltha wouldn't hold with doing for the ungodly."

"Saracens, so I heard."

"That with the towel over his head, 'tis said he's the doctor."

"More devil than doctor from the look of he."

"Cured Prior, so they say, Saracen or not."

"How much do he charge, I wonder?"

"That their fancy piece?" This was addressed over Adelia's head with a nod toward her.

"No, it is not," she said.

The questioner, a man, was taken aback. "Talk English then, maid?"

"Yes. Do you?" Their accent—a chant of oy's, strange inflections, and rising sentence endings—was different from the West Country

English she'd learned at Margaret's knee, but she could just understand it.

She appeared to have amused rather than offended. "Sparky little moggy, in't she?" the man said to the assembly. Then, to her: "That blackie. Mix a good physic, can he?"

"As good as any you'll find round here," she told him. *Probably true,* she thought. The infirmarian at the priory would be a mere herbalist who, though he rendered it freely, gained his knowledge from books—most of them wildly inaccurate, in Adelia's opinion. Those he couldn't treat and who were beyond treating themselves would be at the mercy of the town's quacks, to be sold elaborate, useless, costly, and probably disgusting potions, more intended to impress than cure.

Her new acquaintance took it as a recommendation. "Reckon as I'll pay that a visit, then. Brother Theo up at the priory, he's given up on I."

A grinning woman nudged her neighbor. "Tell her what's wrong with thee, Wulf."

"He do reckon as I've a bad case of malingering," Wulf said obediently, "an he be at a loss how to treat it."

Adelia noticed there were no questions as to why she and Simon and Mansur had come. To Cambridge men and women, it was natural that foreigners should settle in their town. Didn't they come from all parts to do business? Where better? Abroad was dragon country.

She tried to push her way through to get to the gate, but a woman holding up a small child blocked her way. "That ear's hurting him bad. He do need doctoring." Not everybody in the crowd was here out of curiosity.

"He's busy," Adelia said. But the child was whimpering with pain. "Oh, I'll look at it."

Someone in the crowd obligingly held up a lantern while she examined the ear, tutted, opened her bag for her tweezers—"Hold him still, now"—and extracted a small bead.

She might as well have breached a dam. "A wise woman, by lumme," somebody said, and within seconds she was being jostled for her attention. In the absence of a doctor, a wise woman would do.

Rescue came in the form of the one who'd been addressed as Gyltha. She came down the steps and made a path to Adelia by jabbing obstructing bodies with her elbows. "Clear off," she told them. "Ain't even moved in yet. Come back a'morrow." She pushed Adelia through the gate. "Quick, girl." Then she used her bulk to shut the gate and hissed, "You done it now."

Adelia ignored her. "That old man there," she said, pointing. "He has an ague." It looked like malaria and was unexpected; she'd thought the disease to be confined to the Roman marshes.

"That's for the doctor to say," Gyltha said loudly for the benefit of her listeners, then, for Adelia's, "Get in, girl. He'll still have it a'morrow."

There was probably little to be done, anyway. As Gyltha pulled her up the steps, Adelia shouted, "Put him to bed," at a woman supporting the shaking old man. "Try and cool the fever," managing to add, "Wet cloths," before the housekeeper hauled her inside and shut the door.

Gyltha shook her head at her. So did Simon, who'd been watching.

Of course. Mansur was the doctor now; she must remember it.

"But it is interesting if it is malaria," she said to Simon. "Cambridge and Rome. The common feature is marshland, I suppose." In Rome, the disease was attributed by some to bad air, hence its name, by others to drinking stagnant water. Adelia, for whom neither supposition had been proved, kept an open mind.

"Wonderful lot of ague in the fens," Gyltha told her. "Us do treat that with opium. Stops the shakes."

"*Opium?* You grow the poppy round here?" God's rib, with access to opium, she could alleviate a lot of suffering. Her mind reverting to malaria, she muttered to Simon, "I wonder if I might have the chance to look at the old man's spleen when he dies."

"We could ask," Simon said, rolling his eyes. "Ague, child murder: What's the difference? Let's declare ourselves."

"I had not forgotten the killer," Adelia said, sharply. "I have been examining his work."

He touched her hand. "Bad?"

"Bad."

The worn face before her became distressed; here was a man with children, imagining the worst that could happen to them. He has a rare sympathy, Simon, she thought, it's what makes him a fine investigator. But it takes its toll.

Much of his sympathy was for her. "Can you bear it, Doctor?"

"It's what I am trained for," she told him.

He shook his head. "Nobody is trained for what you have seen today." He took in a deep breath and said in his labored English, "This is Gyltha. Prior Geoffrey send her to keep house kindly. She know what we do here."

So, it appeared, did someone who'd been lurking in a corner with an animal. "This is Ulf. Grandson of Gyltha, I think. Also this— what is?"

"Safeguard," Gyltha told him. "And take off thy bloody cap to the lady, Ulf."

Never had Adelia seen a trio more comprehensively ugly. Woman and boy had coffin-shaped heads, big-boned faces, and large teeth, a combination she was to recognize as a fenland trait. If the child Ulf wasn't as alarming as his grandmother, it was because he *was* a child, eight or nine years old, his features still blunted by puppyhood.

The "safeguard" was an overlarge ball of matted wool from which emerged four legs like knitting needles. It appeared ovine but was probably a dog; no sheep smelled as bad.

"Present from Prior," Gyltha said. "You're to do the feeding of it."

Nor was the room they were gathered in any more prepossessing. Cramped and mean, the front door led straight into it, with an equally heavy door opposite giving to the rest of the house. Light from two arrow slits showed bare and broken shelving.

"Where Old Ben did his pawnbroking," Gyltha said, adding with force, "only some bugger's stole all the pledge goods."

Some other bugger, or perhaps the same one, had also used the place as a latrine.

Adelia was clawed by homesickness. Most of all for Margaret, that loving presence. But also, *oh, God,* for Salerno. For orange trees and sun and shade, for aqueducts, for the sea, for the sunken Roman bath in the house she shared with her foster parents, for mosaic floors, for trained servants, for acceptance of her position as *medica,* for the facilities of the school, for *salads*—she hadn't eaten green stuff since arriving in this godforsaken, meat-stuffing country.

But Gyltha had pushed open the inner door, and they were looking down the length of Old Benjamin's hall—which was better.

It smelled of water, lye, beeswax. At their entrance, two maids with buckets and mops whisked out of sight through a door at the far end. From a barrel-vaulted roof hung burnished synagogue lamps on chains, lighting fresh green rushes and the soft polish of elm floorboards. A stone pillar supported a winding staircase leading up to an attic floor and down to the undercroft.

It was a long room, made extraordinary by glazed windows that ran higgledy-piggledy along its left length, their different sizes suggesting that Old Benjamin, on a waste-not-want-not principle, had enlarged or reduced the original casements to fit in their place such unreclaimed glass as came into his possession. There was an oriel, two lattices—both open to allow in the scent of the river—one small sheer pane, and a rose of stained glass that could have originated only in a Christian church. The effect was untidy but a change from the usual bare shuttering, and not without charm.

For Mansur and Simon, however, the ne plus ultra was elsewhere—in the kitchen, a separate building beyond the house. They urged Adelia toward it. "Gyltha is a cook," Simon said as one emerging from the dust of Egypt into Canaan, "our prior . . ."

"May his shadow never grow less," Mansur said.

". . . our good, good prior has sent us a cook on a par with my own dear Becca." Rebecca was his wife. "Gyltha *superba.* Look, Doctor, look what she is preparing."

In a huge fireplace, things were turning on spits, spattering fat into glowing peat; kettles hung from hooks exuded herby, fishy steam; cream-colored pastry lay ready to be rolled on the great floured table. "Food, Doctor, succulent fish, lampreys—*lampreys,* praise to the Lord—duck seethed in honey, suckling lamb."

Adelia had never seen two men so enthused.

The rest of daylight was spent unpacking. There were rooms to spare. Adelia had been allotted the solar, a pleasant room overlooking the river—a luxury after the communal beds of the inns. Its cupboards were bare, having been ransacked by the rioters, leaving her with welcome shelves on which to lay out her herbs and potions.

That evening, Gyltha, calling them to supper, was irritated by the time it took Mansur and Simon to carry out their ritual ablutions, and Adelia, who suspected that dirt was poisonous, to wash her hands before coming to the table. "That'll get cold," she snapped at them. "I ain't cooking for heathens as don't care if good food goes cold."

"You are not," Simon assured her, "Gyltha, you are *not.*"

The dining table was garnished with the riches of a fenland seething with fowl and fish; to Adelia's homesick eyes it lacked sufficient greenstuff, but it was undoubtedly fine.

Simon said, "Blessed are you, HaShem, our God, King of the Universe, who brings forth bread from the earth," and tore a piece from the white loaf on the table to eat it.

Mansur invoked the blessing of Salman the Persian, who had given Mohammed food.

Adelia said, "May good health attend us," and they sat down to dine together.

On the boat from Salerno, Mansur had eaten with the crew, but the last leg of the journey through English inns and around campfires had imposed a democracy that none of them was willing to abandon. In any case, since Mansur now posed as head of the household, it was incongruous to send him to eat with the maids in the kitchen.

Adelia would have reported her findings over dinner, but the men, knowing what they were likely to be, refused to disturb their stomachs with anything except Gyltha's cooking. Or to make any conversation, for that matter. Adelia was amazed by the time and praise two men could lavish on suckling lamb, custards, and cheeses.

For her, food was analogous to the wind—necessary for the propulsion of boats, living beings, and the sails of windmills but otherwise to be unremarked.

Simon drank wine. A barrel from his favorite Tuscan vineyard had traveled with them, English wines reportedly being undrinkable. Mansur and Adelia drank boiled and strained water because they always did.

Simon kept urging Adelia to take some wine and to eat more, despite her protestations that she had breakfasted too well at the priory. He was concerned that her examination of the bodies had sickened her to the point of illness. It was how it would have affected him, but she saw it as a reflection on her professionalism and said sharply, "That was my job. Why else have I come?"

Mansur told him to leave her alone. "Always, the doctor pecks like a sparrow."

The Arab certainly wasn't pecking. "You'll get fat," Adelia warned him. It was his horror; too many eunuchs ate themselves into obesity.

Mansur sighed. "That woman is a siren of cooking. She calls a man's soul through his stomach."

The idea of Gyltha as a siren delighted Adelia. "Shall I tell her so?"

To her surprise, he shrugged and nodded.

"Ooh," she said. In all the years since he had been appointed by her foster parents to be her bodyguard, she had never known him to pay a compliment to a female. That it should be a woman with the face of a horse and with whom he did not share a common language was unexpected and intriguing.

The two maids who served them, both confusingly called Matilda and differentiated by only the initials of their parish saints, therefore answering to Matilda B. and Matilda W., were as wary of Mansur as of a performing bear that had sat down to dine. They emerged from the open passage that led from the kitchen to a door behind the dais, taking and replacing dish after dish without approaching his end of the table, giggling nervously and leaving the food to be passed down to him.

Well, Adelia thought, *they'll have to get used to him.*

At last the table was cleared. Simon metaphorically girded his loins, sighed, and sat back. "And so, Doctor?"

Adelia said, "This is supposition, you understand." It was her invariable caveat.

She waited for both men to acquiesce, then drew in a deep breath. "I believe the children were taken to chalkland to be killed. This may not apply to Little Saint Peter, who seems to have been a different case, perhaps because he was the first victim and the killer had not yet lapsed into routine. But of the three I examined, there was chalk embedded in the heels of both boys, indicating they were dragged through it, and evidence of it on the remains of all of them. Their hands and feet were bound with torn strips of cloth."

She looked toward Simon. "Fine, black wool. I have kept samples."

"I will inquire among the wool merchants."

"He did not bury one of the bodies but kept that, too, somewhere dry and cool." She kept her voice steady. "Also, it may be that the female was stabbed repeatedly in the pubic region, as were the boys. The best preserved of the males lacked his genitals, and I would say the others, too, suffered in the same way."

Simon had covered his face with his hands. Mansur sat very still.

Adelia said, "I believe in each case he cuts off their eyelids, whether before or after death I cannot say."

Simon said quietly, "Fiends walk among us. What do you do, Lord, to allow the torturers of Gehenna to inhabit human bodies?"

Adelia would have argued that to attribute satanic forces to the murderer was partly to absolve him, making him victim to an outside force. To her, the man was rabid, like a dog. But then, she thought, *Perhaps allowing that he is diseased also gives an excuse to what is unpardonable.*

"Mary . . ." She paused. Naming a corpse was a mistake she did not usually make; it did away with objectivity, introduced emotion when it was essential to remain impersonal; she didn't know why she'd done it.

She began again: "The female had something stuck to her hair. At first I thought it to be semen. . . ." Simon's hand gripped the table, and she remembered she was not addressing her students. "However, the object has preserved its original oblong shape, probably a sweet-meat."

Now then.

She said quietly, "We must consider particularly the time and location of the bodies' discovery. They were found on silt; there was a dusting of it on each, but the shepherd who came across them assured Prior Geoffrey that they were not there the day before. Therefore, they had been taken from where they were kept, in chalk, to the site where the shepherd found them yesterday morning, on silt."

It seemed a year ago.

Simon's eyes were on hers, reading them. "We came to Cambridge yesterday morning," he said. "The night before we were . . . what was the name of that place?"

"Part of the Gog Magog hills." Adelia nodded. "On chalk."

Mansur followed what she was implying. "So in the night the dog moved them. For us?"

She shrugged; she pronounced on only what was provable; others must draw the inference. She waited to see what Simon of Naples would make of it. Journeying together had engendered respect for him; the excitability, near gullibility, he displayed in public was not a deliberate disguise but a reaction to *being* in public and in no way represented a mind that calculated with brilliance and at speed. She regarded it as a compliment to herself and to Mansur that when they were alone, they were allowed to see his brain at work.

"He did." Simon's fists gently drummed the table. "It is too immediate for coincidence. How long have the little souls been missing? A year in one case? But when our cavalcade of pilgrims stops on the road and our cart moves up the hillside . . . all at once they are found."

Mansur said, "He sees us."

"He saw us."

"And he moves the bodies."

"He moved the bodies." Simon splayed his hands. "And why? He was afraid we would find where he kept them on the hill."

Adelia, playing devil's advocate, asked, "Why should he be afraid of *us* discovering them? Other people must have walked those hills these past months and not found them."

"Maybe not so many. What was the name, the name of the hill we were on? . . . The prior told me. . . ." He tapped his forehead, then looked up as a maid came in to trim the candlewicks. "Ah. Matilda."

"Yes, master?"

Simon leaned forward. *"Wand-le-bury Ring."*

The girl's eyes widened; she made the sign of the cross and backed out the way she had come.

Simon looked round. "Wandlebury Ring," he said. "What did I say? Our prior was right; it is a place of superstition. Nobody goes there; it is left to sheep. But *we* went there last night. He saw us. Why had we come? He does not know. To spread our tents? To stay? To walk the ground? He cannot be sure what we will do, and he is afraid because that is where the bodies are and we may find them. He moves them." He leaned back in his chair. "His lair is on Wandlebury Ring."

He saw us. Adelia was inflicted by an image of batlike wings cringing over a pile of bones, a snout sniffing the air for intruders, a sudden gripe of the talons.

"So he digs the bodies up? He carries them a distance? He leaves them to be found?" Mansur said, his voice higher than ever with incredulity. "Can he be so foolish?"

"He was trying to lead us away, so we would not know the bodies were first laid in chalk," said Simon. "He didn't reckon with Dr. Trotula here."

"Or does he *want* them to be found?" Adelia suggested. "Is he laughing at us?"

Gyltha came in. "Who's been scaring my Matildas?" She was aggressive and was holding a pair of candle trimmers in a manner that caused Simon to fold his hands over his lap.

"Wand-le-bury Ring, Gyltha," Simon said.

"What about it? Don't you credit that squit they talk about the ring. Wild Hunt? I don't hold with it." She took down a lantern and began snipping. "Just a bloody hill, Wandlebury is. I don't hold with hills."

"Wild Hunt?" Simon asked. "What is Wild Hunt?"

"Pack of bloody hounds with red eyes led by the Prince of Darkness, and I don't credit a word of it, them's ordinary sheep-killers, I reckon, and you come down out of there, Ulf, you liddle grub, afore I set the pack on you."

There was a gallery at the other end of the hall, its staircase hidden by a door in the wainscoting, out of which now sidled the small, unprepossessing figure of Gyltha's grandson. He was muttering and glaring at them.

"What does the boy say?"

"Nothing." She cuffed the child toward the kitchens. "You ask that loafer Wulf about the Wild Hunt; he's full of squit. Reckons he saw it once, and he'll sell you the tale for a drink of ale."

When she'd gone, Simon said, "Wild Hunt, Benandanti, the Chausse Sauvage. *Das Woden here.* It is a superstition encountered all over Europe and varies very little; always hounds with eyes of fire, always a black and terrible horseman, always death to those seeing them."

Quiet fell on the room. Adelia was more aware than she had been of the darkness beyond the two open lattice windows, where things rustled in the long grass. From the reeds by the river, the spring call of a bittern had accompanied their meal; now the notes took on the resonance of a drum heralding an approaching funeral.

She rubbed her arms to rid them of gooseflesh. "So we are to assume that the killer lives on the hill?" she asked.

Simon said, "It may be that he does. Maybe not. As I understand it, the children went missing from around the town; it is unlikely that all three would have ventured so far as the hill at different times under their own volition. There are long odds against a creature spending every minute in such surroundings so that he may guard his lair and espy someone approaching it. Either they were lured there, which is also unlikely—it is a distance of some miles—or they were taken. We may assume, therefore, that our man looks for his victims in Cambridge and uses the hill as his killing ground."

He blinked at his wine cup as if seeing it for the first time. "What would my Becca say to all this?" He took a sip.

Adelia and Mansur stayed quiet; there was more—something that had been prowling outside was going to come in.

"No"—Simon was speaking slowly now—"no, there is another explanation. Not one I like, but it must be considered. Almost certainly, our presence at the hill precipitated the removal of the bodies. What if, instead of being spotted by a killer who was already in situ—a most fortuitous happening—what if *we brought him with us?*"

It was in the room now.

Simon said, "While we were attending Prior Geoffrey, what were the others of our party doing in that long night? Eh? My friends, we have to consider the possibility that our killer is one of the pilgrims we joined at Canterbury."

The night beyond the lattices became darker.

Six

Soft beds were something else Gyltha didn't hold with. Adelia had wanted a mattress stuffed with goosedown such as she'd slept on in Salerno, and said so. Cambridge skies, after all, were stippled with geese.

"Goose feathers is buggers to wash," Gyltha said. "Straw's cleaner, change that every day."

There was an unsought tension between them; Adelia had requested more salad with her meals, a demand Gyltha treated as lèse-majesté. Now, here was a moment of test; the response would decide who had future authority.

On the one hand, the process of running even such a modest household as this was beyond Adelia, who had few accomplishments necessary for it, knowing little of provisioning nor dealing with any merchants other than apothecaries. She could neither spin nor weave; her knowledge of herbs and spices was medical rather than culinary. Her sewing was restricted to mending torn flesh or cobbling together cadavers she had taken apart.

In Salerno, these things had not mattered; the blessed man who was her foster father had early recognized a brain rivaling his own and, because that *was* Salerno, had put her to becoming a doctor as he and his wife were. The organization of their large villa was left to his sister-in-law, a woman who had run it as if on greased wheels without ever raising her voice.

To all this, Adelia added the fact that her stay in England was to be temporary and would leave her no time for domesticity.

On the other hand, she was not prepared to be bullied by a servant. She said sharply, "See to it that the straw is indeed changed every day."

A compromise, honors temporarily in Gyltha's favor, the final outcome still to be decided. Not now, though, because her head ached.

Last night the Safeguard had shared the solar with her—another battle lost. To Adelia's protests that the dog stank too much to bed anywhere but outside, Gyltha had said, "Prior's orders. That's to go where you go." And so the animal's snores had mingled with unaccustomed calls and shrieks from the river, just as her dream had been made terrible by Simon's suggestion that the killer's face would be familiar to them.

Before retiring, he'd expanded on it: "Who slept by that campfire on the road and who left it? A monk? A knight? Huntsman? Tax collector? Did any of them steal away to gather up those poor bones— they were light, remember, and perhaps he took a horse from the lines. The merchant? One of the squires? Minstrel? Servants? We must consider them all."

Whichever one it was had swooped through her solar window last night in the shape of a magpie. It carried a living child in its claws. Sitting on Adelia's chest, it dismembered the body, a lidless eye gleaming perkily at her as it pecked out the child's liver.

It was a visitation so vivid that she woke up gasping, convinced a bird had killed the children.

"Where is Master Simon?" she asked Gyltha. It was early; the west-facing windows of the hall gave onto a meadow that was still shadowed by the house until its decline approached the river, where sunlight was shining on a Cam so polished, so deep and flat and wandering among the willows that Adelia had to suppress a sudden urge to go and dabble in it like a duck.

"Gone out. Wanted to know where there was wool merchants."

Irritably, Adelia said, "We were to go to Wandlebury Hill today." It had been agreed last night that their priority was to discover the killer's lair.

"So he did say, but acause Master Darkie can't go, too, he are going termorrer."

"Mansur," Adelia snapped. "His name's Mansur. Why can't he go?"

Gyltha beckoned her to the end of the hall and into Old Benjamin's shop. "Acause of them."

Standing on tiptoe, Adelia looked through one of the arrow slits.

A crowd of people was by the gate, some of them sitting as if they had been there a long time.

"Waiting to see *Dr.* Mansur," Gyltha said with emphasis. "'S why you can't go pimbling off to the hills."

Here was a complication. They should have foreseen it but, in allowing Mansur to be set up as a doctor, an untried, foreign doctor in a busy town, it had not occurred to them that he would be burdened with patients. News of their encounter with the prior had spread; a cure for ills was to be found in Jesus Lane.

Adelia was dismayed. "But how *can* I treat them?"

Gyltha shrugged. "From the look, most of 'em's dying anyway. Reckon as them's Little Saint Peter's failures."

Little Saint Peter, the small, miraculous skeleton whose bones the prioress had trumpeted like a fairground barker all the way from Canterbury.

Adelia sighed for him, for the desperation that sent the suffering people to him, and, now, the disappointment that brought them to her. The truth was that, except in a few cases, she could do no better.

Herbs, leeches, potions, even belief could not hold back the tide of disease to which most of humanity was subject. She wished it wasn't so. God, she wished it.

It was a long time, in any case, that she'd had to do with living patients—other than those in extremis when no ordinary doctor was available, as the prior had been.

However, pain had gathered outside her door; she could not ignore it; something had to be done. Yet if she were to be seen practicing medicine, every doctor in Cambridge would go running to his bishop. The Church had never approved of human interference in disease, having held for centuries that prayer and holy relics were God's method of healing and anything else was satanic. It allowed treatment to be carried out in the monasteries and, perforce, tolerated lay doctors as long as they did not overstep the mark, but women, being intrinsically sinful, were necessarily banned except in the case of authenticated midwives—and they had to take care not to be accused of witchcraft.

Even in Salerno, that most esteemed center of medicine, the Church had tried to enforce its rule that physicians should be celibate. It had failed, as it had failed in prohibiting the city's women practitioners. But that was Salerno, the exception which proved the rule. . . .

"What are we to do?" she said. Margaret, most practical of women, would have known. *There's ways round everything. Just you leave it to old Margaret.*

Gyltha tutted. "What you whinnicking for? 'S easy as kiss me hand. You act like you'm the doctor's assistant, his potions mixer or summat. They tell you in good English what's up with they. You say it to the doctor in that gobble you talk, he gobbles back, and you tell 'em what to do."

Crudely put but with a fine simplicity. If treatment were needed, it could appear that Dr. Mansur was instructing his assistant. Adelia said, "That's rather clever."

Gyltha shrugged. "Should keep us out the nettles."

Told of the situation, Mansur took it calmly, as he took everything. Gyltha, however, was dissatisfied with his appearance. "Dr. Braose, him over by the market, he's got a cloak with stars on it, and a skull on his table and a thing for telling the stars."

Adelia stiffened, as she did at any suggestion of magic. "This one is practicing medicine, not wizardry." Cambridge would have to settle for a kaffiyeh framing a face like a dark eagle and a voice in the upper ranges. Magic enough for anybody.

Ulf was sent to the apothecaries with a list of requirements. A waiting area was established in the room that had been the pawnshop.

The very rich employed their own doctors; the very poor treated themselves. Those who'd come to Jesus Lane were neither one nor the other: artisans, wage earners who, if the worst came to the worst, could spare a coin or two, even a chicken, to pay for treatment.

The worst *had* come to most of them; home remedies hadn't worked, nor had giving their money and poultry to Saint Radegund's convent. As Gyltha had said, these were Little Saint Peter's failures.

"How did this come about?" Adelia asked a blacksmith's wife, gently swabbing eyes gummed tight with yellow encrustation. She remembered to add, "The doctor wants to know."

It appeared that the woman had been urged by the prioress of Saint Radegund's to dip a cloth into the ooze of decomposing flesh that had been the body of Little Saint Peter after it was dragged from the river, then wipe her eyes with it in order to cure her increasing blindness.

"Somebody should kill that prioress," Adelia said to Mansur in Arabic.

The blacksmith's wife caught the meaning, if not the words, and was defensive. "Weren't Little Saint Peter's fault. Prioress said as I didn't pray hard enough."

"*I'll* kill her," Adelia said. She could do nothing about the woman's blindness but sent her on her way with an eyewash of weak, strained agrimony that, with regular use, should get rid of the inflammation.

The rest of the morning did little to alleviate Adelia's anger. Broken bones had been left too long and set crookedly. A baby, dead in its mother's arms, could have been saved its convulsions by a decoction of willow bark. Three crushed toes had gone gangrenous—a cloth soaked in opium held for half a minute over the young man's nose and swift application of the knife saved the foot, but amputation would not have been necessary if the patient hadn't wasted time appealing to Little Saint Peter.

By the time the amputee had been stitched, bound, rested, and taken home, and the waiting room emptied, Adelia was raving. "God-damn Saint Radegund's and all its bones. Did you see the baby? Did you see it?" In her temper, she turned on Mansur. "And what were you doing, recommending sugar for that child with the cough?"

Mansur had tasted power; he'd begun to make cabalistic arm movements over the patients' heads as they bowed before him. He faced Adelia. "Sugar for a cough," he said.

"Are you the doctor now? Sugar may be the Arab remedy, but it is not grown in this country and is very expensive here; neither, in this case, would it be any damned use."

She stamped off to the kitchen to take a drink from the bouser, flinging the tin cup back into the water when she'd finished. "Blast them, blast their ignorance."

Gyltha looked up from rolling pastry crust; she'd been on hand to interpret some of the more impenetrably East Anglian symptoms— "wambly" had proved to mean unsteadiness of the legs. "You saved young Coker's foot for un, though, bor."

"He's a *thatcher*," Adelia said. "How can he climb ladders with only two toes on one foot?"

"Better'n no bloody foot at all."

There'd been an alteration in Gyltha, but Adelia was too depressed to notice it. This morning twenty-one desperate people had come to her—or, rather, to Dr. Mansur—and she could have helped eight of them if they'd attended sooner. As it was, she'd saved only three—well, four really—the child with the cough might benefit from inhalation of essence of pine if its lungs weren't too affected.

The fact that until now she hadn't been in residence to treat anybody passed her by; they'd been in need.

Absentmindedly, Adelia munched a biscuit Gyltha slid under her hand. Furthermore, she thought, if patients continued to arrive at this rate, she would have to set up her own kitchen. Tinctures, decoctions, ointments, and powders needed space and time for their manufacture.

Shop apothecaries tended to skimp; she'd never trusted them since Signor D'Amelia had been discovered interlacing his more expensive powders with chalk.

Chalk. That's where she and Simon and Mansur should be this minute, searching the chalk of Wandlebury Hill, though she granted that Simon had been right not to go alone to that eerie place if only because it would need more than one person to peer into all those strange pits, let alone the possibility that the killer might peer back, in which case Mansur would come in handy.

"You say Master Simon is visiting wool merchants?"

Gyltha nodded. "Took they strips as that devil tied the childer up with. See if any on 'em sold it, and who to."

Yes. Adelia had washed and dried two of the pieces ready for him. Since Wandlebury Hill must wait, Simon was using the time in another direction, though she was surprised that he had made Gyltha privy to what he was up to. Well, since the housekeeper was in their confidence . . .

"Come upstairs," Adelia told her, leading the way. Then she paused. "That biscuit . . ."

"My honey oatcake."

"Very nourishing."

She took Gyltha to the table in the solar on which stood the contents of her goatskin bag. She pointed to one of them. "Have you seen anything like that before?"

"What is it?"

"I believe it to be a sweetmeat of some sort."

The thing was lozenge-shaped, dried rock-hard and gray. It had taken her sharpest knife to shave a sliver from it, an action that revealed a pinkish interior and released, faint as a sought-for memory, a second's suggestion of perfume. She said, "It was tangled in Mary's hair."

Gyltha's eyes squeezed shut as she crossed herself, then opened to peer closely.

"Gelatine, I would say," Adelia urged her. "Flower-flavored, or fruit. Sweetened with honey."

"Rich man's confit," Gyltha said immediately. "I ain't seen the like. Ulf."

Her grandson was in the room within a second of the call, leading Adelia to suppose he'd been outside the door.

"You seen the like of this?" Gyltha asked him.

"Sweetmeats," the boy growled—so he *had* been outside the door. "I buy sweeties all the time, oh, yes, money to burn, me . . ."

As he grumbled, his sharp little eyes took in the lozenge, the vials, the remaining strips of wool drying by the window, all the exhibits brought back from Saint Werbertha's anchorage.

Adelia threw a cloth over them. "Well?"

Ulf shook his head with compelling authority. "Wrong shape for round here. Twists and balls, this country."

"Cut off then," Gyltha told him. When the boy had gone, she spread her hands. "If he ain't seen the like, it don't swim in our pond."

It was disappointing. Last night the magnitude of suspecting every man in Cambridge had been reduced by the decision to devote their attention to the pilgrims. Even so, discounting wives, nuns, and female servants, the number for investigation was forty-seven. "Surely we may also discount the merchant from Cherry Hinton? He seemed harmless." But consultation with Gyltha had placed Cherry Hinton to the west of Cambridge and therefore on a line with Wandlebury Hill.

"We discount nobody," Simon had said.

In order to narrow suspicion through what evidence they had before starting to ask questions of and about forty-seven people, Simon had taken for himself the task of locating the source of the scraps of wool, Adelia the lozenge.

Which was proving unidentifiable.

"Yet we must suppose that its rarity will strengthen its connection with the killer once we find him," Adelia said now.

Gyltha cocked her head. "You reckon he tempted Mary with it?"

"I do."

"Poor little cosset Mary was, frit of her father—always fetching her and her mother a blow, he was—frit of everything. Never ventured far." Gyltha viewed the lozenge: "Did you tempt her away, you beggar?"

The two women shared a moment's reflection . . . a beckoning hand, the other holding out an exotic sweetmeat, the child attracted closer, closer, a bird drawn by a gyrating stoat . . .

Gyltha hurried off down the stairs to lecture Ulf on the danger of men who offered goodies.

Six years old, Adelia thought. Frightened of everything, six years of a brutal father and then a dreadful death. *What can I do? What shall I do?*

She went downstairs. "May I borrow Ulf? There may be some purpose in seeing the place from which each child disappeared. Also, I should like to examine Little Saint Peter's bones."

"They can't tell you much, girl. The nuns boiled him."

"I know." It was the usual practice with the body of a putative saint. "But bones can speak."

Peter was the primus inter pares of the murdered children, the first to disappear and the first to die. As far as could be deduced, his was the only one whose death did not accord with the others', since, presumably, it had occurred in Cambridge.

Also, his was the only death to be accredited to crucifixion and, unless that could be disproved, she and Simon would have failed in their mission to exonerate the Jews, no matter how many killers they produced from the chalk hills.

She found herself explaining this to Gyltha. "Perhaps the boy's parents can be persuaded to talk to me. They would have seen his body before it was boiled."

"Walter and his missus? They saw nails in them little hands and the crown of thorns on that poor little head and they won't say no different, not without losing themselves a mort of cash."

"They're making money from their son?"

Gyltha pointed upriver. "Get you to Trumpington and their cottage, the which you can't see for folk clamoring to go inside it so's to breathe air as Little Saint Peter breathed and touch Little Saint Peter's shirt, the which they can't acause he was wearing his only one, and Walter and Ethy sitting at their door charging a penny a time."

"How shameful."

Gyltha hung a kettle over the fire and then turned. "Seems you've never wanted for much, mistress." The "mistress" was ominous; such rapport as had been achieved that morning had waned.

Adelia admitted she had not.

"Then s'pose you wait til you got six childer to feed apart from the one that's dead and obliged for the roof over your head to do four days a week plowing and reaping of the nunnery's fields as well as your own, to say nought of Agnes being bonded to do its bloody cleaning. Maybe you don't care for their way, but that's not shameful, that's surviving."

Adelia was silenced. After a while, she said, "Then I shall go to Saint Radegund's and ask to see the bones in its reliquary."

"Huh."

"I shall look around me, at least," Adelia said, piqued. "Shall Ulf guide me or not?"

Ulf would, though not willingly. So would the dog, though it seemed to scowl as horribly as the boy.

Well, perhaps with such companions—but *such* companions—she would blend into the Cambridge scenery.

"Blend into the *scenery*," she said to Mansur with emphasis when he readied himself to accompany her. "You can't come. I'd as easy blend in with a troop of acrobats."

He protested, but she pointed out that it was daylight, there were plenty of people about, and she had her dagger and a dog whose smell could fell an assailant at twenty paces. In the end, she thought, he was not reluctant to stay behind with Gyltha in the kitchen.

She set off.

Beyond an orchard, a raised balk ran along the edge of a common field leading down to the river, angled with cultivated strips. Men and women were hoeing the spring planting. One or two touched their forehead to her. Farther along, the breeze bellied washing that was pinned to tenterhooks.

The Cam, Adelia saw, was a boundary. Across the river was a countryside of gently rising uplands, some forested, some parkland, a mansion like a toy in the distance. Behind her, the town with its noisy quays crowded the right bank as if enjoying the uninterrupted view.

"Where's Trumpington?" she asked Ulf.

"Trumpington," the boy grumbled to the dog. They went left. The angle of the afternoon sun showed that they had turned south. Punts went past them, women as well as men poling themselves about their business, the river their thoroughfare. Some waved to Ulf, the boy nodding back and naming each one to the dog. "Sawney on his way for to collect the rents, the old grub . . . Gammer White with the washing for Chenies . . . Sister Fatty for to supply the hermits, look a her puff . . . Old Moggy finished early at the market . . ."

They were on a causeway that kept Adelia's boots, the boy's bare feet, and Safeguard's paws from sinking into meadows where cows grazed on deep grass and buttercups among willow and alder, their hooves causing a sucking sound as they moved to a fresh patch.

She'd never seen so much greenness in so great a variety. Or so many birds. Or such fat cattle. Pasture in Salerno was burned thin and good only for goats.

The boy stopped and pointed to a cluster of thatch and a church tower in the distance. "Trumpington," he informed the dog.

Adelia nodded. "Now, where is Saint Radegund's tree?"

The boy rolled his eyes, intoned "Saint Raddy's," and set off back the way they had come.

With Safeguard plodding dispiritedly behind them, they crossed the river by a footbridge so that this time they were following the Cam's left bank northward, the boy complaining to the dog at every step. From what Adelia could understand, he resented Gyltha's change of occupation. As errand boy to his grandmother's eel business, he occasionally received pourboires from the customers, a source of money now cut off.

Adelia ignored him.

A hunting horn sounded musically in the hills to the west. Safeguard and Ulf raised their disreputable heads and paused. "Wolf," Ulf told the dog. The echo died and they went on.

Now Adelia was able to look across the water to Cambridge town.

Set without competition against pure sky, its jumbled roofs that were spiked with church towers gained significance, even beauty.

In the distance loomed Great Bridge, a massive, workmanlike arch crammed with traffic. Beyond it, where the river formed a deep pool below the castle on its hill—almost a mountain in this terrain—shipping so crowded the quays it seemed impossible, from this view, that it should disentangle itself. Wooden cranes dipped and rose like bowing herons. Shouts and instructions were being issued in different languages. The crafts were as varied as the tongues; wherries, horse-drawn barges, poled barges, rafts, vessels like arks—even, to Adelia's astonishment, a dhow. She could see men with blond plaits, hung about with animal skins so that they looked like bears, performing a leaping dance back and forth between barges for the amusement of working dockers.

Carried on the breeze, the noise and industry accentuated the quietness of the bank where she walked with the boy and the dog. She heard Ulf informing the dog that they were approaching Saint Radegund's tree.

She'd worked that out for herself. It had been fenced off. A stall stood just outside the palings with a pile of branches on it. Two nuns were breaking off twigs, attaching a ribbon to each, and selling them to relic-seekers.

This, then, was where Little Saint Peter had taken his Easter branches and where, subsequently, Chaim the Jew had been hanged.

The tree stood outside the convent grounds, which were marked here by a wall that, on the river side, led down to gates next to a boathouse and a small quay but which, heading west, ran so far back into the forested countryside that Adelia could see no end to it.

Inside the open gates, other nuns busied themselves among a mass of pilgrims like black-and-white bees directing honey-gatherers into their hive. As Adelia went under the entrance arch, a nun sitting at a table in the sunny courtyard was telling a man and wife ahead of her,

"Penny to visit Little Saint Peter's tomb," adding, "Or a dozen eggs, we're low on eggs, hens ain't laying."

"Pot of honey?" the wife suggested.

The nun tutted, but they were allowed to pass in. Adelia contributed two pennies since the nun was prepared to exclude Safeguard if she did not and Ulf was reluctant to enter without the dog. Her coins clinked into a bowl already nearly full. The argument had held up the line of people that formed behind her, and one of the nuns marshaling it became angry at the delay and almost pushed her through the gates.

Inevitably, Adelia compared this, the first English nunnery she had visited, with Saint Giorgio's, largest of the three female convents in Salerno and the one with which she was most familiar. The comparison was unfair, she knew; Saint Giorgio's was a rich foundation, a place of marble and mosaic, bronze doors opening into courtyards where fountains cooled the air, a place, Mother Ambrose always said, "to feed with beauty the hungry souls who come to us."

If the souls of Cambridge looked for such sustenance from Saint Radegund's, they went empty away. Few had endowed this female house, suggesting that the rich of England did not esteem women's worship. True, there was a pleasing simplicity of line in the convent's collection of plain stone oblong outbuildings, though none of them any bigger nor more ornate than the barn in which Saint Giorgio's kept its grain, but beauty was lacking. So was charity. Here, the nuns were employed in selling rather than giving.

Stalls set up along the path to the church displayed Little Saint Peter talismans, badges, banners, figurines, plaques, weavings from Little Saint Peter's willow, ampullae containing Little Saint Peter's blood, which, if it *were* human blood, had been so watered as to show only the lightest taint of pink.

There was a press to buy. "What one's good for gout? . . . For the flux? . . . For fertility? . . . Can this cure staggers in a cow?"

Saint Radegund's was not waiting on the years it would take for its martyred son to be confirmed in sainthood by the Vatican. But then, neither had Canterbury, where the industry based on the martyrdom of Saint Thomas à Becket was immensely bigger and better organized.

Chastened by Gyltha's strictures on want, Adelia could not blame so poor a convent for exploitation, but she could despise the vulgarity with which it was being done. Roger of Acton was here, striding up and down the line of pilgrims, brandishing an ampulla, urging the crowd to buy: "Whoso shall be washed in the blood of this little one need never wash again." The sour whiff as he passed suggested he took his own advice.

The man had capered the journey from Canterbury, a demented monkey, always shouting. His earflapped cap was still too large for him, his green-black robe daubed with the same mud and food splashes.

On a pilgrimage that had consisted mainly of educated people, the man had appeared an idiot. Yet here, among the desperate, his cracked voice carried compulsion. Roger of Acton said "Buy," and his hearers bought.

It was expected that God's finger infected those it touched with holy madness; Acton was commanding the respect accorded to skeletal men gibbering in the caves of the East, or to a stylite balancing on his pillar. Did not saints embrace discomfort? Had not the corpse of Saint Thomas à Becket been wearing a hair shirt swarming with lice? Dirt, exaltation, and an ability to quote the Bible were signs of sanctity.

He was of a type Adelia had always found to be dangerous; it denounced eccentric old women as witches and hauled adulterers before the courts, its voice inciting violence against other races, other beliefs.

The question was *how* dangerous.

Was it you? Adelia wondered, watching him. *Do you prowl Wandlebury Ring? Do you truly wash in the blood of children?*

Well, she wasn't going to ask him yet, not until she had reason, but in the meantime, he remained a fitting candidate.

He didn't recognize her. Neither did Prioress Joan, who passed them on her way to the gates. She was dressed for riding and had a gyrfalcon on her wrist, encouraging the customers as she went with a "Tallyho."

The woman's confident, bullying manner had led Adelia to expect that the house of which she was the head would prove to be the acme of organization. Instead, slackness was apparent: weeds grew around the church; there were missing tiles on its roof. The nuns' habits were patched, the white linen beneath the black wimples showed mostly dirty; their manners were coarse.

Shuffling behind the line entering the church, she wondered where the money gained from Little Saint Peter was going. Not, so far, to the greater glory of God. Nor on comfort for the pilgrims: no one assisted the sick; there were no benches for the lame while they waited; no refreshment. The only suggestion for overnight accommodation was a curling list of the town's inns pinned to the church gate.

Not that the supplicants shuffling with her seemed to care. A woman on crutches boasted of visits to the glories of Canterbury, Winchester, Walsingham, Bury Saint Edmunds, and Saint Albans as she displayed her badges to those around her, but she was tolerant of the shabbiness here: "I got hopes of this un," she said. "He'm a young saint yet, but he was crucified by Jews; Jesus'll listen to him, I'll be bound."

An English saint, one who'd shared the same fate, and at the same hands, as the Son of God. Who had breathed the air they breathed now. Despite herself, Adelia found herself praying that he would.

She was inside the church now. A clerk sat at a table by the doors, taking down the deposition of a pale-faced woman who was telling him she felt better for having touched the reliquary.

This was too tame for Roger of Acton, who came bounding up. "You were strengthened? You felt the Holy Spirit? Your sins washed away? Your infirmity gone?"

"Yes," the woman said, and then more excitedly: "Yes."

"Another miracle!" She was dragged outside to be displayed to the waiting line. "A cure, my people! Let us praise God and his little saint."

The church smelled of wood and straw. The chalk outline of a maze on the nave suggested that someone had attempted to draw the labyrinth of Jerusalem on the stones, but only a few of the pilgrims were obeying the nun trying to make them walk it. The rest were pushing toward a side chapel where the reliquary lay hidden from Adelia's view by those in front of her.

While she waited she looked around. A fine stone plaque on one wall declaring that "in the Year of Our Lord 1138, King Stephen confirmed the gift which William le Moyne, goldsmith, made to the nuns of the cell newly founded in the town of Cambridge for the soul of the late King Henry."

It probably explained the poverty, Adelia thought. Stephen's war with his cousin Matilda had ended in triumph for Matilda, or, rather, Henry II, her son. The present king would not be happy to endow a house confirmed by the man his mother had fought for thirteen years.

A list of prioresses declared that Joan had taken up her position only two years previously. The church's general disrepair showed she lacked enthusiasm for it. Her more secular interest was suggested by the painting of a horse with the subscription: "Braveheart. A.D. 1151— A.D. 1169. Well Done, Thou Good and Faithful Servant." A bridle and bit hung from the wooden fingertips of a statue to Saint Mary.

The couple in front had now reached the reliquary. They dropped to their knees, allowing Adelia to see it for the first time.

She caught her breath. Here in a white blaze of candles was transcendence to forgive all the grossness that had gone before. Not just the glowing reliquary but the young nun at its head who knelt, still as stone, her face tragic, her hands steepled in prayer, brought to life a scene from the Gospels: a mother, her dead child; together they made a scene of tender grace.

Adelia's neck prickled. She was suddenly ravished by the wish to believe. Here, surely, in this place was radiant truth to sweep doubt up to Heaven for God to laugh at.

The couple was praying. Their son was in Syria—she'd heard them talking of him. Together, as if they'd been practicing, they whispered, "Oh holy child, if you'd mention our boy to the Lord and send him home safe, we'd be grateful evermore."

Let me believe, God, Adelia thought. A plea as pure and simple as this must prevail. *Only let me believe. I am lonely for belief.*

Holding each other, the man and woman moved away. Adelia knelt. The nun smiled at her. She was the shy little one who had accompanied the prioress to Canterbury and back, but now timidity had been transfigured into compassion. Her eyes were loving. "Little Saint Peter will hear you, my sister."

The reliquary was shaped like a coffin and had been placed on top of a carved stone tomb so that it should be on eye level with those who knelt to it. This, then, was where the convent's money had gone—into a long, jewel-encrusted casket on which a master goldsmith had wrought domestic and agricultural scenes depicting the life of a boy, his martyrdom by fiends, and his ascension to Paradise borne upward by Saint Mary.

Inset along one side was mother-of-pearl so thin that it acted as a window. Peering into it, Adelia could see only the bones of a hand that had been propped up on a small velvet pillow to assume the attitude of benediction.

"You may kiss his knuckle, if you wish." The nun pointed to a monstrance lying on a cushion on top of the reliquary. It resembled a Saxon brooch and had a knobbled, tiny bone set in gold among precious stones.

It was the trapezium bone of the right hand. The glory faded. Adelia returned to herself. "Another penny to view the whole skeleton," she said.

The nun's white brow—she was beautiful—furrowed. Then she leaned forward, removed the monstrance, and lifted the reliquary's lid. As she did so, her sleeve crumpled to show an arm blackened with bruises.

Adelia, shocked, looked at her; they beat this gentle, lovely girl. The nun smiled and smoothed her sleeve down. "God is good," she said.

Adelia hoped He was. Without asking permission, she picked up one of the candles and directed its flame toward the bones.

Bless him, they were so small. Prioress Joan had magnified her saint in her mind; the reliquary was too large; the skeleton was lost in it. She was reminded of a little boy dressed in clothes too big for him.

Tears prickled Adelia's eyes even as they took in the fact that the only distortion of the hands and feet was from the missing trapezoid. No nails had been hammered into these extremities, neither was the rib cage or spine punctured. The wound from a spear that Prior Geoffrey had described to Simon had more likely been due to the process of mortification swelling the body beyond what the skin could bear. The stomach had split open.

But there, around the pelvic bones, were the same sharp, irregular chippings she had seen on the other children. She had to stop herself from putting her hand into the reliquary to lift them out for examination, but she was almost sure; the boy had been repeatedly stabbed with that distinctive blade of a kind she had never seen before.

"Hey, missus." The line behind her was becoming restive.

Adelia crossed herself and walked away, putting her penny onto the table of the clerk at the door. "Are you cured, mistress?" he asked her. "I must record any miracles."

"You may put down that I feel better," she said.

"Justified" would have been a more accurate word; she knew where she was now. Little Saint Peter had not been crucified; he had died even more obscenely. Like the others.

And how to declare that to a coroner's inquest? she thought, sourly. I, Dr. Trotula, have physical proof that this boy did not die on a cross but at the hands of a butcher who still walks among you.

Play that to a jury knowing nothing of anatomical sciences and caring less, demonstrated to them by a foreign woman.

It wasn't until she was outside in the air that she realized Ulf had not come in with her. She found him sitting on the ground by the gates with his arms round his knees.

It occurred to Adelia that she had been unthinking. "Were you acquainted with Little Saint Peter?"

Labored sarcasm was addressed to the Safeguard. "Never went to bloody school with un wintertime, did I? 'Course I never."

"I see. I am sorry." She *had* been thoughtless; the skeleton back there was once a schoolfellow and a friend to this one, who, presumably, must grieve for him. She said politely, "However, not many of us can say we attended lessons with a saint."

The boy shrugged.

Adelia was unacquainted with children; mostly she dealt with dead ones. She saw no reason to address them other than as cognitive human beings, and when they did not respond, like this one, she was at a loss.

"We will go back to Saint Radegund's tree," she said. She wanted to talk to the nuns there.

They retraced their steps. A thought struck Adelia. "By any chance did you see your schoolfellow on the day he disappeared?"

The boy rolled his eyes at the dog in exasperation. "Easter that was. Easter me and Gran was still in the fens."

"Oh." She walked on. It had been worth a try.

Behind her, the boy addressed the dog: "Will did, though. Will was with him, wasn't he?"

Adelia turned round. "Will?"

Ulf tutted; the dog was being obtuse. "Him and Will was picking pussy willow both."

There'd been no mention of a Will in the account of Little Saint Peter's last day that Prior Geoffrey had given to Simon and that Simon had passed on to her. "Who is Will?"

When the child was about to speak to the dog, Adelia put her hand on the boy's head and screwed it round to face her. "I would prefer it if you talked directly to me."

Ulf retwisted his neck so that he could look back at the Safeguard. "We don't like her," he told it.

"I don't like you, either," Adelia pointed out, "but the matter at issue is who killed your schoolmate, how, and why. I am skilled in the investigation of such things, and in this case I have need of your local knowledge—to which, since you and your grandmother are in my employment, I am entitled. Our liking for each other, or lack of it, is irrelevant."

"Jews bloody did it."

"Are you sure?"

For the first time, Ulf looked straight at her. Had the tax collector been with them at that moment, he would have seen that, like Adelia's when she was working, the boy's eyes aged the face they were set in. Adelia saw an almost appalling shrewdness.

"You come along o' me," Ulf said.

Adelia wiped her hand down her skirt—the child's hair where it stuck out from his cap had been greasy and quite possibly inhabited—and followed him. He stopped.

They were looking across the river at a large and imposing mansion with a lawn that led down to a small pier. Closed shutters on every window and weeds growing from the gutters showed it to be abandoned.

"Chief Jew's place," Ulf said.

"Chaim's house? Where Peter was assumed to have been crucified?"

The boy nodded. "Only he weren't. Not then."

"My information is that a woman saw the body hanging in one of the rooms."

"Martha," the boy said, his tone putting the name into the same category as rheumatism, unadmired but to be put up with. "That'll say anything to get her bloody noticed." As if he'd gone too far in condemning a fellow Cambriensan, he added, "I ain't saying her never, I'm saying her never bloody see it when her says she did. Like old Peaty. Look here."

They were off again, past Saint Radegund's willow and its stall of branches, to the bridge.

Here was where a man delivering peat to the castle had seen two Jews casting a bundle, presumed to be the body of Little Peter, into the Cam. She said, "The peat seller was also mistaken?"

The boy nodded. "Old Peaty, he'm half blind and a wormy old liar. He didn't see nothing. Acause . . ."

Now they were returning the way they'd come, back to the spot opposite Chaim's house.

"Acause," said Ulf, pointing to the empty pier protruding into the water, "*Acause* that's where they found the body. Caught under them bloody stanchions like. So nobody threw nothing over the bridge acause . . . ?"

He looked at her expectantly; this was a test.

"Because," Adelia said, "bodies do not float upstream."

The worldly wise eyes were suddenly amused, like those of a teacher whose student had unexpectedly come up to scratch. She'd passed.

But if the testimony of the peat seller was so obviously false, thus casting doubt on that of the woman who claimed that only a little while before, she had seen the crucified body of the child in Chaim's house, why had the finger of guilt pointed straight at the Jews?

"Acause they bloody did it," the boy said, "only not then." He gestured with a grubby hand for her to sit down on the grass, then sat beside her. He began talking fast, allowing her entrance into a world of juveniles who formed theory based on data differently observed and at odds with the conclusions of adults.

Adelia had difficulty following not only the accent but the patois; she leaped onto phrases she could recognize as if jumping from tussock to tussock across a morass.

Will, she gathered, was a boy of about Ulf's age, and he had been on the same errand as Peter, to gather pussy willow for Palm Sunday decoration. Will lived in Cambridge proper, but he and the boy from Trumpington had encountered each other at Saint Radegund's tree, where both had been attracted by the sight of the wedding celebrations on Chaim's lawn across the river. Will had thereupon accompanied Peter over the bridge and through the town in order to see what was to be seen in the stables at the back of Chaim's house.

Afterward, Will had left his companion to take the needed willow branches back home to his mother.

There was a pause in the narration, but Adelia knew there was more to come—Ulf was a born storyteller. The sun was warm, and it was not unpleasant to sit in the dappling shade of the willows, though Safeguard's coat had acquired something noisome on the walk that became more pungent as it dried. Ulf, with his prehensile little feet in the river, complained of hunger. "Give us a penny and I'll go to the pie shop for us."

"Later." Adelia prodded him on. "Let me recapitulate. Will went home and Peter disappeared into Chaim's house, never to be seen again."

The child gave a mocking sniff. "Never to be seen by any bugger 'cept Will."

"Will saw him again?"

It had been later that day, getting dark. Will had returned to the

Cam to bring a supper pail to his father, who was working into the night caulking one of the barges ready for the morning.

And Will on the Cambridge side had seen Peter across the river, standing on the left bank—"Here he was, right here. Where we're bloody sitting." Will had called out to Peter that he should be getting home.

"So he ought've," Ulf added, virtuously, "you get caught in them Trumpington marshes of a night, will o'the wisps lead you down to the Pit."

Adelia ignored will o'the wisps, not knowing, nor caring, what they were. "Go on."

"So Peter, he calls back he's going to meet someone for the Jew-Jews."

"Ju-jus?"

"Jew-*Jews*." Ulf was impatient, twice prodding a finger in the air toward Chaim's house. "Jew-Jews, that's what he said. He was going to meet someone *for* the Jew-Jews, and would Will come with him. But Will says no, and he's bloody glad he did, acause *that's* when nobody saw Peter after."

Jew-Jews. Meeting someone *for* the Jew-Jews? Running an errand on the Jew-Jews' behalf? And why that infantile term? There were a hundred derogatory terms for Jews; since she'd been in England she'd heard most of them, but not that one.

She puzzled over it, recreating the scene at the river on that night. Even today in full sunlight, even with the crowd around Saint Rade-gund's tree farther up, this bit of bank was quiet, forest and parkland closing in behind it. How shadowy it would have been then.

Peter's character, she thought, emerged from the narrative as fey, romantic; Ulf had described a child more easily distracted than the dependable Will.

She saw him now: a small figure, waving to his friend, pale among the dusk of the trees, disappearing into them forever.

"Did Will inform anyone of this?"

Will had not, at least not the adults. Too scared the bloody Jews would come after him next. And right to be so, in Ulf's opinion. Only to his peers, that knee-high, hidden, disregarded, secret world of childhood camaraderie, had Will committed his secret.

The result, in any case, had been the desired one: The Jews had been accused and the perpetrator and his wife punished.

Leaving the ground clear for the murderer to kill again, Adelia thought.

Ulf was watching her. "You want more? There's more. Get your boots wet, though."

He showed her his final proof that Peter had returned to Chaim's house later that night, proof of Chaim's guilt. Because she had to scramble down the bank to the river's edge and bend low, it did indeed involve getting her feet wet. And the bottom of her skirt. And a considerable amount of Cambridge silt over the rest of her. Safeguard came with them.

It was when the three emerged back onto the bank that darker shadows than those of the trees fell across them.

"God's eyes, it's the foreign bitch," Sir Gervase said.

"Rising as Aphrodite from the river," Sir Joscelin said.

They were in hunting leathers, sitting their sweat-flecked horses like gods. The corpse of a wolf slung in front of Sir Joscelin had a cloak lain over it from which a dripping muzzle hung down, still caught in the rictus of a snarl.

The huntsman who'd accompanied them on the pilgrimage was in the background, holding three wolfhounds on a leash, each one of which was big enough to pick Adelia up and carry her off. The dogs' eyes watched her mildly from rough, mustachioed faces.

She would have walked away, but Sir Gervase kneed his horse forward so that she and Ulf and Safeguard were in a triangle formed on two sides by horses with the river as its base behind them.

"We should ask ourselves what our visitor to Cambridge is doing paddling in the mud, Gervase." Sir Joscelin was amused.

"We should. We should also damn well tell the sheriff about her magic axes when a gentleman deigns to notice her." More jovial now, but still threatening, Gervase was out to regain the supremacy he'd lost to Adelia in their encounter. "Eh? What about that, witch? Where's your Saracen lover now?" Each question came louder. "What about ducking you back in the water? Eh? Eh? Is that his brat? It looks dirty enough."

She wasn't frightened this time. *You ignorant clod,* she thought. *You dare talk to me.*

At the same time she was fascinated; she didn't take her eyes off him. More hatred here, enough to eclipse Roger of Acton's. He'd have raped her on that hill merely to show that he could—and would now if his friend were not by. Power over the powerless.

Was it you?

The boy beside her was as still as death. The dog had crept behind her legs where the wolfhounds couldn't see him.

"*Gervase,*" Sir Joscelin said sharply. Then, to her: "Pay my friend no mind, mistress. He's waxy because his spear missed old Lupus here"— he patted the wolf's head—"and mine didn't." He smiled at his companion before turning to look down again on Adelia. "I hear the good prior has found you better accommodation than a cart."

"Thank you," she said, "he has."

"And your doctor friend? Is he setting up here?"

"He is."

"Saracen Quack and Whore, that'll look good on the shingle." Sir Gervase was getting restive and more outrageous.

This is what it's like to be among the weak, Adelia thought. *The strong insult you with impunity. Well, we'll see.*

Sir Joscelin was ignoring the man. "I suppose your doctor can do nothing for poor Gelhert here, can he? The wolf sliced his leg." He jerked his head toward one of the hounds. It had a paw raised.

And that, too, is an insult, Adelia thought, *though you may not mean it to be.*

She said, "He is better with humans. You should advise your friend to consult him as soon as possible."

"Eh? What's the bitch say?"

"Do you think him ill then?" Joscelin asked.

"There are signs."

"What signs?" Gervase was suddenly anxious. "What signs, woman?"

"I am not in a position to say," she told Joscelin. Which was true, since there were none. "But it would be as well for him to consult a doctor—and quickly."

Anxiety was turning to alarm. "Oh my God, I sneezed a full seven times this morning."

"Sneezing," Adelia said, reflectively. "There it is, then."

"Oh my God." He wrenched the reins and wheeled his horse, spiking its side with his spurs, leaving Adelia spattered with mud but content.

Smiling, Joscelin raised his cap. "Good day, mistress."

The huntsman bowed to her, gathered the hounds, and followed them.

It could be either of them, Adelia told herself, watching them go. Because Gervase is a brute and the other is not means nothing.

Sir Joscelin, for all his pleasant manner, was as likely a candidate as his objectionable companion, of whom he was obviously fond. He'd been on the hill that morning.

But then, who had not? Hugh, the huntsman with a face as bland as milk that might well harbor as much viciousness as Roger of Acton without showing it. The fat-cheeked merchant from Cherry Hinton. The minstrel, too. The monks—the one they called Brother Gilbert was a hater if ever she'd met one. All had access to Wandlebury Ring that night. As for the inquisitive tax inspector, everything about him was subject to suspicion.

And why do I consider only the men? There's the prioress, nun, merchant's wife, servants.

But, no, she absolved all females; this was not a woman's crime. Not that women were incapable of cruelty to children—she had examined many results of torture and neglect—but the only cases that even approached this one's savage, sexual assault had involved men, always men.

"They *talked* to you." Ulf's stillness, unlike her own, had been the grip of awe. "Crusaders, they are. Both on 'em. Been to the Holy Land."

"Have they indeed," she said flatly.

They had, and had come back rich, having won their spurs. Sir Gervase held Coton manor by knight's fee of the priory. Sir Joscelin held Grantchester manor of Saint Radegund's. Great hunters they were and borrowed Hugh and his wolfhounds from Prior Geoffrey when they had to run down a devil like the one across Sir Joscelin's horse—been taking lambs over Trumpington way, it had—acause Hugh was the best wolf hunter in Cambridgeshire. . . .

Men, she thought, listening to him run on in his admiration. *Even when they are small boys . . .*

But this one was looking up at her now, worldly wise again. "And you stood to 'em," he said.

She, too, had won her spurs.

Companionably, they walked back to Old Benjamin's together, the disgraced Safeguard trailing behind them.

IT WAS DARK by the time Simon returned to the house, hungry for the eel stew with dumplings and fish pie awaiting him—the day was Friday and Gyltha strictly observed it—complaining of the great number of wool merchants plying their trade in and around Cambridge.

"Amiable beings to a man, each one amiably explaining to me that my ties came from an old batch of wool . . . something about its nap, apparently . . . but, oh, dear me, yes, not impossible to trace the bale it came from were I prepared to pursue its history."

For all the insignificance of his looks and dress, Simon of Naples came of a wealthy family and had never considered before the journey that wool made from the sheep to the clothyard. It amazed him.

He instructed Mansur and Adelia as he ate.

"They use urine to clean the fleeces, did you know? Wash it in vats of piss to which whole families contribute." Carding, fulling, weaving, dyeing, mordants. "Can you conceive of the difficulty in achieving of the color black? *Experto crede*. It must be based on deep blue, woad or a combination of tannin and iron. I tell you, yellow is simpler. I have met dyers today who would that we all dressed in yellow, like ladies of the night. . . ."

Adelia's fingers began to tap; Simon's glee suggested that his quest had been successful, but she also had news.

He noticed. "Oh, very well. The ties are deemed to be worsted from their solid, compact surface, but, even so, we could not have traced it if this strip . . ." Simon ran it lovingly through his hand and Adelia saw that in the thrill of investigation he had all but forgotten the use to which it had been put. "If this strip had not included part of a selvedge, a warp-turned selvedge for strengthening edges, distinctive to the weaver . . ."

He caught her eye and gave in. "It is part of a batch sent to the Abbot of Ely three years ago. The abbot holds the concession to supply all religious houses in Cambridgeshire with the cloth in which to dress their monastics."

Mansur was the first to respond. "A habit? It is from a monk's habit?"

"Yes."

There was one of the reflective silences to which their suppers were becoming subject.

Adelia said, "The only monastic we can absolve is the prior, who was with us all night."

Simon nodded. "His monks wear black beneath the rochet."

Mamsur said, "So do the holy women."

"That is true"—Simon smiled at him—"but in this case irrelevant, for in the course of my investigations I came across the merchant from Cherry Hinton again who, as luck would have it, deals in wool. He assures me that the nuns and his wife and the female servants spent the night under canvas, ringed outside and guarded by the males of the company. If one of those ladies is our murderer, she could not have gone unnoticed to tramp the hills carrying bodies."

Which left the three monks accompanying Prior Geoffrey. Simon listed them.

Young Brother Ninian? Surely not. Yet why not?

Brother Gilbert? A displeasing fellow, a possible subject.

The other one?

Nobody could remember either the face or the personality of the third monk.

"Until we make more inquiries, speculation is bootless." Simon said. "A spoiled habit, cast out onto a midden perhaps; the killer could have acquired it anywhere. We will pursue it when we are fresher."

He sat back and reached for his wine cup. "And now, Doctor, forgive me. We Jews so rarely join the chase, you see, that I have become as tedious as any huntsman with a tale of how he ran his quarry down. What news from your day?"

Adelia began her account chronologically and was more brusque about it; the ending of her own day's hunt had been more fruitful than Simon's, but she doubted if he would like it. She didn't.

He was encouraged by her view of Little Saint Peter's bones. "I knew it. Here's a blow for our side. The boy never was crucified."

"No, he wasn't," she said, and took her listeners to the other side of the river and her conversation with Ulf.

"*We have it.*" Simon spluttered wine. "Doctor, you have saved Israel. The child was seen *after* leaving Chaim's house? Then all we must do is gather up this boy Will and take him to the sheriff. 'You see, my lord Sheriff, here is living proof that the Jews had nothing to do with the death of Little Saint Peter. . . .'" His voice trailed away as he saw the look on Adelia's face.

"I am afraid they did," she said.

Seven

Over the year, the watch kept on Cambridge Castle by the towns-people to make sure the Jews inside did not escape from it had dwindled to Agnes, the eel seller's wife and mother to Harold, whose remains still awaited burial.

The small hut she'd built for herself out of withies looked like a beehive against the great gates. By day she sat at its entrance, knit-ting, with one of her husband's eel glaives planted spike end down on one side of her, and on the other a large handbell. By night she slept in the hut.

On the occasion during the winter when the sheriff had tried to smuggle the Jews out through the dark, thinking she was asleep, she had used both weapons. The glaive had near skewered one of the ac-companying sheriff's men; the bell had raised the town. The Jews had been hurried back inside.

The castle postern was also guarded, this time by geese kept there for the purpose of declaring the emergence of anyone trying to get out, much as the geese of the Capitoline had warned Rome that the Gauls were trying to get in. An attempt by the sheriff's men to shoot them from the castle walls had caused such honking that, again, the alarm was raised.

Climbing the steep, winding, fortified road up to the castle, Adelia expressed surprise that commoners were allowed to flout authority for so long. In Sicily a troop of the king's soldiers would have solved the problem in minutes.

"And result in massacre?" Simon said. "Where could it escort the Jews that would not give rise to the same situation? The whole country believes the Jews of Cambridge to be child-crucifiers."

He was downcast today and, Adelia suspected, very angry.

"I suppose so." She reflected on the restraint with which the king of England was dealing with the matter. She could have expected a man like him, a man of blood, to wreak awful revenge on the people of Cambridge for killing one of his most profitable Jews. Henry had been responsible for the death of Becket; he was a tyrant, after all, like any other. But so far he had held his hand.

When asked what she thought might happen, Gyltha had said the town did not look forward to the fine that would be imposed on it for Chaim's death, but she wasn't anticipating wholesale hangings. This king was a tolerant king as long as you didn't poach his deer. Or cross him beyond endurance, as Archbishop Thomas had.

"Ain't like the old days when his ma and uncle Stephen were warring with each other," she'd said. "Hangings? A baron'd come galloping up—didn't matter which side he was on, didn't matter which side *you* was on, he'd hang you just for scratching your arse."

"Quite right, too," Adelia had said. "A nasty habit." The two of them were beginning to get on well.

The civil war between Matilda and Stephen, Gyltha said, had even penetrated the fens. The Isle of Ely with its cathedral had changed hands so many times, you never knew who was abbot and who wasn't. "Like we poor folk was a carcass and wolves was ripping us apart. And when Geoffrey de Mandeville came through . . ." At that point,

Gyltha had shaken her head and fallen silent. Then she said, "Thirteen years of it. Thirteen years with God and saints sleeping and taking no bloody notice."

"Thirteen years when God and his saints slept." Since her arrival in England, Adelia had heard that phrase used about the civil war a score of times. People still blanched at the memory. Yet on the accession of Henry II, it had stopped. In twenty years it had never restarted. England had become a peaceful country.

The Plantagenet was a more subtle man than she'd classified him; perhaps he should be reconsidered.

They turned the last corner of the approach and emerged onto the apron before the castle.

The simple motte and bailey the Conqueror had built to guard the river crossing had gone, its wooden palisade replaced by curtain walls, its keep grown into the accommodation, church, stables, mews, barracks, women's quarters, kitchens, laundry, vegetable and herb gardens, dairy, tiltyards, and gallows and lockup necessary for a sheriff administering a sizable, prosperous town. At one end, scaffolding and platforms clad the growing tower that would replace the one that had burned down.

Outside the gates, two sentries leaned on their spears and talked to Agnes where she sat, knitting, on a stool outside her beehive. Somebody else was sitting on the ground, resting his head against the castle wall.

Adelia groaned. "Is the man ubiquitous?"

At the sight of the newcomers, Roger of Acton leaped to his feet, picked up a wooden board on a stick that had been lying beside him, and began shouting. The chalked message read: "Pray for Littel Saint Peter, who was crucafid by the Jews."

Yesterday he'd favored the pilgrims to Saint Radegund's; today, it appeared, the bishop was coming to visit the sheriff and Acton was ready to waylay him.

Again, there was no recognition of Adelia, nor, despite Mansur's singularity, of the two men with her. He doesn't see people, she thought, only fodder for hell. She noticed that the man's dirty soutane was of worsted.

If he was disappointed that he didn't yet have the bishop to hector, he made do. "They did scourge the poor child till the blood flowed," he yelled at them. "They kept gnashing their teeth and calling him Jesus the false prophet. They tormented him in divers ways and then crucified him. . . ."

Simon went up to the soldiers and asked to see the sheriff. They were from Salerno, he said. He had to raise his voice to be heard.

The elder of the guards was unimpressed. "Where's that when it's at home?" He turned to the yelling clerk. "Shut up, will you?"

"Prior Geoffrey has asked us to attend on the sheriff."

"What? I can't hear you over that crazy bastard."

The younger sentry pricked up. "Here, is this the darky doctor as cured the prior?"

"The same."

Roger of Acton had spotted Mansur now and come up close; his breath was rank. "Saracen, do you acknowledge our Lord Jesus Christ?"

The older sentry cuffed him round the ear. "Shut up." He turned back to Simon. "And that?"

"Milady's dog."

Ulf had, with difficulty, been left behind, but Gyltha had insisted that the Safeguard must go with Adelia everywhere. "He is no protection," Adelia had protested. "When I was facing those damned crusaders, he skulked behind me. He's a skulker."

"Protection ain't his job," Gyltha had said. "He's a safeguard."

"Reckon as they can go in, eh, Rob?" The sentry winked at the woman in the entrance to her withy hut. "All right by you, Agnes?"

Even so, the guard captain was fetched, and was satisfied that the three were not concealing weapons before they were allowed through the wicket. Acton had to be restrained from going in with them. "Kill the Jews," he was shouting, "kill the crucifiers."

The reason for precaution became apparent as they were ushered into the bailey; fifty or so Jews were taking exercise in it, enjoying the sun. The men were mainly walking and talking; women were gossiping in one corner or playing games with their children. As with all Jews in a Christian country, they were dressed like anyone else, though one or two of the men wore the conelike *Judenhut* on their heads.

But what distinguished this particular group as *the* Jews was their shabbiness. Adelia was startled by it. In Salerno there were poor Jews, just as there were poor Sicilians, Greeks, Moslems, but their poverty was disguised by the alms flowing from their richer brethren. In fact, it was held, somewhat sniffily, by the Christians of Salerno that "the Jews have no beggars." Charity was a precept of all the great religions; in Judaism, *"Give unto Him of what is His, seeing that thou and what thou hast are His"* was law. Grace was bestowed on the giver rather than the receiver.

Adelia remembered one old man who'd driven her foster mother's sister to distraction by his refusal to say thank you for the meals he'd taken in her kitchen. "Do I eat what is yours?" he used to ask. "I eat what is God's."

The sheriff's charity to his unwanted guests, it appeared, was not so munificent. They were thin. The castle kitchen, Adelia thought, was unlikely to accord with the dietary laws, and therefore its meals would in many cases remain uneaten. The clothes in which these people had to hurry from their homes the year before were beginning to tatter.

Some of the women looked up expectantly as she and the others crossed the bailey. Their men were too deep in discussion to notice.

With the younger soldier from the gate leading the way, the three passed over the moat bridge, under the portcullis, and across another court.

The hall was cool, vast, and busy. Trestle tables stretched down its length, covered with documents, rolls, and tallies. Clerks poring over them occasionally broke off to run to the dais, where a large man sat in a large chair at another table on which other documents, rolls, and tallies were growing at a rate threatening to topple them.

Adelia was unacquainted with the role of sheriff, but Simon had said that as far as each shire was concerned, this was the man of greatest importance next to the king, the royal agent of the county who, with the diocesan bishop, wielded most of its justice and alone was responsible for the collection of its taxes, the keeping of its peace, pursuing its villains, ensuring there was no Sunday trading, seeing to it that everybody paid church tithes and the Church paid its dues to the Crown, arranging executions, appropriating the hanged one's chattels for the king, as well as that of waifs, fugitives, outlaws, ensuring that treasure trove went into the royal coffers—and twice a year delivering the resultant money and its accounting to the king's Exchequer at Winchester, where, Simon said, a penny's discrepancy could lose him his place.

"With all that, why does anyone want the job in the first place?" Adelia inquired.

"He takes a percentage," Simon said.

To judge from the quality of the clothes the Sheriff of Hertfordshire was wearing and the amount of gold and jewels adorning his fingers, the percentage was a big one, but at the moment, it was doubtful whether Sheriff Baldwin thought it enough. "Harassed" hardly described him; "distracted" did.

He stared with manic vacancy at the soldier who announced his visitors. "Can't they see I'm busy? Don't they know the justices in eyre are coming?"

A tall and bulky man, who'd been bending over some papers at the sheriff's side, straightened up. "I think, my lord, these people may be helpful in the matter of the Jews," Sir Rowley said.

He winked at Adelia. She looked back at him without favor. Another as ubiquitous as Roger of Acton. And perhaps more sinister.

Yesterday a note had arrived for Simon from Prior Geoffrey, warning him against the king's tax collector: "The man was in the town on two occasions at least when a child disappeared. May the good Lord forgive me if I cast doubt where none is deserved, but it behooves us to be circumspect until we are sure of our ground."

Simon accepted that the prior had cause for suspicion, "but no more than for anyone else." He'd liked what he had seen of the tax collector, he said. Adelia, made privy to what lay beyond the amiable exterior when Sir Rowley had forced his presence on her examination of the dead children, did not. She found him disturbing.

It appeared he had the castle in thrall. The sheriff was staring up at him for help, incapable of dealing with any but his own immediate troubles. "Don't they know there's an eyre coming?"

Rowley turned to Simon. "My lord wishes to know your business here."

Simon said, "With the lord's permission, we would speak to Yehuda Gabirol."

"No harm in that, eh, my lord? Shall I show them the way?" He was already moving.

The sheriff grabbed at him. "Don't leave me, Picot."

"Not for long, my lord, I promise."

He ushered the trio down the hall, talking all the way. "The sheriff's just been informed that the justices in eyre are intending to hold an assize in Cambridge. Coming on top of the presentment he must make to the Exchequer, that means considerable extra work, and he finds himself somewhat, shall we say, overwhelmed. So do I, of course."

He smiled chubbily down at them; a less overwhelmed man would have been difficult to find. "One is trying to discover what debts are owed to the Jews and, therefore, to the king. Chaim was the chief moneylender in this county, and all his tallies went up in the tower fire. The difficulty of recovering what is not there to speak for itself is considerable. However . . ."

He gave an odd little sideways bow to Adelia. "I hear Madam Doctor has been dabbling in the Cam. Not a doctorly thing to do, one would have thought, considering what pours into it. Perhaps you had your reasons, ma'am?"

Adelia said, "What is an assize?"

They had gone through an arch and were following Sir Rowley up the winding staircase of a tower, the Safeguard pattering behind them.

Over his shoulder, the tax collector said, "Ah, an assize. A judgment really, by the king's traveling justices. A Day of Judgment—and nearly as terrible as God's for those in its scales. Judgment of ale and punishment for the watering down of. Judgment of bread, ditto for the underweight of. Gaol delivery, guilt or innocence of prisoners therein. Presentments of land, ownership of, presentment of quarrels, justification for . . . the list goes on. Juries to be provided. Doesn't happen every year, but when it does . . . Mother of God help us, these steps are steep."

He was puffing as he led them up. Shafts of sun coming in through arrow slits deep in the stone lit tiny landings, each with its arched door.

"Try losing weight," Adelia told him, her eyes presented with his backside as it ascended.

"I am a man of muscle, madam."

"Fat," she said. She slowed so that he rounded the next twist ahead of her and she could hiss at Simon at her rear, "He is going to listen in to what we have to say."

Simon took his hands off the rail that had been aiding him upward and spread them. "He must know our business here already. He knows—Lord, he's right about these stairs—who you are. Where's the difference?"

The difference was that the man would draw conclusions from what was to be said to the Jews. Adelia distrusted conclusions until she had all the evidence. Also, she distrusted Sir Rowley. "But if he should be the killer?"

"Then he knows already." Simon closed his eyes and groped for the rail.

Sir Rowley was waiting for her at the top of the stairs, much put out. "You think me fat, mistress? I'd have you know that when he heard I was on the march, Nur-ad-Din would pack up his tents and steal away into the desert."

"You went on crusade?"

"The Holy Places couldn't have done without me."

He left them in a small circular room, of which the only amenities were some stools, a table, and two unglazed windows with spreading views, promising that Master Gabirol would attend them in minutes and that he'd send up his squire with refreshments.

While Simon paced and Mansur stood, a statue as usual, Adelia went to the windows, one facing west, the other east, to study the panorama afforded by each.

To the west, among the low hills, she could see battlemented roofs from which flew a standard. Even miniaturized by distance, the manor that Sir Gervase held from the priory was larger than Adelia would have expected of a knight's fee. If Sir Joscelin's, held from the nuns, to the southeast and beyond either window's view, was as big, both gentlemen appeared to have done well from their tenancies and crusading.

Two men came in. Yehuda Gabirol was young, his black earlocks cork-screwed against cheeks that were hollow and tinged with an Iberian pallor.

The uninvited guest was old and had found the climb hard. He clung to the doorpost, introducing himself to Simon in a wheeze. "Benjamin ben Rav Moshe. And if you're Simon of Naples, I knew your father. Old Eli still alive, is he?"

Simon's bow was uncharacteristically curt, as was his introduction of Adelia and Mansur, merely giving their names without explaining their presence.

The old man nodded to them, still wheezing. "Is it you occupying my house?"

Since Simon showed no sign of replying, Adelia said, "We are. I hope you don't mind."

"I should mind?" Old Benjamin said sadly. "In good shape is it?"

"Yes. Better for being occupied, I think."

"You like the hall windows?"

"Very nice. Most unusual."

Simon addressed the younger man. "Yehuda Gabirol, just before Passover a year ago, you married the daughter of Chaim ben Eliezer here in Cambridge."

"The cause of all my troubles," Yehuda said gloomily.

"The boy came all the way from Spain to do it," Benjamin said. "I arranged it. A good marriage, though, I say it myself. If it turned out unfortunate, is that the fault of the *shadchan*?"

Simon continued to ignore him, his eyes on Yehuda. "A child of this town disappeared on that day. Perhaps Master Gabirol could cast light on what happened to him."

Adelia had never seen this side of Simon; he *was* angry.

There was an outburst of Yiddish from both men. The young one's thin voice rose over Benjamin's deeper one: "Should I know? Am I the keeper of English children?"

Simon slapped him across the face.

A sparrow hawk landed on the west windowsill and took off again, disturbed by the vibration inside the room as the sound of Simon's slap reverberated round the walls. Fingermarks rose on Yehuda's cheek.

Mansur stepped forward in case of retaliation, but the young man had covered his face and was cowering. "What else could we do? What else?"

Adelia stood unnoticed by the window as the three Jews recovered themselves enough to drag three stools into the center of the room and sit down on them. *A ceremony even for this,* she thought.

Benjamin did most of the talking while young Yehuda cried and rocked.

A good wedding it had been, Old Benjamin said, an alliance between cash and culture, between a rich man's daughter and this young Spanish scholar of excellent pedigree whom Chaim intended to keep as an *eidem af kest,* a resident son-in-law to whom he would give a dowry of ten marks. . . .

"Get on," Simon said.

A fine early spring day it was; the chuppah in the synagogue was decorated with cowslips. "I myself shattered the glass. . . ."

"Get *on.*"

So back to Chaim's house for the wedding banquet, which, such was Chaim's wealth, had been expected to go on for a week. Fife, drums, fiddle, cymbals, tables weighed with dishes, wine cups filled and refilled, enthronement of the bride under white samite, speeches—all this on the riverside lawn because the house was scarcely big enough to entertain all the guests, some of whom had traveled more than a thousand miles to get there.

"Maybe, maybe a little bit, Chaim was showing off to the town," Benjamin admitted.

Inevitably, he was, Adelia thought. To burghers who would not invite him to their houses yet were quick enough to borrow from him? Of course he was.

"Get on." Simon was remorseless, but at that moment Mansur raised a hand and began tiptoeing to the door.

Him. Adelia tensed. The tax collector was listening.

Mansur opened the door with a pull that took half of it off its hinges. It was not Sir Rowley who knelt on the threshold, ear at keyhole level, it was his squire. A tray with a flagon and cups was on the floor beside him.

In one flowing movement, Mansur scooped up the tray and kicked the eavesdropper down the stairs. The man—he was very young—tumbled to the turn of the stairwell which caught him so that he was doubled with his legs higher than his head. "Ow. *Ow.*" But when Mansur shifted as if to follow him down and kick him again, the boy writhed to his feet and pattered away down the steps, holding his back.

The odd thing was, Adelia thought, that the three Jews sitting on the stools paid the incident little attention, as if it was of no more moment than another bird landing on the windowsill.

Is that plump Sir Rowley the killer? What exercises him about these murdered children?

There were people—she knew because she'd encountered them—who became excited by death, who tried to bribe their way into the school's stone chamber when she was working on a corpse. Gordinus had been obliged to put a guard on his death field to shoo away men, even women, wanting to gaze on the festering carcasses of the pigs.

She hadn't detected that particular salacity in Sir Rowley during the examination she'd carried out in Saint Werbertha's cell; he'd seemed appalled.

But he'd sent his creature—Pipin, *that* was the squire's name—to listen at the keyhole, which suggested that Sir Rowley wished to keep himself abreast of her and Simon's investigation, either through interest—*in which case, why doesn't he ask us directly?*—or through fear that it would lead to him.

What are you?

Not what he seemed was the only answer. Adelia returned her attention to the three men in their circle.

Simon had not yet allowed Mansur to offer round the contents of the tray; he was forcing the two Jews on, through the events of Chaim's daughter's wedding.

To the evening. A chilly dusk descending, the guests had retired back into the house to dance, but the lamps across the garden were left burning. "And maybe, a little bit, the men were getting drunk," Benjamin said.

"*Will you tell us?*" Never had Simon shown anger like this.

"I'm telling you, I'm telling. So the bride and her mother—two women closer than those two ain't been seen—they wander outside for air, talking . . ." Benjamin was slowing up, reluctant to get to whatever it was.

"There was a body." Everybody turned to Yehuda; he'd been forgotten. "In the middle of the lawn, like someone throw it from the river, from a boat. The women saw it. A lamp shone on it."

"A little boy?"

"Perhaps." Yehuda, if he'd seen it at all, had glimpsed it through a haze of wine. "Chaim saw it. The women screamed."

"Did you see it, Benjamin?" Adelia made her first interjection.

Benjamin glanced at her, dismissed her, and said to Simon, as if it was an answer, "I was the *shadchan*." The arranger of this great wedding, feted with wine on all sides? He should be *capable* of seeing anything?

"What did Chaim do?"

Yehuda said, "He put out all the lamps."

Adelia saw Simon nod, as if it was reasonable; the first thing you did when you discovered a corpse on your lawn, you put out the lamps so that neighbors or passersby should not see it.

It shocked her. But then, she thought, she was not a Jew. The libel that at Passover time Jews sacrificed Christian children was attached to them like an extra shadow sewn on their heels to follow them everywhere. "The legend is a tool," her foster father had told her, "used against every feared and hated religion by those who fear and hate it. In the first century, under Rome, the ones accused of taking the blood and flesh of children for ritual purposes were the early Christians."

Now, and for many ages, the child-eaters had been the Jews. So deeply entrenched in Christian mythology was the belief, and so often had Jews suffered for it, that the automatic response to finding the body of a Christian child on a Jewish lawn was to hide it.

"What could we do?" Benjamin shouted. "You tell me what we should have done. Every important Jew in England was with us that night. Rabbi David had come from Paris, Rabbi Meir from Germany, great biblical commentators, Sholem of Chester had brought his family. Did we want lords like these torn to pieces? We needed time for them to get away."

So while his important guests took horse and scattered into the night, Chaim wrapped the body in a tablecloth and carried it to his cellar.

How and why the little corpse had appeared on the lawn, who had done whatever it was that had been done to it, these things hardly entered the discussion among the remaining Cambridge Jews. The concern was how to get rid of it.

They didn't lack humanity, Adelia assured herself, but each Jew had now felt so close to being murdered himself, and his family with him, that any other preoccupation was beyond him.

And they'd botched it.

"Dawn was breaking," Benjamin said. "We'd come to no conclusion—how could we think? The wine, the fear. Chaim it was who decided for us, his neighbors, God rest his soul. 'Go home,' he said to us. 'Go home and be about your business as if nothing has happened. I will deal with it, me and my son-in-law.'" Benjamin raised his cap and clawed his fingers over his scalp as if it still had hair on it. "Yahweh forgive us, that's what we did."

"And how did Chaim and his son-in-law deal with it?" Simon was leaning forward toward Yehuda, whose face was again hidden by his hands. "It was daytime now—you couldn't smuggle it out of the house without someone seeing you."

There was silence.

"Maybe," Simon went on, "maybe at this point perhaps Chaim remembers the conduit in his cellar."

Yehuda looked up.

"What is it?" Simon asked, almost without interest. "A shit hole? An escape route?"

"A drain," Yehuda said sullenly. "There's a stream through the cellar."

Simon nodded. "So there's a drain in the cellar? A large drain? Leading into the river?" For a second his gaze shifted to Adelia, who nodded back at him. "The mouth comes out under the pier where Chaim's barges tie up?"

"How did you know?"

"So," Simon said, still mild, "you pushed the body down it."

Yehuda rocked, crying again. "We said prayers over it. We stood in the dark of the cellar and recited the prayers for the dead."

"You recited the prayers for the dead? Good, that's good. That will please the Lord. *But you didn't go to see if the body floated free when it got to the river.*"

Yehuda stopped crying in surprise. "It didn't?"

Simon was on his feet, raising his arms in supplication to the Lord, who allowed fools like these.

"The river was searched," Adelia interposed in Salernitan patois for Simon's and Mansur's ears only. "The whole town was out. Even if the body had been caught by a stanchion under the pier, a search such as that would have found it."

Simon shook his head at her. "They had been talking," he said, wearily, in the same tongue. "We are Jews, Doctor. We talk. We consider the outcome, the ramifications; we wonder if it is acceptable to the Lord and if we should do it anyway. I tell you, by the time they finished gabbing and made their decision, the searchers had been and gone." He sighed. "They are donkeys and worse than donkeys, but they didn't kill the boy."

"I know." Though there was no court of law that would believe it. Rightly terrified for their own lives, Yehuda and his father-in-law had done a desperate thing and done it badly, gaining themselves only a few days' respite, during which the body, snagged below the waterline under the pier, swelled to the point where it unsnagged itself and floated to the surface.

She turned to Yehuda, unable to wait any longer. "Before it went into the drain, did you examine the body? What condition was it in? Was it mutilated? Was it clothed?"

Yehuda and Benjamin regarded her with disgust. "You bring a female ghoul into our company?" Benjamin demanded of Simon.

"Ghoul? *Ghoul?*" Simon was in danger of hitting somebody again, and Mansur put out a hand to stop him. "You shove a poor little boy down a drain and you talk to me of ghouls?"

Adelia left the room, leaving Simon in full tirade. There was one person still in the castle who could tell her what she wanted to know.

As she crossed the hall on her way to the bailey, the tax collector noted her departure. He left the sheriff's side for a moment to instruct his squire.

"That Saracen's not with her, is he?" Pipin was nervous; he was still favoring his back.

"Just see whom she talks to."

Adelia walked across the sunlit bailey toward the corner where the Jewish women were gathered. She was able to pick out the one she sought by her youth and the fact that, of all the women, she had been given a chair to sit on. And by her distended belly. At least eight months gone, Adelia judged.

She bowed to Chaim's daughter. "Mistress Dina?"

Dark eyes, huge and defensive, turned to look at her. "Yes?"

The girl was too thin for the good of her condition; the rounded stomach might have been an invasive protuberance that had attached itself to a slender plant. Hollowed sockets and cheeks were darkened in a skin like vellum.

The doctor in Adelia thought, *You need some of Gyltha's cooking, lady; I shall see to it.*

She introduced herself as Adelia, daughter of Gershom of Salerno. Her foster father might be a lapsed Jew, but this was not the time to bring up either his or her own apostasy. "May we talk together?" She looked around at the other women, who were gathering close. "Alone?"

Dina sat motionless for a moment. She was veiled to keep off the sun in near-transparent gossamer; her ornate headdress was not everyday wear. Silk encrusted with pearls peeped out from under the old shawl wrapped around her shoulders. Adelia thought with pity, *She's in the clothes she was married in.*

At last, a flap of the hand sent the other women scattering; fugitive as she was, orphaned as she was, Dina still held rank among her sex as daughter of the man who had been the richest Jew in Cambridgeshire. And she was bored; having been cooped up with them for a year, she would have heard everything her companions had to say—and heard it several times.

"Yes?" The girl lifted her veil. She was sixteen, perhaps, no more, and lovely, but her face was setting into bitterness. When she heard what Adelia wanted, she turned it away. "I will not talk about it."

"The real murderer must be caught."

"They are all murderers." She cocked her head to one side in the attitude of listening, raising a finger so that Adelia should listen with her.

Faintly, from beyond the curtain wall, came shouts indicating that Roger of Acton was responding to the arrival of the bishop at the castle gates. "Kill the Jews" was distinguishable among the gabble.

Dina said, "Do you know what they did to my father? What they did to my mother?" The young face crumpled, becoming even younger. "I miss my mother. I miss her."

Adelia knelt beside her, taking the girl's hand and putting it to her cheek. "She would want you to be brave."

"I can't be." Dina put back her head and let the tears gush.

Adelia glanced to where the other women were teetering anxiously and shook her head to stop them coming forward. "Yes, you can," she said. She laid Dina's hand and her own on the swell of the girl's stomach. "Your mother would want you to be brave for her grandchild."

But Dina's grief, having burst out, was mixed with terror. "They'll kill the baby, too." She opened her eyes wide. "Can't you hear them? They're going to break in. They're going *to break in*."

How hideous it was for them. Adelia had imagined the isolation, even the boredom, but not the day-to-day waiting, like an animal with its leg in a trap, for the wolves to come. There was no forgetting that there was a pack outside; Roger of Acton's howl was there to remind them.

She made ineffectual pats of comfort. "The king won't allow them in." And "Your husband's here to protect you."

"*Him.*" It was said with a contempt that dried tears.

Was it the king so derided? Or the husband? The girl would not have set eyes on the man she'd been told to marry until the day she married him; Adelia had never thought it a good custom. Jewish law did not permit a young woman to be married against her will, but too often that meant only that she could not be forced to wed a man she hated. Adelia herself had escaped marriage through the liberality of a foster father who had complied with her wish to remain celibate. "There are good wives aplenty, thank God," he'd said, "but few good doctors. And a good woman doctor is above rubies."

In Dina's case, a fearful wedding day and the incarceration that followed it had not augured well for marital bliss.

"Listen to me," Adelia said briskly. "If your baby is not to spend the rest of its life in this castle, if a killer is not to stay free and murder other children, tell me what I want to know." Out of desperation, she added, "Forgive me but, by extension, he also killed your parents."

Wet-lashed, beautiful eyes studied her as if she were an innocent. "But that was why they did it. Don't you know that?"

"Know what?"

"Why they killed the boy. We know that. They killed him only so that we should be blamed. Why else would they put his corpse in our grounds?"

"No," Adelia said. *"No."*

"Of course they did." Dina's mouth was ugly with a sneer. "It was planned. Then they set the mob on, kill the Jews, kill Chaim the usurer. That's what they shouted, and that's what they did."

"Kill the Jews." The echo came parrotlike from the gate.

"Other children have died since," Adelia said. She was taken aback by a new thought.

"Them too. They were killed so that the mob will have an excuse when they come to hang the rest of us." Dina was inexorable. Then she wasn't. "Did you know my mother stepped in front of me? Did you know that? So they tore her apart and not me?"

Suddenly, she covered her face and rocked back and forth as her husband had done minutes before, only Dina was praying for her dead: *"Oseh sholom bimromov, hu ya'aseh sholom olaynu, v'al kol yisroel. Omein."*

"Omein." He who makes peace in his high holy places, may he bring peace upon us and upon all Israel. If you are there, God, Adelia prayed, *let it be thus.*

Of *course* these people would see their plight as deliberately engineered, a plot by goyim to murder children if, in so doing, they could murder Jews. Dina did not ask why; history was her answer.

Gently, firmly, Adelia pulled Dina's hands down so that she could look into the girl's face. "Listen to me, mistress. One man killed those children, *one.* I have seen their bodies, and he is inflicting injuries on them so terrible that I will not tell you what they are. He is doing it because he has lusts we do not recognize, because he is not human as we understand it. Now Simon of Naples has come to England to free the Jews of this guilt, but I do not ask you to help him because you are a Jew. I ask you because it is against all the law of God and men that children should suffer as those children suffered."

The castle's noise was climbing up its daylong crescendo, diminishing Roger of Acton's ravings to a bird's chirrup.

A bull waiting to be baited was adding its bellow to the rasp of a grindstone where squires were sharpening their master's blades. Soldiers were drilling. Children, newly let out to play in the sheriff's garden, laughed and shouted.

Away in the tiltyard, a tax collector who had decided to shed some of his weight had joined the knights practicing with wooden swords.

"What do you want to know?" Dina asked.

Adelia patted her cheek. "You are worthy of your brave mother." She took in her breath. "Dina, you saw that body on the lawn before the lights were put out, before it was covered by the tablecloth, before it was taken away. What condition was it in?"

"The poor child." This time Dina wept not for herself, nor for her baby, nor for her mother. "The poor little boy. Somebody had cut off his eyelids."

Eight

I had to make sure," Adelia said. "The boy could have died at the hands of someone other than our killer, or even accidentally—the injuries might have been sustained after death."

"They do that," Simon said. "When they're accidentally dead, they leap up on the nearest Jewish lawn."

"It was necessary to make sure he died as the others did. It had to be proved." Adelia was as tired as Simon, though she didn't regard the Jews' treatment of the body on their lawn with the disgust that he did; she was sorry for them. "We can now be certain the Jews didn't kill him."

"And who will believe it?" Simon was determinedly depressed.

They were at supper. The last of the sun coming almost directly through the ridiculous windows was warming the room and touching Simon's pewter flagon with gold. To save the wine, he'd reverted to English beer. Mansur was drinking the barley water that Gyltha made for him.

It was Mansur who asked now, "Why does the dog cut off their eyelids?"

"I don't know." Adelia didn't want to consider the reason.

"Would you know what I think?" Simon said.

She would not. In Salerno, she was presented with bodies, some of which had died in suspicious circumstances; she examined them; she gave her results to her foster father, who, in turn, told the authorities; the bodies were taken away. Sometimes, always later, she learned what happened to the perpetrator—if he or she had been found. This was the first time she had been involved in physically hunting down a killer, and she was not enjoying it.

"I think they die too quickly for him," Simon said. "I think he wants their attention even after they are dead."

Adelia turned her head away and watched midges dancing in a shaft of sun.

"I know what parts I'll cut off when we catch him, *inshallah,*" Mansur said.

"I shall assist you," Simon agreed.

Two men so different. The Arab, looming in his chair, dark face almost featureless against the white folds of his headdress; the Jew, the sun catching the line of his cheek, leaning forward, his fingers turning and turning his flagon. Both in accord.

Why did men think that was the worst thing? Perhaps, for them, it was. But it was trivial, like castrating a rogue animal. The harm done by this particular creature was too vast for human reprisal, the pain it had caused spread too far. Adelia thought of Agnes, mother of Harold, and her vigil. She thought of the parents who'd gathered round the little catafalques in Saint Augustine's church. Of two men in Chaim's cellar, praying as they did violence to their nature by ridding themselves of a fearful burden. She thought of Dina and the shadow fallen over her that could never be lifted.

It accounted for the wish for eternal damnation, she thought, that there could be no reparation made to such dead, nor for the living they'd left behind. Not in this life.

"Do you agree with me, Doctor?"

"What?"

"My theory on the mutilations."

"It is not in my *brief*. I am not here to understand why a murderer does what he does, merely to prove that he did it."

They stared at her.

"I apologize," she said more quietly, "but I will not enter his mind."

Simon said, "We may have to do that very thing before this business is finished, Doctor. Think as he thinks."

"Then you do it," she said. "You're the subtle one."

He took in a sad breath; they were all gloomy this evening. "Let us consider what we know of him so far. Mansur?"

"No killings here before the saint boy. Maybe he came new to this place a year ago."

"Ah, then you think he's done this before, somewhere else?"

"A jackal is always a jackal."

"True," Simon said. "Or he could be a new recruit to the armies of Beelzebub, just starting to slake his desires."

Adelia frowned; that the killer should be a very young man did not accord with her sense of him.

Simon's head came up. "You don't think so, Doctor?"

She sighed; she was to be drawn in despite herself. "Are we supposing?"

"We can do little else."

Reluctantly, because the apprehension came from less than a shadow glimpsed in a fog, she said, "The attacks are frenzied, which argues youth, but they are planned, which argues maturity. He lures them to a special and isolated place, like the hill; I think that must be so because nobody hears their torture. Possibly, he takes his time, not in the case of Little Peter—he was more hurried there—but with the subsequent children."

She paused because the theory was hideous and founded on such little proof. "It *may* be that they are kept alive for some time after their abduction. That would argue a perverted patience and a love of prolonged agony. I would have expected the corpse of the most recent victim, considering the day he was taken, to have displayed more advanced decomposition than it did."

She glared at them. "But that could be due to so many causes that, as a proposition, it bears no weight at all."

"Ach." Simon pushed his cup away as if it offended him. "We are no further. We shall, after all, have to inquire into the movements of forty-seven people, whether they wear black worsted or not. I shall have to write to my wife and tell her I will not be home yet."

"There is one thing," Adelia said. "It occurred to me today when I talked with Mistress Dina. That poor lady believes all the killings are the result of a conspiracy to blame her people. . . ."

"They are not." Simon said. "Yes, he tries to implicate the Jews with his Stars of David, but that is not why he kills."

"I agree. Whatever the prime motive for these murders, it is not racial; there is too much sexual ferocity involved."

She paused. Having sworn not to enter the mind of the killer, she could feel it reaching out to enmesh her. "Nevertheless, he may see no reason why he should not gain from it. Why did he cast Little Peter's body on Chaim's lawn?"

Simon's eyebrows went up; the question didn't need asking. "Chaim was a Jew, the eternal scapegoat."

"It worked damn well, too," Mansur said. "No suspicion on the killer. And"—he dragged a finger across his throat—"good-bye, Jews."

"Exactly," said Adelia. "Good-bye, Jews. Again, I agree it is probable that the man wanted to implicate the Jews while he was about it. But why choose that particular Jew? Why not put the body near one of the other houses? They were deserted and dark that night because all Jewry was attending Dina's wedding. If he were in a boat—and presumably he was—the killer could have lain the corpse here; this house,

Old Benjamin's, is near the river. Instead, he took unnecessary risk and chose Chaim's lawn, which was well lighted, to throw the body onto."

Simon leaned even further forward until his nose almost touched one of the table's candlesticks. "Continue."

Adelia shrugged. "I merely look at the end result. The Jews are blamed; a mob is fired into madness; Chaim, the biggest moneylender in Cambridge, is hanged. The tower holding the records of all those owing money to the usurers goes up in flames, Chaim's with it."

"He owed money to Chaim? Our killer having satisfied his perversion also wants his debt canceled?" Simon considered it. "But could he have reckoned on the mob burning the tower down? Or that it would turn on Chaim and hang him, for that matter?"

"He is in the crowd," Mansur said, and his boy's voice went into a shriek: "Kill the Jews. Kill Chaim. No more filthy usury. To the castle, people. Bring torches."

Startled by the sound, the head of Ulf peeped over the rail of the gallery, a white and unruly dandelion clock in the growing darkness. Adelia shook a finger at it. "Go to bed."

"Why you talking that foreign gobble?"

"So you can't eavesdrop. Go to bed."

More of Ulf appeared over the rail. "You reckon the Judes didn't do for Peter and them after all, then?"

"No," Adelia told him and added, because, after all, it was Ulf who had discovered and shown her the drain, "Peter was dead when they found him on the lawn. They were frightened and put him into the drain to take suspicion off themselves."

"Mighty clever of 'em, weren't it?" The boy gave a grunt of disgust. "Who *did* do for him, then?"

"We don't know. Somebody who wanted to see Chaim blamed, perhaps someone who owed him money. Go to bed."

Simon held up his hand to detain the boy. "We do not know who, my son. We try to find out." To Adelia he said in Salernitan, "The child is intelligent; he has already been of use. Perhaps he can scout for us."

"No." She was surprised by her own vehemence.

"I can help." Ulf left the balustrade to come pattering down the stairs in a rush. "I'm a tracker. I got my hoof all over this town."

Gyltha came in to light the candles. "Ulf, you get to bed afore I feed you to the cats."

"Tell 'em, Gran," Ulf said desperately. "Tell how I'm a fine tracker. And I hear things, don't I, Gran? I hear things nobody else don't acause nobody don't notice me, I can go places. . . . I got a right, Gran, Harold and Peter was my friends."

Gyltha's eyes met Adelia's and the momentary terror in them told Adelia that Gyltha knew what she knew: The killer would kill again.

A jackal is always a jackal.

Simon said, "Ulf could come with us tomorrow and show us where the three children were found."

"That's at the foot of the ring," Gyltha objected. "I don't want the boy near it."

"We have Mansur with us. The killer is not on the hill, Gyltha, he is in town; from the town, the children were abducted."

Gyltha looked toward Adelia, who nodded. Safer that Ulf should be in their company than wandering Cambridge following a trail of his own.

Gyltha considered. "What about the sick?"

"Surgery will be closed for the day," Simon said firmly.

Equally firmly, Adelia said, "On his way to the hill, the doctor will call on yesterday's worst cases. I want to make sure of the child with the cough. And the amputation needs his dressing changed."

Simon sighed. "We should have set up as astrologers. Or lawyers.

Something useless. I fear the spirit of Hippocrates has lain a yoke of duty across our shoulders."

"It has." In Adelia's limited pantheon, Hippocrates ruled supreme.

Ulf was persuaded to the undercroft where he and the servants slept, Gyltha retired to the kitchen, and the three others resumed their discussion.

Simon drummed his fingers on the table, thinking. He stopped. "Mansur, my good, wise friend, I believe you are right, our killer was in the crowd a year ago, urging the death of Chaim. Doctor, you agree?"

"It could be so," Adelia said cautiously. "Certainly Mistress Dina believes the mob was being set on with intent."

Kill the Jews, she thought, the demand beloved of Roger of Acton. How fitting if that creature proved as horrid in action as in person.

She said so out loud, then doubted it. The children's murderer was surely persuasive. She could not imagine the timorous Mary being tempted by Acton, however many sweetmeats he offered her. The man lacked guile; he was a ranting buffoon, ugly. Nor, despising the race as he did, was he likely to have borrowed from a Jew.

"Not necessarily so," Simon told her. "I have seen men leave my father's counting house, condemning his usury while their purses bulged with his gold. Nevertheless, the fellow wears worsted, and we must see if he was in Cambridge on the requisite dates."

His spirits had risen; he would not be long returning to his family after all. *"Au loup!"* Beaming at their puzzlement, he said, "We are on the scent, my friends. We are Nimrods. Lord, if I had known the thrill of the chase, I would have neglected my studies for the hunting field. *Tyer-hillaut!* Is that not the call?"

Adelia said kindly, "I believe the English cry halloo and tallyho."

"Do they? How quickly language corrupts. Ah, well. However, our quarry is in sight. Tomorrow I shall return to the castle and use this excellent organ"—he tapped his nose, which was twitching like a questing shrew's—"to sniff out which man it is in this town that owed Chaim money he was reluctant to repay."

"Not tomorrow," Adelia said. "Tomorrow we go to Wandlebury Hill." To search, it would need all three of them. And Ulf.

"The day after, then." Simon was not to be put off. He raised his flagon first to Adelia, then Mansur. "We are on his track, my masters. A man of maturity in age, on Wandlebury Hill three nights ago, in Cambridge on such and such a day, a man in heavy debt to Chaim and leading the crowd as it bays for the moneylender's blood. With access to black worsted." He drank deep and wiped his mouth. "Almost we know the size of his boots."

"Who may be someone entirely different," Adelia said.

To that list she would have added a cloak of geniality, for surely if, like Peter, the children had gone willingly to meet their killer, they had been persuaded by charm, even humor.

She thought of the big tax collector.

Gyltha didn't hold with her employers staying up too late and came in to clear the table while they were yet sitting at it.

"Here," she said, "let's have a look at that confit of yourn. I got Matilda B.'s uncle in the kitchen; he's in the confectionary trade. Might be as he's seen the like."

It wouldn't do in Salerno, Adelia thought, as she trudged upstairs. In her parents' villa, her aunt made sure that servants not only knew their place but kept to it, speaking—and with respect—when spoken to.

On the other hand, she thought, *which is preferable? Deference? Or collaboration?*

She brought down the sweetmeat that had been entangled in Mary's hair and put it with its square of linen on the table. Simon shrank from it. Matilda B.'s uncle poked at it with a finger like pasty and shook his head.

"Are you sure?" Adelia tipped a candle to give better light.

"It's a jujube," Mansur said.

"Made with sugar, I reckon," the uncle said. "Too dear for my trade, we do sweeten with honey."

"What did you say?" Adelia asked of Mansur.

"It's a jujube. My mother made them, may Allah be pleased with her."

"A *jujube.*" Adelia said. "Of course. They make them in the Arab quarter in Salerno. Oh, God . . ." She sank into a chair.

"What is it?" Simon was on his feet. *"What?"*

"It wasn't Jew-Jews, it was jujubes." She squeezed her eyes shut, hardly able to bear a renewal of the picture in which a little boy looked back before disappearing into the darkness of trees.

By the time she opened them, Gyltha had ushered Matilda B. and her uncle out of the room and then come back to it. Uncomprehending faces stared into hers.

Adelia said in English, *"That's* what Little Saint Peter meant. Ulf told us. He said Peter called across the river to his friend Will that he was going for the Jew-Jews. But he didn't. He said that he was going for the jujubes. It's a word Will can't have heard before; he translated it as 'Jew-Jews.' "

Nobody spoke. Gyltha had taken a chair and sat with them, elbows on the table, her hands to her forehead.

Simon broke the silence: "You are right, of course."

Gyltha looked up. "That's what they was tempted with, sure enough. But I never heard of un."

"An Arab trader may bring them," Simon pointed out. "They are a sweetmeat of the East. We look for someone with Arab connections."

"Crusader with a sweet tooth, maybe," Mansur said. "Crusaders bring them back to Salerno, maybe one brings them to here."

"That's right." Simon was becoming excited again. "That's right. Our killer has been to the Holy Land."

Once again, Adelia thought not of Sir Gervase nor Sir Joscelin, but of the tax collector, another crusader.

SHEEP, LIKE HORSES, will not willingly tread on the fallen. The shepherd called Old Walt, following his flock to its day's grazing on Wandlebury Hill, had seen a gap appear in its woolly flow as if an unseen prophet had called on it to divide. By the time he'd reached the obstruction it had avoided, the ongoing sea of sheep had become seamless once more.

But his dog had set to howling.

The sight of the children's bodies, a strange weaving laid on the chest of each one, had broken the tenor of a life into which the only enemy was bad weather, or came on four legs and could be chased away.

Now Old Walt was mending it. His dry, creased hands were folded on his crook, a sack over his bent head and shoulders, eyes like beads set deep, contemplating the grass where the corpses had lain, muttering to himself.

Ulf, who sat close by, said he was praying to The Lady. "To heal the place, like."

Adelia had moved some yards away, had chosen a tussock, and was sitting on it, Safeguard by her side. She'd tried questioning the shepherd, but, though his glance had swept over her, he had not seen her. She'd *seen* him not seeing her, as if a foreign woman was so far outside his experience as to be invisible to him.

This must be left to Ulf, who, like the shepherd, was a fenlander and therefore claimed a solid position in the landscape.

Such a weird landscape. To her left the land descended to the flatness of the fens and the ocean of alder and willow that kept its secrets. Away to her right, in the distance, was the bare hilltop with its wooded sides where she, Simon, Mansur, and Ulf had spent the last three hours examining the strange depressions in its ground, bending to peer under bushes, looking for a lair where murder had been done—and not finding it.

Light rain came and went as clouds obscured the sun and then let it shine again.

Knowing that a Golgotha was nearby had affected natural sound: the song of warblers, leaves trembling in the rain, the breeze creaking an ancient apple tree, the puffing of Simon the townsman as he stumbled. The crisp sound of sheep tearing mouthfuls of grass had, for her, been overlaid by a heavy silence still vibrating with unheard screams.

She'd been glad of an excuse when, far off, she saw the shepherd, the priory's shepherd—for these were Saint Augustine sheep—and had gone with Ulf to talk to him, leaving the two men still searching.

For the tenth time, she went over the reasoning that had brought them all to this place. The children had died in chalk, no doubt of it.

They had been found on silt—down there, on a muddy sheepwalk that led eventually to the hill. And, what's more, found on the very morning after the hill had been disturbed by an ingress of strangers.

Ergo, the corpses had been moved in the night. From their chalk graves. And the nearest chalk, the only possible chalk outcrop from which they could have been carried in the time, was Wandlebury Ring.

She looked toward it, blinking away rain from the latest shower, and saw that Simon and Mansur had disappeared.

They would be scrambling among the deep, dark avenues, made darker by overhanging trees, that had once been the hill's encircling ditches.

What ancient people had fortified the place with those ditches and for what purpose? She found herself wondering if the children's was the only blood that had been shed there. Could a place be intrinsically evil and attract to itself the blackness in men's souls as it had attracted the killer's?

Or was Vesuvia Adelia Rachel Ortese Aguilar as prey to superstition as an old man muttering spells over a stretch of grass?

"Is he going to talk to us or not?" she hissed at Ulf. "He must know if there's a cave up there. Something."

"He don't go up there no more," Ulf hissed back. "Says Old Nick dances on that of nights. Them hollows is his footprints."

"He allows his sheep up there."

"Best grazing for miles this time of year. His dog's with 'em. Dog allus tells un if aught's amiss."

An intelligent dog, and a mere lift of its lip had sent Safeguard cowering.

She wondered which lady the shepherd was praying to. Mary, mother of Jesus? Or a more ancient mother?

The Church had not managed to banish all the earth gods; for this old man, the depressions on the hilltop would be the hoofprints of a horror that predated Christianity's Satan by thousands of years.

Into her mind's eye came the picture of a giant horned beast trampling on the children. She grew cross with herself in consequence— what was the matter with her?

She was also becoming wet and cold. "Ask him if he's actually seen Old Nick up there, blast him."

Ulf put the question in a low-voiced singsong that she couldn't catch. The old man replied in the same tone.

"He don't go near, he says. And I won't blame un. He seen the fire o' nights, though."

"What fire?"

"Lights. Old Nick's fire, Walt reckons. The which he dances round."

"What sort of fire? When? Where?"

But the staccato of questions had disturbed the peace the shepherd was making with the spirit of the place. Ulf gestured for quiet and Adelia returned to her contemplation of the spiritual, good and bad.

Today on the hill, she had been glad that beneath her tunic was the little wooden crucifix that Margaret had given to her, though it was for Margaret's sake that she always wore it.

It wasn't that she had anything against the faith of the New Testament; left alone, it would be a tender and compassionate religion; indeed, on her knees beside her dying nurse, it had been Margaret's Jesus she had beseeched to save her. He hadn't, but Adelia forgave him that; Margaret's loving old heart had grown too tired to go on—and at least the end had been peaceful.

No, what Adelia objected to was the Church's interpretation of God as a petty, stupid, moneygrubbing, retrograde, antediluvian tyrant who, having created a stupendously varied world, had forbidden any inquiry into its complexity, leaving His people flailing in ignorance.

And the lies. At seven years old, learning her letters at Saint Giorgio's convent, Adelia had been prepared to believe what the nuns and the Bible told her—until Mother Ambrose had mentioned the ribs . . .

The shepherd had finished his prayers and was telling Ulf something.

"What does he say?"

"He's saying about the bodies, what the devil done to them."

It was noticeable that Old Walt addressed Ulf as an equal. Perhaps, Adelia thought, the fact that the boy could read raised him to a level in the shepherd's eyes that obviated the difference in their ages.

"What's he saying now?"

"He's saying the which he never saw the like of it, not since Old Nick was here last time and did similar to some of the sheep."

"Oh." A wolf or something.

"Says he'd hoped he'd seen the last of the bugger then, but he's come back."

What Old Nick did to the sheep. Sharply, Adelia asked, "What did he do?" And *then* she asked, "What sheep? When?"

Ulf put out the question and received the answer. "Year of the great storm, that was."

"For God's sake. Oh, never mind. *Where did he put the carcasses?*"

AT FIRST ADELIA AND ULF used tree branches as spades, but the chalk was too friable to be raised in chunks, and they were reduced to digging with their hands. "What we looking for?" Ulf had asked, not unreasonably.

"Bones, boy, bones. Somebody, not a fox, not a wolf, not a dog . . . some*body* attacked those sheep, he said so."

"Old Nick, he said."

"There isn't any Old Nick. The wounds were similar, didn't he say?"

Ulf's face went dull, a sign—she was beginning to know him—that he hadn't enjoyed hearing the shepherd's description of the wounds.

And perhaps he should not have heard it, she thought, but it was too late now. "Keep digging. In what year was the great storm?"

"Year Saint Ethel's bell tower fell down."

Adelia sighed. Seasons went by uncounted in Ulf's world, birthdays passed without recognition, only unusual events recorded the passage of time. "How long ago was that?" She added, helpfully, "In yuletides?"

"Weren't yuletide, were prim-e-rose time." But the look on Adelia's chalk-streaked face urged Ulf to put his mind to it. "Six, seven Christmases gone."

"Keep digging."

Six, seven years ago.

That, then, was when there had been a sheep stall on Wandlebury Ring. Old Walt said he used to shut the flock in it overnight. Not anymore, not since the morning he'd found its door torn open and carnage in the grass around it.

Prior Geoffrey, on being told, had discounted his shepherd's tale of the devil. A wolf, Prior Geoffrey had said, and set the hunt to find it.

But Walt knew it wasn't a wolf; wolves didn't do that, not *that*. He had dug a pit at the bottom of the hill, away from the grazing, and carried the carcasses down one by one to bury them in it, "laying them out reverent," as he told Ulf.

What human soul was so tormented that it would knife and knife a sheep?

Only one. Pray God, only one.

"Here we go." Ulf had uncovered an elongated skull.

"Well done." On her side of the pit they'd made, Adelia's fingers also encountered bone. "It's the hindquarters we want."

Old Walt had made it easy for them; in his attempt to give peace to the spirits of his sheep, he had arranged the corpses neatly in rows, like dead soldiers on a battlefield.

Adelia dragged out one of the skeletons and, sitting back, laid its tail end across her knees, brushing away chalk. She had to wait for another shower to pass before the light was bright enough to examine it. At last it was.

She said, quietly, "Ulf, fetch Master Simon and Mansur."

The bones were clean, the wool no longer clinging to them, consistent with them having lain here for a long time. There was terrible damage to what, in a pig—the only animal skeleton with which she was familiar—would have been the pelvis and pubes. Old Walt had been right; no toothmarks, these. Here were stab wounds.

When the boy had gone, she felt for her purse, loosened the drawstring, brought out the small traveling slate that went everywhere with her, opened it, and began to draw.

The gouges in these bones corresponded to those inflicted on the children; not caused by the same blade, perhaps, but by one very similar, crudely faceted like the end of a flattish piece of wood that had been whittled to a point.

What in hell's weaponry was it? Certainly not wood. Not a steel blade, not necessarily iron, too roughly shaped. Sharp, though, hideously sharp—the animal's spine had been severed.

Was this where the killer's shocking sexual rage had first shown itself? On defenseless animals? Always the defenseless with him.

But why the hiatus between six, seven years ago and this last year? Compulsions like his could surely not be held in for so long. Presumably, they hadn't been; other animals had been killed elsewhere and their death put down to a wolf. When had animals ceased to satisfy him? When had he graduated to children? Was Little Saint Peter his first?

He moved away, she thought. *A jackal is always a jackal.* There have been other deaths in other places, but that hill up there is his favored killing place. It is the ground where he dances. He's been away, and now he's come back.

Carefully, Adelia closed the slate against the rain, put the skeleton aside, and lay down on her front so that she could reach into the pit for more bones.

Somebody bade her good morning.

He's come back.

For a moment she was very still, then she rolled over, awkward and exposed, her hands on the skeletons in the pit behind her in order to support her upper body from collapsing on top of them.

"Talking to bones again?" the tax inspector asked with interest. "What will these say? *Baa?*"

Adelia became aware that her skirt had ridden up to show a considerable amount of bare leg, and she was in no position to pull it down.

Sir Rowley leaned down to put his hands under her armpits and raise her like a doll. "A lady Lazarus from the tomb," he said, "complete with gravedust." He began patting at her person, releasing clouds of sour-smelling chalk.

She pushed his hand away, no longer frightened but angry, very angry. "What do you do here?"

"Walking for my health, Doctor. You should approve."

He gleamed with health and good humor; he was the most defined thing in the gray landscape, ruddy cheeks and cloak; he looked like an oversized robin. He swept off his cap to bow to her and in the same movement picked up her slate. With apparent clumsiness, he knocked it open, exposing the drawings for him to look at.

Geniality went. He bent down to peer at the skeleton. Slowly, he straightened. "When was this done?"

"Six or seven years ago," she said.

She thought, *Was it you? Is there madness behind those jaunty blue eyes?*

"So he began with sheep," he said.

"Yes." A swift intelligence? Or the cunning to assume it, knowing what she had surmised already?

His jaw had tightened. It was a different, much less good-natured man, who stood in front of her now. He seemed to have gotten thinner.

The rain was increasing. No sign of Simon or Mansur.

Suddenly he had her by the arm and was pulling her along. Safeguard, having given no warning of the man's approach, scampered happily behind them. Adelia knew she should be afraid, but all she felt was outrage.

They stopped under a sheltering beech tree, where Picot shook her. "Why are you ahead of me each time? Who *are* you, woman?"

She was Vesuvia Adelia Rachel Ortese Aguilar, and she was being manhandled. "I am a doctor of Salerno. You will show me respect."

He looked at his big hands that were clutching her arms and released her. "I beg your pardon, Doctor." He tried smiling. "This won't do, will it?" He took off his cloak, laid it carefully at the foot of the tree, and invited her to sit on it. She was glad to do so; her legs were still shaking.

He sat down beside her, talking reasonably. "But do you see, I have a particular interest in discovering this killer, yet each time I follow a thread that might take me into the depth of his labyrinth, I find not the Minotaur but Ariadne."

And Ariadne finds you, she thought. She said, "May I ask what thread it was led you here today?"

Safeguard lifted a leg against the tree trunk, then settled itself on an unoccupied corner of the cloak.

"Oh, that," Sir Rowley said. "Easily explained. You were good enough to employ me in writing down the story those poor bones told you in the hermit's hut, their removal from chalk to silt. A moment's reflection even suggested *when* that removal took place." He looked at her. "I assume your menfolk are searching the hill?"

She nodded.

"They won't find anything, I know damn well they won't, because I've been prowling it myself for the last two evenings and believe me, lady, it is no place to be when night comes down."

He slammed his fist down on the stretch of cloak between them, making Adelia jump and Safeguard look up. "But it's there, god-dammit. The clue to the Minotaur leads there. Those poor youngsters told us it did." He looked at his hand as if he hadn't seen it before, uncurling it. "So I made my excuses to the lord sheriff and rode over to have yet another look. And what do I find? Madam Doctor listening to more bones. There, now you know all about it."

He'd become cheery again.

Rain had been pattering while he talked; now the sun came out. He's like the weather, Adelia thought. And I don't know all about it.

She said, "Do you like jujubes?"

"Love 'em, ma'am. Why? Are you offering me one?"

"No."

"Oh." He squinted at her as at someone whose mind shouldn't be disturbed further, then spoke slowly and kindly. "Perhaps you would tell me who sent you and your companions on this investigation?"

"The King of Sicily," she said.

He nodded cautiously. "The King of Sicily."

She began to laugh. It might have been the Queen of Sheba or the Grand Inquisitor; he couldn't recognize the truth because he didn't use it. *He thinks I am mad.*

As she laughed the sun sent its light through the young beech leaves to fall on her like a shower of newly minted copper pennies.

His face changed so that she sobered and looked away from him.

"Go home," he said. "Go back to Salerno."

Now she could see Ulf leading Simon and Mansur toward them from the direction of the sheep pit.

The tax collector was all reasonableness again. Good day, good day, my masters. Having attended the good doctor while she was performing the postmortem on the poor children . . . he, like them, had suspected the hill as being the site of . . . had searched the ground yet found nothing . . . Should they not, all four, exchange what knowledge they possessed to bring this fiend to justice?

Adelia moved away to join Ulf, who was slapping his cap against his leg to shake off raindrops. He waved it in the direction of the tax collector. "Don't like that un."

"I don't either," Adelia said, "but the Safeguard seems to."

Absentmindedly—and she thought he would be sorry for it later—

Sir Rowley was caressing the dog's head where it leaned against his knee.

Ulf growled in disgust. Then he said, "You reckon them sheep were done for by him as did for Harold and the others?"

"Yes," she said. "It was a similar weapon."

Ulf mused on it. "Wonder where he's been killing betwixt times?"

It was an intelligent question; Adelia had asked it of herself immediately. It was also the question the tax collector should have asked. And hadn't.

Because he knows, she thought.

DRIVING BACK TO TOWN in the cart, like a good medicine vendor after a day picking herbs, Simon of Naples expressed gratification at having joined forces with Sir Rowley Picot. "A quick brain, for all his size, none quicker. He was most interested in the significance we place on the appearance of Little Saint Peter's body on Chaim's lawn and, since he has access to the county's accounts, he has promised to assist me in discovering which men owed Chaim money. Also, he and Mansur are going to investigate the Arab trade ships and see which of them carries jujubes."

"God's rib," Adelia said. "Did you tell him *everything*?"

"Most everything." He smiled at her exasperation. "My dear Doctor, if he is the killer, he knows everything already."

"If he's the killer, he knows we're closing him round. He knows enough to wish us away. He told me to go back to Salerno."

"Yes, indeed. He is concerned for you. 'This is no matter to involve a woman,' he told me. 'Do you want her murdered in her bed?'"

Simon winked at her; he was in a good mood. "Why is it that we are always murdered in our beds, I wonder. We are never murdered at breakfast time. Or in our bath."

"Oh, stop it. I don't trust the man."

"I do, and I have considerable experience of men."

"He disturbs me."

Simon winked at Mansur. "Considerable experience of women, too. I believe she likes him."

Furiously, Adelia said, "Did he tell you he was a crusader?"

"No." He turned to look at her, grave now. "No, he did not tell me that."

"He was."

Nine

It was the custom of those in Cambridge who had been on pilgrimage to hold a feast after their return. Alliances had been made on the journey, business conducted, marriages arranged, holiness and exaltation experienced; the world in general had been widened; and it was pleasurable for those who had shared these things to be brought together once more to discuss them and give thanks for a safe return.

This pilgrimtide it was the turn of the Prioress of Saint Radegund's to host the feast. Since, however, Saint Radegund was yet a poor, small convent—a situation soon to be altered if Prioress Joan and Little Saint Peter had anything to do with it—the honor of holding it on her behalf had been awarded to her knight and tenant, Sir Joscelin of Grantchester, whose hall and lands were considerably larger and richer than hers, a not unusual anomaly in the case of those who held part in fee of the lesser religious houses.

A famous feast-giver, Sir Joscelin. It was said that when he'd entertained the Abbot of Ramsay last year, thirty beeves, sixty pigs, a hundred and fifty capon, three hundred larks (for their tongues), and two knights had died in the cause, the latter in a melee laid on for the abbot's entertainment that had gotten gloriously out of hand.

Invitations were therefore valued; those who had not been on the pilgrimage but were closely associated with it, stay-at-home wives, daughters, sons, the good and the great of the shire, canons, and nuns, thought themselves ill-used not to be included. Since most of them were, the caterers to Cambridge's finery had been kept busy with barely a spare breath to bless the names of Saint Radegund's prioress and her loyal knight, Sir Joscelin.

It was not until the morning of the day itself that a Grantchester servant arrived with an invitation for the three foreigners in Jesus Lane. Dressed for the occasion, complete with a horn to blow, he was put out when Gyltha took him in at the back door.

"No use going by the front way, Matt, Doctor's physicking."

"Let's just blow a call, Gylth. Master sends his invites with a call."

He was taken into the kitchen for a cup of home brew; Gyltha liked to know what was going on.

Adelia was in the hall, wrangling with Dr. Mansur's last patient of the day; she always kept Wulf to the end.

"Wulf, there is nothing wrong with you. Not the strangles, not ague, not the cough, not distemper, not diper bite, whatever that is, and you are certainly not lactating."

"Do the doctor say that?"

Adelia turned wearily to Mansur. "Say something, Doctor."

"Give the idle dog a kick up his arse."

"The doctor prescribes steady work in fresh air," Adelia said.

"With my back?"

"There is nothing wrong with your back." She regarded Wulf as a phenomenon. In a feudal society where everybody, except the growing mercantile class, owed work to somebody else for their existence, Wulf had escaped vassalage, probably by running away from his lord and certainly by marrying a Cambridge laundress who was prepared to labor for them both. He was, quite literally, afraid of work; it made him ill. But in order to escape the derision of society, he needed to be adjudged ill in order to avoid becoming so.

Adelia was as gentle with him as with all her patients—she wondered if his brain could be pickled postmortem and sent to her so that she might examine it for some missing ingredient—but she refused to compromise her duty as a doctor by diagnosing or prescribing for a physical complaint where none existed.

"How about malingering? I'm still a-suffering from that, ain't I?"

"A bad case," she said and shut the door on him.

It was still raining and therefore chilly and, since Gyltha didn't hold with lighting a fire in the hall from the end of March to the beginning of November, the warmth of Old Benjamin's house lay in its kitchen outside, a roaring place equipped with apparatus so fearful that it could be a torture chamber if it weren't for its ravishing smells.

Today it held a new object, a wooden barrel like a washerwoman's *lessiveuse*. Adelia's best saffron silk underdress, as yet unworn in England, hung from a flitch hook above it to steam out the wrinkles. She had thought the gown to be still in the clothes press upstairs.

"What's that for?"

"Bath. You," Gyltha said.

Adelia was not unwilling; she hadn't bathed since last climbing out of the tiled and heated pool in her stepparents' villa that the Romans had installed nearly fifteen hundred years before. The bucket of water carried to the solar every morning by Matilda W. was no replacement. However, the scene before her prefigured an event, so she asked, "Why?"

"I ain't having you let me down at the feast," Gyltha said.

Sir Joscelin's invitation to Dr. Mansur and his two assistants, so Gyltha said, having put his man to the inquisition, was at Prior Geoffrey's prompting—if not true pilgrims, they had at least joined the pilgrimage on its return journey.

To Gyltha it was a challenge; the stoniness of her face showed that she was excited. As she had allied herself with these three queer fish, it was necessary for her self-esteem and social standing that they appear well when exposed to the scrutiny of the town's illustrious. Her limited knowledge of what such an occasion demanded was being augmented by Matilda B., whose mother was scrubwoman at the castle and had witnessed preparations for the tiring of the sheriff's lady on feast days, if not the tiring itself.

Adelia had spent too much of her girlhood in study to join the festivity of other young women; later, she had been too busy. Nor, since she was not to marry, had her foster parents encouraged her in the higher social graces. She had subsequently been ill-equipped to attend the masques and revelry in the palaces of Salerno and, when forced to do so, had passed most of the time behind a pillar, both resentful and embarrassed.

This invitation, therefore, sounded an old alarm. Her immediate instinct was to find an excuse to refuse. "I must consult Master Simon."

But Simon was at the castle, closeted with the Jews in an effort to discover whose indebtedness might have spurred Chaim's death.

"He'll say as you all got to go," Gyltha told her.

He probably would; with almost everyone they suspected gathered under one roof, tongues loosened by drink, it would be an opportunity to find out who knew what about whom.

"Nevertheless, send Ulf to the castle to ask him."

Truth to tell, now that she thought about it, Adelia was not unwilling to go. Death had overlain her days in Cambridge with the murdered children, also with some of her patients; the little one with the cough had given way to pneumonia, the ague had died, so had the kidney stone, so had a new mother brought in too late. Adelia's successes—the amputation, the fever, the hernia—were discounted in the sum of what she regarded as her failures.

It would be nice, for once, to forgather with the living healthy at play. As usual, she could hide in the background; she would not be noticed. After all, she thought, a feast in Cambridge could not compete with the sophistication of its Salerno equivalent in the palaces of kings and popes. She need not be daunted by what, inevitably, would be a bucolic affair.

And she wanted that bath. Had she known that such a thing were possible, she would have demanded one before now; she'd assumed that preparing baths was one of the many things Gyltha didn't hold with.

She had no choice, anyway; Gyltha and the two Matildas were determined. Time was short; an entertainment that could last six or seven hours began at noon.

She was stripped and plunged into the lessiveuse. Washing lye was poured in after her, along with a handful of precious cloves. She was scrubbed with a bathbrick until nearly raw and held under while her hair was attacked with more lye and a brush before being rinsed with lavender water.

Hauled out, she was wrapped in a blanket and her head inserted into the bread oven.

Her hair was a disappointment, more had been expected of its emergence from the cap or coif she always wore; she habitually sheared it off at shoulder length.

"Color's all right," Gyltha said grudgingly.

"But that's too short," Matilda B. objected. "Us'll have to put that in net pockets."

"Net costs."

"I don't know that I'm going yet," Adelia shouted from the oven.

"You bloody are."

Oh, well. Still on her knees at the oven, she directed her tiring women to her purse. Money was plentiful; Simon had been provided with a letter of credit on Luccan merchant bankers with agents in England and had drawn on it for them both.

She added, "And if you're for the market, it's time you three had new kirtles. Buy an ell of best camlet for yourselves." Their goodwill made her ashamed that they should be shabby while she was resplendent.

"Linen'll do," Gyltha said shortly, pleased.

Adelia was pulled out, put into her shift and underdress, and set on a stool to have her hair brushed until it gleamed like white gold. Silver net had been purchased and stitched into little pockets that were now being pinned over the plaits round her ears. The women were still working on it when Simon arrived with Ulf.

At the sight of her, he blinked. "*Well.* Well, well, well . . ."

Ulf's mouth had fallen open.

Embarrassed, Adelia said crossly, "All this fuss, and I don't know if we should go at all."

"Not go? Dear Doctor, if Cambridge were denied the sight of you now, the very skies would weep. I know of only one woman as beautiful, and she is in Naples."

Adelia smiled at him. Subtle little man that he was, he knew she would be comfortable with a compliment only if it was without coquetry. He was always careful to mention his wife, whom he adored, not just to point out that *he* was out-of-bounds but to reassure her that she, Adelia, was out-of-bounds to him. Anything else would have jeopardized a relationship that was close of necessity. As it was, it had allowed them to be comrades, he respecting her professionalism, she respecting his.

And it was nice of him, she thought, to put her on a par with the wife whom he still saw in his mind's eye as the slim, ivory-skinned maiden he had married in Naples twenty years before—though, probably, having since borne him nine children, the lady was not as slim as she had been.

He was triumphant this morning.

"We shall soon be home," he told her. "I shall not say too much until I have uncovered the requisite documents, but there *are* copies of the burned tallies. I was sure there must be. Chaim had lodged them with his bankers and, since they are extensive—the man seems to have lent money to all East Anglia—I have taken them to the castle in order that Sir Rowley may assist me in perusing them."

"Is that wise?" Adelia asked.

"I think it is, I think it is. The man is versed in accounting and as eager as we are to discover who owed what to Chaim and who regretted it so mightily as to want him dead."

"*Hmm.*"

He would not listen to Adelia's doubts; Simon thought he knew the sort of man Sir Rowley was, crusader or not. A hasty change into his best clothes so as to be ready for Grantchester and he was out of the door, heading back to the castle.

Left to herself, Adelia would have put on her gray overdress in order to tone down the brightness of the saffron that would therefore only show at bosom and sleeves. "I don't want to attract attention."

The Matildas, however, plumped for the only other item of note in her wardrobe, a brocade with the colors of an autumn tapestry, and Gyltha, after a short waver, agreed with them. It was slid carefully over Adelia's coiffure. The pointed slippers Margaret had embroidered with silver thread went on with new white stockings.

The three arbiters stood back to consider the result.

The Matildas nodded and clasped their hands. Gyltha said, "Reckon as she'll do," which was as near as she approached to hyperbole.

Adelia's brief glimpse of her reflection in the polished but uneven bottom of a fish kettle showed something like a distorted apple tree, but obviously she passed muster with the others.

"Ought to be a page as'll stand behind Doctor's at the feast," Matilda B. said. "Sheriff and them allus takes a page to stand behind their chairs. Fart-catchers, Ma calls them."

"Page, eh?"

Ulf, who had been staring at Adelia without closing his mouth, became aware that four pairs of eyes rested on him. He began running.

The ensuing chase and battle were terrible. Ulf's screams brought neighbors round to see if another child was in danger of its life. Adelia, standing well back in case she be splashed by the lessiveuse's turmoil, was in pain from laughing.

More cash was expended, this time at the business premises of Ma Mill, whose ragbags contained an old but serviceable tabard of almost the right size that responded nicely to a rub with vinegar. Dressed in it and with his flaxen hair bobbed around a face like a gleaming, discontented pickled onion, Ulf too passed muster.

Mansur eclipsed them both. A gilded agal held the veil of his kaffiyeh in place; silk flowed long and light around a fresh white woollen robe. A jeweled dagger flashed on his belt.

"O Son of the Noonday," Adelia said, bowing. *"Eeh l-Halaawa di!"*

Mansur inclined his head, but his eyes were on Gyltha, who took a poker to the fire, face averted. "Girt great maypole," she said.

Oh ho, Adelia thought.

THERE WAS MUCH to smile at in the aping of fine manners, at the reception of hoods, swords, and gloves from guests whose boots and cloaks were muddied by the walk from the river—nearly everybody had been punted from town—at the stiff use of titles by those who had known each other intimately for years, at the rings on female fingers toughened by the making of cheese in their owner's home dairy.

But there was also much to admire. How friendlier it was to be greeted at the arched door with its carved Norman chevrons by Sir Joscelin himself than announced by an ivory-wanded, high-chinned majordomo. To be handed warming spiced wine on a cool day, not iced wine. To smell mutton, beef, and pork sizzling on spits in the courtyard rather than to pretend with one's host, as one did in southern Italy, that food was being conjured by a wave of the hand.

Anyway, with the scowling Ulf and Safeguard at her heels rather than the lapdogs carried by pages attendant on some of the other ladies, Adelia was in no position to be supercilious.

Mansur, obviously, had gained status in Cambridge's eyes, and his dress and height came in for attention. Sir Joscelin welcomed him with a graceful salute and a *"Salaam alaikum."*

The matter of his kard was also resolved with charm. "The dagger is not a weapon," Sir Joscelin told his porter, who was struggling to wrest it from Mansur's belt and put it with the guests' swords. "It is a decoration for such a gentleman as this, as we old crusaders know."

He turned to Adelia, bowing, and asked her to translate his apology to the good doctor for the tardiness of their invitation. "I feared he would be bored by our rustic amusements, but Prior Geoffrey assured me otherwise."

Though he had always shown her civility, even when she must have seemed to him to be a foreign trollop, Adelia realized that Gyltha had circulated word that the doctor's assistant was virtuous.

The prioress's welcome was offhand through lack of interest, and she was taken aback by her knight's greeting to both Mansur and Adelia. "You have had dealing with these people, Sir Joscelin?"

"The good doctor saved the foot of my thatcher, ma'am, and probably his life." But the blue eyes, amused, were directed at Adelia, who feared that Sir Joscelin knew who had performed the amputation.

"My dear girl, my dear girl." Prior Geoffrey's grip on her arm propelled her away. "How beautiful you look. *Nec me meminisse pigebit Adeliae, dum memor ipse mei, dum spiritus hos regit artus.*"

She smiled up at him; she had missed him. "Are you well, my lord?"

"Pissing like a racehorse, I thank you." He bent toward her ear so that she should hear him above the noise of conversation. "And how goes the investigation?"

They had been remiss not to keep him informed; that they had been able to investigate as much as they had was due to this man, but they'd been so busy. "We have made ground and hope to make more tonight," she told him. "May we report to you tomorrow? Particularly, I want to ask you about . . ."

But there was the tax collector himself, two yards away and staring at her over the head of the crowd. He began to wade through an intervening group toward her. He looked less plump than he had.

He bowed. "Mistress Adelia."

She nodded to him. "Is Master Simon with you?"

"He is delayed at the castle." He gave her a conspiratorial wink. "Having to escort the sheriff and his lady here, I was forced to leave him to his studies. He begged me to tell you he will attend later. May I say . . ."

Whatever he wished to say was interrupted by a trumpet call. They were to dine.

Her fingers raised high on his, Prior Geoffrey joined the procession to take Adelia into the hall, Mansur at his side. There they had to separate, he to the top table that stood across the dais at one end, she and Mansur to their more lowly position. She was interested to see where this would be; precedence was a formidable concern for host and guest alike.

Adelia had witnessed her Salerno aunt near to collapse from the worry of placing highborn guests at table in an order that would not mortally offend one or the other. Theoretically, the rules were clear: a prince to equal an archbishop, bishop to an earl, baron in fief before a visiting baron, and so on down the line. But suppose a legate, equal to a visiting baron, was papal—where did he sit? What if the archbishop had crossed the prince, as was so often the case? Or vice versa? Which was even more frequent. Fisticuffs, feuds could result from the unintended insult. And the poor host always to blame.

It was a matter that had exercised even Gyltha, whose vicarious honor was involved, and who had also been called to Grantchester for the night to do interesting things with eels in its kitchens. "I'll be a-watching, and if Sir Joscelin do put any of you below the salt, that's the last barrel of eels he do get from me."

As she entered, Adelia glimpsed Gyltha's head poking out anxiously from behind a door.

She could sense tension, see eyes glancing left and right as Sir Joscelin's marshal ushered the guests to their places. The lower pecking orders, particularly self-made men whose ambition outran their birth, were as sensitive as the high, perhaps more so.

Ulf had already done some scouting. "He's up here, and you're down there," he said, jerking a thumb back and forth between Adelia and Mansur. He adopted the slow, careful baby talk he always used to Mansur. "You. Sitty. Here."

Sir Joscelin had been generous, Adelia thought, relieved for Gyltha's sake—and also for her own; Mansur was touchy about his dignity, and, decoration or not, he had a dagger in his belt. While he hadn't been put at the top table with the host and hostess, prior, sheriff, et cetera, nor could he expect to be, he was quite near it on one of the long trestles that ran the length of the great hall. The lovely young nun who had allowed Adelia to look at Little Saint Peter's bones was on his left. Less happily, Roger of Acton had been placed opposite him.

Positioning the tax collector must have called for considerable reflection, she thought. Unpopular in his calling, but nevertheless the king's man and, at the moment, the sheriff's right hand. Sir Joscelin had opted for safety as far as Sir Rowley Picot was concerned. He was next to the sheriff's wife, making her laugh.

As ostensibly a mere female potion-mixing doctor's attendant, and foreign at that, Adelia found herself on another of the trestles in the body of the hall toward its lower end—though several positions above the ornate salt cellar that marked the division between guests and those serfs who were present to fulfill Christ's command that the poor be fed. The even poorer were gathered in the courtyard round a brazier, waiting for the scraps.

She was joined on her right by the huntsman, Hugh, his face as impassive as ever, though he bowed to her courteously enough. So did an elderly little man she did not know who took his place on her left.

She was unhappy to see that Brother Gilbert had been placed directly across from her. So was he.

Trenchers were brought round, and there was covert slapping by parents of their young people's hands as they reached to break off a piece, for there was much to happen before the bread could have food put upon it. Sir Joscelin must declare his fealty for his liege, Prioress Joan, which he did on one knee and with a presentation of his rent, six milk-white doves in a gilt cage.

Prior Geoffrey must say grace. Wine cups must be filled for the dedicatory toast to Thomas of Canterbury and his new recruit to martyred glory, Little Peter of Trumpington, the raisons d'être of the feast. *A curious custom,* Adelia thought, as she stood to drink to the health of the dead.

A discordant shriek cut across the respectful murmurs. "The infidel insults our holy saints." Roger of Acton was pointing in triumphant outrage at Mansur. "He drinks to them in water."

Adelia closed her eyes. *God, don't let him stab the swine.*

But Mansur stayed calm, sipping his water. It was Sir Joscelin who administered a rebuke clear to the entire hall: "By his faith, this gentleman forswears liquor, Master Roger. If you cannot hold yours, may I suggest you follow his example."

Nicely done. Acton collapsed onto his bench. Adelia's opinion of her host rose.

Do not be charmed, though, she told herself. *Memento mori.* Literally, re-member death. He may be the killer; he is a crusader. So is the tax collector.

And so was another man on the top table; Sir Gervase had watched every step of her progress into the hall.

Is it you?

Adelia was assured now that the man who had murdered the chil-dren had been on crusade. It was not merely identification of the sweetmeat as an Arab jujube, but that the hiatus between the attack on the sheep and the one on the children coincided exactly with a pe-riod when Cambridge had responded to the call of Outremer and sent some of its men to answer it.

The trouble was that there had been the absence of so many. . . .

"Who left town in the Great Storm year?" Gyltha had said when applied to. "Well, there was Ma Mill's daughter as got herself in the family way by the peddler. . . ."

"Men, Gyltha, men."

"Oh, there was a mort of young men went. See, the Abbot of Ely called for the country to take the Cross." By "country" Gyltha meant "county." "Must of been hundreds went off with Lord Fitzgilbert to the Holy Places."

It had been a bad year, Gyltha said. The Great Storm had flattened crops, flood swept away people and buildings, the fens were inun-dated, even the gentle Cam rose in fury. God had shown His anger at Cambridgeshire's sins. Only a crusade against His enemies could pla-cate Him.

Lord Fitzgilbert, looking for lands in Syria to replace his drowned estates, had planted Christ's banner in Cambridge's marketplace. Young men with livelihoods destroyed by the storm came to it, and so did the ambitious, the adventurous, rejected suitors, and husbands with nagging wives. Courts gave criminals the option of going to prison or taking the Cross. Sins whispered to priests in confession were absolved—as long as the perpetrator joined the crusade.

A small army marched away.

Lord Fitzgilbert had returned pickled in a coffin and now lay in his own chapel under a marble effigy of himself, its mailed legs crossed in the sign of a crusader. Some arrived home and died of the diseases they carried with them, to lie in less exalted graves with a plain sword carved into the stone above. Some were merely a name on a mortuary list carried by survivors. Some had found a richer, drier life in Syria and opted to stay there.

Others came back to take up their former occupation so that, according to Gyltha, Adelia and Simon must now take a keen look at two shopkeepers, several villeins, a blacksmith, and the very apothecary who supplied Dr. Mansur's medicines, not to mention Brother Gilbert and the silent canon who had accompanied Prior Geoffrey on the road.

"Brother Gilbert went on crusade?"

"That he did. Nor it ain't no good suspecting only them as came back rich like sirs Joscelin and Gervase," Gyltha had said relentlessly. "There's lots borrow from Jews, small amounts maybe but big enough to them as can't pay the interest. Nor it ain't certain a fellow yelling for the Jew to swing was the same devil killed the little uns. There's plenty like to see a Jew's neck stretch *and* they call theyselves Christians."

Daunted by the size of the problem, Adelia had grimaced at the housekeeper for her logic even as she'd acknowledged it as inescapable.

So now, looking around, she must attach no sinister significance to Sir Joscelin's obvious wealth. It could have been gained in Syria, rather than from Chaim the Jew. It had certainly transformed a Saxon holding into a flint-built manor of considerable beauty. The enormous hall in which they ate possessed a newly carved roof as fine as any she'd seen in England. From the gallery above the dais issued music played with professional skill on recorder, vielle, and flute. The personal eating irons that a guest usually took to a meal had been made redundant by a knife and spoon laid at each place. Saucers, finger bowls waiting on the table were of exquisite silverwork, the napkins of damask.

She expressed her admiration to her companions. Hugh the huntsman merely nodded. The little man on her left said, "But you ought to've seen that in old days, wonderful wormy barn of a place near to falling down that was when Sir Tibault had un, him as was Joscelin's father. Nasty old brute he was, God rest him, as drank hisself to death in the end. Ain't I right, Hugh?"

Hugh grunted. "Son's different."

"That he is. Different as chalk and cheese. Brought the place back to life, Joscelin has. Used un's gold well."

"Gold?" Adelia asked.

The little man warmed to her interest. "So he told me. 'There's gold in Outremer, Master Herbert,' he said to me. 'Hatfuls of it, Master Herbert.' See, I'm by way of being his bootmaker; a man don't fib to his bootmaker."

"Did Sir Gervase come back with gold as well?"

"A ton or more, so they say, only he ain't so free with his money."

"Did they acquire this gold together?"

"Can't answer for that. Probable they did. They ain't hardly apart. David and Jonathan, them."

Adelia glanced toward the high table at David and Jonathan, good-looking, confident, so easy together, talking over the prioress's head.

If there were *two* killers, both in accord . . . It hadn't crossed her mind, but it should have. "Do they have wives?"

"Gervase do, a poor, dribblin' little piece as stays home." The bootmaker was happy to display his knowledge of great men. "Sir Joscelin now, he's atrading for the Baron of Peterborough's daughter. Good match that'd be."

A shrill horn blasted away all talk. The guests sat up. Food was coming.

AT THE HIGH TABLE, Rowley Picot allowed his knee to rub against that of the sheriff's wife, keeping her happy. He also winked at the young nun seated at the trestle below to make her blush, but found that his eyes were more often directed toward little Madam Doctor down among the toilers and hewers. Washed up nicely, he'd give her that. Creamy, velvety skin disappeared into that saffron bodice, inviting touch. Made his fingertips twitch. Not the only thing to twitch, either; that gleaming hair suggested she was blonde all over. . . .

Damn the trollop—Sir Rowley shook off a lubricious reverie—she was finding out too much, and Master Simon with her, relying on their bloody great Arab for protection, a eunuch, for God's sake.

TO HELL, thought Adelia, *there's more.*

For the second time, a blast on the horn had announced another course from the kitchen, led by the marshal. More and even larger platters, piled like petty mountains, each needing two men to carry them, were greeted with cheers from the merry diners, who were getting merrier.

The wreckage from the first course was removed. Gravy-stained trenchers were put into a wheelbarrow and taken outside to where ragged men, women, and children waited to fall on them. Fresh ones took their place.

"*Et maintenant, milords, mesdames . . .*" It was the head cook again. "*Venyson en furmety gely. Porcelle farce enforce. Pokokkye. Crans. Venyson roste.*

Conyn. Byttere truffée. Pulle endore. Braun freyes avec graunt tartez. Leche Lumbarde. A soltelle."

Norman French for Norman food.

"That's France talk," explained Master Herbert, the bootmaker, to Adelia kindly, as if he hadn't said so the first time, "as Sir Joscelin brought that cook from France."

And I wish he might go back there. Enough, enough.

She was feeling strange.

To begin with, she had refused wine and asked for boiled water, a request that had surprised the servant with the wine pitcher and had not been fulfilled. Persuaded by Master Herbert that the mead being offered as an alternative to wine and ale was an innocuous drink made from honey, and being thirsty, she had emptied several cups.

And was still thirsty. She waved frantically at Ulf to bring her some of the water from Mansur's ewer. He didn't see her.

It was Simon of Naples who waved back. He'd just entered and bowed a deep apology to Prioress Joan and Sir Joscelin for his late arrival.

He's learned something, Adelia thought, sitting up. She could tell from his very walk that his time with the Jews had yielded fruit. She watched him talking excitedly to the tax collector at the end of the high table before he disappeared from her view to take his seat farther up the trestle and on the same side of it as herself.

Week-dead peacocks still displaying their tail were on the board; litters of crispy baby pigs sucked sadly on the apple between their jaws. The eye of a roasted bittern, which would have looked better unroasted among the fenland reeds where it belonged, stared accusingly into Adelia's.

Silently, she apologized to it. *I'm sorry. I'm sorry they stuffed truffles up your arse.*

Again, she glimpsed Gyltha's face peering round the kitchen door. Adelia sat up straight again. *I am doing you credit, I am, I am.*

Venison in a stew of corn appeared on her clean trencher. It was joined by "gely" from a saucer. Red currant, probably. "I want salads," she said hopelessly.

The prioress's rent had escaped from their cage and joined the sparrows in the rafters to plop droppings on the tables below.

Brother Gilbert, who'd been ignoring the nuns on either side of him and was staring at Adelia instead, leaned across the table. "I should think you ashamed to show your hair, mistress."

She glared back. "Why?"

"You would better hide your locks beneath a veil, better dress in mourning garments, neglect your exterior. O Daughter of Eve, don the penitential garb that women must derive from Eve's ignominy, the odium of it being the cause of the fall of the human race."

"Wasn't her fault," said the nun on his left. "Fall of the human race wasn't her fault. Wasn't mine, neither."

She was a skinny, middle-aged woman who had been drinking heavily, as had Brother Gilbert. Adelia liked the cut of her jib.

The monk turned on her. "Silence, woman. Would you argue with the great Saint Tertullian? You, from your house of loose living?"

"Yah," the nun said, crowing, "we got a better saint than you got. We got Little Saint Peter. Best you've got is Saint Etheldreda's big toe."

"We have a piece of the True Cross," Brother Gilbert shouted.

"Who ain't?" said the nun on his other side.

Brother Gilbert descended from his high horse into the blood and dust of the battleground. "A muck of good Little Saint Peter'll do you when the archdeacon investigates your convent, you slut. And he will. Oh, I know what goes on at Saint Radegund's—slackness, holy office neglected, men in your cells, hunting parties, sliding upriver to provision your anchorites. I *don't* think. Oh, I know."

"So we do provision 'em." This was the nun on Brother Gilbert's right, as plump as her sister in God was thin. "If I visit my aunty after, where's the harm?"

Ulf's voice repeated itself in Adelia's head. *Sister Fatty for to supply the hermits, look a her puff.* She squinted at the nun. "I saw you," she said happily. "I saw you poling a punt upriver."

"I'll wager you didn't see her poling back." Brother Gilbert was spitting in his fury. "They stay out all night. They comport themselves in licentiousness and lust. In a decent house, they'd be whipped until their arses bled, but where's their prioress? Out hunting."

A man who hates, Adelia thought, *a hateful man.* And a crusader. She leaned across the table. "Do you like jujubes, Brother Gilbert?"

"What? *What?* No, I loathe confits." He turned from her to resume his denunciation of Saint Radegund's.

A quiet, sad voice on Adelia's right said, "Our Mary liked confits." Appallingly, tears were running down the sinewy cheeks of Hugh the huntsman and plopping into his stew.

"Don't cry," she said, "don't cry."

A whisper came from the bootmaker on her left: "She was his niece. Little Mary as was murdered. His sister's child."

"I'm sorry." Adelia touched the huntsman's hand. "I'm so sorry."

Bleary, infinitely sad, his blue eyes looked into hers. "I'll get him. I'll tear his liver out."

"We'll both get him," she said and became irritated that Brother Gilbert's harangue should be intruding on such a moment. She stretched across the board to poke the monk in his chest. "Not *Saint* Tertullian."

"What?"

"Tertullian. Fellow you quoted on Eve. He wasn't a saint. Did you think he was a saint? He wasn't. He left the Church. He was"—she said it carefully—"heterodoxal. That's what *he* was. Joined the Montanists, Subsequently never declared a saint."

The nuns rejoiced. "Didn't know that, did you?" the skinny one said.

Brother Gilbert's reply was drowned by yet another trumpet blast and another course processing by the high table.

"Blaundersorye. Quincys in comfyte. Curlews en miel. Pertyche. Eyround angels. Pety-perneux . . ."

"What's petty-perno?" asked the huntsman, still crying.

"Little lost eggs," Adelia told him and began to weep uncontrollably.

The part of her brain that hadn't totally lost its battle with mead got her to her feet and carried her to a sideboard containing a jug of water. Clutching it, she aimed for the door, Safeguard behind her.

The tax collector watched her go.

Several guests were already in the garden. Men were contemplatively facing tree trunks; women were scattering to find a quiet place to squat. The more modest were forming an agitated queue for the shrouded benches with bottom-sized holes that Sir Joscelin had provided over the stream running down to the Cam.

Drinking fiercely from her jug, Adelia wandered off, past stables and the comforting smell of horses, past dark mews where hooded raptors dreamed of the swoop and kill. There was a moon. There was grass, an orchard . . .

The tax collector found her asleep beneath an apple tree. As he reached out, a small, dark, smelly shape beside her raised its head and another, much taller and with a dagger at its belt, stepped from the shadows.

Sir Rowley displayed empty hands to them both. "Would I hurt her?"

Adelia opened her eyes. She sat up, feeling her forehead. "Tertullian wasn't a saint, Picot," she told him.

"I always wondered." He squatted down beside her. She'd used his name as if they were old friends—he was dismayed by the pleasure that gave him. "What were you drinking?"

She concentrated. "It was yellow."

"Mead. You need a Saxon constitution to survive mead." He pulled her to her feet. "Come along, you'll have to dance it off."

"I don't dance. Shall we go and kick Brother Gilbert?"

"You tempt me, but I think we'll just dance."

The hall had been cleared of its tables. The gentle musicians of the gallery had transformed into three perspiring, burly men on the dais, a tabor player and two fiddlers, one of them calling the steps in a howl that overrode the squealing, laughing, stamping whirl on what was now a dance floor.

The tax collector pulled Adelia into it.

This was not the disciplined, fingertip-holding, toe-pointing, complex dancing of Salerno's high society. No elegance here. These people of Cambridge hadn't time to attend lessons in Terpsichore, they just danced. Indefatigably, ceaselessly, with sweat and stamina, with zest, compelled by savage ancestral gods. A stumble here or there, a wrong move, what matter? Back into the fray, dance, dance. "Strike." Left foot to the left, the right stamped against it. "Back to back." Catch up one's skirt. Smile. "Right shoulder to right shoulder." "Left circle hey." "Straight hey." "Corner." "Weave, my lords and ladies, *weave*, you buggers." "Home."

The flambeaux in their holders flickered like sacrificial fires. Bruised rushes on the floor released green incense into the room. No time to breathe, this is "Horses Brawl," back, circle, up the middle, under the arch, again, again.

The mead in her body vaporized and was replaced by the intoxication of cooperative movement. Glistening faces appeared and disappeared, slippery hands grasped Adelia's, swung her: Sir Gervase, an unknown, Master Herbert, sheriff, prior, tax collector, Sir Gervase again, swinging her so roughly that she was afraid he might let go and send her propelling into the wall. Up the middle, under the arch, gallop, weave.

Vignettes glimpsed for a second, and then gone. Simon signaling to her that he was leaving but his smile—she was being revolved with speed by Sir Rowley at that moment—telling her to stay and enjoy herself. A tall prioress and a small Ulf swinging round on the centrifuge of their crossed hands. Sir Joscelin talking earnestly to the little nun as they passed back-to-back in a corner. An admiring circle round Mansur, his face impassive as he danced over crossed swords to an intoned *maqam*. Roger of Acton trying to make a circling carole go to the right: "Those that turn to the left are perverse, and God hates them. Proverbs twenty-seven." And being trampled.

Dear Lord, the cook and the sheriff's lady. No time to marvel. Right shoulder to right shoulder. Dance, dance. Her arms and Picot's forming an arch, Gyltha and Prior Geoffrey passing under it. The skinny nun with the apothecary. Now Hugh the huntsman and Matilda B. Those below the salt, those above it in thrall to a democratic god who danced. *Oh, God, this is joy on the wing. Catch it, catch it.*

Adelia danced her slippers through and didn't know it until friction burns afflicted the soles of her feet.

She spun out of the melee. It was time to go. A few guests were leaving, though most were congregating at the sideboards on which supper was being set out.

She limped to the doorway. Mansur joined her. "Did I see Master Simon leave?" she asked him.

He went to look and came back from the direction of the kitchen with a sleeping Ulf in his arms. "The woman says he went ahead." Mansur never used Gyltha's name; she was always "the woman."

"Are she and the Matildas staying?"

"They help to clear up. We take the boy."

It seemed that Prior Geoffrey and his monks had long gone. So had the nuns, except for Prioress Joan, who was at a sideboard with a piece of game pie in one hand and a tankard in the other; she was so far mellowed as to smile on Mansur and wave a benediction with the pie over Adelia's curtseyed thanks.

Sir Joscelin they met coming in from the courtyard where firelit figures gnawed on bones.

"You honored us, my lord," Adelia told him. "Dr. Mansur wishes me to express our gratitude to you."

"Do you go back via the river? I can call my barge. . . ."

No, no, they had come in Old Benjamin's punt, but thank you.

Even with the flambeau burning in its holder on a stanchion at the river's edge, it was almost too dark to distinguish Old Benjamin's punt from the others waiting along the bank, but since all of them, bar Sheriff Baldwin's, were uniformly plain, they took the first in line.

The still-sleeping Ulf was lain across Adelia's lap where she sat in the bow; Safeguard stood unhappily with his paws in bilge. Mansur took up the pole. . . .

The punt rocked dangerously as Sir Rowley Picot leaped into it. "To the castle, boatman." He settled himself on a thwart. "Now, isn't this nice?"

A slight mist rose from the water and a gibbous moon shone weakly, intermittently, sometimes disappearing altogether as overarching trees on the banks turned the river into a tunnel. A lump of ghastly white transformed into a flurry of wings as a protesting swan got out of their way.

Mansur, as he always did when he was poling, sang quietly to himself, an atonal reminiscence of water and rushes in another land.

Sir Rowley complimented Adelia on her boatman's skill.

"He is a Marsh Arab," she said. "He feels at home in fenland."

"Does he now? How unexpected in a eunuch."

Immediately, she was defensive. "And what *do* you expect? Fat men lolling around a harem?"

He was taken aback. "Yes, actually. The only ones I ever saw were."

"When you were crusading?" she asked, still on the attack.

"When I was crusading," he admitted.

"Then your experience of eunuchs is limited, Sir Rowley. I fully expect Mansur to marry Gyltha one day." *Oh, damn it*, her tongue was still loose from the mead. Had she betrayed her dear Arab? And Gyltha?

But she would not have this, this *fellow*, this possible murderer, denigrate a man whose boots he was not fit to lick.

Rowley leaned forward. "Really? I thought his, er, condition would put marriage out of the question."

Damn and blast and hellfire, now she had placed herself into the position of having to explain the circumstances of the castrated. *But how to put it?* "It is only that children of such a union are out of the question. Since Gyltha is past childbearing age anyway, I doubt that will concern them."

"I see. And the other, er, condolences of marriage?"

"They can sustain an erection," she said sharply. To hell with euphemisms; why sheer away from physical fact? If he hadn't wanted to know, he shouldn't have asked.

She'd shocked him, she could tell; but she hadn't finished with him. "Do you think Mansur chose to be as he is? He was taken by slavers when he was a small child and sold for his voice to Byzantine monks, where he was castrated so that he might keep his treble. It is a common practice with them. He was eight years old, and he had to sing for the monks, *Christian* monks, his torturers."

"May I ask how you acquired him?"

"He ran away. My foster father found him on a street in Alexandria and brought him home to Salerno. My father specializes in acquiring the lost and abandoned."

Stop it, stop it, she told herself. *Why this wish to inform? He is nothing to you;*

he may be worse than nothing. That you have just spent the time of your life with him is nothing.

A moorhen clooped and rustled in the reeds. Something, a water rat, slid into the water and swam away, leaving a wake of moonlit ripples. The punt entered another tunnel.

Sir Rowley's voice sounded in it. "Adelia."

She closed her eyes. "Yes?"

"You have contributed all you can to this business. When we reach Old Benjamin's, I shall come in with you and have a word with Master Simon. He must be made to see that it is time you went home to Salerno."

"I do not understand," she said. "The killer is not yet uncovered."

"We're closing on his coverts; if we flush him, he'll be dangerous until we can bring him down. I don't want him leaping on one of the beaters."

The anger the tax collector always inspired in her came hot and sharp. *"One of the beaters?* I am qualified, *qualified,* and chosen for this mission by the King of Sicily, not by Simon, and certainly not by you."

"Madam, I am merely concerned for your safety."

It was too late; he would not have suggested that a man in her position go home; he had insulted her professional ability.

Adelia lapsed into Arabic, the only tongue in which she could swear freely, because Margaret had never understood it. She used phrases overheard during Mansur's frequent quarrels with her foster parents' Moroccan cook, the one language that could counteract the fury Sir Rowley Picot ever inspired in her. She spoke of diseased donkeys and his unnatural preference for them, of his doglike attributes, his fleas, his bowel performance, and his eating habits. She told him what he could do with his concern, an injunction again involving his bowels. Whether Picot knew what she was saying or didn't was irrelevant; he could get the gist.

Mansur poled them out of the tunnel, grinning.

The rest of the journey passed in silence.

When they reached Old Benjamin's house, Adelia would not let Picot accompany her to it. "Shall I take him on to the castle?" Mansur wanted to know.

"Anywhere, take him anywhere," she said.

THE NEXT MORNING, when a water bailiff came to tell Gyltha that Simon's corpse was being delivered to the castle, Adelia knew she had been swearing as their punt passed his body where it had floated, face down, in the Trumpington reeds.

Ten

Is she hearing me?" Sir Rowley asked Gyltha.

"They're hearing you in Peterborough," Gyltha said. The tax collector had been shouting. "She just ain't listening."

She was listening, but not to Sir Rowley Picot. The voice she heard was that of Simon of Naples, clear as clear, and saying nothing significant, merely chatting as he'd used to chat in his light, busy tenor—actually, at the moment, about wool and its processes. *"Can you conceive of the difficulty in achieving of the color black?"*

She wanted to tell him that her difficulty now was of conceiving him to be dead, that she was delaying the moment because the loss was too great and must therefore be ignored, a life removed revealing a chasm that she had not seen because he'd filled it.

They were mistaken. Simon was not the sort of person to be dead.

Sir Rowley looked around Old Benjamin's kitchen for help. Were all its women poleaxed? And the boy? Was she going to sit and stare into the fire forever?

He appealed to the eunuch, who stood with folded arms, staring out the doorway at the river.

"Mansur." He had to go close so that their faces were level. "*Mansur.* The body is at the castle. Any minute the Jews are going to discover that it is there and bury it themselves. They know him to be one of their own. Listen to me." He reached up to the man's shoulders and shook him. "There's no time for her to mourn. She must examine the corpse first. He was murdered, don't you see?"

"You speak Arabic?"

"What do you *think* I'm speaking, you great camel? Wake her up, make her move."

Adelia put her head on one side to consider the balance that had been maintained, the sexless affection and acceptance, respect with humor, a friendship so rare between a man and a woman that such a one was unlikely to be granted to her again. She knew now something of what it would be like to lose her foster father.

She grew angry, accusing Simon's shade of culpability. *How could you be so careless? You were of value to us all; it is a deprivation; dying in a muddy English river is so* silly.

That poor woman he had loved so much. His children.

Mansur's hand was on her shoulder. "This man is saying Simon was murdered."

It took a minute, then she was on her feet. *"No."* She was facing Picot. "It was an accident. That man, the waterman, told Gyltha it was an accident."

"He'd found the tallies, woman, *he knew who it was.*" Sir Rowley clenched his teeth with exasperation, then began to speak slowly. "Listen to me. Are you listening?"

"Yes."

"He came late to Joscelin's feast. Are you hearing me?"

"Yes," she said, "I saw him."

"He came to the top table to make his apologies for being late. The marshal showed him to his place, but as he went by me, he stopped and patted a wallet on his belt. And he said . . . Are you listening? He said, 'We have him, Sir Rowley. I have found the tallies.' He spoke low, but that's what he said."

"'We have him, Sir Rowley,'" Adelia repeated.

"That's what he said. I've this minute seen his body. There's no wallet on his belt. He was killed for it."

Adelia heard Matilda B. squeaking with distress, Gyltha uttering a moan. Were she and Picot speaking English? They must be.

"Why should he tell you that?" she asked.

"Great heavens, woman, we'd been attending to it together all day. It was inconceivable that the only debt tallies were those that were burnt. The damned Jews could have laid their hands on them any day if they'd only realized it; they were with Chaim's banker."

"Don't you say that about them." She had a hand on his chest and was pushing him. "Don't *say* it. Simon was a Jew."

"*Exactly.*" He caught her hands. "It's because he was a Jew that you must come with me now and examine his body before the Jews get hold of it." He saw her expression and stayed remorseless. "What happened to him. When. From that, with even more luck, we may be able to deduce who. You taught me that."

"He was my friend," she said. "I cannot." Her soul rebelled at the thought, and so would Simon's—to be exposed, fingered, cut, and by her. Autopsy was against Jewish law in any case. She would defy the Christian Church any day, but, for Simon's dear sake, she would not offend the Jewish.

Gyltha stepped in between them to peer carefully into the tax collector's face. "What you're saying. Master Simon was killed by him as killed the children? Is that right?"

"Yes, *yes.*"

"And she can tell from looking at his poor corpse?"

Sir Rowley recognized an ally and nodded. "She might."

Gyltha addressed Matilda B. "Get her cloak." And to Adelia, "We'll go together." And to Ulf, "You stay here, boy. Give the Matildas a hand."

Between them, with Mansur and the Safeguard following, Adelia was hustled through the streets toward the bridge. She was still gabbling her protest. "It can't have been the killer. He only attacks the defenseless. This is different, this is . . ." She slowed as she tried to think what it was. "This is everyday awfulness."

To the water bailiff, who had come to tell them, bodies in his river were commonplace. Nor had she questioned his verdict of simple drowning, she who had examined so many waterlogged corpses on the marble table in Salerno's mortuary. People drowned in their baths; sailors fell overboard, like most sailors, unable to swim; freak waves plucked victims into the sea. Children, men, and women drowned in rivers, pools, fountains, puddles. People made tragic misjudgments, took an unwary step. It was an ordinary way of dying.

She heard the tax collector's huff of impatience as he hurried her on. "Our man is a wild dog. Wild dogs leap for the throat when they're threatened. Simon had become a threat."

"He weren't very big, neither," Gyltha said. "Nice little man, but no more to un than a rabbit."

No, there wasn't. But to be murdered. Adelia's mind fought against it. She and Simon had come to resolve a predicament that the people of a minor town in a foreign country had gotten themselves into, not to enter into the same predicament with them. She had regarded the two of them as excluded from it by some special dispensation given to investigators. And so, she knew, had Simon.

She halted in her tracks. "We've been at risk?"

The tax collector stopped with her. "Well, I'm glad you've seen it. Did you think you had exemption?"

They were bustling her on again, the two of them talking over her head.

"Did you see him leave, Gyltha?"

"Not to say leave. He looked into the kitchen with compliments to the cook and say good-bye to me." Gyltha's voice wavered for a mo-ment. "Always the polite gentleman he was."

"Was that before the dancing began?"

Gyltha sighed. It had been busy in Sir Joscelin's kitchen last night.

"Beggared if I can remember. Might've been. He said as he must apply himself to study afore he went to bed, that I do recall. The which he was a-leaving early."

" 'Apply himself to study.' "

"His very words."

"He was going to look through the tallies."

As usual, the bridge was crowded; they had trouble walking in line and, with Sir Rowley keeping a firm grip on her, Adelia was bumped into by passersby, most of them clerks, all in a hurry, each with a dis-tinctive chain around his neck, lots of them. Officialdom had come to Cambridge. Vaguely, she wondered why.

Question and answer went on over her head.

"Did he say he was walking home? Or going by boat?"

"With never a blink of light? He'd never walk, surely." Like most Cambridge people, Gyltha regarded the boat as the only form of transport. "There'd be someone leaving the same time as would've of-fered to drop un off home."

"I fear that is what somebody did."

"Oh, dear God, help us all."

No, no, Adelia thought. Simon was not unwary; he was not a child to be tempted by jujubes. Foolishly, townsman that he was, he had at-tempted to walk back along the riverbank. He slipped in the dark; it was an accident.

"Who *did* leave at the same time?" Picot's voice.

But Gyltha could not tell him. Anyway, they had reached the castle. No Jews in the inner court today; instead, there were more clerks, dozens, like an infestation of beetles.

The tax collector was answering Gyltha: "Royal clerks, here to get all ready for the assize. It takes days to be prepared for the justices in eyre. Come on, this way. They took him to the chapel."

So they had, but, by the time the three reached it, the chapel was empty except for the castle priest, who was busily swinging a thurible up and down the nave to resanctify it. "Did you know the corpse was that of a Jew, Sir Rowley? Such a thing. We thought him to be Christian, but when we laid it out . . ." Father Alcuin took the tax collector by the arm and led him away so that the women should not hear. "When we unclothed it, we saw the evidence. It was circumcised."

"What's been done with him?"

"It could not stay here, for all heaven. I called for it to be taken away. It cannot be buried here, however the Jews fuss for it. I have sent for the prior, though it is more a matter for the bishop, but Prior Geoffrey knows how to quiet the Israelites."

Father Alcuin caught sight of Mansur and paled. "Will you bring another paynim into this holy place? Get him out, get him out."

Sir Rowley saw the despair in Adelia's face and took the little priest by the front of his robe, raising him several inches off the ground. "Where have they taken the body?"

"I do not know. Let me down, you fiend." As he regained his feet, he said defiantly, "Nor do I care." He returned to clanking the thurible, disappearing in a cloud of incense and bad temper.

"They're not treating him with respect," Adelia said. "Oh, Picot, see that he has a proper Jewish burial." Cosmopolitan humanist he might have appeared, but au fond Simon of Naples had been a devout Jew; her own nonobservance had always troubled him. For his body to be merely disposed of, the rites of his religion ignored, was terrible to her.

"That's not right," Gyltha agreed. "It's like the Good Book says, *They have taken away my Lord and I know not where they have laid him.*'"

Blasphemy perhaps, but it was said with indignation and sorrow.

"Ladies," Sir Rowley Picot said, "if I have to go to the Holy Ghost for it, Master Simon will be buried with reverence." He went off and came back. "The Jews have already taken him, it seems."

He set off toward the Jews' tower. As they followed him, Adelia slipped her hand into that of her housekeeper.

Prior Geoffrey was at its door, talking to a man Adelia did not know but whom she recognized at once to be a rabbi. It wasn't the locks or the untrimmed beard; he was dressed much the same, and as shabbily, as his fellow Jews. It was the eyes; they were scholarly, sterner than Prior Geoffrey's but with the same breadth of knowledge and a wearier amusement. Men with eyes like those had gently disputed Jewish law with her foster father. A Talmudic scholar, she thought, and was relieved; he would care for Simon's body as Simon would have wished. But he would not, since it was forbidden, allow the corpse to be subject to an autopsy, despite anything Sir Rowley could do—and that also was a relief to Adelia.

Prior Geoffrey was holding her hands. "My dear girl, such a blow, such a blow for us all. The loss to you must be incalculable. God's grace and how I liked the man, ours was a brief acquaintance, yet I per-ceived the sweetness of soul in Master Simon of Naples and I grieve at his passing."

"Prior, he must be buried according to Jewish law, which means he has to be buried today." To keep a corpse above ground any longer than twenty-four hours was to humiliate it.

"Ah, as to that . . ." Prior Geoffrey was uneasy. He turned to the tax collector, as did the rabbi—this was men's business. "A situation has arisen, Sir Rowley. Indeed, I am surprised it has not come up before, but it appears—happily, of course—that none of Rabbi Gotsce's people here in the castle have died during their year of incarceration. . . ."

"It must be the cooking." It was a deep voice, Rabbi Gotsce's, and, if he'd made a joke, his face showed no sign of it.

"Accordingly," the prior went on, "and I admit my fault in this, no arrangement has yet been made. . . ."

"There is no burial ground for Jews in the castle," Rabbi Gotsce said.

Prior Geoffrey nodded. "I fear Father Alcuin is claiming the entire precinct as Christian ground."

Sir Rowley grimaced. "Perhaps we can smuggle him down to the town tonight."

"There is no burial ground for Jews in Cambridge," Rabbi Gotsce said.

They all stared at him, except the prior, who looked ashamed.

"What was done for Chaim and his wife, then?" Rowley asked.

Reluctantly, the prior said, "In unsanctified ground, with the suicides. Anything else would have inflamed another riot."

The open door of the tower before which they all stood showed a to-do in progress behind it. Women with basins and cloths in their arms were running up and down the circular stair while a group of men stood in the hallway, talking. Adelia saw Yehuda Gabirol in the middle of it, clutching his forehead.

She clutched her own because, on top of everything else, confusing the issue, somebody was in pain. The conversation of prior, rabbi, and tax collector was being interrupted every now and then by a loud and deep sound issuing from one of the tower's upper windows, something between a groan and the huff of a faulty pair of bellows. The men were ignoring it.

"Who is that?" she asked, but nobody attended to her.

"Where do you usually take your dead, then?" Rowley asked the rabbi.

"To London. The king is good enough to allow us a cemetery near the Jewish quarter in London. It has always been so."

"It's the only one?"

"The only one. If we die in York or on the border to Scotland, in Devon or Cornwall, we must take our coffin to London. We have to pay a special toll, of course. And then there's the hiring of the dogs that bark at us as we pass through the towns." He smiled without mirth. "It comes expensive."

"I didn't know," Rowley said.

The little rabbi bowed politely. "How should you?"

"We are at an impasse, you see," Prior Geoffrey said. "The poor body cannot be interred in the castle grounds, yet I doubt we could elude the townspeople long enough, or safely enough, to smuggle it to London."

London? Smuggle? Adelia's distress grew into anger she could hardly contain.

She stepped forward. "Forgive me, but Simon of Naples is not an inconvenience to be disposed of. He was sent to this place by the King of Sicily to root out a killer in your midst, and if this man here is right"—she pointed to the tax collector—"he died for it. In the name of God, the least all of you can do is bury him with respect."

"She's right, Prior," Gyltha said. "Good little man, he was."

The two women were embarrassing the men. Further embarrassment came from the upper window in another groan that turned into an unmistakably feminine shriek.

Rabbi Gotsce felt called upon to explain. "Mistress Dina."

"The baby?" demanded Adelia.

"A little before its time," the rabbi told her, "but the women have hopes of its safe arrival."

She heard Gyltha say, "The Lord giveth and the Lord taketh away."

Adelia did not ask how Dina did, for at that moment, Dina obviously did badly. Adelia's shoulders drooped as a little of the anger went out of her. Something would be gained, then, some new, good thing in a wicked world.

The rabbi saw it. "You are a Jew, madam?"

"I was brought up by a Jew. I am nothing except Simon's friend."

"So he told me. Be at peace, my daughter. For us of this poor little community, your friend's burial is a sacred task obligatory to us all. Already we have performed the Tahara, the washing and cleansing of his body as it begins its journey to its next stage. He has been clad in the simple white shroud of the Tachrichim. A coffin of willow twigs as commanded by the great sage, Rabban Gamliel, is even now being prepared for him. See? I tear my clothes for him." The rabbi ripped the front of his already somewhat ragged tunic in the gesture of ritual mourning.

She should have known. "Thank you, Rabbi, thank you." However, there was one more thing. "But he should not be left alone."

"He is not alone. Old Benjamin acts as *shomer* and keeps vigil over him and is reciting the appropriate psalms." Rabbi Gotsce looked around. The prior and the tax collector were deep in discussion. He lowered his voice. "As to the burial. We are a flexible people, we have had to be, and the Lord recognizes what is impossible for us. He is not unkind if we adapt a little." His voice lowered almost to a whisper. "We have always found that Christian laws, too, are flexible, especially when it comes to money. We are collecting what little cash we have between us to buy a plot in the earth of this castle where our friend may be laid with reverence."

Adelia smiled for the first time that day. "I have money, and plenty."

Rabbi Gotsce stood back. "Then what need to worry?" He took her hand to pronounce the blessing prescribed for those that mourned, *"Blessed is the Eternal our God, Ruler of the universe, the true judge."*

For a moment, Adelia felt a grateful peace; perhaps it was the blessing, perhaps it was being in the presence of well-intentioned men, perhaps it was the advent of Dina's baby.

Yet, she thought, *however they bury him, Simon is dead; something of great value has been withdrawn from the world. And you, Adelia, are called upon to establish whether it was taken accidentally or through murder—no one else can.*

She still felt a reluctance to examine Simon's body, which, she realized, was partly a fear of what it might tell her. If the beast at large had killed him, it had made a mortal thrust not only at Simon but at her resolve to continue their mission. Without Simon, the responsibility was hers only, and without Simon she was a lonely, broken, and very frightened reed.

But the rabbi, to whom Sir Rowley had been speaking very fast, wasn't intending to let her near the body of Simon of Naples. "No," he was saying, "not at all, and certainly not a woman."

"Dux femina facti," interjected Prior Geoffrey helpfully.

"Sir, the prior is right," Rowley pleaded. "In this matter, the leader of our enterprise is a woman. The dead speak to her. They tell her the cause of the death, from which we may deduce who caused it. We owe it to the dead man, to justice, to see if the children's killer was also his. Lord's sake, man, he was acting for your people. If he was murdered, don't you want him avenged?"

"Exoriare aliquis nostris ex ossibus ultor." The prior was still being helpful. "Rise up from my dead bones, avenger."

The rabbi bowed. "Justice is good, my lord," he said, "but we have found that it is only in the next world that it can be achieved. You ask that this be done for the Lord's sake, yet how can we please the Lord by breaking His laws?"

"Stubborn beggar, that one," Gyltha said to Adelia, shaking her head. "It's what makes him a Jew."

Sometimes Adelia wondered how both the race and the religion had survived at all in the face of an almost universal and, to her, inexplicable hostility. Homelessness, persecution, degradation, attempted genocide, all these things had been visited on the Jewish people—who clung even more tenaciously to their Jewishness. During the First Crusade, Christian armies, filled with religious zeal and liquor, seeing it as their evangelic duty to convert such Jews they came across, had presented them with the alternative of baptism or death. The answer had been thousands of dead Jews.

A reasonable man, Rabbi Gotsce, but he would die on the steps of this tower before a tenet of his faith was broken and a woman was allowed to touch the corpse of a man, however gainful that touch might prove.

Which only showed, Adelia thought, that the three great religions were at least united when it came to the inferiority of her sex. Indeed, a devout Jew at his prayers thanked God every day that he had not been born a woman.

While her mind was occupied, there had been energetic talk in progress in which Sir Rowley's voice was uppermost. He came over to her now. "I've gained this much," he said. "The prior and I are to be allowed to look at the body. You may stay outside and tell us what to look *for*."

Ludicrous, but it seemed to suit everybody, including herself. . . .

With considerable labor, the Jews had carried the corpse to the room at the top of the tower, the only one unoccupied, in which she and Simon and Mansur had first encountered Old Benjamin and Yehuda.

As if afraid that she might invade it in an excess of zeal, the rabbi made Adelia wait on the landing of the staircase below, the Safeguard with her. She heard the door of the room open. A quick burst of Old Benjamin's voice chanting the Tehillim came down the stairwell to her before the door closed again.

Picot is right, she thought. *Simon should not be put into the ground unheard.* The spirit of the man himself would see it as greater desecration that nobody should listen to what his body had to say.

She sat down on a stone stair and composed herself, directing her mind to the mechanism of death by drowning.

It was difficult. Without being able to cut a section of lung to see if it had ballooned and contained silt or weed, the diagnosis would largely depend on excluding other causes of death. In fact, she thought, there was unlikely to be any sign at all to tell them if it were murder. She could probably establish that it *was* drowning, whether or not Simon was alive when he went into the water, but that would still beg the question: Had he fallen or been pushed?

Old Benjamin's voice, *"Lord, thou has been our dwelling place in all generations. . . ."* And the thud of the tax collector's boots coming heavily down the stairs to her.

"He looks peaceful. What do we do?"

She said, "Is there froth coming from the mouth and nostrils?"

"No. They've washed him."

"Press on the chest. If there is froth, wipe it away and press again."

"I don't know if the rabbi will let me. Gentile hands."

Adelia stood up. "Don't ask him, just do it." She had become doctor to the dead again.

Rowley hurried back upstairs.

". . . Thou shalt not be afraid for the terror by night, nor for the arrow that flieth by day. . . ."

She leaned on the triangle of the arrow slit beside her, absentmindedly stroking Safeguard's head and looking out at the view she had seen before, of the river and the trees and hills beyond it, a Virgilian pastoral.

But I am *afraid of the terror by night*, she thought.

Sir Rowley was beside her again. "Froth," he said, shortly, "both times. Pinkish."

Alive in the water, then. Indicative but not proof; he could have suffered a disruption of the heart and toppled into the river because of it. "Is there bruising?" she asked.

"I can't see any. There are cuts between his fingers. Old Benjamin said they found plant stalks in them. Does that mean something?"

Again, it meant that Simon was alive when he went into the river; in the terrible minute or so that it took for him to die, he'd torn at reeds and weed that had been retained as his hands closed in the fatal spasm.

"Look for bruising on his back," she said, "but don't lay him on his face; it's against the law."

This time she could hear him arguing with the rabbi, Rowley's voice and Rabbi Gotsce's both sharp. Old Benjamin ignoring them both. *"He maketh me to lie down in green pastures; he leadeth me beside the still waters."*

Sir Rowley won. He came back to her. "There's a spread of bruising here and here," he said, putting his hand over one shoulder and then the other to indicate a line across his upper back. "Was he beaten?"

"No. It happens sometimes. The struggle to get back to the surface ruptures muscles around the shoulders and neck. He drowned, Picot. That is all I can tell you, Simon drowned."

Rowley said, "There's one very distinct bruise. Here." This time he crooked his arm around his back, waggling his fingers and turning round so that she could see them. It was a spot between the lower shoulder blades. "What caused that?"

Seeing her frown, he spat on the stair at his feet and knelt down to stir a small wet circle on the stone. "Like this. Round. Distinct, as I say. What is it?"

"I don't know." Exasperation overtook her. With their petty laws, with their fear of women's incipient impurity, with their *nonsense*, they were erecting a barrier between doctor and patient. Simon was calling out to her, and they wouldn't let her hear him. "Excuse me," she said.

She went up the stairs and marched into the room. The body lay on its side. It took less than a moment before she marched out again.

"He was murdered," she told Rowley.

"A barge pole?" he asked.

"Probably."

"They held him down with it?"

"Yes," she said.

Eleven

The curtain wall was a rampart from which archers could repel—
and during the war of Stephen and Matilda *had* repelled—an
attack on the castle. Today it was quiet and empty except for a sentry doing his rounds of the allure and the cloaked woman with a
dog standing by one of the crenels to whom he bade an unanswered
good-day.

A fine afternoon. The westerly breeze had pushed the rain farther
east and was scudding lambswool clouds across a laundered blue sky,
making the pretty, busy scene Adelia looked down on prettier and
busier by billowing the canvas roofs of the market stalls, fluttering the
pennants of the boats moored by the bridge, swaying the willow
branches farther down into a synchronized dance, and whisking the
river into glistening irregular wavelets.

She didn't see it.

How did you do it? she was asking Simon's murderer. *What did you say to
tempt him into the position enabling you to push him into the water? It would not have
taken much strength to hold him down by the pole jabbed into his back; you would have
leaned your weight on it, making it impossible to dislodge.*

A minute, two, while he scrabbled like a beetle, until that life of complexity and goodness was extinguished.

Oh, dear heaven, what had it been like for him? She saw flurries of silt cloud the encompassing, entrapping weed, watched the rising bubbles of the last remnants of breath. She began to gasp in vicarious panic . . . as if she were taking in water, not clean Cambridge air.

Stop it. This does not serve him.

What will?

Undoubtedly, to bring his killer, who was also the children's, to the seat of justice, but how much more difficult that would be without him. *"We may have to do that very thing before this business is finished, Doctor. Think as he thinks."*

And she had answered, *"Then you do it. You're the subtle one."*

Now she must try to enter a mind that saw death as an expedient: in the case of children, pleasurable.

But she could see only the diminution it had brought about. She had become smaller. She knew now that the anger she had felt at the children's torture had been that of a deus ex machina called down to set matters right. She and Simon had been apart, above the action, its finale, not its continuance. For her, she supposed, it had been a form of superiority—it was not in the play that its gods become protagonists—which Simon's murder had now removed, casting her among the Cambridge players, as ignorant and as helpless as any of those tiny, breeze-blown, fate-driven figures down there.

She was joined in a democracy of misery to Agnes, sitting outside her beehive hut below; to Hugh the huntsman, who had wept for his niece; to Gyltha and every other man and woman with some beloved soul to lose.

It wasn't until she heard familiar footsteps approaching along the rampart that she knew she had been waiting for them. The only plank she had been given to hold on to in this maelstrom was the knowledge that the tax collector was as innocent of the murders as she herself.

She would have been happy, very happy, to apologize humbly to him for her suspicion—except that he added to her confusion.

To all but her intimates, Adelia liked to appear imperturbable, putting on the kindly but detached manner of one called to profession by the god of medicine. It was a veneer that had helped deflect the impertinence and overfamiliarity and, occasionally, the downright physical presumption with which her fellow students and early patients had offered to treat her. Indeed, she actually thought of herself as withdrawn from humanity, a calm and hidden resort that it could call on in need, though one which did not involve itself in its vulnerability.

But to the owner of the coming footsteps, she had shown grief and panic, called for help, pleaded, had leaned on him, even in her misery had been grateful that he was with her.

Accordingly, the face Adelia turned up to Sir Rowley Picot was blank. "What was the verdict?"

She had not been called to give evidence to the jurors hastily assembled for the inquest on Simon's body. Sir Rowley had felt that it would not be in her interest, nor that of the truth, if she were exposed as an expert on death. "You're a woman, for one thing, and a foreigner, for another. Even if they believed you, you would achieve notoriety. I will show them the bruise on his back and explain that he was trying to investigate the finances of the children's killer and therefore became the murderer's victim, though I doubt whether coroner or jury—they're all bumpkins—will have the wit to follow that tangled skein with any credence."

Now, from his look, she saw that they had not. "Accidental death by drowning," he told her. "They thought I was mad."

He put his hands on the crenel and expelled an exasperated breath at the town below. "All I may have achieved is to sap their conviction by an inch or two that it was one of their own and not the Jews who murdered Little Saint Peter and the others."

For a second, something reared in the turbulence of Adelia's mind, showing hideous teeth, then sank again, to be hidden by grief, disappointment, and anxiety.

"And the burial?" she asked.

"Ah," he said. "Come with me."

Slavishly, the Safeguard was on its spindle legs in a minute and trotting after him. Adelia followed more slowly.

Building was in progress in the great courtyard. The chatter of gathered clerks was being drowned by an insistent, deafening banging of hammer on wood. A new scaffold was going up in one corner to hold the triple gallows for use in the assizes when the justices in eyre emptied the county's gaols and tried the cases of those thus brought before them. Almost as high as the nooses would be, a long table and a bench reached by steps were being erected near the castle doors to place the judges above the multitude.

Some of the din faded as Sir Rowley led Adelia and her dog round a corner. Here, sixteen years of royal Plantagenet peace had allowed Cambridgeshire's sheriffs to throw out an abutment, an attachment to their quarters from which steps led down to this sunken walled garden approached from outside by a gate in an arch.

Inside, going down the steps, it was quieter still, and Adelia could hear the first bees of spring blundering in and out of flowers.

A very English garden, planted for medicine and strewing rather than spectacle. At this time of year, color was lacking except for the cowslips between the stones of the paths and a mere impression of blue where a bank of violets crowded along the bottom of a wall. The scent was fresh and earthy.

"Will this do?" Sir Rowley asked casually.

Adelia stared at him, dumb.

He said with exaggerated patience, "This is the garden of the sheriff and his lady. They have agreed to let Simon be buried in it." He took her arm and led her down a path to where a wild cherry tree drifted delicate white blossoms over untended grass sprinkled with daisies. "Here, we thought."

Adelia shut her eyes and breathed in. After a while, she said, "I must pay them."

"Certainly not." The tax collector was offended. "When I say that this is the sheriff's garden, I should more properly call it the king's, the king being the ultimate owner of England's every acre, except those belonging to the Church. And since Henry Plantagenet is fond of his Jews and since I am Henry Plantagenet's man, it was merely a matter of pointing out to Sheriff Baldwin that by accommodating the Jews, he would also be accommodating the king, which, in another sense, he will—and soon, since Henry is due to visit the castle shortly, another factor I pointed out to his lordship."

He paused, frowning. "I shall have to press the king for Jewish cemeteries to be put in each town; the lack is a scandal. I cannot believe he's aware of it."

No money was involved, then. But Adelia knew whom she should pay. It was time to do it, and do it properly.

She bent her knee to Rowley Picot in a deep bow. "Sir, I am in your debt, not only for this kindness, but for ill suspicion that I have harbored against you. I am truly sorry for it."

He looked down at her. "What suspicion?"

She grimaced with reluctance. "I believed you might be the killer."

"*Me?*"

"You have been on crusade," she pointed out, "as, I think, has he. You were in Cambridge on the pertinent dates. You were among those near Wandlebury Ring on the night the children's bodies were moved. . . ." God's rib, the more she expounded the theory, the more reasonable it seemed; why should she apologize for it? "How else would I think?" she asked him.

He had become statuelike, his blue eyes staring at her, one finger pointing at her in disbelief and then at himself. "Me?"

She became impatient. "I see it was a base suspicion."

"It damned well was," he said with force, and startled a robin into flying away. "Madam, I would have you know I *like* children. I suspect I may have fathered quite a few, even if I can't claim any. Goddammit, I've been hunting the bastard, I told you I was."

"The killer could have said as much. You did not explain why."

He thought for a moment. "I didn't, did I? Strictly speaking, it is nobody's business except mine and . . . though in the circumstances . . ." He stared down at her. "This will be a confidence, madam."

"I shall keep it," she said.

There was a turfed seat farther up the garden where young hop leaves formed a tapestry against the brick of the wall. He pointed her to it and then sat beside her, his linked hands cradling one of his knees.

He began with himself. "You should know that I am a fortunate man." He had been fortunate in his father, who was saddler to the lord of Aston in Hertfordshire and had seen to it that he had schooling, fortunate in the size and strength that made people notice him, fortunate in possessing a keen brain. "You should also know that my mathematical prowess is remarkable, as is my grasp of languages. . . ."

Not backward in coming forward, either, Adelia thought, amused. It was a phrase she'd picked up from Gyltha.

Young Rowley Picot's abilities had early been recognized by his father's lord, who had sent him to the School of Pythagoras here in Cambridge where he had studied Greek and Arab sciences and where, in turn, he'd been recommended by his tutors to Geoffrey De Luci, chancellor to Henry II, and taken into his employment.

"As a tax collector?" Adelia asked innocently.

"As a chancery clerk," Sir Rowley said, "to begin with. Eventually, I came to the attention of the king himself, of course."

"Of course."

"Will I proceed with this narrative?" he wanted to know. "Or shall we discuss the weather?"

Chastened, she said, "I beg you to continue, my lord. Truly, I am interested." *Why am I teasing him,* she wondered, *on this day of all days? Because he makes it bearable for me with everything he does and says.*

Oh, dear God, she thought with shock, *I am attracted to him.*

The realization came like an attack, as if it had been gathering itself in some cramped and secret place inside her and had grown suddenly too big to remain unnoticed any longer. *Attracted?* Her legs were weak with it, her mind registering intoxication as well as something like disbelief at the improbability and protest at the sheer inconvenience.

He is too light a man for me; not in weight certainly, but in gravitas. This is an infliction, a madness wreaked on me by a garden in springtime and his unsuspected kindness. Or because I am desolate just now. It will pass; it has to pass.

He was talking with animation about Henry II. "I am the king's man in all things. Today his tax collector, tomorrow—whatever he wants me to be." He turned to her. "Who *was* Simon of Naples? What did he do?"

"He was . . ." Adelia tried to gather her wits "Simon? Well . . . he worked secretly for the King of Sicily, among others." She clenched her hands—he must not see that they trembled; he must not see that. She concentrated. "He told me once that he was analogous to a doctor of the incorporeal, a mender of broken situations."

"A fixer. 'Don't worry, Simon of Naples will see to it.'"

"Yes. I suppose that is what he was."

The man beside her nodded, and because she was now furiously interested in who he was, in everything about him, she understood that he, too, was a fixer and that the King of England had said in his Angevin French, *"Ne vous en faites pas, Picot va tout arranger."*

"Strange, isn't it," the fixer said now, "that the story begins with a dead child."

A royal child, heir to the throne of England and the empire his father had built for him. William Plantagenet, born to King Henry II and Queen Eleanor of Aquitaine in 1153. Died 1156.

Rowley: "Henry doesn't believe in crusade. Turn your back, he says, and while you're away, some bastard'll steal your throne." He smiled. "Eleanor does, however; she went on one with her first husband."

And had created a legend still sung throughout Christendom—though not in churches—and brought to Adelia's mind images of a bare-breasted Amazon blazing her naughty progress across desert sands, trailing Louis, the poor, pious king of France, in her wake.

"Young as he was, the child William was forward and had vowed he would go on crusade when he grew up. They even had a little sword made for him, Eleanor and Henry, and after the boy died, Eleanor wanted it taken to the Holy Land."

Yes, Adelia thought, touched. She had seen many such pass through Salerno, a father carrying his son's sword, a son his father's, on their way to Jerusalem on vicarious crusade as a result of a penance or in response to a vow, sometimes their own, sometimes that of their dead, which had been left unfulfilled.

Perhaps a day or so ago she would not have been so moved, but it was as if Simon's death and this new, unsuspected passion had opened her to the painful loving of all the world. How pitiable it was.

Rowley said, "For a long time the king refused to spare anybody; he held that God would not refuse Paradise to a three-year-old child because he hadn't fulfilled a vow. But the queen wouldn't let it rest and so, what was it, nearly seven years ago now, I suppose, he chose Guiscard de Saumur, one of his Angevin uncles, to take the sword to Jerusalem."

Again, Rowley grinned. "Henry always has more than one reason for what he does. Lord Guiscard was an admirable choice to take the sword: strong, enterprising, and acquainted with the East, but hot-tempered like all Angevins. A dispute with one of his vassals was threatening peace in the Anjou, and the king felt that Guiscard's absence for a while would allow the matter to calm down. A mounted guard was to go with him. Henry also felt that he should send a man of his own with Guiscard, a wily fellow with diplomatic skills, or, as he put it, 'Someone strong enough to keep the bugger out of trouble.'"

"You?" Adelia asked.

"Me," Rowley said smugly. "Henry knighted me at the same time because I was to be the sword carrier. Eleanor herself strapped it to my back, and from that day until I returned it to young William's tomb, it never left me. At night, when I took it off, I slept with it. And so we all set off for Jerusalem."

The place's name overcame the garden and the two people in it, filling the air with the adoration and agony of three inimical faiths, like planets humming their own lovely chords as they hurtled to collide.

"Jerusalem," Rowley said again, and his words were those of the Queen of Sheba: "Behold, the half was not told me."

As a man entranced, he had trodden the stones made sacred by his Savior, shuffled on his knees along the Via Dolorosa, prostrated himself, weeping, at the Holy Sepulchre. It had seemed good to him, then, that this navel of all virtue should have been cleansed of heathen tyranny by the men of the First Crusade so that Christian pilgrims should once more be able to worship it as he worshipped. He had floundered in admiration for them.

"Even now I don't know how they did it." He was shaking his head, still wondering. "Flies, scorpions, thirst, the heat—your horse dies under you, just touching your damned armor blisters your hands. And they were outnumbered, ravaged by disease. No, God the Father was with those early crusaders, else they could never have recaptured His Son's home. Or that's what I thought then."

There were other, profane pleasures. The descendants of the original crusaders had come to terms with the land they called Outremer;

indeed, it was difficult to distinguish between them and the Arabs whose style of living they now imitated.

The tax collector described their marble palaces, courtyards with fountains and fig trees, their baths—"I swear to you, great Moorish baths sunk into the floor"—and the rich, pungent scent of seduction drenched the little garden.

Rowley, particularly, of all his group of knights, had been bewitched, not just by the outlandish, exotic holiness of the place but by its diffusion and complexity. "That's what you don't expect—how tangled it all is. It's not plain Christian against plain Saracen, nothing as straightforward as that. You think, God bless, that man's an enemy because he worships Allah. And, God bless, that fellow kneeling to a cross, he's a Christian, he must be on our side—and he *is* a Christian, but he isn't necessarily on your side, he's just as likely to be in alliance with a Moslem prince."

That much Adelia knew. Italian merchant-venturers had traded happily with their Moslem counterparts in Syria and Alexandria long before Pope Urban called for the deliverance of the Holy Places from Mohammedan rule in 1096, and they had cursed the crusade to hell then and cursed again in 1147, when men of the Second Crusade went into the Holy Land once more with no more understanding than their predecessors had had of the human mosaic they were invading, thus disrupting a profitable cooperation that had existed for generations between differing faiths.

As Rowley described a mélange that had delighted him, Adelia was alarmed at how the last of her defenses against him crumbled. Always one to categorize, quick to condemn, she was finding in this man a breadth of perception rare in crusaders. *Don't,* don't. *This infatuation must be dispelled; it is necessary for me not to admire you. I do not wish to fall in love.*

Unaware, Rowley went on. "At first I was amazed that Jew and Moslem were as ardent in their attachment to the Holy Temple as I was, that it was equally holy to them." While he did not allow the realization to put a creep of doubt into his mind about the rightness of the crusading cause—"that came later"—he nevertheless began to find distasteful the loud, bullying intolerance of most of the other newcomers. He preferred the company and way of life of crusaders who were descendants of crusaders and who had accommodated themselves to its melting pot. Thanks to their hospitality, the aristocratic Guiscard and his entourage were able to enjoy it.

No question of returning home, not yet. They learned Arabic, they bathed in unguent-scented water, joining their hosts in hunting with ferocious little Barbary falcons, enjoying loose robes and the company of compliant women, sherbet, soft cushions, black servants, spiced food. When they went to war, they covered their armor with burnooses against the sun, indistinguishable from the Saracen enemy apart from the crosses on their shields.

For go to war Guiscard and his little band did, so completely had they turned from pilgrims into crusaders. King Amalric had issued an urgent call to arms to all the Franks in order to prevent the Arab general Nur-ad-Din, who had marched into Egypt, from uniting the Moslem world against Christians.

"A great warrior, Nur-ad-Din, and a great bastard. It seemed to us, then, you see, that in joining the King of Jerusalem's army, we were also joining the King of Heaven's."

They marched south.

Until now, Adelia noticed, the man next to her had spoken in detail, building for her white and golden domes, great hospitals, teeming streets, the vastness of the desert. But the account of his crusade itself was sparse. "Sacred madness" was all he had to say, though he added, "There was chivalry on both sides, even so. When Amalric fell ill, Nur-ad-Din ceased fighting until he was better."

But the Christian army was followed by the dross of Europe. The

Pope's pardon to sinners and criminals as long as they took the cross had released into Outremer men who killed indiscriminately—certain that, whatever they did, they would be welcomed into Jesus' arms.

"Cattle," Rowley said of them, "still stinking of the farmyards they came from. They'd escaped servitude; now they wanted land and they wanted riches."

They'd slaughtered Greeks, Armenians, and Copts of an older Christianity than their own because they thought they were heathens. Jews, Arabs, who were versed in Greek and Roman philosophy and advanced in the mathematics and medicine and astronomy that the Semitic races had given to the West, went down before men who could neither read nor write and saw no reason to.

"Amalric tried to keep them in check," Rowley said, "but they were always there, like the vultures. You'd come back to your lines to find that they'd slit open the bellies of the captives because they thought Moslems kept their jewels safe by swallowing them. Women, children, it didn't matter to them. Some of them didn't join the army at all; they roamed the trade routes in bands, looking for loot. They burned and blinded, and when they were caught, they said they were doing it for their immortal souls. They probably still are."

He was quiet for a moment. "And our killer was one of them," he said.

Adelia turned her head quickly to look up at him. "You know him? He was there?"

"I never set eyes on him. But he was there, yes."

The robin had come back. It fluttered up onto a lavender bush and peered at the two silent people in its territory for a moment before flying off to chase a dunnock out of the garden.

Rowley said, "Do you know what our great crusades are achieving?"

Adelia shook her head. Disenchantment did not belong on his face, but it was there now, making him look older, and she thought that perhaps bitterness had been beneath the jollity all along, like underlying rock.

"I'll tell you what they're achieving," he was saying. "They're inspiring such a hatred amongst Arabs who used to hate each other that they're combining the greatest force against Christianity the world has ever seen. It's called Islam."

He turned away from her to go into the house. She watched him all the way. Not chubby now—how could she have thought that? Massive.

She heard him calling for ale.

When he came back, he had a tankard in each hand. He held one out to her. "Thirsty work, confession," he said.

Was that what it was? She took the pot and sipped at it, unable to move her eyes away from him, knowing with a dreadful clarity that whatever sin it was he had to confess, she would absolve him of it.

He stood looking down at her. "I had William Plantagenet's little sword on my back for four years," he said. "I wore it under my mail so that it should not be damaged when I fought. I took it into battle, out of it. It scarred my skin so deep that I'm marked with a cross, like the ass that carried Jesus into Jerusalem. The only scar I'm proud of." He squinted. "Do you want to see it?"

She smiled back at him. "Perhaps not now."

You are a drab, she told herself, *seduced into infatuation by a soldier's tale. Outremer, bravery, crusade, it is illusory romance. Pull yourself together, woman.*

"Later, then," he said. He sipped his ale and sat down. "Where was I? Oh, yes. By this time we were on our way to Alexandria. We had to prevent Nur-ad-Din from building his ships in the ports along the Egyptian coast; not, mind you, that the Saracens have taken to sea warfare yet—there's an Arab proverb that it is better to hear the flatulence of camels than the prayers of fishes—but they will one day. So there we were, fighting our way through the Sinai."

Sand, heat, the wind the Moslems called *khamsin* scouring the eye-

balls. Attacks coming out of nowhere by Scythian mounted archers—
"Like damned centaurs they were, loosing arrows at us thick as a locust
swarm so that men and horses ended up looking like hedgehogs."
Thirst.

And in the middle of it, Guiscard falling sick, very sick.

"He'd rarely been ill in his life, and he was all at once frightened by
his own mortality—he didn't want to die in a foreign land. 'Carry me
home, Rowley,' he said, 'Promise to take me to Anjou.' So I promised
him."

On behalf of his sick lord, Rowley had knelt to the King of Jerusalem to beg for and be granted leave to return to France. "Truth to
tell, I was glad. I was tired of the killing. Is this what the Lord Christ
came to earth for? I kept asking myself that. And the thought of the
little boy in his tomb waiting for his sword was beginning to trouble
my sleep. Even so . . ."

He drank the last of his ale, then shook his head, tired. "Even so,
the guilt when I said good-bye . . . I felt a traitor. I swear to you, I'd
never have left with the war unwon if it hadn't fallen to me to see
Guiscard home."

No, she thought, *you wouldn't. But why apologize? You are alive, and so are the
men you would have killed if you had stayed. Why feel more shame for leaving such a
war than pursuing it? Perhaps it is the brute in men—and dear heaven, it is certainly
the base brute in me that I thrill to it.*

He had begun organizing the journey back. "I knew it wouldn't be
easy," he said. "We were deep in the White Desert at a place called Baharia, a biggish settlement for an oasis, but if God has ever heard of it,
I'll be surprised. I intended to head back west to strike the Nile and
sail up to Alexandria—it was still in friendly hands then—and take
passage to Italy from there. But apart from the Scythian cavalry, assas-
sins behind every bloody bush, wells poisoned, there were our own
dear Christian outlaws looking for booty—and over the years, Guiscard had acquired so many relics and jewels and samite that we were

going to be traveling with a pack train two hundred yards long, just asking to be raided."

So he'd taken hostages.

Adelia's tankard jerked in her hand. "You took hostages?"

"Of course I did." He was irritated. "It's the accepted thing out there. Not for ransom as we do in the West, you understand. In Outremer, hostages are security."

They were a guarantee, he said, a contract, a living form of good faith, a promise that an agreement would be kept, part and parcel of the diplomacy and cultural exchange between different races. Frankish princesses as young as four years old were handed over to ensure an alliance between their Christian fathers and Moorish captors. The sons of great sultans lived in Frankish households, sometimes for years, as warranty for their family's good behavior.

"Hostages save bloodshed," he said. "They're a fine idea. Say you're besieged in a city and want to make terms with the besiegers. Very well, you demand hostages to ensure that the bastards don't come in raping and killing and that the surrender takes place without reprisals. Then again, suppose you have to pay a ransom but can't raise all the cash immediately, ergo you offer hostages as collateral for the rest. Hostages are used for just about anything. When Emperor Nicepheros wanted to borrow the services of an Arab poet for his court, he gave hostages to the poet's caliph, Harun al-Rashid, as surety that the man would be returned in good order. They're like pawnbrokers' pledges."

She shook her head in wonder. "Does it work?"

"To perfection." He thought about it. "Well, nearly always. I never heard of a hostage paying the penalty while I was there, though I gather the early crusaders could be somewhat hasty."

He was eager to reassure her. "It's an excellent thing, you see. Keeps the peace, helps both sides understand each other. Those Moorish baths now—we men of the West would never have known about them if some high-born hostage hadn't demanded that one be installed."

Adelia wondered how the system worked in reverse. What did the European knights, of whose cleanliness she had no great opinion, teach their captors in return?

But she knew this was wandering from the point. The narrative was slowing. *He doesn't want to arrive at it,* she thought. *I don't want him to, either; it will be terrible.*

"So I took hostages," he said.

She watched his fingers crease the tunic on his knees.

He had sent an emissary to Al-Hakim Biamrallah at Farafra, a man who ruled over most of the route he would have to take.

"Hakim was of the Fatimid persuasion, you see, a Shia, and the Fatimids were taking our side against Nur-ad-Din, who wasn't." He cocked an eye at her. "I told you it was complicated."

With the emissary had gone gifts and a request for hostages to ensure the safe passage of Guiscard, his men, and pack animals to the Nile.

"That's where we were going to leave them. The hostages. Hakim's men would pick them up from there."

"I see," she said very gently.

"Cunning old fox, Hakim," Rowley said in tribute, one cunning fox to another. "White beard down to here but more wives than you could shake a stick at. He and I had already met several times on the march; we'd gone hunting together. I liked him."

Adelia, still watching Rowley's hands, nice hands, grip and grip again like a raptor's on a wrist. "And he agreed?"

"Oh, yes, he agreed."

The emissary had returned minus the gifts and plus hostages, two of them, both boys: Ubayd, Hakim's nephew, and Jaafar, one of his sons. "Ubayd was nearly twelve, I think; Jaafar . . . Jaafar was eight, his father's favorite."

There was a pause, and the tax collector's voice became remote. "Pleasant boys, well-mannered, like all Saracen children. Excited to be hostages for their uncle and father. It gave them status. They regarded it as an adventure."

The large hands curved, showing bone beneath the knuckles. "An adventure," he said again.

The gate to the sheriff's garden creaked and two men came in carrying spades, and walked past Sir Rowley and Adelia with a tug of their caps and on down the path to the cherry tree. They began digging.

Without comment, the man and woman on the turf bench turned their heads to watch as if observing shapes across a distance, nothing to do with them, something happening in another place entirely.

Rowley was relieved that Hakim had sent not only mule and camel drivers to help with Guiscard's goods but also a couple of warriors as guards. "By this time, our own party of knights was diminished. James Selkirk and D'Aix had been killed at Antioch; Gerard De Nantes died in a tavern brawl. The only ones left of the original group were Guiscard and Conrad De Vries and myself."

Guiscard, too weak to mount a horse, rode in a palanquin that could go only at the pace of the slaves who carried it, so it was a long, slow train that began the journey across the parched countryside—and Guiscard's condition worsened to the point where they couldn't go on.

"We were midway, as far to go back as to continue, but one of Hakim's men knew of an oasis a mile or so off the track, so we took Guiscard there and pitched our pavilions. Tiny place it was, empty, a few date palms, but, by a miracle, its spring was sweet. And that's where he died."

"I am sorry," Adelia said. The dreariness descending on the man beside her was almost palpable.

"So was I, very." He lifted his head. "No time to sit and weep, though. You of all people know what happens to bodies, and in that heat it happens fast. By the time we reached the Nile, the corpse would have been . . . well."

On the other hand, Guiscard had been a lord of Anjou, uncle to Henry Plantagenet, not some vagabond to be buried in a nameless hole scratched out of Egyptian grit. His people would need something of him returned over which to perform the funeral rites. "Besides, I'd promised him to take him home."

It was then, Rowley said, that he made the mistake that would pursue him to the grave. "May God forgive me, I split our forces."

For the sake of speed, he decided to leave the two young hostages where they were while he and De Vries with a couple of servants made a dash back to Baharia, carrying the corpse with them in the hope of finding an embalmer.

"We were in Egypt, after all, and Herodotus goes into quite disgusting detail on how the Egyptians preserve their dead."

"You read Herodotus?"

"His Egyptian stuff, very informative about Egypt is Herodotus."

Bless him, she thought, *prancing about the desert with a thousand-year-old guide.*

He went on. "They were content with the situation, the boys, quite happy. They had Hakim's two warriors to guard them, plenty of servants, slaves. I gave them Guiscard's splendid bird to fly while we were away—they were keen falconers, both. Food, water, pavilions, shelter at night. And I did everything I could; I sent one of the Arab servants to Hakim to tell him what had occurred and where the boys were, just in case anything happened to me."

A list of excuses to himself; he must have gone over it a thousand times. "I thought we were the ones taking the risk, De Vries and I, being just the two of us. The boys should have been safe enough." He turned to her as if he would shake her. *"It was their damned country."*

"Yes," Adelia said.

From the bottom of the garden where the men were digging Simon's grave came the regular scrape and scatter, scrape and scatter, of earth being lifted and discarded. They might have been three thousand miles away from the crucible of hot sand in which, by now, she could barely breathe.

A harness had been constructed to carry the palanquin containing Guiscard's corpse between a couple of pack animals and, with only two mule drivers as accompaniment, Sir Rowley Picot and his fellow knight had ridden with it as fast as they could.

"It turned out there wasn't an embalmer in Baharia, but I found some old shaman who cut the heart out for me and put it in pickle while the rest was boiled down to the skeleton."

That had proved a lengthier process than Rowley was expecting, but at last, with Guiscard's bones in a satchel and the heart in a stoppered jar, he and De Vries had set off back to the oasis, approaching it eight days after they'd left it.

"We saw the vultures while we were still three miles off. The camp had been raided. All the servants were dead. Hakim's warriors had given a good account of themselves before they were hacked to pieces, and there were three bodies belonging to the raiders. The pavilions had gone, the slaves, the goods, the animals."

In the terrible desert silence, the two knights heard a whimper coming from the top of one of the date palms. It was Ubayd, the older boy, alive and physically unhurt. "The attack had been at night, you see, and in the darkness he and one of the slaves had managed to shin up a tree and hide in the fronds. The boy had been there a day and two nights. De Vries had to climb up and unhook his hands to get him down. He'd seen everything; he couldn't move."

The one they couldn't find was eight-year-old Jaafar.

"We were still scouring the place for him when Hakim and his men arrived. He'd received news that there was a raiding party loose in the land just about the same time that he'd gotten my message. He'd immediately ridden like a wind from hell for the oasis."

Rowley's great head went down as if to receive coals of fire. "He didn't blame me. Hakim. Not a word, not even later when we found . . . what we found. Ubayd explained, told the old man it wasn't my fault, but these last years I've known whose fault it was. I should never have left them; I should have taken the boys with me. They were my responsibility, you see. My hostages."

Adelia's fingers covered the gripping hands for a moment. He didn't notice.

When, eventually, Ubayd had been able to speak of it, he'd told them that the raiding party had been twenty to twenty-five strong. He'd heard different languages spoken as the slaughter below him went on. "Frankish mainly," he'd said. He'd heard his little cousin cry to Allah for help.

"We tracked them. They had a lead of thirty-six hours, but we reckoned that they'd be slowed by all the loot. On the second day we saw the hoofprints of a lone horse that had broken away from the rest and turned south."

Hakim sent some of his men after the raiders' main party while he and Rowley followed the tracks of the single horseman.

"Looking back, I don't know why we did that; the man could have veered off for a dozen reasons. But I think we knew."

They knew when they saw the vultures circling over a single object behind one of the dunes. The naked little body was curled in the sand like a question mark.

Rowley had his eyes shut. "He'd done such things to that little boy as no human being should look on or describe."

I looked on them, Adelia thought. *You were angry when I looked on them in Saint Werbertha's hut. I described them, and I'm sorry. I am so sorry for you.*

"We'd played chess together," Rowley said, "the boy and I. On the journey. He was a clever child, he used to beat me eight times out of ten."

They'd wrapped the body in Rowley's cloak and taken it to

Hakim's palace, where it was buried that night to the sound of ululating, grieving women.

Then the hunt began in earnest. Such a strange chase it was, led by a Moslem chieftain and a Christian knight, skirting battlefields where the crescent and the cross were at war with each other.

"The devil was loose in that desert," Rowley said. "He sent sandstorms against us, obliterating tracks, resting places were waterless and devastated either by crusader or Moor, but nothing was going to stop us, and at long last we caught up with the main party."

Ubayd had been right, it was a ragtag.

"Deserters, mainly, runaways, the prison sweepings of Christendom. Our killer had been their captain, and in carrying off the boy, he'd also taken most of the jewels and abandoned his men to their own devices, which weren't much. They hardly put up any resistance; most of them were silly with hasheesh, and the rest were fighting among themselves over the remaining booty. We questioned each one of them before he died: Where's your leader gone? Who is he? Where does he come from? Where will he make for? Not one of them knew much about the man they'd followed. A ferocious leader, they said. A lucky man, they said."

Lucky.

"Nationality means nothing to scum like those; to them he was just another Frank, which means he could have originated anywhere from Scotland to the Baltic. Their descriptions weren't much better, either: tall, medium-height, darkish, fairish—mind you, they were saying anything they thought Hakim wanted to know, but it was as if each saw him differently. One of them said he had horns growing out of his head."

"Did he have a name?"

"They called him Rakshasa. It's the name of a demon. Moors frighten naughty children with it. From what I could gather from Hakim, the Rakshasi came out of the Far East—India, I think. The

Hindus set them on the Moslems in some ancient battle. They take different shapes and ravage people at night."

Adelia leaned out and picked a lavender stalk, rubbing it between her fingers, looking around the garden to root herself in its English greenness.

"He's clever," the tax collector said, and then corrected himself. "No, not clever, he has instinct, he can sniff danger on the air like a rat. He knew we were after him, I know he knew. If he'd made for the Upper Nile, and we were sure he would, we'd have taken him—Hakim had sent word to the Fatimid tribes—but he cut northeast, back into Palestine."

They picked up the scent again in Gaza, where they found he'd sailed from its port of Teda on a boat bound for Cyprus.

"How?" asked Adelia. "How did you pick up his scent?"

"The jewels. He'd taken most of Guiscard's jewels. He was having to sell them one by one to keep ahead of us. Every time he did, word got back through the tribes to Hakim. We were given his description—a tall man, almost as tall as me."

At Gaza, Sir Rowley lost his companions. "De Vries wanted to stay in the Holy Land; anyway, he wasn't under the obligation that I was; Jaafar hadn't been his hostage, and he hadn't taken the decision that got the boy killed. As for Hakim . . . good old man, he wanted to come with me, but I told him he was too ancient and anyway would stick out in Christian Cyprus like a houri among a huddle of monks. Well, I didn't put it like that, though such was the gist. But there and then I knelt to him and vowed by my Lord, by the Trinity, by the Mother Mary, that I'd follow Rakshasa if necessary to the grave and I'd cut the bastard's head off and send it to him. And so, with God's help, I shall."

The tax collector slipped to his knees, took off his cap, and crossed himself.

Adelia sat still as stone, confused by the repulsion and the terrible comfort she found in this man. Some of the loneliness into which she'd been cast by Simon's death had gone. Yet he was not another Simon; he had stood by, perhaps assisted in, questioning the raiders; "questioning" undoubtedly being a euphemism for torture until death, something Simon would not and could not have done. This man had sworn by Jesus, whose attribute was mercy, to exact revenge, was praying for it at this minute.

But when she had covered his clawing hand, the back of her own had been wetted with his tears and, for a moment, the space that Simon had left had been filled by someone whose heart, like Simon's, could break for the child of another race and faith.

She composed herself; he was getting up so that he could pace while he told her the rest.

Just as he had taken her with him on his every step across the wasteland of Outremer, now she went with him as, still carrying his relics of the dead, he followed the man they called Rakshasa back through Europe.

From Gaza to Cyprus. Cyprus to Rhodes—just one boat behind, but a storm had separated chase and chaser so that Rowley had not picked up the trail again until Crete. To Syracuse, and from there up the coast of Apulia. To Salerno . . .

"Were you there then?" he asked.

"Yes, I was there."

To Naples, to Marseilles, and then overland through France.

A more curious passage no man ever took in a Christian country, he told her, because Christians played so little part in it. His helpers were the disregarded: Arabs and Jews, artisans in the jewel trade, trinket makers, pawnbrokers, moneylenders, workers in alleys where Christian townsmen and women sent their servants with objects for mending, ghetto dwellers—the sort of people to whom a pursued and desperate killer with a jewel to sell was forced to apply for money.

"It wasn't the France I knew; I might have been in a different country altogether. I was a blind man in it, and they were my knotted string. They'd ask me, 'Why do you hunt this man?' And I would answer, 'He killed a child.' It was enough. Yes, their cousin, aunt, sister-in-law's son had heard of a stranger in the next town with a bauble to sell—and at a knockdown price, for he must sell it quickly."

Rowley paused. "Are you aware that every Jew and Arab in Christendom seems to know every other Jew and Arab?"

"They have to," Adelia said.

Rowley shrugged. "Anyway, he never stayed anywhere long enough for me to catch up with him. By the time I got to the next town, he'd taken the road north. Always north. I knew he was heading for somewhere particular."

There were other, dreadful knots in the string. "He killed at Rhodes before I got there, a little Christian girl found in a vineyard. The whole island was in uproar." At Marseilles there'd been another death, this time of a beggar boy snatched from the roadside, whose corpse had suffered such injuries that even the authorities, not usually troubled by the fate of vagabonds, had issued a reward for the killer.

In Montpellier another boy, this one only four years old.

Rowley said, "'*By their deeds ye shall know them,*' the Bible tells us. I knew him by his. He marked my map with children's bodies; it was as if he couldn't go more than three months without sating himself. When I lost him, I only had to wait to hear the scream of a parent echoing from one town to another. Then I took horse to follow it."

He also found the women Rakshasa left in his wake. "He has an attraction for women, the Lord only knows why; he doesn't treat them well." All the bruised creatures Rowley had questioned refused to help him in his quest. "They seemed to expect and hope he would come back to them. It didn't matter; by this time, anyway, I was following the bird he had with him."

"A *bird*?"

"A mynah bird. In a cage. I knew where he'd bought it, in a *souq* in

Gaza. I could even tell you how much he paid for it. But *why* he kept it with him . . . perhaps it was his only friend." There was the rictus of a smile on Rowley's face. "It got him noticed, thanks be to God; more than once I received word of a tall man with a birdcage on his saddle. And in the end, it told me where he was going."

By this time hunter and hunted were approaching the Loire Valley, Sir Rowley distracted because Angers was the home of the bones he carried. "Should I follow Rakshasa as I had sworn? Or fulfill my vow to Guiscard and take him to his last resting place?"

It was in Tours, he said, that his dilemma took him to its cathedral to pray for guidance. "And there Almighty God, in His wonder and grace and seeing the justice of my cause, opened His hand unto me."

For, as Rowley left the cathedral by its great west door and went blinking into the sunlight, he heard the squawk of a bird coming from an alley where its cage hung in the window of a house.

"I looked up at it. It looked down at me and said good-day in English. And I thought, the Lord has led me to this alley for a purpose; let us see if this is Rakshasa's pet. So I knocked on the door and a woman opened it. I asked for her man. She said he was out, but I could tell that he was there and that it was him—she was just such a one as the others, draggled and frightened. I drew my sword and pushed past her, but she fought me as I tried to go up the stairs, clinging to my arm like a cat and screaming. I heard him shout from the upstairs room, then a thump. He'd leapt out of the window. I turned back down, but the woman hampered me all the way, and by the time I regained the alley, he'd gone."

Rowley ran his hands over his thick, curly hair in despair at describing the fruitless chase that had followed. "In the end, I went back to the house. The woman had left, but in the upstairs room the bird was fluttering in its cage on the floor where he'd knocked it down as he jumped. I picked the cage up and the bird told me where I would find him."

"How? How did it tell you?"

"Well, it didn't give me his address. It looked at me out of that wattled, cocky eye they have and said I was a pretty boy, a clever boy—all the usual things, their banality made shocking by the knowledge that I was hearing Rakshasa's voice. He had trained it. No, there was nothing special in *what* it said but in *how* it said it. It was the accent. It spoke in a Cambridgeshire accent. The bird had copied the speech of its master. Rakshasa was a Cambridgeshire man."

The tax collector crossed himself in gratitude to the god who had been good to him. "I let the bird prattle through its repertoire," he said. "There was time enough now, I could take Guiscard to Angers. I knew where Rakshasa was heading; he was going home to settle down with what remained of Guiscard's jewels. So he did and so he has, and this time he shall not escape me."

Rowley looked at Adelia. "I've still got the cage," he said.

"What happened to the bird?"

"I wrung its neck."

The gravediggers had left, unnoticed, their work done. The long shadow of the wall at the end of the garden had reached the turf seat.

Adelia, shivering from the chilly descent of evening, realized she had been cold for some time. Perhaps there was more to say, but at the moment she could not think of it. Nor could he. He got up. "I must see to the arrangements."

Others had seen to them for him.

A sheriff, an Arab, a tax collector, an Augustine prior, two women, and a dog stood at the top of the steps outside the house as Simon of Naples in his willow coffin, preceded by torchbearers and followed by every male Jew in the castle, was carried to his place beneath the cherry tree at the other end of the garden. They were invited no nearer. Under a waxing, gibbous moon the figures of the mourners appeared very dark and the cherry blossom very white, a flurry of suspended snow.

The sheriff fidgeted. Mansur put his hands on Adelia's shoulders and she leaned back against him, listening more to the cascade of the rabbi's deep notes as he repeated the ninety-first Psalm than able to distinguish its words.

What she disregarded, what all of them paid no attention to because they were used to a noisy castle, was the sound of raised voices down by the main gates to which Father Alcuin, the priest, had taken his discontent.

There, having listened to it, Agnes had left her hut and run into town, and Roger of Acton had begun to persuade the guards that their castle was being desecrated by the secret burial of a Jew in its precincts.

The mourners under the cherry tree heard it; their ears were attuned to trouble.

"*El ma'aleh rachamim.*" Rabbi Gotsce's voice didn't falter. "*Sho-chayn bahm-ro . . .* Lord, filled with Motherly Compassion, grant a full and perfect rest to our brother Simon under the wings of Your sheltering presence among the lofty, holy, and pure, radiant as the shining firmament, and to the souls of all those of all Your peoples who have been killed in and around the lands where Abraham our Forebear walked. . . ."

Words, thought Adelia. *An innocent bird can repeat the words of a killer. Words can be said over the man he killed and pour balm on the soul.*

She heard the hit, hit, hit of earth being thrown onto the coffin. Now the procession was filing up through the garden to go out of its gate and, although she was not a Jew and a mere woman at that, each man gave her a blessing as he passed the foot of the steps on which she stood. "*Hamakom y'nachem etchem b'toch sh'ar availai tziyon ee yerushalayim.* May God comfort you among all the mourners of Zion and Jerusalem."

The rabbi paused and bowed to the sheriff. "We are grateful for your beneficence, my lord, and may you be spared trouble because of it." Then they were gone.

"Well," Sheriff Baldwin said, brushing his gown, "we must get back to work, Sir Rowley. If the devil does indeed find work for idle hands, he will discover none here tonight."

Adelia expressed her gratitude. "And may I visit the grave tomorrow?"

"I suppose so, I suppose so. You might bring Senor Doctor here with you. All this worry has produced a fistula that makes my sitting uncomfortable."

He looked toward the gate. "What is that turmoil, Rowley?"

It was ten or so men armed with a variety of domestic weapons, garden forks, eel glaives, led by Roger of Acton, and all of them feverish with a rage that had been pent up too long, all rushing into the garden screaming in so many different curses that it took a moment to distinguish the theme of "child-killer" and "Jew."

Acton was coming to the steps, waving a flambeau in one hand and a garden fork in the other. He was shouting. "The Jew shall be sunk in the pit he hath made, for the Lord has redeemed us from his filth. We have come to cast him out from our inheritance. O fear the name of the Lord, thou traitors." His mouth sprayed spit. Behind him, a big man was brandishing a wicked-looking kitchen cleaver.

The other men were scattering in a search and he turned to them. "Find the grave, my brothers, so we may execute our fury upon his carcass. For ye have been promised that he who chastiseth the heathen shall not be corrected."

"No," Adelia said. They had come to dig him up. They had come to dig Simon up. *"No."*

"Trollop." Acton was ascending the steps, the fork pointing at her. "Thou hast gone a-whoring after the child-killers, but we shall not bear thy shame anymore."

One of the men was standing by the cherry tree, shouting and gesticulating at the others. "Here, it's here."

Adelia dodged Acton as she went down the steps and began running toward the grave. What she would do when she got there was not in her mind—she could think only of stopping this terrible thing.

Sir Rowley Picot went after her, Mansur just behind him, Roger of Acton on his heels, the other intruders running to intercept. Everybody met in a crashing, howling, punching, beating, stabbing, trampling confluence. Adelia went down under it.

Such violence was unknown to her; it wasn't the pain but the whacking shock of men's sudden, furious strength. A boot broke her nose; she covered her head while above her the world fractured into jagged pieces.

Somewhere a voice dominated all, steady and commanding—the prior's.

Bit by bit, the shards fell away. There was nothing. Then there was something and she was able to stagger to her feet and see figures retreating from the place were Rowley Picot lay with a cleaver end down in his groin, blood overflowing from around the buried part of its blade.

Twelve

"Am I dead?" asked Sir Rowley of nobody in particular.

"No," Adelia told him.

A weak, pale hand searched beneath the bedclothes. There was a cry of raw agony. "Oh, Jesus God, where's my prick?"

"If you mean your penis, it is still there. Under the pads."

"Oh." The sunken eyes opened again. "Will it work?"

"I am sure," Adelia said clearly, "that it will function satisfactorily in every respect."

"Oh."

He'd gone again, comforted by the brief exchange while unaware that it had taken place.

Adelia leaned over and pulled the blanket straight. "But it was a damned near thing," she told him softly. Not just the loss of his *membrum virilis* but his life. The cleaver had struck the artery, and she'd had to keep her fist in the wound while he was carried indoors to stop him bleeding to death before she could use Lady Baldwin's needle and embroidery thread—and even then to be so hampered by pumping blood that she knew, if none of those gathered anxiously about her did, it was a matter of blind luck whether or not the sutures were in the right place.

That had been only half the battle. She'd managed to extract the pieces of tunic that the cleaver had pushed into the wound, but how much detritus remained from the blade itself had been anyone's throw of the dice. Foreign matter could, and usually did, lead to poisoning, which led to death. She'd recalled dismembering resultant gangrenous corpses—recalled, too, the remote curiosity with which she'd looked for the site that had spread its fatality.

This time she had not been remote. When Rowley's wound inflamed and he went into delirium from fever she had never prayed so hard in her life as she bathed him in cold water and dripped cooling draughts between lips that were flaccid and ghastly as a dead man's.

And to what had she prayed? Something, anything. Pleading, begging, *demanding* that it should help her pull him back to life.

Damn it. What had she vowed to all the gods she'd called on? Belief? Then she was now a follower of Jehovah, Allah, and the Trinity, with Hippocrates thrown in, and had wept with gratitude to all of them as the sweat broke out on the patient's face and his breathing returned from stertor to a soft and natural snore.

The next time he woke up, she watched his hand make its instinctive exploration. Such primitive beings, men.

"Still there." The eyes closed with relief.

"Yes," she said. Even facing death's portals, they retained consciousness of their sexuality. Prick, indeed—such an aggressive euphemism.

The eyes opened. "You still here?"

"Yes."

"How long?"

"Five nights and . . ." She looked toward the window, where the afternoon sun was sending stripes of light through its mullions onto the floorboards. "Approximately seven hours."

"So long? Blind me." He tried lifting his head. "Where is this?"

"The top of the tower." Shortly after the operation, which had been performed on the sheriff's kitchen table, Mansur had carried the patient to the Jews' upper room—an amazing feat of strength—so that doctor and patient should have privacy and quiet while she engaged in the battle for his life.

The room had no garderobe; on the other hand, Adelia had been blessed with people willing—nay, eager—to go up and down the stair carrying chamber pots, most of them Jewish women grateful to Sir Rowley for his defense of a Jewish grave. Indeed, saving Sir Rowley had been a cooperative effort, and if Adelia had refused most of the help on offer, it was in order not to offend Mansur and Gyltha, who made the cause their own.

A breeze came through the room's unglazed windows, free of the bad airs circulating at the lower level of the castle and its open cesspits, sullied only by a whiff of Safeguard that entered through the gap under the door to the stairs, to which he had been banished. Even after a bath, the dog's pelt almost immediately acquired a stink that attacked the nose. It was the only thing about him that did attack; he had been notably absent from the melee in the sheriff's garden, in which, by rights, he should have involved himself on his mistress's behalf.

The voice from the bed asked now, "Did I kill the bastard?"

"Roger of Acton? No, he is well, though incarcerated in the donjon. You managed to lame Quincy the butcher and hack Colin of Saint Giles in the neck, and there's a blacksmith whose prospects of fatherhood are not as sanguine as your own, but Master Acton escaped unharmed."

"*Merde.*"

Even this much conversation had tired him; he drifted off.

Copulation as the first priority, she thought. *Battle as the second. And although you are now considerably thinner, gluttony has been in evidence, so has arrogance.*

That represents most of the cardinal sins. So why, out of all humanity, are you the one for me?

Gyltha had guessed. At the height of Rowley's fever, when Adelia had refused to let the housekeeper replace her at the bedside, Gyltha had said, "Love un you may, woman, but that'll not help un iffen you drop."

"Love him?" It was a screech. "I am caring for a patient; he's not . . . oh, Gyltha, what am I to do? He's not my sort of man."

"What sort's got bugger-all to do with it," Gyltha had said, sighing.

And, indeed, Adelia was compelled to confess that it hadn't.

True, there was much to be said for him. As he had demonstrated for the Jews, he was an incipient defender of the defenseless. He was funny, he made her laugh. And in his fever, he had visited again and again the dune where a child's torn body lay—to suffer once more the same guilt and grief. His mind had pursued the killer through a delirium as hot and terrible as desert sands until Adelia had fed him an opiate for fear that it would wear out the weakened body.

But there was as much to be said against him. In the same fever he had babbled with carnal appreciation of the women he had known, often confusing their attributes with food he'd also enjoyed in the East. Small, slender Sagheerah, tender as an asparagus spear; Samina, sufficiently fleshed for a full-course meal; Abda, black and beautiful as caviar. It had been not so much a list as a menu. As for Zabidah . . . Adelia's narrow knowledge of what men and women got up to in bed had been stretched to shocked amazement by the antics of that acrobatic and communally minded female.

More chilling was the revelation of a driving ambition. At first Adelia, listening to the fantastical conversations he was holding with an unseen person, had mistaken his frequent use of "my lord" as being directed at his heavenly king—until it turned out he was referring to Henry II. The compelling need to find and punish Rakshasa had allied itself to serving the King of England at the same time. If he should

rid Henry of a nuisance that was depriving the Exchequer of its income from Cambridge's Jews, Rowley expected royal gratitude and
advancement.

Very considerable advancement, too. "Baron or bishop?" he would
ask in his dementia, clutching at Adelia's hand as it tried to soothe
him, as if it were her decision. "Bishopric or barony?"

The golden prospect of either would add to his agitation—"It
won't move, I can't move it"—as if the wagon he had attached to the
royal star was proving too heavy to stir.

Such, then, was the man. Undoubtedly brave and compassionate
but a gourmandizing, womanizing, cunning, and greedy seeker after
status. Imperfect, licentious. Not a man Adelia had expected, or
wanted, to love.

But did.

When that suffering head had turned on the pillow, exposing the
line of the throat, and he had pleaded for her—"Doctor, are you there?
Adelia?"—his sins, like her heart, had melted away.

As Gyltha said, the sort of man he was had bugger-all to do with it.

Yet it *must* matter. Vesuvia Adelia Rachel Ortese Aguilar had her
own fixity of purpose. It did not aspire to preferment or riches but to
serving the particular gift she had been given. For a gift it was, and with
it had come the obligation not to give birth to life as other women did
but to discover more about life's nature and thereby save it.

She had always known, and still knew it, that romantic love was not
for her; in that respect, she was as bound to chastity as any nun married to God. As long as that chastity had been cloistered in the Medical School of Salerno, she had envisaged its untroubled continuance
into a quiet, useful, and respected old age, contemptuous—she admitted it—of women who surrendered to flailing passion.

Sitting in this tower room, she accused that former self of plain
damned ignorance. *You didn't know.* Didn't know of this rampage that
makes the mind lose its reason against all better judgment.

But you must *reason, woman,* reason.

The hours during which she had labored to save the man had been a privilege; saving anybody's life was a privilege; his, her joy. She had begrudged being called away from his side to treat the patients whom the Matildas redirected to the castle so that she and Mansur could heal them, though she had done it.

Now it was time for common sense.

Marriage was out of the question, even supposing he offered it, which was unlikely. Adelia had a strong estimation of her own worth, but she doubted it if he could recognize it. For one thing, to judge from the color of the pubic hair he had described during his more lubricious ravings, his preference was for brunettes. For another, she could not—would not—enter the lists against the likes of Zabidah.

No, a reserved, plain-faced woman doctor was unlikely to attract him; such yearning as he had shown for her in his fever had been a request for relief.

In any case, he thought of her as sexless or his account of his crusade would not have been so frank and so full of swear words. A man talked to a friendly priest in those terms, to a Prior Geoffrey perhaps, not to the lady of his fancy.

In any case, with a bishopric in his sights, he could not offer marriage to anybody. And a bishop's mistress? There were plenty of them, some being ostentatious, shameless strumpets, others a rumor, a thing of gossip and sniggers, hidden away in a secret bower, dependent on the whim of their particular diocesan lover.

Welcome to the Gates of Heaven, Adelia, and what did you do with your life? My lord, I was a bishop's whore.

And if he became a baron? He would look for an heiress to increase his estates, as they all did. Poor heiress, a life devoted to store cupboard, children, entertaining, and setting one's husband's bloody deeds to song when he came back from whatever battlefield his king had dragged him off to. Where, undoubtedly, said husband had taken other

women—brunettes, in this case—and fathered bastards on them with
the concupiscence of a rutting rabbit.

Deliberately, exhausted, she worked herself into such a fury at the
hypothetically adulterous Sir Rowley Picot with his hypothetical and
illegitimate brats that, Gyltha now coming into the room with a bowl
of gruel for him, Adelia told her, "You and Mansur look after the
swine tonight. I'm going home."

Yehuda waylaid her at the bottom of the steps to inquire after
Rowley and to drag her off to see his new son. The baby nuzzling at
Dina's breast was tiny but seemed to have all its requisites, though its
parents were concerned that it was not gaining sufficient weight.

"We've agreed with Rabbi Gotsce that Brit Mila should be delayed
beyond the eight days. Do it when he is stronger," Yehuda said, anxiously. "What do you think, mistress?"

Adelia said that it was probably wise not to subject the child to cir-
cumcision until it was a better size.

"Is it my milk, do you think?" Dina said. "I don't have enough?"

Midwifery was not Adelia's field; she knew the principles, but
Gordinus had always taught his students that the practice was better
left to wise women of whatever denomination unless there were com-
plications in the case. His belief, based on observation, was that more
babies survived when delivered by experienced women than by male
doctors. It was not a teaching that made him popular with either the
general medical profession or the Church, both of which found it
profitable to condemn most midwives as witches, but the death toll in
Salerno not only among babies but their mothers whose accouche-
ment had been attended by male physicians suggested that Gordinus
was right.

However, the baby *was* very small and seemed to be sucking without profit, so Adelia ventured, "Have you considered a wet nurse?"

"And where do we find one of those?" Yehuda demanded with an
Iberian sneer. "Did the mob that drove us in here make sure we had

lactating mothers among our number? They overlooked it, I don't know why."

Adelia hesitated before saying, "I could ask Lady Baldwin if there is one in the castle."

She waited for condemnation. Margaret had originally been her wet nurse, and Adelia knew of other Christian women employed in that capacity by Jewish households, but whether this stiff-necked little enclave would contemplate its newest recruit being put to a goy's breast . . .

Dina surprised her. "Milk's milk, my husband. I would trust Lady Baldwin to find a clean woman."

Yehuda put his hand gently on his wife's head. "As long as she understands that it is not your fault. With all you have suffered, we are lucky to have a son at all."

Oh ho, Adelia thought, *fatherhood is improving you, young man.* And Dina, though anxious, looked happier than the last time she'd seen her; this had the makings of a better marriage than its beginning had promised.

As she left them, Yehuda followed her out. "Doctor . . ."

Adelia turned on him fast. "You must not call me that. The doctor is Master Mansur Khayoun of Al 'Amarah. I am but his helper."

Obviously, the tale of the operation in the sheriff's kitchen had circulated, and she had enough troubles without the inevitable opposition she would encounter from Cambridge's physicians, let alone the Church, if her profession became generally recognized.

Perhaps she could put down the presence of Mansur—he had stood by during the procedure—to that of a master overseeing the work. Claim it had been a Moslem holy day and that Allah wouldn't allow him to touch blood during its hours. Something like that.

Yehuda bowed. "Mistress, I only wish to say that we are naming the baby Simon."

She took his hand. "Thank you."

Though still tired, the day altered for her; life itself had altered with a swing. She felt, quite literally, uplifted by the naming of the child—she experienced a curious feeling of bobbing.

It was being in love, she realized. Love, however doomed, had the capacity to attach buoys to the soul. Never had seagulls circled with such purity against the eggshell-blue sky, never had their cries been so thrilling.

Visiting the other Simon was a priority, and on her way to the sheriff's garden, Adelia toured the bailey, looking for flowers to take to his grave. This part of the castle was strictly utilitarian, and its roaming hens and pigs had stripped it of most vegetation, but some Jack-by-the-hedge had colonized the top of an old wall and a blackthorn was flowering on the Saxon mound where the original wooden keep had stood.

Children were sliding down the slope on a plank of wood, and while she painfully snapped off some twigs, a small boy and girl came up to chat.

"What's that?"

"It's my dog," Adelia told them.

They considered the statement and animal for a moment. Then, "That blackie you come with, lady, is he a wizard?"

"A doctor," she told them.

"Is he mending Sir Rowley, lady?"

"He's funny, Sir Rowley," the little girl said. "He says it's a mouse in his hand but it's a farthing really, what he gives us. I like him."

"So do I," Adelia said helplessly, finding it sweet to make the confession.

The boy said, pointing, "That's Sam and Bracey. Shouldn't have let 'em in, should they? Not even to kill Jews, my pa says."

He was indicating to a spot near the new gallows on which stood a double pillory with two heads protruding from it, presumably those of the guards on the gate when Roger of Acton and the townspeople had gained entrance to the castle.

"Sam says he didn't mean to let them in," the girl said. "Sam says the buggers rushed him."

"Oh, dear," Adelia said. "How long have they been there?"

"Shouldn't have let 'em in, should they?" the boy said.

The little girl was more forgiving. "They free 'em of nights."

So bad for the back, the pillory. Adelia hurried over to it. A wooden sign had been hung about each man's neck. It read: "Failed in Duty."

Carefully avoiding the ordure that was collecting round the feet of the pillory's victims, Adelia placed her posy on the ground and lifted one of the signs. She settled the guard's jerkin so that it formed a buffer between his skin and the string that had been cutting into his neck. She did the same for the other man. "I hope that's more comfortable."

"Thank you, mistress." Both stared straight ahead with military directness.

"How much longer must you remain here?"

"Two more days."

"Oh, dear," Adelia said. "I know it cannot be easy, but if you let your wrists take the weight from time to time and incline your legs backwards, it will reduce the strain on the spine."

One of the men said flatly, "We'll bear it in mind, mistress."

"Do."

In the sheriff's garden, the sheriff's wife, who was at one end overseeing the division of tansy roots, was holding a shouted conversation with Rabbi Gotsce at the other, where he bent over the grave.

"You should wear it in your shoes, Rabbi. I do. Tansy is a specific against the ague." Lady Baldwin's voice carried effortlessly to the ramparts.

"Better than garlic?"

"Infinitely better."

Charmed and unseen, Adelia lingered in the gateway until Lady

Baldwin caught sight of her. "There you are, Adelia. And how is Sir Rowley today?"

"Improving. I thank you, ma'am."

"Good, good. We cannot spare such a brave fighter. And what of your poor nose?"

Adelia smiled. "Mended and forgotten." The race to halt Rowley's hemorrhage had obliterated everything else. She'd only become aware of the fracture to her nose two days later, when Gyltha commented on the fact that it had become humped and blue. Once the swelling went down, she'd clicked the bone into place without trouble.

Lady Baldwin nodded. "What a pretty posy, very green and white. The rabbi is seeing to the grave. Go down, go down. Yes, the dog too—if that's what it is."

Adelia went down the path to the cherry tree. A simple wooden board had been laid over the grave. Carved into it was the Hebrew for "Here lies buried" followed by Simon's name. On the bottom were the five letters for "May his soul be bound up in the bond of life eternal."

"It will do for now," Rabbi Gotsce said. "Lady Baldwin is finding us a stone to replace it, one that's too heavy to lift, she says, so Simon cannot be desecrated." He stood up and dusted his hands. "Adelia, that is a fine woman."

"Yes, she is." Much more than the sheriff's, this was his wife's garden; it was where her children played and from which she took the herbs to flavor her food and scent her rooms. It had been no mean sacrifice to surrender part of it to the corpse of a man despised by her religion. Admittedly, since this was ultimately royal ground, it had been imposed on her force majeure, but whatever she felt in private, Lady Baldwin had acceded with grace.

Better still, the principle that giving imposes obligation on the giver as well as the recipient had come into play, and Lady Baldwin was showing concern for the welfare of the strange community in her castle. The newest little Baldwin's baby clouts had been passed on to Dina and the suggestion made that the community should have a share in the castle's great bread oven instead of baking for themselves.

"They're really human beings just like us, you know," Lady Baldwin had lectured Adelia when visiting the sickroom bearing calf's-foot jelly for the patient. "And their rabbi is quite knowledgeable on the subject of herbs, really quite knowledgeable. Apparently they eat a lot of them at Easter, though they seem to choose the bitter ones, horseradish and such. Why not a little angelica, I asked him. To sweeten it up?"

Smiling, Adelia had said, "I think they're supposed to be bitter."

"Yes, so he told me."

Now, asked if she knew of a wet nurse for Baby Simon, Lady Baldwin promised to supply one. "And not one of the castle trollops, either," she said. "That baby needs *respectable* Christian milk."

The only one who had failed Simon, Adelia thought as she placed her posy, was herself. His name on the simple board should shriek of murder instead of portraying a supposed victim of his own negligence.

"Help me, Rabbi," she said. "I must write to Simon's family and tell his wife and children he is dead."

"So write," Rabbi Gotsce said. "We shall see to sending the letter; we have people in London who correspond with Naples."

"Thank you, I would be grateful. It's not that, it's . . . *what* shall I write? That he was murdered but his death has been recorded as an accident?"

The rabbi grunted. "If you were his wife, what would you want to know?"

She said immediately, "The truth." Then she considered. "Oh, I don't know." Better for Simon's Rebecca to grieve over a drowning accident than to envisage again and again Simon's last minutes as she did, to have her mourning polluted by horror, as was Adelia's, to desire justice on his killer so much that she could not take ease in anything else.

"I suppose I shall not tell them," she said, defeated. "Not while he is unavenged. When the killer is found and punished, perhaps then we can give them the truth."

"The truth, Adelia? So simple?"

"Isn't it?"

Rabbi Gotsce sighed. "To you, maybe. But as the Talmud tells us, the name of Mount Sinai comes from our Hebrew word for hatred, *sinah,* because truth produces hate for those who speak it. Now, Jeremiah . . ."

Oh, dear, she thought. *Jeremiah, the weeping prophet.* None of the slow, worldly-wise, clever Jewish voices lecturing in the sunlit atrium of her foster parents' villa had ever mentioned Jeremiah without prophesying evil. And it was such a nice day, and there was beautiful detail in the flowers of the cherry blossom.

". . . we should remember the old Jewish proverb that truth is the safest lie."

"I've never understood it," she said, coming to.

"No more have I," the rabbi said. "But by extension it tells us that the rest of the world never wholly believes a Jewish truth. Adelia, do you think that sooner or later the real killer will be revealed and condemned?"

"Sooner or later," she said. "God send it be sooner."

"Amen to that. And on that happy day, the good people of Cambridge will line up outside this castle, weeping and sorry, so sorry, for killing two Jews and keeping the rest imprisoned? That also you believe? The news will speed through Christendom that Jews do not crucify children for their pleasure? You believe that, too?"

"Why not? It is the truth."

Rabbi Gotsce shrugged. "It's your truth, it's mine, it was truth for the man who lies here. Maybe even the townsfolk of Cambridge will believe it. But truth travels slowly and gets weaker as it goes. Suitable lies are strong and run faster. And this was a suitable lie; Jews put the

Lamb of God to the cross, therefore they crucify children—it fits. A nice, agreeable lie like that, it scampers through all Christendom. Will the villages in Spain believe the truth if it limps so far? Will the peasants of France? Russia?"

"Don't, Rabbi. Oh, don't." It was as if this man had lived a thousand years; perhaps he had.

He bent to remove a piece of blossom from the grave and stood up again, taking her arm and walking her to the gate. "Find the killer, Adelia. Deliver us from this English Egypt. But in the end, it will still be the Jews who crucified that child."

Find the killer, she thought as she went down the hill. *Find the killer, Adelia. No matter that Simon of Naples is dead and Rowley Picot is out of action, leaving only me and Mansur. Mansur doesn't speak the language and I am a doctor, not a bloodhound. And that's on top of the fact that we're the only people who think there is a killer yet to be found.*

The ease with which Roger of Acton had enlisted recruits for his attack on the castle garden showed that Cambridge still believed the Jews to be responsible for ritual murder, despite the fact that they were incarcerated when three of the killings had been committed. Logic played no part in it; the Jews were feared because they were different and, for the townspeople, that fear and difference endowed supernatural ability. The Jews had killed Little Saint Peter, ergo they had killed the others.

Despite this, despite the rabbi and Jeremiah, despite grief for Simon, her decision to renounce carnal love and pursue science in chastity, the day persisted in presenting itself as beautiful to her.

What is this? I am extended, stretched thin, vulnerable to death and other people's pain but also to life in its infinite width.

The town and its people swam in pale gold effervescence like the wine from Champagne. A bunch of students touched their caps to her. She was forgiven the toll for the bridge when, fumbling in her pocket for a halfpenny, it was found that she didn't have one. "Oh, get on, then, and good day to you," the tollman said. On the bridge itself, carters raised their whips in salute to her, pedestrians smiled.

Taking the longer way along the riverbank to Old Benjamin's house, willow fronds brushed her in good fellowship and fish came to the surface of the river in bubbles that responded to those in her veins.

There was a man on Old Benjamin's roof. He waved at her. Adelia waved back.

"Who is that?"

"Gil the thatcher," Matilda B. told her. "Reckons his foot's better and reckons there's a tile or two on that roof as needs fixing."

"He's doing it for nothing?"

"A'course for nothing," Matilda said, winking. "Doctor mended his foot for un, didn't he?'

Adelia had put down as bad manners the lack of gratitude shown by Cambridge patients who rarely, if ever, said they were obliged for the treatment they received from Dr. Mansur and his assistant. Usually, they left the room looking as surly as when they'd arrived, in sharp contrast to Salernitan patients who would spend five minutes in her praise.

But as well as the mending of the tiles, there was to be duck for dinner, provided by the woman, whose growing blindness was at least made less miserable by eyes that no longer suppurated. A pot of honey, a clutch of eggs, a pat of butter, and a crock of a repellent-looking something that turned out to be samphire, all left wordlessly at the kitchen door, suggested that Cambridge folk had more concrete ways of saying thank you.

Something important was lacking. "Where's Ulf?"

Matilda B. pointed toward the river where, under an alder, the top of a dirty brown cap was just apparent above the reeds. "Catching trout for supper, but tell Gyltha as we're keeping an eye on un. We told un he's not to shift from that spot. Not for jujubes, not for nobody."

Matilda W. said, "He's missed you."

"I missed him." And it was true; even in the fury to save Rowley Pi-cot, she had regretted her absence from the boy and sent him mes-sages. She had almost wept over the bunch of primroses tied with a bit of string that he had sent her via Gyltha, "to say he was sorry for your loss." This new love she felt radiated outward in its incandescence; with the death of Simon, its glow fell on those whom, she realized now, had become necessary to her well-being, not least the small boy sitting and scowling on an upturned bucket among the reeds of the Cam with a homemade fishing line in his grubby hands.

"Move over," she told him. "Let a lady sit down."

Grudgingly, he shifted and she took his place. To judge from the number of trout thrashing in the creel, Ulf had picked the spot well; not actually on the Cam proper, he was fishing a stream that welled in the reeds and cut through the silt, forming a decent-sized channel be-fore reaching the river.

Compared with the King's Ditch on the other side of town, a stinking and mostly stagnant dike that had once served to repel invad-ing Danes, the Cam itself was clean, but the fastidious Adelia, though perforce she ate them on Fridays, entertained a suspicion of fish from a river that received effluent from humans and cattle as it meandered through the county's southern villages.

She appreciated Ulf's choice of springwater into which to make his casts. She sat in silence for a while, watching the fish move, sliding through the water, as clear as if they swam in air. Dragonflies flashed, gemlike, among the reeds.

"How's Rowley-Powley?" It was a sneer.

"Better, and don't be rude."

He grunted and got on with his fishing.

"What worms are you using?" she asked politely. "They work well."

"These?" He spat. "Wait til the hangings when the 'sizes start, then you'll see proper worms, take any fish they will."

Unwisely, she asked, "What have hangings to do with it?"

"Best worms is them under a gallows with a rotting corpse on it. I thought ev'body knew that. Take any fish, gallows' worms will. Di'n't you know that?"

She hadn't and wished she didn't. He was punishing her.

"You're going to have to talk to me," she said. "Master Simon is dead, Sir Rowley's laid up. I need someone who thinks to help me find the killer—and you're a thinker, Ulf, you know you are."

"Yes, I bloody am."

"And don't swear."

More silence.

He was using a float, a curious contraption of his own invention that ran his line through a large bird's quill so that the bait and tiny iron hooks were kept to the surface of the water.

"I missed you," she said.

"Huh." If she thought that was going to placate him . . . but after a while he said, "Do we reckon as he drowned Master Simon?"

"Yes. I know he did."

Another trout rose to a worm, was unhooked, and thrown into the creel. "It's the river," he said.

"What do you mean?" Adelia sat up.

For the first time, he looked at her. The small face was screwed up in concentration. "It's the river. That's what takes 'em. I been asking about . . ."

"*No.*" She almost screamed it. "Ulf, whatever . . . you mustn't, you must not. Simon was asking questions. Promise me, *promise* me."

He looked at her with contempt. "All I done was talk to the kin. No harm in that, is there? Was *he* a-listening when I done it? Turns hisself into cra and perches on trees, does he?"

A crow. Adelia shivered. "I wouldn't put it past him."

"That's dizzy talk. You want to know or not?"

"I want to know."

He pulled in his line and detached it from rod and float, arranged both carefully in the wicker box that East Anglians called a frail, then sat cross-legged facing Adelia, like a small Buddha about to deliver enlightenment.

"Peter, Harold, Mary, Ulric," he said. "I talked with their kin, the which nobody else seems to have listened to. Each of un, *each of un,* was seen last at the Cam here or heading for un."

Ulf lifted a finger. "Peter? By the river." He lifted another. "Mary? She was Jimmer the wildfowler's young un—Hugh Hunter's niece— and what was she about, last seen? Deliverin' a pail o' fourses to her pa in the sedge up along Trumpington way."

Ulf paused. "Jimmer was one of them rushed the castle gates. Still blames the Jews for Mary, Jimmer does."

So Mary's father had been among that terrible group of men with Roger of Acton. Adelia remembered that the man was a bully and, quite probably, easing his own guilt for the treatment of his daughter by attacking the Jews.

Ulf continued with his list. He jerked a thumb upriver. "Harold?" A frown of pain. "Eel seller's boy, Harold'd gone for water as to put the elvers in. Disappeared . . ." Ulf leaned forward. *"Making for the Cam."*

Her eyes were on his. "And Ulric?"

"Ulric," said Ulf, "lived with his ma and sisters on Sheep's Green. Taken Saint Edward's Day. And what day was Saint Edward's last?"

Adelia shook her head.

"Monday." He sat back.

"Monday?"

He shook his head at her ignorance. "You frimmocking me? Wash-day, woman. Mondays is washday. I talked to his sister. Run out of rainwater to boil, they had, so Ulric was sent with a yoke o' pails . . ."

"Down to the river," she finished for him in a whisper.

They stared at each other and then, together, turned their heads to look toward the Cam.

It was full; there had been heavy rain during the week; Adelia had shuttered the window of the tower room to stop it coming in. Now, innocent, polished by the sun, it fitted the top edge of its banks like sinuous marquetry.

Had others noticed it as a common factor in the children's deaths? *They must have,* Adelia thought; even the sheriff's coroner wasn't entirely stupid. The significance, however, could have escaped them. The Cam was the town's larder, waterway, and washpot; its banks provided fuel, roofing, and furniture; everybody used it. That all the children had disappeared while in its vicinity was hardly less surprising than if they had not.

But Adelia and Ulf knew something else; Simon had been deliberately drowned in that same water—a coincidence stretched too far.

"Yes, " she said, "it's the river."

As evening drew on, the Cam became busy, boats and people outlined against the setting sun so that features were indistinguishable. Those going home after a day's work in town hailed workers coming back from the field to the south, or cursed as their craft caused a jam. Ducks scattered, swans made a fuss as they took flight. A rowing boat carried a new calf that was to be fed by hand at the fireside.

"Reckon as it took Harold and the others to Wandlebury?" Ulf asked.

"No. There's nothing there."

She had begun to discount the hill as the site where the children were murdered; it was too open. The extended suffering they had been subjected to would have required their killer to have more privacy than a hilltop could offer, a chamber, a cellar, somewhere to contain them and their screams. Wandlebury might be lonely, but agony was noisy. Rakshasa would have been fearful of it being heard, unable to take his time.

"No," she said again. "He may take the bodies to it, but there's somewhere else. . . ." She was going to say "where they're put to death," then stopped; Ulf was only a little boy, after all. "And you're right," she told him. "It's on or near the river."

They continued to watch the moving frieze of figures and boats.

Here came three fowlers, their punt low in the water from its piles of geese and duck destined for the sheriff's table. There went the apothecary in his coracle—Ulf said he had a lady friend near Seven Acres. A performing bear sat in a stern while his master rowed it to their hovel near Hauxton. Market women went by with their empty crates, poling easily. An eight-oared barge towed another behind it bearing chalk and marl, heading for the castle.

"Why d'you go, Hal?" Ulf was muttering. "Who was it?"

Adelia was thinking the same thing. Why had any of the children gone? Who was it on that river had whistled them to the lure? Who had said, "Come with me?" and they'd gone. It couldn't have been merely the temptation of jujubes; there must have been authority, trust, familiarity.

Adelia sat up as a cowled figure punted past. "Who's that?"

Ulf peered through the fading light. "Him? That's old Brother Gil."

Brother Gilbert, eh? "Where's he going?"

"Taking the host to the hermits. Barnwell's got hermits, same as the nuns, and near all of 'em live along the banks upriver in the forests." Ulf spat. "Gran don't hold with them. Dirty old scarecrows, she reckon, cuttin' theyselves off from everybody else. Ain't Christian, Gran says."

So Barnwell's monks used the river to supply the recluses just as the nuns did.

"But it's evening," Adelia said. "Why do they go so late? Brother Gilbert won't be back in time for Compline."

The religious lived by the tolling of holy hours. For Cambridge generally, the bells acted as a daytime clock; appointments were made by them, sandglasses turned, business begun and closed; they rang laborers to their fields at Lauds, sent them home at vespers. But their clanging by night allowed sleeping laity the schadenfreude of staying in bed while nuns and monks were having to issue from their cells and dorters to sing vigils.

An appalling knowingness spread over Ulf's unlovely little features. "That's why," he said. "Gives 'em a night off. Good night's sleep under the stars, bit of hunting or fishing next day, visit a pal, maybe, they all do it. 'Course the nuns take advantage, Gran says, nobody don't know *what* they get up to in them forests. But . . ."

Suddenly, he was squinting at her. *"Brother Gilbert?"*

She squinted back, nodding. "He could be." *How vulnerable children were,* she thought. If Ulf with all his mother-wit and knowledge of the circumstances was slow to suspect someone of standing that he knew, the others had been easy prey.

"He's grumpy, old Gil, I grant," the child said, reluctant, "but he speaks fair to young 'uns and he's a cru—" Ulf clapped his hands over his mouth and for the first time Adelia saw him discomposed. "Oh my arse, he went on crusade."

The sun was down now and there were fewer boats on the Cam; those that were had lanterns at the prow so that the river became an untidy necklace of lights.

Still the two of them sat where they were, reluctant to leave, attracted and repelled by the river, so close to the souls of the children it had taken that the rustle of its reeds seemed to carry their whispers.

Ulf growled at it. "Why don't you run backwards, you bugger?"

Adelia put her arm round his shoulders; she could have wept for him. Yes, reverse nature and time. Bring them home.

Matilda W.'s voice shrieked for them to come in for their supper.

"How's about tomorrow, then?" Ulf asked as they walked up to the house. "We could take old Blackie. He punts well enough."

"I wouldn't dream of going without Mansur," she said, "and if you don't show him respect, you will stay behind."

She knew, as Ulf did, that they must explore the river. Somewhere along its banks there was a building, or a path leading to a building, where such horror had occurred that it must declare itself.

It might not have a sign outside to that effect, but she would know it when she saw it.

THAT NIGHT, there was a figure standing on the far bank of the Cam.

Adelia saw it from her open solar window when she was brushing her hair and was so afraid she could not move. For a moment, she and the shadow under the trees faced each other with the intensity of lovers separated by a chasm.

She backed away, blowing out her candle and feeling behind her for the dagger she kept on her bedside table at night, not daring to take her eyes off the thing on the other bank in case it leaped across the water and in through the window.

Once she had steel in her hand she felt better. Ridiculous. It would need to have wings or a siege ladder to reach Old Benjamin's windows. It couldn't see her now; the house was in darkness.

But she knew it watched as she closed the lattice. Felt its eyes piercing the walls as she padded on bare feet downstairs to make sure everywhere was bolted, Safeguard reluctantly following.

Two arms raised a weapon above her head as she reached the hall.

"Gor bugger," said Matilda B. "You gone and scared the shit out of I."

"Likewise," Adelia told her, panting. "There's somebody across the river."

The maid lowered the poker she'd been holding. "Been there every night since your lot went to the castle. Watching, always watching. And little Ulf the only man in the place."

"Where *is* Ulf?"

Matilda pointed toward the stairs to the undercroft. "Safe asleep."

"You're sure?"

"Certain."

Together the two women peered through a pane in the rose window.

"Gone now."

That the figure had disappeared was worse than if it were still there.

"Why didn't you tell me?" Adelia wanted to know.

"Reckon as you had enough on your shoulders. Told the watch, though. Shit lot of good they were. Didn't see nobody nor nothin', not surprising, the rumpus they made marching over the bridge to get there. Peeping Tom, they reckoned it was."

Matilda B. went to the middle of the room to replace the poker. For a second, it vibrated against the bars of the fire grate as if the hand that held it was shaking too much to release it. "Ain't a Peeping Tom, though, is it?"

"No."

The next day, Adelia moved Ulf into the castle tower to stay with Gyltha and Mansur.

Thirteen

Y ou will *not* go without me," Sir Rowley said, struggling out of bed and falling. "Ow, *ow,* God rot Roger of Acton. Give me a cleaver and I'll chop his privates for him, I'll use them for fish bait, I'll . . ."

Trying not to laugh, Adelia and Mansur raised her patient from the floor and put him back to bed. Ulf retrieved his nightcap and replaced it on his head.

"It will be safe enough with Mansur and Ulf—and we are going in daylight," she said. "You, on the other hand, will indulge in light exercise. A gentle walk round the room to strengthen the muscles, that is all you are capable of at the moment, as you see."

The tax collector let out a snarl of frustration and hammered his bedclothes, an action that caused another moan, this time of pain.

"Stop that nonsense," Adelia told him. "Anyway, it wasn't Acton who wielded the cleaver. I'm not sure who it was, there was such a confusion."

"I don't care. I want him hanged before the assize judges look at his bloody tonsure and let him go."

"He should be punished," she said. Acton was certainly responsible for whipping into a frenzy the group that had forced their way in to desecrate Simon's grave. "But I hope he is not hanged."

"He attacked a royal castle, woman, he damn near neutered me, he needs basting over a slow fire with a spit up his arse." Sir Rowley shifted his position and looked at her sideways. "Have you at all dwelt on the fact that you and I were the only ones to receive injury in the melee? Apart from the likely lads I put out of action, I mean."

She had not. "In my case, a broken nose hardly merits the title of injury."

"It could have been a great deal worse."

It could, but it had been accidental; in a sense, her own fault for running into battle.

"Moreover," Rowley said, still cunning, "the rabbi remained unhurt."

She was becoming confused. "Are you implicating the Jews?"

"Of course not. I am merely pointing out that the good rabbi was not set upon. What I'm saying is that only two people remain inquiring into the death of the children now that Simon is dead. You and I. And we were hurt."

"And Mansur," she said absently. "He wasn't hurt."

"They didn't see Mansur until he came into the fight. Besides, he hasn't been asking questions, his English isn't good enough."

Adelia pondered it. "I don't follow your argument," she said. "Are you saying that Roger of Acton is the children's killer? *Acton?*"

"I'm saying, damn it"—physical weakness was making Rowley testy—"I'm *saying* that he was put up to it. The suggestion was made to him or to one of his gang that you and I were Jew lovers better off dead."

"All Jew lovers are better off dead in his view."

"*Somebody,*" the tax collector said between gritted teeth, "somebody is after us. *Us,* you and me."

You, oh, dear God, she thought. *Not us; you. You've been asking questions, Simon and you. At the feast, Simon was addressing you: "We have him, Sir Rowley."*

She groped for the edge of the bed and sat down on it.

"Ah ha," Rowley said, "*Now* it's dawning. Adelia, I want you away from Old Benjamin's. You can move in here with the Jews for a while."

Adelia thought of last night's figure among the trees. She had not told Rowley what she and Matilda B. had seen; he could do nothing about it, and there was no point in adding to his frustration because he could not.

It was Ulf the thing had menaced; it was after another child, had specified this particular one for itself. She'd known it then and she knew it now; it was why the boy must spend his nights in the castle and his days always with Mansur nearby.

But, dear God, if the creature considered Rowley a threat to itself— it was so *clever;* it had resources—two people she loved were in danger.

Then she thought: *Damn it, Rakshasa is achieving what he likes at our expense and locking us all in this damned castle. We shall never find him like this. I, at least, must have the freedom to move.*

She said, "Ulf, tell Sir Rowley your theory about the river."

"No. He'll say that's squit."

Adelia sighed at the incipient jealousy between these two males in her life. "Tell him."

The boy did so sullenly and without conviction.

Rowley pooh-poohed it. "Everybody's near the river in this town." He was equally dismissive of Brother Gilbert as an object of suspicion. "You think he's Rakshasa? A weedy monk like him couldn't cross Cambridge Heath, let alone the desert."

The argument swayed back and forth. Gyltha entered carrying Rowley's breakfast tray and joined in.

While it lasted, though they spoke of horror and suspicion, some of the sting was drawn for Adelia. They were dear to her, these people.

To banter with them, even about life and death, was so pleasurable to her who had never bantered that for this moment she knew a piercing happiness. *Hic habitat felicitas.*

As for the big, flawed, magical man in the bed, cramming ham into his mouth, he had been hers, his life hers, gained not only by her expertise but by the strength that had flowed out of her into him, a grace sought and granted.

Though marvelous to her, it was a sadly one-sided love affair, and she would have to live on it for the rest of her life. Every moment spent in his company confirmed that to show her vulnerability to him would be ruinous; he would use it either to reject or, even worse, to manipulate. His and her intents were mutually destructive.

Already, it was ending. With the wound scabbing nicely, he refused to let her dress it, depending instead on the ministrations of Gyltha or Lady Baldwin. "It's indecent for a maiden female to be finicking about in that man's part," he'd said crossly.

She had forborne asking him where he would be if she hadn't finicked in the first place; she was no longer his necessity; she must withdraw.

"At any rate," she said now, "we must explore the river."

"In the name of God, don't be so bloody stupid," Rowley said.

Adelia got up; she was prepared to die for the swine but not to be insulted. As she tucked the bedclothes more firmly around him, he was enveloped in the smell of her, a mixture of the bogbean tincture that she administered to him three times a day and the chamomile in which she washed her hair—a scent quickly obliterated by the stink of the dog as it passed the bed to follow her out of the room.

Rowley looked around in the silence she left. "Am I not right?" he said in Arabic to Mansur, and then fractiously, because he was exhausted, "I won't have her exploring that scum-sucking river."

"Where *would* you have her, effendi?"

"Flat on her back where she belongs." If he hadn't been weak and pettish, he wouldn't have said it—at least, not out loud. He looked nervously at the Arab, who was advancing; he was in no state to fight the bastard. "I didn't mean it," he said hastily.

"That is as well, effendi," Mansur said, "or I should be forced to re-open your wound and extend it."

Now Rowley was enveloped in a smell that took him back to the *souqs*, a mixture of sweat, burnt frankincense, and sandalwood.

The Arab bent over him and placed the tips of his left fingers and thumb together in front of Rowley's face, then touched them with his right forefinger, a delicate movement that nevertheless cast doubt on Sir Rowley's parentage by indicating that he had five fathers.

Then he stood back, bowed, and left the room, followed by the dwarfish child whose own gesture was simpler, cruder, but just as explicit.

Gyltha gathered up the tray and its wreckage before going after them. "Don't know what you said, bor, but there's better ways of putting it."

Oh, Lord, he thought, sinking back, *I am become childish. Lord, deliver me, though, it is true. That's where I want her, in bed, under me.*

And he wanted her so much that he'd had to stop her dressing his wound with that green muck—*What was it? Comfrey?*—because his adjacent part had gotten its strength back and tended to rise every time she touched him.

He berated his god and himself for putting him in such a fix; she was not at all his type of woman. Remarkable? Never a woman more so; he owed her his life. On top of that, he could talk to her as he could to no other, male or female. He had revealed more of himself while telling her about his hunt for Rakshasa than he had when he'd related it to the king—and, he was afraid, had revealed a damn sight more in his delirium. He could swear in her company—though not *at* her, as her departure from the room had just proved—making her an easy as well as desirable companion.

Could she be seduced? Quite probably; she might be conversant with all the functions of the body, but she was undoubtedly naïve about what made its heart beat faster—and Rowley had learned to have faith in his considerable, though little understood, attraction for women.

Seduce her, however, and at one stroke you removed not only her clothing but her honor and, of course, her remarkableness, thus rendering her just another woman in another bed.

And he wanted *her* as she was; her *hmm*s as she concentrated, her appalling dress sense—though she had looked very nice indeed at the Grantchester feast—the importance she ascribed to all humanity, even its dregs, *especially* its dregs, the gravity which could dissolve into an astonishing laugh, the way she squared her shoulders when she felt daunted, the way she mixed his dreadful medicines and the kindness of her hands as she held the cup to his mouth, the way she walked, the way she did everything. She had a quality he had never known; she *was* quality.

"Oh to hell," said Sir Rowley to the empty room. "I'll have to marry the woman."

THE VENTURE UPRIVER, while beautiful, proved fruitless. Considering its purpose, Adelia was ashamed of enjoying so much a day spent in drifting through tunnels formed by overbranching trees from which they emerged into sunlight where women momentarily ceased laundering to wave and call, where an otter swam craftily by the side of the punt while men and hounds on the far side hunted for it, where fowlers spread their nets, where children tickled for trout, where mile-long stretches of bank were empty except for warblers balancing perilously on the reeds as they sang.

The Safeguard loped dolefully along the bank, having rolled in something that made his presence in the punt untenable, while

Mansur and Ulf took turns poling, competing with each other in a skill seeming so easy that Adelia asked if she might try, eventually clinging to the pole like a monkey as the punt proceeded without her and having to be rescued by Mansur because Ulf was laughing too hard to move.

Shacks, huts, fowlers' hides aplenty lined the river—each one likely to be deserted by night and each desolate enough for any scream issuing from it to be heard only by the wildlife—so many that it would have taken a month to investigate them all and a year to follow the little beaten paths and bridges through the reeds that led to others.

Tributaries flowed into the Cam, some of them mere streams, some of considerable size and navigable. These great flatlands, Adelia realized, were veined with waterways; causeways, bridges, roads were ill-kept and often impassable, but anybody could go anywhere with a boat.

While Safeguard chased birds, the other three explorers ate some of the bread and cheese and drank half the cider that Gyltha had provided, sitting on a bank by the boathouse at Grantchester where Sir Joscelin stored his punts.

Water sent quiet, wobbling reflections onto walls that held oars, poles, and fishing tackle; nothing spoke of death. In any case, a look toward the great house in the distance showed that, like all manors, Sir Joscelin's was too occupied for horror to take place unnoticed. Unless dairymaids, cowherds, stablers, fieldhands, and the house servants were all complicit in the children's abduction, the crusader was not a murderer in his own home.

Going back down the river toward town, Ulf spat into the water. "Waste of bloody time that was."

"Not entirely," Adelia told him. The excursion had brought home something she should have recognized before. Whether they went willingly with their abductor or not, the children would have been seen. Every boat on these stretches below the Great Bridge had a shallow draft and low gunwales, making it impossible to conceal the presence of anyone bigger than a baby—unless he or she were lying flat under the thwarts. Therefore, either the children had hidden themselves or they had been rendered unconscious and a coat, a piece of sacking, something, had been thrown over them for the journey that had taken them to the place of their death.

She pointed this out in Arabic and English.

"He does not use a boat, then," Mansur said. "The devil throws them across his saddle. Takes a route across country unseen."

It was possible; most habitation in this part of Cambridgeshire was on a waterway, its interior virtually deserted apart from grazing cloven-hoofed beasts, but Adelia didn't think so; the predominance of the river in each child's disappearance argued against it.

"Then it is the thebaicum," Mansur suggested.

"Opium?" That was more likely. Adelia had been gratified by how extensively the Eastern poppy was grown in this unlikely area of England and by the availability of its properties, but also alarmed. The apothecary, he who visited his mistress by night, distilled it in alcohol, calling it Saint Gregory's Cordial, and sold it to anybody, though keeping it below his counter out of sight from clerics who condemned the mixture as godless for its ability to relieve pain, an attribute that should be left exclusively to the Lord.

"That's it," Ulf said. "He gives 'em a drop of the Gregory's." He crinkled up his eyes and exposed his teeth. *"Take a sip of this, my pretty, and come along of me to paradise."*

It was a caricature of wheedling malevolence that chilled the warmth of spring.

ADELIA WAS CHILLED AGAIN when, next morning, she sat in the sanctum of a leaded-windowed countinghouse on Castle Hill. The room was stacked with documents and chests bound by chains with locks, a

hard-cornered, masculine room built to intimidate would-be borrow-
ers and to accommodate women not at all. Master De Barque, of De
Barque Brothers, received her into it with reluctance and met her request with a negative.

"But the letter of credit was in the name both Simon of Naples and
myself," Adelia protested and heard her voice being absorbed into the
walls.

De Barque extended a finger and pushed a roll of vellum with a
seal on it across the table to her. "Read it for yourself, mistress, if you
are capable of understanding Latin."

She read it. Among the "heretofores" and "wherebys" and "compliance therewith" the Luccan bankers in Salerno, the issuers, promised
to pay on behalf of the applicant, the King of Sicily, to the Brothers De
Barque of Cambridge such sums as Simon of Naples, the beneficiary,
should require. No other name was mentioned.

She looked up into the fat, impatient, disinterested face. How vulnerable to insult you were if you lacked money. "But it was understood," she said. "I was Master Simon's equal in the enterprise. I was
chosen for it."

"I am sure you were, mistress," Master De Barque said.

He thinks I came along as Simon's strumpet. Adelia sat up, squar-
ing her shoulders. "An application to the Salerno bank or to King
William in Sicily will verify me."

"Then make it, mistress. In the meantime . . ." Master De Barque
picked up a bell on the table and rang it to summon his clerk. He was
a busy man.

Adelia sat where she was. "It will take months." She didn't have
enough money to pay even what it would cost to send the letter. There
had been only a few clipped pennies in Simon's room when she'd gone
to look; either he had been preparing to apply to these bankers for
more or he had kept what he had in the wallet his killer had taken.
"May I borrow until—"

"We do not lend to women."

She resisted the clerk taking her by the arm to lead her out. "Then what am I to do?" There was the apothecary's bill to pay, Simon's headstone to be inscribed by a stonemason, Mansur needed new boots, *she* needed new boots . . .

"Mistress, we are a Christian organization. I suggest you apply to the Jews. They are the king's chosen usurers, and I understand you are close to them."

There it was, in his eye. She was a woman and a Jew lover.

"You know the Jews' situation," she said desperately. "At present they have no access to their money."

For a moment the flesh on Master De Barque's face creased into warmth. "Have they not?" he said.

As they went up the hill, Adelia and Safeguard were passed by a prison cart containing beggars; the castle beadle was rounding them up ready for sentence at the coming assize. A woman was shaking its bars with skeletal hands.

Adelia stared after her. How powerless we are when we're destitute.

Never in her life had she been without money. *I must go home. But I cannot, not until the killer is found, and even then, how can I leave?* She turned her mind from the name; she would have to leave him sooner or later. . . . *In any case, I cannot travel. I have no money.*

What to do? She was a Ruth amid alien corn. Ruth had solved her situation by marrying, which was not an option in this case.

Could she even exist? Patients had been redirected to the castle while she'd been there, and, in between looking after Rowley, she and Mansur had attended to them. But nearly all were too poor to pay cash.

Her anxiety was not placated when, on entering the castle's tower room with Safeguard, she found Sir Rowley up and dressed, sitting on the bed, and chatting with Sir Joscelin of Grantchester and Sir Gervase of Coton. As she bustled toward him, she said irritably to Gyltha, who stood sentinel-like in a corner, "He's supposed to be resting." She ignored the two knights who had risen at her entrance—Gervase reluctantly and only at a signal from his companion. She took the patient's pulse. It was steadier than her own.

"Don't be angry with us, mistress," Sir Joscelin said. "We came to sympathize with Sir Rowley. It was God's mercy you and the doctor were by. The wretch Acton . . . we can only hope the assize will not allow him to escape the rope. We are all agreed hanging's too good for him."

"Are you, indeed?" she snapped.

"The lady Adelia does not countenance hanging; she has crueler methods," Rowley said. "She'd treat all criminals with a hearty dose of hyssop."

Sir Joscelin smiled. "Now that *is* cruel."

"And your methods are effective, are they?" Adelia asked. "Blinding and hanging and cutting off hands makes us all safer in our beds, does it? Kill Roger of Acton and there will be no more crime?"

"And the killer of the children, mistress," Sir Joscelin asked gently. "What would you have done to him?"

Adelia was slow to answer.

"She hesitates," Sir Gervase said with disgust. "What sort of woman is she?"

She was a woman who regarded legislated death as an effrontery by those imposing it—so easily and sometimes for so little cause—because life, to her, who wished to save it, was the only true miracle. She was a woman who never sat with the judge or stood with the executioner but always clung to the bar with the accused. *Would I have come to this place in his or her circumstances? Had I been born to what he or she was born to, would I have done differently? If someone other than two doctors from Salerno had picked up the baby on Vesuvius, would it cower where this man or woman cowers?*

For her, the law should be the point at which savagery ended because civilization stood in its path. We do not kill because we stand for betterment. She supposed the killer had to die and most certainly would, the putting down of a rabid animal, but the doctor in her would always wonder why it had turned rabid and grieve for not knowing.

She turned away from them to go to the medicine table and noticed for the first time how rigidly Gyltha was standing. "What's the matter?"

The housekeeper looked worn, suddenly aged. Her hands were flat and supporting a small reed casket in much the same manner as the faithful received consecrated bread from the priest before putting it into the mouth.

Rowley called from his bed, "Sir Joscelin has brought me some sweetmeats, Adelia, but Gyltha won't let me have them."

"Not I," Joscelin said. "I am merely their porter. Lady Baldwin asked me to carry them up the stairs."

Gyltha's eyes held Adelia's, then looked down at the casket. Letting it rest on one hand, she raised its lid slightly with the other.

Inside, lying on pretty leaves, like eggs in a nest, was an assortment of colored, scented, lozenge-shaped jujubes.

The two women stared at each other. Adelia felt ill. With her back to the men, she silently shaped the word: *"Poison?"*

Gyltha shrugged.

"Where's Ulf?"

"Mansur," Gyltha mouthed back. *"Safe."*

Adelia said slowly, "The doctor has forbidden Sir Rowley confits."

"Hand them round to our visitors, then," Rowley called from his bed.

We can't hide from Rakshasa, Adelia thought. *We are targets; wherever we are, we stand exposed like straw men for him to shoot at.*

She nodded her head toward the door and turned to the men, while behind her, Gyltha left the room, carrying the casket with her.

The medicines. Hurriedly, Adelia checked them. All stoppers were in place, the boxes piled neatly as she and Gyltha always left them.

You are being absurd, she thought; *he is somewhere outside; he cannot have tampered with anything.* But last night's horror of a Rakshasa with wings was on her and she knew she would change every herb, every syrup on the table before administering them.

Is *he outside? Has he been here?* Is he here now?

Behind her, the conversation had turned to horses as it always did among knights.

She was aware of Gervase lolling in his chair because she felt *his* awareness of *her.* His sentences were grunted and abstracted. When she glanced at him, his look turned to a deliberate sneer.

Killer or not, she thought, *you're a brute and your presence is an insult.* She marched to the door and held it open. "The patient is tired, gentlemen."

Sir Joscelin rose. "We are sorry not to have seen Dr. Mansur, aren't we, Gervase? Pass on our compliments to him, if you would."

"Where is he?" Sir Gervase demanded.

"Improving Rabbi Gotsce's Arabic," Rowley told him.

As he passed her on his way out, Gervase muttered, as if to his companion, "That's rich, a Jew and a Saracen in a royal castle. Why to hell did we go on crusade?"

Adelia slammed the door behind him.

Rowley said crossly, "Damn it, woman, I was edging the talk round to Outremer to find out who was where and when; one might let something slip about the other."

"Did they?" she demanded.

"You ushered them out too fast, damn it." Adelia recognized the irritability of recuperation. "Oddly enough, though, Brother Gilbert admitted to being in Cyprus at about the right time."

"Brother Gilbert was here?"

And Prior Geoffrey *and* Sheriff Baldwin *and* the apothecary—with a concoction he'd sworn would heal a wound within minutes—*and* Rabbi Gotsce. "I'm a popular man. What's the matter?" For Adelia had slammed a box of powdered burdock so hard on the table that its lid came off, emitting a cloud of green dust.

"You are not popular," she said, teeth gritted. "You are a corpse. Rakshasa would poison you."

She went back to the door, calling for Gyltha, but the housekeeper was already coming up the stairs, still holding the casket. Adelia snatched it from her, opened it, and shoved it under Rowley's nose. "What are those?"

"Dear Christ," he said. "Jujubes."

"I been asking round," Gyltha said. "Little girl handed 'em to one of the sentries, saying as they was from her mistress for the poorly gentleman in the tower. Lady Baldwin was going to carry 'em up, but Sir Joscelin said he'd save her legs. Always the polite gentleman, he is, not like t'other."

Gyltha didn't hold with Sir Gervase.

"And the little girl?"

"Sentry's one of them sent from London by the king to help guard the Jews. Barney, his name is. Didn't know her, he says."

Mansur and Ulf were summoned so that the matter could be gone over in conference.

"They could be merely jujubes, as they seem," said Rowley.

"Suck one an' see," Ulf told him sharply. "What you think, missus?"

Adelia had picked one up in her tweezers and was smelling it. "I can't tell."

"Let's test them," Rowley said. "Let's send them down to the cells for Roger of Acton, with our compliments."

It was tempting, but instead Mansur took them down to the court-yard to throw the casket on the smithy fire.

"There will be no more visitors to this room," Adelia instructed. "And none of you, especially Ulf, is to leave the castle or wander in it alone."

"Goddammit, woman, we'll never find him like that."

Rowley, it appeared, had been carrying on his own investigation from his bed, using his role as tax inspector to question his visitors.

From the Jews he had learned that Chaim, according to his code, had never talked about his clients nor mentioned the size of their debts. His only records were those that had burned or been stolen from Simon's body.

"Unless the Exchequer in Winchester has a list of tallies, which it may well do—I've sent my squire there to find out—the king will not be best pleased; the Jews provide a large part of this nation's income. And when Henry isn't pleased . . ."

Brother Gilbert had announced that he would rather burn than approach Jews for money. The crusading apothecary as well as Sir Joscelin and Sir Gervase had said the same, though less forcefully. "They're not likely to tell me if they did, of course, but all three seem finely set up from their own efforts."

Gyltha nodded. "They done well out of the Holy Land. John was able to start his 'pothecary shop when he got back. Gervase, nasty lit-tle turd he was as a boy and he ain't any pleasanter now, but he's get-ting hisself more land. And young Joscelin as didn't have a rag to his arse thanks to his pa, he's made a palace out of Grantchester. Brother Gilbert? He's allus Brother Gilbert."

They heard labored breathing on the stairs and Lady Baldwin came in, holding her side with one hand and a letter in the other. "Sickness. At the convent. Lord help us. If it be the plague . . ."

Matilda W. followed her in.

The letter was for Adelia and had been delivered first to Old Benjamin's house whence Matilda W. had brought it. It was a scrap of parchment torn from some manuscript, showing its terrible urgency, but the writing on it was strong and clear.

"Prioress Joan presents her compliments to Mistress Adelia, assistant to Dr. Mansur, of whom she has heard good reports. Pestilence has broken out amongst us and I ask in the name of Jesus and his dear Mother for said Mistress Adelia to visit this convent of the blessed Saint Radegund that she may then report to the good doctor and solicit his advice on what may alleviate the sisters' suffering, it being very severe and some near to death."

A postscript read: "To be no haggling over fees. All this to be done with discretion so as to avoid the spread of alarm."

A groom and horse were awaiting Adelia in the courtyard below.

"I shall send you with some of my beef tea," Lady Baldwin told Adelia. "Joan is not usually alarmed. It must be dire."

It must be, Adelia thought, *for a Christian prioress to beg the aid of a Saracen doctor.*

"The infirmaress have gone down with it," Matilda W. said—she'd heard the groom's report. "Spewing and shitting fit to bust, the lot of 'em. God help us if it be the plague. Ain't this town suffered enough? What's Little Saint Peter at that the holy sisters ain't spared?"

"You will not go, Adelia," Rowley said.

"I must."

"I fear she should," said Lady Baldwin. "The prioress does not allow a man in the nuns' inner sanctum, despite those wicked rumors, except a priest to hear their confession, of course. With the infirmaress hors de combat, Mistress Adelia is the next best thing, an excellent thing. If she keeps a clove of garlic up each nostril, she cannot succumb." She hurried away to prepare her beef tea.

Adelia was giving explanations and instruction to Mansur. "O friend of the ages, look after this man and this woman and this boy while I am absent. Let them go nowhere alone. The devil is abroad. Guard over them in the name of Allah."

"And who shall guard over you, little one? The holy women will not object to the presence of a eunuch."

Adelia smiled. "It is not a harem, the women safeguard their temple from all men. I shall be safe enough."

Ulf was tugging at her arm. "I can come. I ain't growed yet, they know me at Saint Raggy's. And I don't never catch nothing."

"You're not going to catch this, either," she said.

"You will not *go*," Rowley said. Wincing, he dragged Adelia to the window away from the others. "It's a bloody plot to get you unprotected. Rakshasa's in it somewhere."

Back on his feet, Adelia was reminded of how big he was and what it was for a powerful man to be kept powerless. Nor had she realized that, for him, Simon's murder had seemed a preliminary to her own. Just as she was frightened for him, so was he for her. She was touched, gratified, but there were things to attend to—Gyltha must be told to change the medicines on the table; she had to collect others from Old Benjamin's . . . she didn't have time for him now.

"You're the one who's been asking questions," she said gently. "I beg you to take care of yourself and my people. You merely need nursing at this stage, not a doctor. Gyltha will look after you." She tried to disengage herself from him. "You must see that I have to go to them."

"For God's sake," he shouted. "You can stop playing the doctor for once, can't you?"

Playing the doctor. *Playing the doctor?*

Though his hand was still on her, it was as if the ground had fallen between them, and looking up into his eyes, she saw herself across the chasm—a pleasant little creature enough but a deluded one, merely busying itself, a spinster filling in time until she should be claimed by what was basic for a woman.

But if so, what was the line of suffering that waited for her every day? What was Gil the thatcher who was able to climb up ladders?

And what are you, she thought, amazed, looking into his eyes, *who should have bled to death and didn't?*

She knew in absolute certainty now that she should never marry him. She was Vesuvia Adelia Rachel Ortese Aguilar, who would be very, very lonely but always a doctor.

She shook herself free. "The patient can resume solid food, Gyltha, but change all those medicaments for fresh," she said and went out.

Anyway, she thought, *I need that fee the prioress promised.*

SAINT RADEGUND'S CHURCH and its outhouses near the river were deceptive, having been built after the Danes stopped invading and before the foundation ran out of money. The main body of the convent, its chapel and residences, was larger and lonelier and had known the reign of Edward the Confessor.

It stood away from the river hidden among trees so that Viking longboats snaking through the shallow waters of the Cam tributaries might not find it. When the monks, who'd inhabited it originally, died out, the place had been granted to religious women.

All this Adelia learned over the shoulder of Edric as, with Safeguard following, his horse carried them both into the convent estate via a side gate in its wall, the main gates having been barred against visitors.

Like Matilda W., the groom was aggrieved by Little Saint Peter's failure to do his job. "It do look bad shutting up, with the pilgrim season just starting proper," he said. "Mother Joan's right put out."

He set Adelia down by a stable block and kennels, the only well-kept convent buildings she had seen so far, and pointed to a path skirting a paddock. "God go with you, missis." Obviously, he would not.

Adelia, however, was not prepared to be cut off from the outside world. She ordered the man to go to the castle each morning, taking any message she might need to send and asking how her people did, and to bring back the answer.

She set off with Safeguard. The clatter of the town across the river faded. Larks rose around her, their song like bursting bubbles. Behind her the prioress's hounds sent up a belling and a roe deer barked somewhere in the forest ahead.

The same forest, she remembered, that contained the manor of Sir Gervase, and into which Little Saint Peter had disappeared.

"CAN THIS BE MANAGED?" Prioress Joan demanded. She was more haggard than when Adelia had last seen her.

"Well, it isn't the plague," Adelia told her, "nor typhus, Lord be thanked; none of the sisters has the rash. I believe it to be cholera."

She added, because the prioress went pale, "A milder form than the one found in the East, though bad enough. I am concerned for your infirmaress and Sister Veronica." The oldest and the youngest. Sister Veronica was the nun who, praying over Little Saint Peter's reliquary, had presented Adelia with an image of imperishable grace.

"Veronica." The prioress appeared distraught—and Adelia liked her better for it. "The sweetest-natured of them all, may God attend her. What is to be done?"

What indeed? Adelia glanced in dismay across to the other side of the cloister, where, beyond the pillars of its walk, rose what looked like an outsize pigeon-loft, two rows of ten doorless arches, each giving to a cell less than five feet wide, inside which lay a prostrate nun.

There was no infirmary—the title "infirmaress" seemed to be an honorary designation settled on the elderly Sister Odilia merely because she was skilled in herbs. No dorter, either—nowhere, in fact, for the nuns to be cared for collectively.

"The original monks were ascetics who preferred the privacy of individual cells," the prioress said, catching Adelia's look. "We keep to them because as yet we have had no money to build. Can you manage?"

"I shall need assistance." Caring single-handedly for twenty women severely afflicted with diarrhea and vomiting would be hard enough in a ward, but to fetch and carry from cell to cell, up and down the wickedly narrow and railless flight of steps that led to the upper cells, would cut down the carer herself.

"I fear our servants fled at the mention of plague."

"We don't want them back in any case," Adelia said firmly. A glimpse of the convent house suggested that those who should have kept it ordered had allowed slovenliness to reign long before disease overtook it, a slackness that might have caused the disease itself.

She said, "May I ask if you eat with your nuns?"

"And what has that to do with the price of fish, mistress?" The prioress was offended, as if Adelia was accusing her of dereliction.

So Adelia was, in a way. She remembered Mother Ambrose's care for the physical and spiritual nourishment of her nuns while presiding over meals in Saint Giorgio's immaculate refectory, where wholesome food was accompanied by a reading from the Bible, where a nun's lack of appetite for either could be noted and acted on. But she did not want confrontation so early and said, "It may have something to do with the poisoning."

"Poisoning? Do you suggest that someone is trying to murder us?"

"Deliberately, no. Accidentally, yes. Cholera is a form of poisoning. Since you yourself seem to have escaped it . . ."

The prioress's expression suggested that she was beginning to regret calling Adelia in. "As it happens, I have my own quarters, and I am usually too occupied by convent business to eat with the sisters. I have been at Ely this last week, consulting with the abbot on . . . on religious matters."

Buying one of the abbot's horses, so Edric the groom had said.

Prioress Joan went on: "I suggest you confine your interest to the matter in hand. Inform your doctor that there are no poisoners here and, in the name of God, ask him what is to be done."

What had to be done was to solicit help. Satisfied that it was not the convent's air causing the nuns' sickness—though the place was dank and smelled of rot—Adelia walked back to the kennels and sent Edric the groom for the Matildas.

They arrived, and Gyltha with them. "The boy's safe in the castle with Sir Rowley and Mansur," she said when Adelia reproved her. "Reckon you need me more than he do."

That was undoubted, but it was dangerous for them all.

"I shall be glad of you by day," Adelia told the three women. "You shall not stay by night because, while the pestilence lasts, you will not eat any of the convent's food nor drink its water. I insist on this. Also, buckets of brandy will stand in the cloister, and after touching the nuns, or their chamber pots, or anything that is theirs, you must lave your hands in them."

"*Brandy?*"

"Brandy."

Adelia had her own theory concerning diseases such as the one ravaging the nuns. Like so many of her theories, it did not accord with that of Galen or any other medical influences in vogue. She believed that the flux in cases like this was the body's attempt to rid itself of a substance it could not tolerate. Poison in one form or another had gone in and, ergo, poison was coming out. Water itself was so often contaminated—as in the poorer districts of Salerno, where disease was ever-present—it must be treated as a source of the original poison until proved otherwise. Since anything distilled, in this case brandy, frequently stopped wounds from putrefying, it might also act on any ejected poison that touched the hands of a nurse and prevent her from ingesting it herself.

So Adelia reasoned and acted on.

"My brandy?" The prioress expressed dissatisfaction at seeing the cask from her cellar poured into two buckets.

"The doctor insists on it," Adelia told her, as if the messages Edric brought from the castle had contained instructions from Mansur.

"I would have you know that is best Spanish," Joan said.

"An even stronger specific."

Since they were all in the kitchen at that moment, Adelia had the prioress at a disadvantage; she suspected the woman of never having entered it. The place was dark and verminous; several rats had fled at their entrance—Safeguard yelping after them with the most animation Adelia had ever seen in him. The stone walls were encrusted with grease. Such grooves of the pine table block that could be seen beneath litter were filled with grime. There was a smell of rotting sweetness. Pots hanging from hooks retained furred remnants of meals, flour bins were uncovered, and there was a suggestion of movement in their contents, the same applied to the open vats of cooking water— Adelia wondered if it was in one of these that the nuns had boiled Little Saint Peter's corpse and whether it had been cleaned afterward. Shreds clinging to the blade of a meat cleaver stank like pus.

Adelia looked up from sniffing them. "No poisoner here, you say? Your cooks should be arrested."

"Nonsense," the prioress said. "A bit of dirt never hurt anybody." But she pulled at the collar of her pet gazehound to stop him from licking an unidentified mess sticking to a platter on the floor. Rallying, she said, "I am paying Dr. Mansur that my nuns be made well, not for his subordinate to spy on the premises."

"Dr. Mansur says that to treat the premises is to treat the patient."

Adelia would not give way on this. She had fed a pill of opium to the worst cases in the cells in order to relieve their cramps, and now, apart from washing the rest and giving them sips of boiled water— which Gyltha and Matilda W. were already about—little could be done for the invalids until the kitchen was fit to use on their behalf.

Adelia turned to Matilda B., whose Herculean task this was to be. "Can you do it, little one? Cleanse these Augean stables?"

"Kept horses in here as well, did they?" Rolling up her sleeves, Matilda B. looked around her.

"Quite probably."

Followed resentfully by the prioress, Adelia went on a tour of inspection. An aumbry in the refectory contained labeled jars that spoke well of Sister Odilia's knowledge of herbology, though it also held a plentiful supply of opium—*too* plentiful, in the opinion of Adelia, who, knowing the drug's power, kept her own cache to a minimum in case of theft.

The convent's water proved healthy. A peat-colored but pure ground spring had been enclosed in a conduit that ran through the buildings, first to serve the kitchen before supplying the fish in the convent's stew outside, then on to the nuns' laundry, lavatorium, and, finally, to course along a helpful slope under the long, many-holed bench in the outhouse that was the privy. The bench was clean enough, though nobody had brushed out the runnel beneath it for many a long month—a job that Adelia reserved for the prioress, seeing no reason why Gyltha or the Matildas should have to do it.

But that was for later. Having done her best to ensure that the condition of her patients was not made worse, Adelia turned her energy to saving their lives.

Prior Geoffrey came to save their souls. It was generous of him, considering the feud between him and the prioress. It was also brave; the priest who usually heard the sisters' confession had refused to risk the plague and instead sent a letter containing a generalized absolution for any sins that might come up.

It was raining. Gargoyles spouted water from the roof of the cloister walk into the unkempt garden at its center. Prioress Joan received the prior, thanking him with stiff politeness. Adelia took his wet cloak to the kitchen to dry.

By the time she returned, Prior Geoffrey was alone. "Bless the woman," he said. "I believe her to suspect me of trying to steal Little Saint Peter's bones while she is yet at this disadvantage."

Adelia was happy to see him. "Are you well, Prior?"

"Well enough." He winked at her. "Functioning nicely so far."

He was leaner than he had been and looked fitter. She was relieved for that, and also by his mission. "Their sins seem so little, except to them," she said of the nuns. In their more terrible moments, when they thought themselves near death, she had heard most of her patients' reasons for dreading hellfire. "Sister Walburga ate some of the sausage she was taking upriver for the anchorites, but you'd think from her distress that she was a Horseman of the Apocalypse and the Whore of Babylon rolled into one."

Indeed, Adelia had already discounted the accusations made by Brother Gilbert against the nuns' behavior. A doctor learned many secrets from an acutely ill patient, and Adelia found these women to be slapdash perhaps, undisciplined, mostly illiterate—all failings that she put down to the negligence of their prioress—but not immoral.

"She shall be reconciled through Christ for the sausage," Prior Geoffrey said solemnly.

By the time he had finished confessing the sisters on the ground floor, it was dark. Adelia waited for him outside Sister Veronica's cell at the end of the row, to light him to the upper cells.

He paused. "I have given Sister Odilia the last rites."

"Prior, I hope to save her yet."

He patted her shoulder. "Not even you can perform miracles, my child." He looked back to the cell he had just left. "I worry for Sister Veronica."

"So do I." The young nun was ill beyond what she should be.

"Confession has not eased that child's sense of sin," Prior Geoffrey said. "It can be the cross of those who are holy-minded, like her, that they fear God too much. For Veronica, the blood of our Lord is still moist."

Having seen him, complaining, up steps that were slippery from the rain, Adelia went back down the row to Odilia's cell. The infirmaress lay as she had for days, her twiggy, soil-engrained hands plucking at her blanket in an effort to throw it off.

Adelia covered her, wiped away some of the unction trickling down her forehead, and tried to feed her Gyltha's calf's-foot jelly. The old woman compressed her lips. "It will give you strength," Adelia pleaded. It was no good; Odilia's soul wanted free of the empty, exhausted body.

It felt like desertion to leave her, but Gyltha and the Matildas had gone for the night, though reluctantly, and with only the prioress and herself to do it, Adelia had to see the other sisters fed.

Walburga, she who had been Ulf's "Sister Fatty" and was now much thinner, said, "The Lord has forgiven me; the Lord be praised."

"I thought he might. Here, open your mouth."

But after a few spoonfuls, the nun again showed concern. "Who'll be a-feeding our anchorites now? 'Tis wicked to eat if they be starving."

"I'll speak to Prior Geoffrey. Open up. One for the Father. Good girl. One for the Holy Ghost . . ."

Sister Agatha, next door, had another bout of sickness after taking three spoonfuls. "Don't you worry," she said, wiping her mouth, "I'll be better tomorrow. How's the others doing? I want the truth now."

Adelia liked Agatha, the nun who had been brave enough, or drunk enough, to provoke Brother Gilbert at the Grantchester feast. "Most are better," she said, and then, in response to Agatha's quizzical look, "but Sister Odilia and Sister Veronica are still not as well as I'd like."

"Oh, not Odilia." Agatha said, urgently, "Good old stick, she is. Mary, Mother of God, intercede for her."

And Veronica? No intercession for her? The omission was strange; it had been evident when other nuns asked after their sisters in Christ; only Walburga, who was about the same age, had inquired for her.

Perhaps the girl's beauty and youth were resented, as was the fact that she was the prioress's obvious favorite.

Favorite, indeed, Adelia thought. There had been agony in Joan's face that spoke of great love when she looked on Veronica's suffering. Being sensitive to the existence of love in all its forms now, Adelia found herself sincerely pitying the woman and wondered if the energy she put into her hunting was a way of redirecting a passion for which, as a nun, and especially one in authority, she must be clawed by guilt.

Had Sister Veronica been aware of being an object of desire? Probably not. As Prior Geoffrey said, there was an otherworldliness to the girl that spoke of a spiritual life the rest of the convent lacked.

The other nuns must know of it, though. The young nun didn't complain, but the bruises on her skin suggested she'd been physically bullied.

When he'd finished in the upper cells, Adelia made the prior wash his hands in the brandy. The procedure bemused him. "Usually, I take it internally. However, I no longer question anything you would have me do."

She lit him to the gate, where a groom waited for him with their two horses. "A heathenish place, this," he said, lingering. "Perhaps it is the architecture or the barbarous monks who built it, but I am always more conscious of the Horned One than of sanctity when I am in it, and for once I am not referring to Prioress Joan. The arrangement of those cells alone . . ." He grimaced. "I am reluctant to leave you here—and with so little help."

"I have Gyltha and the Matildas," Adelia told him, "and the Safeguard, of course."

"Gyltha is with you? Why did I not see her? Then there's no need for worry; that woman can dispel the forces of darkness single-handed."

He gave her his blessing. The groom took the chrismatory box from him, put it in a saddlebag, heaved him up on his horse, and they were gone.

It had stopped raining, but the moon, which should have been full, was heavily clouded. Adelia stood for a minute or two after they had disappeared, listening to the sound of hooves diminishing into the blackness.

She hadn't told the prior that Gyltha did not stay at night and that it was at night when she became afraid.

"Heathenish," she said out loud. "Even the prior feels it." She went back into the cloister but left the gates open; it was nothing outside the convent that frightened her, it was the convent itself; there was no air to it, nothing of God's light, no windows even in the chapel, just arrow slits set into walls of heavy, unadorned stone that reflected the savagery they had been built to withstand.

But it has gotten in, Adelia thought. The hideously ancient, hogback tomb in the chapel was carved with wolves and dragons biting each other. Scrollwork on the altar circled a figure with arms upheld, Lazarus perhaps, though candlelight gave it a demonic quality. The foliage surrounding the arches of the cells imitated the encroaching forest that tangled buttresses in ivy and creepers.

At night, sitting by a nun's cot, she, who did not credit the devil, found herself listening for him and being answered by the shriek of an owl. For Adelia, as for Prior Geoffrey, the twenty gaping holes, ten below, ten above, in which the nuns were stacked, reinforced the barbarity. Called to another cell, she had to urge herself to brave the wicked, black steps and narrow ledge that led to it.

By day, when Gyltha and the Matildas returned, bringing with them noise and common sense, she allowed herself an hour or two's rest in the prioress's quarters, but even then the two rows of cells infiltrated her exhausted dozes with reproach, as if they were graves of troglodyte dead.

Tonight, when she walked the length of the cloister to look in on Sister Veronica, the light of her lantern flickered the ugly heads of the pillars' capitals into life. They grimaced at her. She was glad of the dog by her side.

Veronica lay tossing in her cot, apologizing to God for not dying. "Forgive me, Lord, that I am not with you. Suspend Thy wrath at my transgressions, Dear Master, for I would come to You if I could. . . ."

"Nonsense," Adelia told her. "God is perfectly happy with you and wants you to live. Open your mouth and have some nice calf's-foot jelly."

But Veronica, like Odilia, would not eat. Eventually, Adelia gave her half an opium pill and sat with her until it took effect. It was the barest cell of the twenty, its only ornament a cross that, like all the nuns' wall crucifixes, was woven from withies.

Somewhere out in the marsh, a bittern boomed. Water dripped on the stones outside with a regularity that made Adelia's nerves twitch. She heard retching from Sister Agatha's cell farther along the cloister, and went to her.

Emptying the chamber pot meant leaving the cloister. A shift of cloud allowed some moonlight on her return, and Adelia saw the figure of a man by one of the walk's pillars.

She closed her eyes against it, then opened them and went forward.

It was a trick of shadow and the glistening of rain. There was nobody there. She put her hand on the pillar to lean against it for a moment, breathing hard; the figure had been wearing horns. Safeguard appeared to have noticed nothing, but then he rarely did.

I am very tired, she thought.

Prioress Joan cried out sharply from Odilia's cell. . . .

WHEN THEY'D SAID THE PRAYERS, Adelia and the prioress wrapped the infirmaress's body in a sheet and carried it between them to the chapel. They laid it on a makeshift catafalque of two tables covered by a cloth and lit candles to stand at the head and the foot.

The prioress stayed to chant a requiem. Adelia went back to the cells to sit with Agatha. All the nuns were asleep, for which she was thankful; they need not know of the death until the morning, when they would be stronger.

That is, if morning ever comes to this awful place, she thought. "Heathenish," the prior had said. At this distance, the strong, single contralto echoing from the chapel sounded not so much a Christian requiem as a lament for a fallen warrior. Had it been Odilia's death or some element in the very stones that conjured the horned figure in the cloister?

Fatigue, Adelia told herself again. *You are tired.*

But the image persisted, and to rid herself of it, she used her imagination to transpose it with another figure, this one more rotund, more funny, infinitely beloved, until Rowley stood there in the horror's stead. With that comforting presence on guard outside, she fell asleep.

Sister Agatha died the next night. "Her heart seems to have just stopped beating," Adelia wrote in a message to Prior Geoffrey. "She was doing well. I did not expect it." And had cried for it.

With rest and Gyltha's good food, the remaining nuns recovered swiftly. Veronica and Walburga, being younger than the others, were up and about sooner than Adelia would have liked, though it was difficult to resist their high spirits. However, their insistence that they should go upriver to supply the neglected anchorites was not sensible, especially as, in order to take sufficient food and fuel, one nun would be poling one punt and her sister yet another.

Adelia went to Prioress Joan with an appeal that they be stopped from exhausting themselves.

Being worn out herself, she did so tactlessly: "They are still my patients. I cannot allow it."

"They are still my nuns. And the anchorites my responsibility. From time to time, Sister Veronica, especially, needs the freedom and solitude to be found among them; she has sought it, and I have always granted it."

"Prior Geoffrey promised to supply the anchorites."

"I have no opinion of Prior Geoffrey's promises."

It was not the first time, nor the second, nor the third, that Joan and Adelia had locked horns. The prioress, conscious that her many absences had brought both convent and nuns to the brink of ruin, involuntarily tried to retain her authority by opposing Adelia's.

They had argued over Safeguard, the prioress saying that he stank, which he did—but not more than the living conditions of the nuns. They had argued over the administration of opium, on which the prioress had decided to take the side of the Church. "Pain is God-sent, only God should take it away."

"Who says so? Where in the Bible does it say that?" Adelia had demanded.

"I am told the plant is addictive. They will form a habit of taking it."

"They won't. They don't know what they are taking. It is a temporary panacea, a soporific to relieve their suffering."

Perhaps because she had won that argument, she lost this. The two nuns were given their superior's permission to take supplies to the anchorites—and Adelia, knowing she could do no more for it, left the convent two days later.

Which was the same time the assize arrived in Cambridge.

THE NOISE WAS TREMENDOUS in any case, but for Adelia, whose ears had become accustomed to silence, it was like being battered. Weighted by her heavy medicine case, the walk from the convent house had been a hard one, and now, wanting only to get back to

Old Benjamin's and rest, she stood in a crowd on the wrong side of Bridge Street as the parade passed.

At first she didn't realize this *was* the assize; the cavalcade of musicians in livery blowing trumpets and beating tabors took her back to Salerno, to the week before Ash Wednesday when the *carnevale* came to town despite all the Church could do to prevent it.

Here came more drums—and beadles, such ornate livery, with great gold maces over their shoulders. And heavens, mitered bishops and abbots on caparisoned horses, one or two actually waving. And a comic executioner with hood and ax . . .

Then she knew the executioner wasn't comic; there would be no tumblers and dancing bears. The three Plantagenet leopards were blazoned everywhere, and the lovely palanquins now going by on the shoulders of tabarded men contained the judges of the king come to weigh Cambridge in their scales and, if Rowley was correct, find much of it wanting.

Yet the people around her cheered as if starved of entertainment, as if the trials and fines and death sentences to come would provide it.

Bewildered by hubbub, Adelia suddenly saw Gyltha pushing to the front of the crowd across the street, her mouth open as if she, too, were cheering. But she wasn't cheering.

Dear God of All, don't let her be saying it. It is unsayable, not to be borne. Don't look like that.

Gyltha ran into the street so that a rider had to rein in, swearing, his horse jittering to one side to avoid trampling her. She was talking, looking, clutching. She was coming close, and Adelia stood back to avoid her, but the shriek penetrated everything. "Any of you seen my little boy?"

She might have been blind. She caught at Adelia's sleeve without recognizing her. "You seen my little boy? Name's Ulf. I can't find un."

Fourteen

S he sat on the Cam's bank in the same spot, on the same upturned
pail that Ulf had sat on to do his fishing.

She watched the river. Nothing else.

Behind the house at her back, the streets were full of noise and
bustle, some of it to do with the assize, much of it caused by the search
for Ulf. Gyltha herself, Mansur, the two Matildas, Adelia's patients,
Gyltha's customers, friends, neighbors, parish reeve, and those merely
concerned all were looking for the child—with increasing despair.

"The boy was restive in the castle and wished to go fishing,"
Mansur had told Adelia, so stolid as to be almost rigid. "I came with
him. Then the small, fat one"—he referred to Matilda B.—"called me
into the house to mend a table leg. When I came outside again, he was
gone." The Arab refused to meet her eye, which told her how upset he
was. "You may tell the woman I am sorry," he'd said.

Gyltha hadn't blamed him, hadn't blamed anybody; the terror was
too great to convert into anger. Her frame wizened into that of a
much smaller, older woman; she would not stay still. Already she and
Mansur had been upriver and down, asking everybody they met if they

had seen the boy and jumping into boats to tear the cover off anything hidden. Today they were questioning traders by the Great Bridge.

Adelia did not go with them. All that night she'd stayed in the solar window, watching the river. Today she sat where Ulf had sat and went on watching it, gripped by a grief so terrible that she was immobilized—although she would have stayed on the bank in any case. *"It's the river,"* Ulf had said, and in her head she listened to him say it over and over again, because, if she stopped listening, she would hear him scream.

Rowley came crashing through the reeds, limping, and tried to take her away. He said things, held her. He seemed to want her to go to the castle, where he was forced to stay, being so busy with the assize. He kept mentioning the king; she hardly heard him.

"I'm sorry," she said, "but I must remain here. It's the river, you see. The river takes them."

"How can the river take them?" He spoke gently, thinking her mad, which, of course, she was.

"I don't know," she told him. "I have to stay here until I do."

He nagged at her. She loved him but not enough to go with him; she was under the direction of a different, more commanding love.

"I shall come back," he said at last.

She nodded, barely noticing that he had gone.

It was a beautiful day, sunny and warm. Some of the passing boat people who knew what had happened shouted encouragement to the woman on the bank sitting on her upturned bucket with a dog beside her. "Don't worry, my duck. He's maybe playing some'eres. He'll turn up like a bad penny." Others averted their eyes from her and remained silent.

She didn't see or hear them, either. What she saw was Ulf's naked, skinny little body struggling in Gyltha's hands as she held it over the bath preparatory to letting it drop into the water.

It's the river.

She made up her mind when, in the late afternoon, Sister Veronica and Sister Walburga came by in their punt. Walburga saw her and poled to the bank. "Now don't you lecture us, mistress. Prior didn't send enough supplies upriver to feed a kitten, and we got to go up again with more. But we're strong again, ain't we, Sister? Strong in the power of God."

Sister Veronica was concerned. "What is it, mistress? You look tired."

"Not to be wondered at," Walburga said. "Wearied from a-looking after us. Angel, she is, blessings on her."

It's the river.

Adelia got up from her bucket. "I shall come with you, if I may."

Pleased, they helped her into the punt and sat her on the stern thwart, her knees bent up to her chin with a crate of hens under her feet. They laughed when Safeguard—"Old Smelly," they called him— disgruntledly set off to follow them by the towpath.

Prioress Joan, they said, was telling the world that Little Saint Peter had been vindicated, for when had so many been so ill and only two died, one of those elderly? The saint had been tested and not found wanting.

The two nuns took turn-and-turn-about at poling with a frequency that showed they hadn't recovered all their strength yet, but they made little of it. "Harder yesterday," Walburga said, "when us was poling separate punts. But we got the Lord's strength on our side." She could go the farthest before she rested; nevertheless, Veronica was the more lissome and economic in movement and made a lovelier shape as her slim arms pressed on the pole and raised it, hardly stirring water that was turning amber in the setting of the sun.

Trumpington flowed past. Grantchester . . .

They were on a part of the river left unexplored on Adelia's day with Mansur and Ulf. Here it divided, becoming two rivers, the Cam to the south, the other entering it from the east.

The punt turned east. Walburga, who was poling, answered Adelia's question—the first she had asked. "This? This be the Granta. This un takes us to the anchorages."

"And your auntie," Veronica said, smiling. "It takes us to your auntie as well, Sister."

Walburga grinned. "That it do. Her'll be surprised seeing me twice in a week."

The countryside changed with the river, becoming something re-sembling flat upland where reed and alder fell back to be replaced by firm grass and taller trees. In the twilight, Adelia could see hedges and fences rather than dikes. The moon, which had been a thin, round wafer in the evening sky, gained substance.

Safeguard was beginning to limp, and Veronica said he should travel with them, poor thing. Once the hens stopped protesting at his presence, there was silence broken only by the last twittering of birds.

Walburga took the punt to an inlet from which a path led to a farm. As she lumbered out, she said, "Now don't you go lifting all that stuff on your own, Sister. Get the old codgers to help you."

"They will."

"And you can manage it back on your own?"

Veronica nodded and smiled. Walburga curtsied to Adelia, then waved them off.

The Granta became narrower and darker, finding its way through a winding, shallow valley in which beeches occasionally came down to the water and Veronica had to crouch to avoid branches. She stopped to light a lantern, which she placed on the board at her feet so that it lit the black water ahead for a yard or so and reflected the green eyes of some animal that looked at them before turning away into the undergrowth.

As they cleared the trees, the moon reached them again to silver a black-and-white landscape of pasture and hedge. Veronica poled to the left bank. "Journey's end, the Lord be praised," she said.

Adelia peered ahead and pointed to a huge, flattopped shape in the distance. "What's that?"

Veronica turned to look. "There? That's Wandlebury Hill."

Of course, it would be.

A tiny, twinkling star seemed to have landed on the hill's head, deceptive in the nature of stars so that a blink sent it away and another blink brought it back.

She shifted in order to let Veronica lift the hen crate from under her legs. "I shall wait here," she said.

The nun looked at her doubtfully, and then at the baskets still in the punt needing to be carried to the unseen anchorages.

Adelia said, "Would you leave the lantern with me?"

Sister Veronica cocked her head. "Feared of the dark?"

Adelia considered the question. "Yes."

"Keep it then, and the Lord take care of you. I'll be back in a while." The nun hefted a sack over her shoulder and, gripping the crate in her other hand, set off up a moonlit track leading into trees.

Adelia waited until she'd gone, then lifted Safeguard onto the bank, picked up the lantern, raised it to see that its candle was good and stout, and began walking.

For a while, the river and its accompanying path meandered in the general direction in which she headed, but, after perhaps a mile, she saw that it would take her too far to the south. She left it to keep due east as the crow flew—except that a crow wouldn't have been impeded by the obstacles that now met Adelia: great stretches of brambles, hillocks, and dips made slippery by the recent rain, hurdle fences that sometimes could be climbed or crawled through and sometimes couldn't.

If human eyes watched from Wandlebury Hill, they saw a tiny, errant light straying across the dark country, going this way and that

with apparent aimlessness as Adelia circumambulated one obstruction, then another. Sometimes the light paused because she fell, and
fell awkwardly in an attempt to keep the lantern from hitting the
ground and going out, Safeguard standing by until she got up.

Occasionally, not having heard it, she was startled by a deer or fox
fleeing across her path—her own sobbing breath being too loud to
hear anything else, though she sobbed not from grief nor exhaustion
but from effort.

However, the watcher on Wandlebury Hill, if there were a watcher,
could have seen that for all its vagaries, the little light was coming
closer.

And Adelia, struggling through her valley of shadows, saw the hill
slowly swell until it dominated everything else ahead. The star that
had gotten entangled on its brow was no longer intermittent but sent
out a steady glow.

She nearly retched as she went, sick with her own stupidity. *Why
didn't I go here straight away? The bodies of the children told me, told me. Chalk, they
said. We were killed on chalk. The river fixated me. But the river leads to Wandlebury
Hill. I should have known.*

Scratched and bleeding, limping, yet with the lantern still lit, she
heaved herself up onto a flat surface and found it to be the spot on the
Roman road where Prior Geoffrey had once screamed to anyone who
would listen that he could not piss.

There was nobody about; indeed, it was late now and the moon
was high, but Adelia was encapsulated away from time; there was no
past where people lived; there wasn't a child called Ulf, she had
stopped hearing or seeing him; there was a hill, and she must reach its
top. Followed by the dog, she took the steep track without recalling
the occasion on which she had first taken it, merely knowing that it
was the way to go.

When she gained the top, she had to look for the twinkling light,
bewildered that it had led her from a distance but was no longer ap-

parent. *Oh, God, don't let it be put out.* In darkness and among this vast expanse of hummocks, she'd never find the place.

She saw it, a glow through some bushes ahead, and ran, forgetting the depressions in the ground. This time, when she fell, the lantern went out. No matter. She began to crawl.

It was a strange light, neither a fire nor the diffusion of candles—more like a beam directed upward. Scrabbling toward it, her hands touched nothing and she was jerked forward so that she was humped over a slope. Safeguard was looking straight ahead, and there it was, three yards away from her in the center of the bowl-like depression. It wasn't a fire or lanterns. There was nobody there. The light came from a hole in the ground. It was the gaping mouth of hell lit by the flames below.

All Adelia's training had to come to her aid then, every nut of natural philosophy, every hypothesis proved, every yardstick of common sense had to be set against unreason in order to fight the howling panic that sent her scrabbling away from the hole, wailing. She prayed for deliverance: *From terror by night, Almighty God defend me.*

"It's not *the* Pit," a voice said, primly, in her head, "It's *a* pit."

Of course it was. A pit. Just a pit. And Ulf was in it.

She started to crawl forward and struck her knee against something that lay in the grass and had seemed merely part of the ground but which, after a minute, her exploring hands discovered to be manufactured—a huge and solid wheel. She crawled over it, finding it covered with turf.

She put out her hand to stop Safeguard from coming too close, then, with the slowness of a turtle, extended her neck to look over the pit's edge.

Not a pit. A shaft, some six feet across and the Lord only knew how deep—the light rising from its bottom confused distance—but deep. A ladder led down into whiteness—white, all white, as far as she could see.

Chalk. Of course it was chalk, the chalk on the dead children.

Rakshasa hadn't dug it; excavation such as this had involved the labor of hundreds. He'd found it and used it; *how* he'd used it.

Is that what all the depressions on the hill were? The filled-in entrances to mines? But who had needed chalk on such a scale?

It doesn't matter; their purpose doesn't matter now. Ulf is down there.

So is the killer. He's lit the place—those are flambeaux down there; this is the light the shepherd saw. *Dear Lord, we should have found it; we walked this stinking hill, skirting every depression to look into it; how did we miss this open invitation to the underworld?*

Because it wasn't open, she thought. The turfed wheel she'd crawled across wasn't a wheel at all, it was a cover, a lid, a wellhead. When it was in place, it made this dip in the ground look like any other.

Such a clever fellow, Rakshasa.

But some of Adelia's skin-crawling horror of the killer left her because she knew that when Simon's cart had carried Prior Geoffrey up the track to Wandlebury Hill, Rakshasa had panicked. Like the guilty thing he was, he had taken the bodies from the shaft by night and carried them down the hill, so that his lair would be kept secret.

This shaft is your place, she thought, *so precious it makes you vulnerable. It glares for you as it does for me now, even when the lid is on; it is the tunnel into your body, the entrance to your rotting soul, your doom to be discovered. For you, its existence cries to God, whom it outrages.*

And I've found it.

She listened. The hill around her rustled with life, but the shaft delivered no sound. She should not have come alone, oh, mercy, she should not. What service was she providing that little boy by bringing no reinforcement and in telling nobody where she had gone?

Yet the moment had demanded it; she could not think of what else she might have done. Anyway, it *was* done, the milk was spilt and, somehow, she had to mop it up.

If Ulf were dead, she could pull out the ladder and push the wheel into place, entombing the living killer, and walk away while Rakshasa thrashed around in his own sepulchre.

But she had followed the belief that Ulf wasn't dead, that the other children had been kept alive in Rakshasa's larder until he was ready for them—a hypothesis based on what the body of a dead boy had once told her. Such frail evidence, such a gossamer of belief, yet it had pulled her into the nuns' punt and marched her across country to this hellhole so that . . .

So that what?

Lying prone, with her head over the pit, Adelia considered her choices with the chill logic of despair. She could run for help, which, considering how long it would take, was no option at all—the last habitation she'd seen had been Sister Walburga's auntie's farm—and now that she was close to Ulf, she could not leave him. She could descend the shaft and be killed, which in the end she must be prepared to do if, thereby, Ulf could escape.

Or, and this had considerably more merit, she thought, she could descend and kill the killer. Which entailed finding a weapon. Yes, she must look for a stick, or a stone, anything sharp . . .

Beside her, the Safeguard shifted suddenly. A pair of hands seized Adelia's ankles and raised them so that she slid forward. Then, with a grunt of effort, somebody threw her down the pit.

What saved her was the ladder. It met her fall halfway down, breaking some of her ribs on impact but allowing her body to slither the rest of the way on its lower rungs. She had time—it seemed quite a long time—to think *I must stay conscious* before her head struck the ground and she wasn't.

AWARENESS WAS A LONG TIME coming to her, traveling slowly through a misty crowd of people who insisted on moving about and shifting her and talking, which irritated her to the point where, if she hadn't been in such pain, she'd have told them to stop. Gradually, they went away and the sound of voices dwindled down to one that persisted in being just as irritating.

"Do be quiet," she said and opened her eyes, but the effort hurt so much that she decided to stay unconscious for a while, which was just as impossible because there was horror waiting for her and someone else, so that her mind, determined on her own and the someone else's survival, insisted on working.

Stay still and think. *God, the* pain; her head was being trepanned. That would be concussion—how severe it was impossible to estimate without knowing for how long she'd been unconscious; the length of time would indicate the severity. *Damnation, it* hurt. And so did her ribs, possibly two fractures there but—she experimented with a deep breath, wincing—probably no puncture of the lung. It wasn't helped by the fact that she seemed to be standing with her arms over her head, causing compression on her chest.

It doesn't matter. You're in such danger, your medical condition doesn't matter. Think and survive.

So. She was in the shaft. She remembered being at its top; now she was at its bottom; her brief glimpse had shown enclosing whiteness all around. What she couldn't remember was getting from one to the other—the natural result of concussion. Pushed or fallen, obviously.

And somebody else had fallen, or had been brought down before or after Adelia herself, because the attempt at opening her eyes had shown a figure against the opposite wall. It was this someone who was ceaselessly and so irritatingly making a noise.

"Save-and-preserve-me, dear-Lord-and-Master-and-I-shall-follow-Thee-all-my-days-I-will-abase-myself-unto-Thee. Punish-me-with-Thy-whips-and-scorpions-yet-keep-me-safe. . . ."

The babbling was Sister Veronica's. The nun stood ten or so feet away on the other side of the ceilingless chamber that was the pit of the shaft. Her wimple and coif had been torn down to her neck and her hair hung over her face like wisps of dark mist. Her hands were stretched above her head where, like those of Adelia, they were manacled to a bolt.

She was out of control with terror, spittle running down her chin, her body shaking so that the iron manacles about her wrists rattled an accompaniment to the prayer for release issuing from her mouth.

"I wish you'd be quiet," Adelia said petulantly.

Veronica's eyes widened with shock and, a little, with justified accusation. "I followed you," she said. "You'd gone, and I followed you."

"Unwise," Adelia told her.

"The Beast is here, Mary, Mother of God, protect us, he took me, he's down here, he'll eat us, oh, Jesus, Mary, save us both, he's *horned.*"

"I dare say he is, just stop shouting."

Enduring the pain, Adelia turned her head to look around. Her dog lay sprawled at the bottom of the ladder, his neck broken.

A sob forced itself out of her throat. *Not now, not now,* she told herself; *there's no room for it; you can't grieve now. To survive you must think. But oh, Safeguard . . .*

Flames from two torches stuck into holders at head height on either side of the chamber illuminated rough, round walls of whiteness marred here and there by a green algae so that she and Veronica stood as if at the bottom of a massive tube of thick, dirty, crumpled paper.

They stood alone; there was no sign of the nun's Beast, though leading off from either side were two tunnels. The opening to the one on Adelia's left was small, a crawling space barred by an iron grating. The one to the right was lit by unseen torches and had been enlarged to admit a man without bending. A curve in it blocked her view of its length, but just inside the entrance, propped against the wall and reflecting the chalk opposite, stood a battered, polished shield engraved with the cross of crusade.

And in the place of honor, in the center of this torture chamber, midway between her and Veronica and the dead dog, stood the Beast's altar.

It was an anvil. So ordinary in its rightful place, so awful here; an anvil heaved from the thatched warmth of a smithy so that children might be penetrated on it. The weapon lay on its top, shiny among the stains, a spearhead. It was faceted—as were the wounds it had inflicted.

Flint, dear God, flint. Flint that occurred in chalk, seams of it. Ancient devils had labored to dig this mine in order to reach flint that they might shape it and kill with it. As primitive as they, Rakshasa used an implement made by a dark people in a dark time.

She shut her eyes.

But the bloodstains were dull; nobody had died on that anvil recently.

"Ulf," she shrieked, opening her eyes. *"Ulf."*

To her left, from far up the darkness of the left-hand tunnel, deadened by the porous chalk yet audible, came a mumbling groan.

Adelia turned her face up to the circle of sky above her head and gave thanks. The sickness of concussion, nausea from the smell of obliterating chalk, from the stink of whatever resin it was the torches were burning, gave way to a waft of fresh, May air. The boy lived.

Well now. There, on the anvil, just a couple of yards away, lay a weapon all ready for her hand.

Though her hands were tethered, from what she could see of Sister Veronica's situation and if it resembled her own, the manacles holding their upstretched arms were attached to a bolt that went into the bare chalk. And chalk was chalk; it crumbled—as much use for retaining a fixture as sand.

Adelia flexed her elbows and pulled at the bolt above her head. *Oh, God, oh, hell.* Pain like hot wire through the chest. This time, she'd surely, *surely* punctured a lung. She hung, puffing, waiting for blood to come into her mouth. After a while, she realized it wasn't going to, but if that blasted nun didn't cease moaning . . .

"Stop gibbering," she yelled at the girl. "Look, pull. *Pull,* damn you. The bolt. In the wall. It'll come out if you tug it." Even in pain, she'd felt a tiny give in the chalk above.

But Veronica couldn't, *wouldn't,* comprehend; her eyes were wide and wild like a deer facing the hounds; she was gibbering.

It is up to me.

Another full tug was to be avoided, but wiggling the manacles might shift the bolt sufficiently to create a cavity around it and enable it to be eased out.

Frantically, she began jiggling her hands up and down, oblivious now to everything except a piece of iron, as if she were enclosed in chalk with it, moving it grain by grain, hurting, hurting, but *seeing* the near end of the protesting bolt separating from . . .

The nun screamed.

"Quiet," Adelia screamed back. "I'm concentrating."

The nun went on screaming. "He's coming."

There had been a flicker of movement to the right. Reluctantly, Adelia turned her head. The tunnel's bend, which was in Veronica's view, prevented Adelia, opposite her, from seeing the thing itself, but she saw it mirrored in the shield. The uneven, convex surface threw back a reflection of dark flesh, at once diminished and monstrous. The thing was naked and looking at itself. Preening, it touched its genitals and then the apparatus on its head.

Death was preparing for his entrance.

In that extremity of terror, everything abandoned Adelia. If she could have sunk to her knees, then she'd have crawled to the creature's feet: *Take the nun, take the boy, leave me.* If her hands were free, she'd have bolted for the ladder, leaving Ulf behind. She lost courage, rationality, everything except self-preservation.

And regret. Regret pierced the panic with a vision, not of her Maker but of Rowley Picot. She was going to die, and disgustingly, without having loved a man in the only health there was.

The thing came out of the tunnel; it was tall, made taller by the antlers on its head. Part of a skinned stag's mask covered the upper face and nose, but the body was human, with dark hair on chest and pubis. Its penis was erect. It pranced up to Adelia, pushing itself against her. Where deer eyes should have been, there were holes from which blue, human eyes blinked at her. The mouth grinned. She could smell animal.

She vomited.

As it sheered back to avoid her spew, the antlers rocked and she saw that bits of string tied the antlered contraption to Rakshasa's head, though not tightly enough to prevent them from wobbling when he made a sudden movement.

How vulgar. Contempt and fury engulfed her; she had better things to do than stand here threatened by a mountebank in a homemade headdress.

"You stinking crap-hound," she told him. "You don't frighten me." At that moment, he hardly did.

She'd discomfited him; the eyes in the mask shifted; a hiss came from between the teeth. As he retreated, she saw that the penis had drooped.

But he was feeling behind him with one arm while looking at Adelia. His hand found Sister Veronica's body, crawled upward until it reached the neck of her habit, and ripped it down to the waist. She screamed.

Still watching Adelia, the thing swaggered for a moment, then turned and bit Veronica on the breast. When it turned back to see Adelia's reaction, its penis was rampant again.

Adelia began to swear; language was the only missile she had, and she pelted him with it: "You turd-mouthed, stench-sucking lummox, what are you good for? Hurting women and children when they're tied? Not excited any other way? Dress like a dog's beef, you son of a pox-ridden sow, under it all you're no man, just a betty-buttered mother's boy."

Who this screaming self was, Adelia didn't know, didn't care. It was going to be killed, but it wasn't going to die in debasement like Veronica; it would go cursing.

Lord Almighty, she'd hit the gold; the thing had lost his erection again. He hissed and, still looking at her, wrenched the nun's clothes down to the crotch.

Arabic, Hebrew, Latin, and Gyltha's Saxon English, Adelia used them all; filth from unknown gutters came to her aid now.

A jellybag, she called him, a snot-faced, arse-licking, goat-fucking, bum-bellied, farting, turd-breathed apology, *Homo insanus*.

As she shouted, she watched the thing's penis; it was a flag, a signal to her victory or his. The act of killing would bring it to emission, she knew, but, in order for it to be in a condition *to* emit, the Beast needed his victim's fear. There were creatures . . . her stepfather had told her . . . reptiles that dragged humans underwater and stashed them until their flesh was soft enough to make a pleasurable meal. For this one, terror was the tenderizer. "You . . . you *corkindrill*," she yelled at it. Fear nourished Rakshasa; it was his excitement, his soup. Deny it to him and, dear God grant it, he couldn't kill.

She shrieked at him. He was a farting, pudding-pulling *chaser*, a maggot-brained hog with a cock like a winkle; she'd seen bigger balls on a raspberry.

No time to be amazed at herself. *Survive. Taunt.* Keep blood in your veins and out of his. With every word, she jiggled the iron cuffs around her hands—and the bolt in the chalk moved more and more easily.

There was blood on Veronica's stomach—her fear had gone beyond terror into a state where her body remained flaccid to the thing's abuse—her head back, eyes closed, her mouth in the rictus of a skull.

Adelia kept swearing.

But now Rakshasa was himself tearing the nun's manacles out of the wall. He stood back to hit the girl across the mouth and then took her by the scruff of her neck to march her toward the small tunnel where he slammed her to her knees. He removed the grating with one pull. He pointed. "Fetch," he said.

Adelia's cursing faltered. He was going to bring the child into this uncleanness and befoul him.

Veronica, on her knees, looked up at her torturer, apparently bewildered. Rakshasa kicked her backside and pointed into the hole, but he was watching Adelia. "Fetch the boy."

The nun crawled into the tunnel and the clank of the manacles on her hands as she moved became muffled.

Adelia prayed a silent scream: *Almighty God, take my soul; I am past what can be borne.*

Rakshasa had picked up the body of Safeguard. He threw it on the anvil so that it was on its back. Still watching Adelia, his hand reached for the flint knife and ran its point experimentally down the back of his wrist. He put up his arm to show her the blood.

He needs my fear, she thought. *He has it.*

The antlers wobbled as, for the first time, he took his gaze off Adelia and looked down. He raised the knife. . . .

She closed her eyes. It was a reenactment, and she would not watch it. He will cut off my eyelids, and I shall not watch it.

But she had to listen to the knife striking into flesh and the squelch and the splinter of bone. On and on.

There was no more swearing in her now, no defiance; her hands were still. *If there is a hell,* she thought dully, *his will be set apart.*

The noises stopped. She heard the approaching pad of his feet, smelled his stink. "Watch," he said.

She shook her head and felt a blow on her left arm that brought her eyes open. He'd stabbed her to get her attention. He was pettish. *"Watch."*

"No."

They both heard it: a scuffling from the little tunnel. Teeth showed beneath the stag's mask. He looked toward the entrance where Ulf was stumbling out. Adelia looked with him.

God save him, the boy was so small, so plain, too real, too *normal* against the monstrous stage the creature had set for him; he skewed it so that Adelia was ashamed to be on it in his presence.

He was fully dressed but tottering and semiconscious, his hands tied in front of him. There were blotches round his mouth and nose. Laudanum. Held over his face. To keep him quiet.

His eyes traveled slowly to the shredded mess on the anvil and widened.

She shouted, "Don't be frightened, Ulf." It wasn't an exhortation but a command: don't show fear; don't feed him.

She saw him try to concentrate. "I ain't," he whispered.

Courage returned to Adelia. And hatred. And ferocity. No pain on earth could stop her from this. Rakshasa had turned half away from her in Ulf's direction. She jerked her hands and the bolt came out of the wall. In the same movement she brought her arms down so that the chain connecting the manacles to each other should go over Rakshasa's neck that she might throttle him with it.

She hadn't achieved enough height, and the chain caught on the antlers. She swung on it so that the headdress tilted ludicrously backward and to one side, its strings dragging tight under Rakshasa's nose and across his eyes.

For a moment he was blinded, and the assault took him off balance. His foot slid and he went down, Adelia with him—into the segments of dog intestines that made the floor slippery.

There was grunting, hers or Rakshasa's, and she hung on, she couldn't do anything else, linked by chain to the antlers, to which he was linked by string; they were joined together, his body crooked under hers, her knees on his outstretched knife arm. Awkwardly placed, he struggled to throw her off so that he could strike backward with it; she struggled so that he shouldn't displace and kill her. All the time she was shouting: "Get out, Ulf. The ladder. Get *out*."

The back beneath her rose; she rose with it and then went down as Rakshasa slipped again. The knife went out of his hand into the slick. Still carrying Adelia, he crawled for it, shoving against Ulf and Veronica in his effort so that they fell into the melee. The four of them rolled back and forth across the mess of the floor in an intricate bundle.

There was a new element somewhere. A sound. It meant nothing; Adelia was blind and deaf. Her hands had found the antlers and were awkwardly twisting them so that a point should go into Rakshasa's skull. The new noise was nothing, her own agony nothing. *Twist. Into the brain. Twist. Mustn't bump me off. Mustn't let go. Twist. Kill.*

The string on the antlers broke, leaving them in her hands. The body beneath slithered away from her and, turning, crouched to spring.

For a second they were opposite each other, glaring and panting. The noise was loud now; it came from the top of the shaft, a combination of familiar sounds so inappropriate to this struggle that Adelia paid them no mind.

But they meant something to the Beast; its eyes changed; she saw a dulling; the alert joy of the kill went from them. The thing was still a beast with teeth exposed, but its head was up, sniffing, considering; it was scared.

Dear God, she thought, and was afraid to think, *that's what it is; beautiful, oh beautiful, the blow of a horn and the belling of hounds.*

The hunt had come for Rakshasa.

Her lips split into a grin as bestial as his. "Now you die," she said.

A shout came down the shaft. "Halloooo." *Beautiful, oh beautiful.* It was Rowley's voice. And Rowley's big feet coming down the ladder.

The thing's eyes were everywhere, looking frantically for the knife. Adelia saw it first. *"No."* She fell on it, covering it. *You shan't have it.*

Rowley, sword in hand, was nearing the bottom of the ladder, obstructed in getting off it by the bodies of Ulf and Veronica.

From the floor, Adelia reached to grip Rakshasa's heel as it went past, but her fingers slipped on its grease. Rowley was kicking the nun and boy out of his way. Adelia's view of Rakshasa's legs and buttocks as he sprinted for the big tunnel was blocked by Rowley's sprinting after him. She saw Rowley fall, flailing, as he tripped over the shield; she heard him curse—and then he was gone.

She sat and looked up. The baying of hounds was loud now; she could see snouts and teeth poking round the head of the shaft. The ladder was shaking; somebody else was clambering onto it, ready to come down.

There was nowhere in her body that didn't hurt. To collapse would be nice, but she dare not do it yet. It wasn't over—the knife had gone.

And so had Veronica and the child.

Rowley came rushing out of the tunnel, kicking the shield out of the way so that it skidded and hit the anvil. He grabbed a flambeau from the wall and disappeared with it into the tunnel again.

She was in darkness; the other torch was gone. A flicker of light showed her a puff of chalk dust and the hem of a black habit disappearing into the tunnel Ulf had come out of.

Adelia crawled after it. *No. No, not now. We're rescued. Give him to me.*

It was a wormhole, an exploratory dig that had not been worked because the flare of Veronica's torch when it came showed a gnarled, glistening line of flint running along it like a dado. The tunnel turned with the seam, cutting her off from the light ahead, and she was in a blackness so deep she might have gone blind. She went on.

No. Not now. Now we're rescued.

It was lopsided crawling; her left arm was weakening where Rakshasa had stabbed it. *Tired, so tired. Tired of being frightened. No time to be tired,* no. *Not now.* Nodules of chalk crumbled under her right hand as her palm pressed her forward. *I shall have him from you. Give him to me.*

She came on them in a tiny chamber, huddled together like a couple of rabbits, Ulf limp in the nun's grasp, his eyes closed. Sister Veronica held the torch high in one hand; the other, around the child, had the knife.

The nun's lovely eyes were thoughtful. She was reasonable, though dribble emerged from the corner of her mouth. "We must protect him," she told Adelia. "The Beast shall not have this one."

"He won't," Adelia said, carefully. "He's gone, Sister. He will be hunted down. Give me the knife now."

Some rags lay next to an iron post planted deep in the ground with a dog lead trailing from it, the collar just big enough for a child's neck. They were in Rakshasa's larder.

Circular walls were turned red by the flickering torchlight. The drawings on them wriggled. Adelia, who daren't take her eyes away from those of the nun, would not have looked at them in any case; in this obscenity of a womb, the embryos had waited not to be born but to die.

Veronica said, "Whoso shall offend one of these little ones, it were better for him that a millstone be hanged about his neck."

"Yes, Sister," Adelia said, "it would be." She crawled forward and took the knife out of the nun's hand.

Between them, they dragged Ulf through the wormhole. As they came out, they saw Hugh the hunter looking around him like a dazed thing with a lantern in his hand. Rowley emerged from the other tunnel. He was swearing and frantic. "I lost him; there's dozens of bloody tunnels along there, and my bloody torch went out. The bastard knows his way, I don't." He turned on Adelia as if he was furious with her—he *was* furious with her. "Is there another shaft somewhere?" As an afterthought, he asked, "Are you women hurt? How's the boy?"

He urged them up the ladder, tucking Ulf under his arm.

For Adelia the climb was interminable, each rung an achievement gained through pain and a faintness that would have toppled her to the bottom again if she'd not had Hugh's hand supporting her back. Her arm stung where the creature had stabbed it, and she became concerned that it might be poisoned. How ridiculous to die now. *Put brandy on it*, she kept thinking, *or sphagnum moss would do; mustn't die now, not when we've won.*

And as her head reached above the shaft and air touched it . . . *We have won. Simon, Simon, we've won.*

Clinging to the top rung, she looked down toward Rowley. "Now they'll know the Jews didn't do it."

"They will," he said. "Get on." Veronica was clinging to him, crying and gabbling. Adelia, struggling to get off the ladder, was nosed by hounds, their tails in frantic motion as if with pleasure at a job well done. Hugh called to them, and they backed away. When Rowley emerged, Adelia said, "You tell them. Tell them the Jews didn't do it."

Two horses were grazing nearby.

Hugh said, "That where our Mary died? Down there? Who done it?" She told him.

He stood still for a moment, the lantern lighting his face from below so that terrible shadows distorted it.

Teetering with frustration and indecision, Rowley shoved Ulf into

Adelia's arms. He needed men to hunt the tunnels below, but neither of the two women was in a condition to fetch them, and he dared not go himself or send Hugh.

"Somebody's got to guard this shaft. He's under this bloody hill, and sooner or later he'll pop out like a bloody rabbit, but there's maybe another exit somewhere. " He snatched Hugh's lantern and set off across the hilltop in what he knew, they all knew, was a hopeless attempt to find it.

Adelia laid Ulf on the grass above the edge of the depression, taking off her cloak to pillow it under his head. Then she sat down beside him and breathed in the smell of the night—how could it still be night? She caught the scent of hawthorn and juniper. Sweet grass reminded her that she was filthy with sweat and blood and urine, probably her own, and the stink of Rakshasa's body, which, she knew, if she spent her life in a bath, would never again quite leave her nostrils.

She felt expended, as if everything had gone from her and left just a trembling slough of skin.

Beside her, Ulf jerked into a sitting position, gasping at the reviving air, his fists clenched. He looked around, at the landscape, the sky, Hugh, the dogs, Adelia. He had trouble enunciating. "Where's . . . this at? Am I out?"

"Out and safe," she told him.

"They . . . got un?"

"They will." God send they would.

"He never . . . scared me," Ulf said, beginning to shake. "I fought the bugger . . . shouted . . . kept fighting."

"I know," Adelia told him. "They had to quiet you with poppy juice. You were too brave for them." She put her arm round his shoulders as his tears began. "No need to be brave anymore."

They waited.

A suspicion of gray in the sky to the east suggested that the night would actually have an end. Across the other side of the depression, Sister Veronica was on her knees, her whispered prayers like the rustle of leaves.

Hugh was keeping one foot on the top of the shaft's ladder so that he might feel any movement on it, one hand on the hunting knife at his belt. He soothed his dogs, murmuring their names and telling them they were brave.

He glanced at Adelia. "Followed the scent of that old mongrel of yourn all the way, my lads did," he said.

The hounds looked up as if they knew they'd been mentioned. "Sir Rowley, he were in rare old taking. 'She's gone after the boy,' he said, 'and very like got herself killed doing it.' Called you a fair few names in his temper, like. But I told un. 'That's a fine old stinker, that ol' dog of hers. My lads'll track un,' I said. Was that the old boy down there?"

Adelia roused herself. "Yes," she said.

"I'm right sorry for that. Did his job, though."

The hunter's voice was controlled, dull. Somewhere in the tunnels below their feet ran the creature that had slaughtered his niece.

A rustle that caused Hugh to take the knife from his belt was the launch of a long-eared owl on its last foray of the night. There was sleepy twittering as small birds woke up. Rowley himself, and not just his lantern, could be seen now, a big, busy shape using its sword as a stick to prod the ground. But every bush on the studded, uneven ground flaked the moonlight with a shadow that could conceal a more sinuous darkness wriggling away.

The sky to the east became extraordinary, a lowering, threatening red band with streaks of jagged black.

"Shepherd's warning," Hugh said, "devil's dawn."

Listlessly, Adelia watched it. Ulf, beside her, showed equal indifference.

He is damaged, Adelia thought, *as I am; we have been to places beyond experi-*

ence and are stained by them. Perhaps I can bear it, but can he? He especially has been betrayed.

With that, energy came back to her. Painfully, she got to her feet and walked round the rim of the depression to where Veronica knelt, her hands steepled high so that the growing dawn light shone on them, her graceful head lowered in prayer, as Adelia had first seen it.

"Is there another exit?" Adelia asked.

The nun didn't move. Her lips stilled for a moment before she resumed the whispered paternoster.

Adelia kicked her. "Is there another exit?"

There was a rasp of protest from Hugh.

Ulf's gaze, which had followed Adelia, transferred to the nun. His treble rang out across Wandlebury Hill. "It was *her*." He was pointing to Veronica. "Wicked, *wicked* female, she is."

Hugh, shocked, whispered, "Hush, lad."

Tears were plopping down Ulf's ugly little face, but it had regained intelligence and intent and bitter anger. "'Twas her. As put stuff over my face, as took me. *She's in with un.*"

"I know she is," Adelia said. "She threw me down the shaft."

The nun's eyes stared up at her, beseeching. "The devil was too strong for me," she said. "He tortured me—you saw him. I never wanted to do it." Her eyes shifted and glowed red as they reflected the dawn behind Adelia's back.

Hugh and Ulf, too, had turned suddenly to the east. Adelia spun round. The sky had flamed into savagery like an entire hemisphere alight and advancing to overwhelm them all. And there, as if he had conjured it, was the devil himself outlined in black against it, naked and running like a stag.

Rowley, fifty yards away, hared to intercept it. The figure capered for a second and changed direction. The watchers heard Rowley's howl: "Hugh. He's getting away. *Hugh.*"

The huntsman knelt, whispering to his hounds. He unleashed

them. With the ease of rocking horses, they began the chase toward the sunrise.

The devil ran—God, how he ran—but now the hounds were outlined against the same stretch of sky.

There was a moment that stayed with those who saw it like a detail of hell on an illuminated manuscript, black on red gold, the dogs in mid-leap and the man with hands upraised as if he would climb the air, before the pack fell on Sir Joscelin of Grantchester and tore him to pieces.

Fifteen

Adelia and Ulf were helped onto one of the horses that Rowley and the huntsman had ridden to the hill. Hugh hoisted the nun onto the other. Taking the reins, the men picked their way down the hill, avoiding rough patches so that Adelia should not be jounced about.

They went in silence.

In his free hand, Rowley carried a bag made out of his cloak. The object in it was round and attracted attention from the hounds until Hugh called them off. After a first glance, Adelia avoided looking at it.

The rain that the dawn had threatened began when they reached the road. Peasants on their way to work put up their hoods, glancing from under them at the little procession with its following of red-jowled dogs.

Passing an area of bog, Rowley pulled the horse up and spoke to Hugh, who squelched off the road and came back with a handful of bog moss.

"Is this the muck you put on wounds?"

Adelia nodded, squeezed some of the water out of the sphagnum moss, then applied it to her arm.

It would be nonsensical to die of putrefaction now, though at the moment she had no feeling left in which to wonder why that should be so.

"Better put some on your eye as well," Rowley said, and she realized that there was yet another pain and that her left eye was closing.

The nun's horse had drawn level. Adelia saw without interest that the girl sat with her face hidden by the cloak Hugh had wrapped her in for decency's sake.

Rowley saw her look. "May we go on now?" he asked, as if she had demanded the delay. He pulled on the reins without waiting for a reply.

Adelia roused herself. "I haven't thanked you," she told him, and felt the pressure of Ulf's hand on her shoulders. "We thank you. . . ." There weren't words for it.

She might have dislodged a stone from a dam.

"What in hell did you think you were doing? Do you know what you put me through?"

"I'm sorry," she told him.

"Sorry? Is that an apology? Are you *apologizing*? Have you any conception . . . ? Let me tell you it was God's mercy I left the assize early. I set out for Old Benjamin's because I was sorry for you in your misery. *Misery*? Mary of God, what was it for *me* when I found you gone?"

"I'm sorry," she said again. Somewhere, deep in the impassivity of exhaustion that encased her, a tiny shift, a bubble of movement.

"Matilda B. said you'd likely gone to church to pray. But I knew, oh, I knew. She was waiting for the bloody river to tell her something, I said. It's told her. She's gone after the bastard like the witless female she is."

The bubble grew and was joined by others. She heard Ulf snuffling, like he did when he was amused. "You see . . ." she said.

But Rowley was remorseless, his wrongs too great. He'd heard Hugh's horn blowing on the other bank and had waded the bloody river to get to him. Immediately, the huntsman had suggested tracking Adelia by Safeguard's scent.

"Hugh said Prior Geoffrey attached the bloody animal to you for that very purpose, having worried for your safety in an alien town and no other canine leaving a scent so rank. I always wondered why you went everywhere with the cur, but at least it had the sense to leave a trail, which was more than you did "

Bless him, so cross. Adelia looked down at the tax inspector and breathed in the magic of the man.

He'd made a dash into Old Benjamin's house and up to Adelia's room, he said. Grabbed the mat the Safeguard slept on and came down again to shove it under Hugh's hounds' noses. He'd acquired the horses by snatching them from under passing, innocent, protesting riders.

Galloping along the towpath . . . following the scent along the Cam, then the Granta. Nearly losing it across country . . . "And would have if that dog of yours hadn't stank the heavens out. And years off my life with it, you shatterbrained harpy. Do you know what I've suffered?"

Ulf was now openly guffawing. Adelia, hardly able to breathe, thanking Almighty God for such a man. "I do love you, Rowley Picot," she managed.

"That's neither here nor there," he'd said. "And it's not *funny*."

She began drifting off to sleep and was kept in the saddle only by the pressure of Ulf's hands on her shoulders—for him to clasp her round the body was too painful.

Later, she was to remember passing through Barnwell priory's great gates and thinking of the last time she and Simon and Mansur had entered them in a peddler's cart, as ignorant as babes unborn of what faced them. *They'll know now, Simon. Everybody will know.*

After that, the dozes deepened into a long unconsciousness in which she was only vaguely aware of Rowley's voice like the rap of a drum issuing explanation, orders, and Prior Geoffrey's, appalled but also giving instruction. They were overlooking the most important thing, and Adelia woke up long enough to voice it—"I want a bath"— before relapsing to sleep.

". . . AND IN THE NAME OF GOD, *stay* there," Rowley told her. A door slammed.

She and Ulf were alone on a bed in a room, and she was looking up at the timber beams and purlins of a ceiling she'd seen before. Candles—*candles?* Wasn't it day? Yes, but shutters were closed against rain that beat on them.

"Where are we?"

"Prior's guesthouse," Ulf said.

"What's happening?"

"Dunno."

He sat beside her with his knees drawn up, staring at nothing.

What is he seeing? Adelia put her undamaged arm round him and hugged him close. *He is my only companion,* she thought, *as I am his.* The two of them had survived a travail that no one now living had made; only they knew how great was the distance they'd traveled and how long it had taken them and, indeed, how far they had yet to go. Exposure to the extremes of darkness had made them aware of things, not least about themselves, that they should not have known.

"Tell me," she said.

"Nothin' *to* tell. She poles up to where I was fishing and it's *'Oh, Ulf, I think the punt's leaking.'* Nice as honey. Next thing there's stuff over my face and I'm gone. Woke up in the pit."

He threw back his head and an incredulous cry that spoke for the shattered innocence of the ages rang through the room. *"Why?"*

"I don't know."

Desperately, the little boy turned on her. "She was a lily. He was a crusader."

"They were freaks. It didn't show in their countenance, but they were freaks that found each other. Ulf, there are more of us than there are of those. Infinitely more. Hold fast to that." She was trying to hold fast to it herself.

The child's eyes fed off hers. "You come after me."

"They were not going to have you."

He considered it for a while, and then something of its old self crept back into the ugly little face. "I heard you. Gor, you didn't half swear. I ain't heard cussing like that, not even when the troopers came to town."

"You ever tell anybody and it's back to the pit."

Gyltha was in the doorway. Like Rowley, who loomed behind her, she was furious with relief. Tears ran down her face. "You little maggot," she shouted at Ulf. "Didn't I tell you? I'll wallop your backside for you."

Sobbing, she ran to gather up her grandson, who gave a sigh of contentment and held out his arms to her.

"Out," Rowley told them. There were laden servants behind him; Adelia saw the concerned face of Brother Swithin, the priory guestmaster.

As Gyltha headed for the door with Ulf in her arms, she paused to ask Rowley, "Sure as I can't do nothing for her?"

"No. Out you go."

Gyltha still lingered, looking at Adelia. "Was a good day when you came to Cambridge," she said. She went out.

Men came in with a huge tin bath and began pouring steaming jugs of water in it; one had bars of yellow soap resting on a pile of the harsh segments of old sheeting that passed for towels in the monastery.

Adelia watched the preparations hungrily; if she could not wash the filth the killers had imposed on her mind, she could at least scrub it from her body.

Brother Swithin was troubled by the arrangements. "The lady is injured, I should fetch the infirmarian."

Rowley said, grimly, "When I found the lady, she was rolling on the ground in battle with the forces of darkness; she will survive."

"There should at least be a female attendant. . . ."

"Out," Rowley said. "Out now." He opened his arms and scooped the whole boiling of them to the door and shut it on them. He was a massive man, Adelia realized. The fat she'd derided was lessened; he was still heavy, but great strength of muscle had been revealed.

Lumbering to where she lay, he put his hands under her armpits, lifted her so that she stood on the floor, and began undressing her, picking her dreadful clothes off with surprising delicacy.

She felt very small. *Was this seduction?* For certain he would stop when he reached her shift.

It wasn't and he didn't; this was care. As he picked up her naked body and slipped it into the bath, she looked into his face; it might have been Gordinus's, intent over an autopsy.

I should be embarrassed, she thought. *I would be embarrassed, but I am not.*

The bath was warm and she slid down it, grabbing one of the soaps before she went completely underwater, scrubbing, rejoicing in the harshness against her skin. Raising her arms was difficult, so she surfaced long enough to ask him to wash her hair and felt his fingers strong against her scalp. The servants had left ewers of fresh water that he poured over her hair to rinse it.

She couldn't bend to reach her feet without pain, so he laved those as well, intent, meticulously going between the toes.

She thought, watching him, *I am in a bath, naked in a bath with no bubbles, and a man is washing me; my reputation is doomed and to hell with it. I've been to hell and all I wanted in it was to be alive for this man. Who carried me out of it.*

It was as if she and Ulf, all of them, had fallen into a world not even

nightmare had prepared them for but which coexisted with the normal so closely that an unguarded step gained access to it. It was at the
end of everything, or perhaps at the beginning, a savagery that, though
they had survived it, revealed convention as an illusion. The thread of
her life had so nearly been sheared that never again would she depend
on having a future.

And in that moment, she had wanted this man. Still wanted him.

Adelia, who'd thought she was conversant with all conditions of
the body, was new to this one. She felt soapy, *lubricated*, within as well as
without; it was as if she were bursting into foliage, her skin rising
toward him, desperate for him to touch it—he who, at the moment,
was regarding not her breasts but the bruises across her poor ribs.

"Did he hurt you? *Truly* hurt you, I mean?" he asked.

She wondered what he considered the bruises and the wound in
her arm to be, and her eye. Then she thought: *Ah, was I raped? It matters
to them. Virginity is their holy grail.*

"And if he did?" she asked gently.

"That's the thing," he said. He was kneeling beside the bath now so
their heads could be on a level. "All the way to the hill, I was seeing
what he could do to you, but, as long you survived it, *I didn't care.*" He
shook his head at the extraordinary. "Fouled or in pieces, I wanted you
back. You were mine, not his."

Oh, oh.

"He didn't touch me," she said, "apart from this and this. I'll mend."

"Good," he said briskly, and got up. "Well, there's much to do. I
can't be dallying with women in baths; there's arrangements to be
made, not least for our marriage."

"Marriage?"

"I shall speak to the prior, of course, and he will speak to Mansur;
these things must be done with propriety. And there's the king . . . tomorrow, perhaps, or the day after, when all's settled."

"Marriage?"

"You have to marry me now, woman," he said, surprised. "I've seen you in your bath."

He was going, actually leaving.

She hauled herself painfully out of the bath, grabbing one of the towels. There wouldn't be a tomorrow, didn't he realize? Tomorrows were full of awful things. Today, *now*, was the essential. There was no time for propriety.

"Don't leave me, Rowley. I can't endure to be alone."

And that was true. Not all the forces of darkness were vanquished; one was still somewhere in this building; some would stalk her memory always. Only he could keep them out.

Wincing, she slid her arms round his neck and felt the warm, damp softness of her skin against his.

Gently, he disengaged them. "This is another thing, don't you see, woman? This is a marriage between us; it must be in accordance with holy law."

A fine moment, she thought, for him to worry about holy law. "There isn't time, Rowley. There isn't any time beyond that door."

"No, there isn't. I've got a great deal to see to." But he was beginning to pant. Her bare feet were standing on his boots, the towel had slipped, and every inch of her body that could reach it was pressed against his.

"You're making this very hard for me, Adelia." His mouth quirked. "In more ways than one."

"I know." She could feel it.

He pretended to sigh. "It won't be easy making love to a woman with broken ribs."

"Try," she said.

"Oh, dear Christ," he said harshly. And carried her to the bed. And tried. And did very well, first cradling her and crooning to her in Arabic as if neither English nor French was sufficient to express how beautiful she was to him, black eye or not, and after that, supporting his weight on his arms so as not to crush her.

And she knew herself to be beautiful to him, just as he was beautiful to her, and this was sex, was it, this throbbing, slippery ride to the stars and back.

"Can you do it again?" she asked.

"Good God, woman. No, I can't. Well, not yet. It's been a difficult day." But again, after a while, he tried and did equally well.

Brother Swithin was not generous with his candles, and they went out, leaving the room in semidarkness from the rain still lashing against the shutters. She lay crooked in her lover's arm, breathing in the wonderful smell of soap and sweat.

"I love you so much," she said.

"Are you crying?" He sat up.

"No."

"Yes, you are. Coitus does that to some women."

"You'd know, of course." Wiping her eyes with the back of her hand.

"Sweetheart, this is completion. He's gone, she will be . . . well, we'll see. I shall be rewarded as I deserve, and you, too—not that you deserve anything. Henry will give me a nice barony that we can both get fat on and rear dozens of nice, fat little barons."

He got out of bed and reached for his clothes.

His cloak is missing, she thought. *It is somewhere outside this room with Rakshasa's head in it. Everything terrible is beyond that door; the only completion you and I shall ever have is with us now.*

"Don't go," she said.

"I'll be back." His mind had already moved away from her. "I can't stay here all day, forced to swive insatiable women against my will. There's things to do. Go to sleep."

And he'd gone.

Still watching the door, she thought, *I could have him for always. I could have him and our little barons. What is playing the doctor compared to happiness like that? Nothing. Who are the dead to rob me of life?*

With that settled, she lay back and closed her eyes, yawning, replete. But as she drifted into sleep, her last coherent thought was of the clitoris. *What an organ of surprise and wonder it is. I must pay it more attention the next time I dissect a female.*

Always and ever the doctor.

She came to, protesting at someone's repetition of her name, determined to stay asleep. She sniffed in the pungency of clothes kept in pennyroyal against the moth.

"Gyltha? What time is it?"

"Night. And time you was up, girl. I brought you fresh clothes."

"No." She was stiff and her bruises were aching; she was staying in bed. She made a concession by squinting out of one eye. "How's Ulf?"

"Sleepin' the sleep of the just." Gyltha's rough hand cupped Adelia's cheek for a moment. "But you both got to get up. There's some high-and-mighties gatherin' over the way as want answers to their questions."

"I suppose so," she said wearily. They were quick with their trial. Her evidence and Ulf's would be essential, but there were things better left unremembered.

Gyltha went for food, collops of bacon swimming in a beany, delicious broth, and Adelia was so hungry that she hoisted herself into a sitting position. "I can feed myself."

"No, you bloody can't." Since words failed her, Gyltha's gratitude for the safe return of her grandson could best be expressed by stuffing huge spoonfuls into Adelia's mouth as into a baby bird's.

There was one question that had to be asked through the bacon. "Where have they put . . . ?" She couldn't bring herself to name the madwoman. *And I suppose,* Adelia thought with even greater weariness, *because she is a madwoman, I must see to it that they do not torture her.*

"Next door. Being waited on like Lady Muck-a-muck." Gyltha's lips shriveled as if touched by acid. "They don't believe it."

"Don't believe what? Who don't?"

"As her did them . . . things, along of *him.*" Neither could Gyltha bring herself to use the names of the killers.

"Ulf can tell them. So can I. Gyltha, she threw me down the shaft."

"See her do it, did you? And what's Ulf's word worth? A ignorant little slip as sells eels along of his ignorant old gran?"

"It was her." Adelia spat out food because panic was rising in her throat. It was one thing for the nun to be spared torture, quite another that she be set free; the woman was insane; she could do it again. "Peter, Mary, Harold, Ulric . . . of *course* they went with her; they trusted her. A holy sister? Offering jujubes a crusader taught her how to make? Then the laudanum over their noses—believe me, there's a plentiful supply at the convent." Afresh, Adelia saw delicate hands upraised in prayer turn downward into clawed iron bands. "Almighty God . . ." She rubbed her forehead.

Gyltha shrugged. "Saint Raddy's nuns don't do that, seemingly."

"But it was the *river.* I knew, that's why I got into her boat. She had the freedom of the river, up and down—to Grantchester, to *him.* She was familiar; people waved at her or didn't notice her at all. A saintly nun taking supplies to anchorites? Nobody to check her movements, certainly not Prioress Joan. And Walburga, if she was with her, Walburga always went off to her aunt's. What do they think she was doing when she stayed out all night?"

"I know this, Ulf do knows it. But see . . ." Gyltha was a dogged devil's advocate. "She's near as hurt as you are. They brought in one of the sisters to bathe her on account of I wouldn't touch the hag, but I took a look. Bruises all over, bites, eye closed like yourn. The nun as was

a-washing her wept for how the poor thing suffered, and all for coming to help you."

"She . . . liked it. She enjoyed him hurting her. *It's true.*" For Gyltha
had drawn back, frowning with incomprehension. How to explain to
her, to *anybody,* that the nun's screams of terror during the beast's attack had mingled with shrieks of insane, exquisite joy?

She can't understand such perversity, Adelia thought in despair, *and I can't
either.* Dully, she said, "She procured those children for him. And she
killed Simon."

The bowl slipped out of Gyltha's hand and rolled across the room,
spilling broth over the wide, elm floorboards. "Master Simon?"

Adelia was back in Grantchester on the night of the feast, watching
Simon of Naples talk excitedly to the tax collector at the end of the
high table, the tallies in his wallet, only a few places from the chair
in which sat the giver of the feast, whom they incriminated, only a
few more from the woman who had procured the murderer's victims
for him.

"I saw him tell her to kill Simon." And she saw them again now,
dancing together, the crusader and the nun, the one instructing the
other.

Dear Lord, she should have realized then. Irascible, woman-hating
Brother Gilbert had as good as told her without knowing the import:
*"They stay out all night. They comport themselves in licentiousness and lust. In a de-
cent house, they'd be whipped until their arses bled, but where's their prioress? Out
hunting."*

Simon leaving early, to examine the tallies he'd gained and find out
who it was who had a financial reason for implicating Jews in the murders. His host coming back from the garden after a short absence, having seen his creature on her way.

"She left the feast early, Grantchester. I think I saw the other nuns
later on, but not her. Did I? Yes, I'm sure I did. And the prioress
stayed even later."

And then what? The gentlest and most angelic of the sisters . . . ?
"So far to walk on this dark night, Master Simon, may I not punt you home? Yes, yes,
there is room. I am alone, glad of your company."

Adelia thought of the Cam's willow-dark stretches and a slim figure
with wrists strong as steel stabbing a pole into the water, pressing it
down on a man as on a speared fish while he floundered and drowned.

"He told her to kill Simon and steal his wallet," Adelia said. "She
did what he told her; she was enslaved to him. In the pit I had to take
Ulf from her. I think she was going to kill him so that he couldn't give
her away."

"Don't I know?" Gyltha asked, even as her hands made pushing
notions against the knowledge. "Ain't Ulf told me what she did? And
me knowing what both *would* have done to the boy if the good Lord
hadn't sent you to stop 'em. What they did to the others . . ." Her eyes
went into slits and she stood up. "Let's you and me go next door and
stick a pillow on her face."

"No. Everyone must know what she did, what *he* did."

Rakshasa had escaped justice. His terrible end . . . Adelia shut her
mind to avoid the vision against the sunrise . . . had not been justice.
Eliminating that creature from the earth it sullied had not weighted
its side of the scales against the pile of little bodies it had left in its passage from the Holy Land.

Even if they had captured it, dragged it to the assize, put it on trial,
and executed it, the scales would have remained unbalanced for those
whose children had been torn from them, but at least people would
have known what it had done and seen it pay. The Jews would have
been publicly exonerated. Most important, the law that brought order
from chaos, that separated civilized humanity from the animals,
would have been upheld.

While Gyltha helped her to dress, Adelia examined her conscience
to see whether her objection against capital punishment had been
abandoned. No, it had not; it was a principle. The mad must be re-

strained, certainly, yet not judicially killed. Rakshasa had escaped legal exposure: His collaborator must not. Her actions had to be recounted in full common view so that some equilibrium was brought into the world.

"She has to stand trial," Adelia said.

"You think she's a-going to?"

A knock on the door was Prior Geoffrey's. "My dear girl, my poor, dear girl. I thank the Lord for your courage and deliverance."

She brushed his prayers aside. "Prior, the nun . . . She was his accomplice in everything. As much a killer as he was, she murdered Simon of Naples without a thought. You *do* believe that?"

"I fear I must. I have listened to Ulf's account, which, though confused by whatever soporific she gave him, leaves no doubt that she abducted him to that place where he was put in danger of his life. I have also heard what Sir Rowley and the hunter had to tell. This very evening I visited that hole with them. . . ."

"You've been to Wandlebury?"

"I have," the prior said wearily. "And never was I so close to hell. Oh, dear, the equipment we found there. One can only rejoice that Sir Joscelin's soul will burn for eternity. *Joscelin* . . ." The emphasis was to help him believe it. "A local boy. I had marked him as a future sheriff of the county." A spark of indignation enlivened the prior's tired eyes. "I even accepted a donation toward our new chapel from those heinous hands."

"Jews' money," Adelia said. "He owed it to the Jews."

He sighed. "I suppose it was. Well, at least our friends in the tower have been absolved."

"And is the town to be made aware that they *are* absolved?" Adelia jerked an inelegant thumb toward the room in which the nun was housed. "She *will* be put on trial?" She was getting restive; there was a reservation, a fogginess, in some of the prior's answers.

He went to the window and opened the shutter a crack. "They said it would rain. The dawn was a true shepherd's warning, apparently. Well, the gardens need it after a dry spring." He closed the shutter. "Yes, an announcement declaring the Jews' innocence shall be trumpeted in full assize—thank heaven it is still in progress. But as for the . . . female . . . I have asked for a convocation of all those concerned to get to the truth of the matter. They are gathering now."

"A convocation? Why not a trial?" *And why at nighttime?*

As if she hadn't spoken, he said, "I expected it to meet at the castle, but the clerk of the assize deemed that an inquiry be better held here so that the legal processes should not be confused. And after all, it is here that the children are buried. Well, we shall see, we shall see."

Such a good man, her first friend in England and she had not thanked him. "My lord, I owe you my life. If it hadn't been for your gift of the dog, bless him . . . Did you see what was done to him?"

"I saw." Prior Geoffrey shook his head, then smiled a little. "I ordered his remnants gathered and given to Hugh, whom Brother Gilbert suspects of secretly burying his hounds in the priory graveyard when no one is by. The Safeguard may well lie with human beings who are less faithful."

It had been a small grief among all the rest but a grief nevertheless; Adelia was comforted.

"However," the prior went on, "as you and I know, you also owe your life to someone with more right to it, and, in part, I am here for him."

But her mind had reverted to the nun. *They're going to let her go. None of us saw her kill: not Ulf, not Rowley, not me. She's a nun; the Church fears a scandal. They're going to let her go.*

"I won't have it, Prior," she said.

Prior Geoffrey's mouth had been shaping words that obviously pleased him; now it stopped, open. He blinked. "A somewhat hasty decision, Adelia."

"People must know what was done. She must be brought to trial, even if she is adjudged too mad for sentence. For the children's sake, for Simon's, for mine; I found their lair and was near killed for it. I will have justice—and it must be seen to be done." Not from blood-lust, nor even revenge, but because, without a completion, the night-mares of too many people would be left open-ended.

Then something the prior had said caught up with her. "I beg your pardon, my lord?"

Prior Geoffrey sighed and began again. "Before he was forced to re-turn to the assize—the king has arrived, you know—he approached me. For lack of anyone else, he seems to regard me as in loco parentis. . . ."

"The king?" Adelia wasn't keeping up.

The prior sighed once more. "Sir Rowley Picot. Sir Rowley has asked me to approach you with a request—indeed, his manner sug-gested it to be a foregone conclusion—for your hand in marriage."

It was all one with this extraordinary day. She had gone down into the pit and been raised from it. A man had been torn to death. Next door was a murderess. She had lost her virginity, gloriously lost it, and the man who had taken it now reverted to etiquette, using the good offices of a surrogate father to request her hand.

"I should add," Prior Geoffrey said, "that the proposal is made at some cost. At the assize, the king offered Sir Rowley the bishopric of Saint Albans, and with my own ears I heard Picot reject the position on the grounds that he wished to remain free to marry."

He wants me as much as that?

"King Henry was not pleased," the prior went on. "He has a partic-ular wish to appoint our good tax collector to the see of Saint Albans, nor is he used to being thwarted. But Sir Rowley was not to be moved."

Now it was Adelia's mouth that remained paused over the answer she had known she must make, unable to make it.

With the rush of love came fear that she would accept because she so very much wanted to, because this morning Rowley had soothed away the mental damage done and purified it. Which, of course, was the danger in itself. *He has made such sacrifice for me. Isn't it right, and beautiful, that I make similar sacrifice for him?*

Sacrifice.

Prior Geoffrey said, "He may have disappointed King Henry, but he charges me to tell you that he is still well regarded and marked for high position so that there can be no disadvantage to you by the match." When Adelia still didn't answer, he went on: "Indeed, I have to say I would be content to see you bound to him."

Bound.

"Adelia, my dear." Prior Geoffrey took her hand. "The man deserves an answer."

He did. She gave it.

The door opened and Brother Gilbert stood on the threshold, rendering the scene before him—his superior in the company of two women in a bedroom—into something naughty. "The lords are assembled, Prior."

"Then we must attend them." The prior raised Adelia's hand and kissed it, but it was his wink at Gyltha—who winked back—that was naughty.

THE CONVOKED LORDS were met in the monastery's refectory rather than its church so that the canons were free to keep the hours of vigil where and when they always did; nor, having taken supper and it being some hours until breakfast, need they disturb the convocation at its business.

Or even know it has taken place, Adelia thought.

They called it a convocation, but it was, in effect, a trial. *Not* of the young nun who stood suitably chaperoned between her prioress and Sister Walburga, her head modestly bowed and her hands meekly folded.

The accused was Vesuvia Adelia Rachel Ortese Aguilar, a foreigner, who, according to an angry Prioress Joan called from her bed, had made an unwarranted, obscene, *devilish* accusation against an innocent and godly member of the holy order of Saint Radegund, and must be whipped for it.

Adelia stood in the middle of the hall with the imps that studded the beams of its hammer roof grinning down at her. Its long table with its benches had been pushed to one side against a wall, so that the line of chairs at the far end in which the judges sat was off-center, skewing the room's otherwise lovely proportions for her and giving another scrape to nerves already quivering from disbelief, anger, and, it had to be said, plain fear.

For facing her were three of the several justices in eyre who had come to Cambridge for its assize—the Bishops of Norwich and Lincoln, and the Abbot of Ely. They represented England's legal authority. They could close their jeweled fists and crush Adelia like a pomander. Also, they were cross at being summoned from a sleep they deserved after the long day's hearings at the assize, at traveling from the castle to Saint Augustine's in darkness and pouring rain—and at her. She could feel hostility emanating from them strong enough to blow the floor's rushes down its length and into a pile at her feet.

Most hostile of all was an Archdeacon of Canterbury, not a judge but someone who regarded himself, and, apparently, was regarded by the others, as a mouthpiece for the late, sainted Thomas à Becket and seemed to think that any attack on a member of the Church—such as Adelia's denunciation of Veronica, sister of Saint Radegund—was comparable to Henry II's knights spilling Becket's brains on his cathedral floor.

That they were all churchmen had taken Prior Geoffrey aback. "My lords, I'd hoped that some lords temporal might also attend."

They silenced him; they were, after all, his spiritual superiors. "It is purely a Church matter."

With them was a young man in nonclerical dress, slightly amused
by the whole proceeding and using a portable writing desk to make
notes of it on a parchment. Adelia knew his name only because one of
the others addressed him by it—Hubert Walter.

Behind their chairs were ranged a selection of assize attendants,
two clerks, one of them asleep where he stood, a man-at-arms who'd
forgotten to take off his nightcap before putting on his helmet, and
two bailiffs with manacles at their belt, each carrying a mace.

Adelia stood apart and alone, though for a while Mansur had stood
beside her.

"What is . . . that, Prior?"

"He is Mistress Adelia's attendant, my lord."

"A Saracen?"

"A distinguished Arab doctor, my lords."

"She has no need of either a doctor or an attendant. Nor have we."

Mansur had been banished from the room.

Prior Geoffrey was standing to one side of the line of chairs with
Sheriff Baldwin—Brother Gilbert behind them both.

He had done his best, bless him; the dreadful story had been told,
Adelia's and Simon's part in it explained, their discoveries and Simon's death recounted, the evidence delivered of the prior's own eyes
as to what lay beneath Wandlebury Hill—and he had outlined the
charge against Sister Veronica.

He had carefully mentioned neither Adelia's examination of the
children's bodies nor her qualification for it—a neglect for which she
thanked God; she was in enough trouble, she knew, without facing an
accusation of witchcraft.

Hugh the hunter had been called into the refectory with his frank-
pledges, the men who, under England's legal system, answered for his
honesty. He'd stood with his hat on his heart to state that, looking
down the shaft, he had seen a bloody, naked figure that he recognized

as Sir Joscelin of Grantchester. That he had later descended into the tunnels. That he had examined the flint knife. That he had recognized the dog collar attached to the chain in the womblike chamber. . . .

"'Twas Sir Joscelin's, my lords. I'd seen it a dozen times on his own hound in former days—had his seal embossed in its leather, so it did."

The dog collar was produced, the seal examined.

No doubt that Sir Joscelin of Grantchester had killed the children— the judges had been appalled. *"Joscelin of Grantchester shall be declared base felon and murderer. The remains of his corpse shall hang in Cambridge market square for all to see and shall not be accorded Christian burial."*

As for Sister Veronica . . .

There was no direct evidence against her, because Ulf was not allowed to give it.

"How old is the child, Prior? He may not be accorded frankpledge until he is twelve."

"Nine, my lord, but a percipient and honest boy."

"Of what degree?"

"He is free, my lords, not a villein. He works for his grandmother and sells eels."

At this point, there was an interjection from Brother Gilbert, who whispered treacherously into the ear of the archdeacon with every sign of satisfaction.

Ah, the grandmother was not married, never had been, possibly the progenitor of illegitimate children. The boy was likely a bastard, then, of no degree whatsoever: "The law does not recognize him."

So Ulf, like Mansur, was banished to the kitchen that lay behind the refectory, with Gyltha's hand over his mouth to stop him from shouting out, both of them listening on the other side of the open hatch from which a smell of bacon and broth came to mingle with that of the rich, rain-dampened ermine lining the judges' cloaks, while Rabbi Gotsce, also in the kitchen, translated into English for them proceedings that were being held in Latin.

The court had been scandalized by his very presence.

"*You would bring a Jew before us, Prior Geoffrey?*"

"*My lords, the Jews of this town have been grossly maligned. It can be shown that Sir Joscelin was one of their chief debtors, and it was part of his wickedness to see them accused of murder and their tallies burned.*"

"*Has the Jew evidence of this?*"

"*The tallies were destroyed, my lord, as I said. But surely the rabbi is entitled to . . .*"

"*The law does not recognize him.*"

The law didn't recognize, either, that a nun whose purity of soul shone in her face could do what Adelia had said she had done.

Her prioress spoke for her. . . .

"Like Saint Radegund, our beloved foundress, Sister Veronica was born in Thuringia," she said. "But her father, a merchant, settled in Poitiers, where she was offered to the convent at the age of three and sent to England while still a child, though one whose devotion to God and His Holy Mother was in evidence then and has been ever since."

Prioress Joan had tempered her voice; her rein-callused hands were in her sleeves; she was every inch the superior of a well-ordered house of God. "My lords, I stand for this nun's modesty and temperance and her devotion to the Lord—many a time when the other nuns were at recreation, Sister Veronica has been on her knees beside our blessed little saint, Peter of Trumpington."

There was a muffled squeak from the kitchen.

"Whom she lured to his death," Adelia said.

"Hold your tongue, woman," the archdeacon told her.

The prioress turned on Adelia, finger pointing, her voice a hunting horn. "*Judge,* my lords. Judge between *that,* a slandering viper, and *here,* this exemplar of saintliness."

It was a pity that the dress Gyltha had brought her from Old Benjamin's was the one Adelia had worn to the Grantchester feast, too low in the bodice and too high in color to compare well with the nuns' sleekly sober black and white. A pity, too, that in her joyous fluster over Ulf's return, Gyltha had forgotten to bring a veil or cap and that, therefore, Adelia, whose previous cap lay somewhere under Wandlebury Hill, was as bareheaded as a harlot.

No one except Prior Geoffrey spoke for her.

Not Sir Rowley Picot; he wasn't there.

The Archdeacon of Canterbury rose to his feet, which were still in slippers. He was a tiny old man, full of energy. "Let us expedite this matter, my lords, that we may return to our beds and, should we find it has been raised out of malice"—the face he turned on Adelia was that of a malevolent monkey—"let those responsible be sent to the whipping post. Now, then . . ."

One by one, the bricks on which Adelia had built her case were examined and discarded.

The word of an eel-selling bastard minor to condemn a bride of Christ?

The good sister's familiarity with the river? But who was not familiar with boatmanship in this waterlogged town?

Laudanum? Was it not generally available at any apothecary's?

Spending the occasional night away from her convent? Well . . .

For the first time, the young man called Hubert Walter raised his voice, and his head from his note-taking: "Perhaps that does call for explanation, my lord. It is . . . unusual."

"If I may speak, your lordships." Prioress Joan stepped forward again. "Taking supplies to our anchorites is an act of charity that exhausts Sister Veronica's strength—see how frail she is. Accordingly, I have allowed her permission to spend such nights in rest and contemplation with one of our lady eremites before returning to the convent."

"Laudable, laudable." The eyes of the judges rested appreciatively on Sister Veronica's willow-wand figure.

Which lady eremite, Adelia wondered, *and why should she not be hauled be-*

fore this court to be asked how many nights she and the frail Veronica have spent in contemplation?

None, I'll warrant.

But it was useless; the anchorite, *being* an anchorite, would not come. Demanding that she attend could only confirm Adelia's stridency as opposed to Veronica's respectful silence.

Where are you, Rowley? I cannot stand here alone. Rowley, they're going to let her go.

The dismemberment went on. Who had seen Simon of Naples die? Had not the inquest confirmed that the Jew drowned accidentally?

The walls of the great room were closing in. A bailiff studied the manacles he carried as if to judge them small enough for Adelia's wrists. Above her head, the gargoyles gibbered in glee and the eyes of the judges stripped the skin off her.

Now the archdeacon was questioning her motive in going to Wandlebury Hill at all. "What led her to that infamous place, my lords? How did she know what went on there? Can we not assume that it was she who was in league with the devil of Grantchester, and not the holy sister she accuses—whose only crime, it seems, was to follow her out of concern for her safety?"

Prior Geoffrey opened his mouth but was forestalled by the clerk Hubert Walter, still amused. "I think we must accept, my lords, that all four children died before this female set foot in England. We may at least acquit her of their murder."

"Really?" The archdeacon was disappointed. "Nevertheless, we have proved her a slanderer and, by her own statement, she had knowledge of the pit and its circumstances. I find that curious, my lords. I find it suspicious."

"So do I." The Bishop of Norwich broke in, yawning. "Take the damned female to the whipping post and be done with it."

"Is that the verdict of you all?"

It was.

Adelia shouted, not for herself but for Cambridgeshire's children. "Don't let her go, I beg you. She can kill again."

The judges weren't listening, not looking at her—their attention had been claimed by somebody who'd entered the refectory from the kitchen, where he'd taken himself a bowl of bacon broth and was now eating it.

He blinked at the assembly. "A trial, is it?"

Adelia waited for this plainly dressed man in leather to be blasted back to where he came from. A couple of boar hounds had slouched in with him—a hunter, then, who'd wandered here by mistake.

But the lord judges were standing. Were bowing. Were remaining on their feet.

Henry Plantagenet, King of England, Duke of Normandy and Aquitaine, Count of Anjou, hoisted himself up on the refectory table, letting his legs dangle, and looked around. "Well?"

"Not a trial, my lord." The Bishop of Norwich was as awake and fluttering as a lark now. "A convocation, merely a preliminary inquiry into the matter of the town's murdered children. The killer has been identified, but *that*"—he pointed in the direction of Adelia—"that female has brought an accusation of complicity against this nun of Saint Radegund."

"Ah, yes," the king said, pleasantly, "I *thought* our lords spiritual were somewhat overrepresented. Where's De Luci? De Glanville? The lords temporal?"

"We did not wish to disturb their rest, my lord."

"Very thoughtful," Henry said, still pleasant though the bishop quailed. "And how are we getting on?"

Hubert Walter had left his place to stand by the king, holding out his parchment.

Henry took it, putting down his bowl of broth. "I hope nobody minds if I make myself familiar with the case—it's been causing me some trouble, you see; my Cambridge Jews have been incarcerated in the castle tower because of it."

He added mildly enough, but, again, the judges shifted in discomfort, "And I've lost revenue accordingly."

Scanning the parchment, he leaned down and took a handful of rushes from the floor. There was silence as he read, except for the beat of rain against the high windows and a contented gnawing from one of the dogs, who'd found a bone under the table.

Adelia's legs were trembling so much that she didn't know whether they'd hold her up; this plain, casual-seeming man had brought a directionless terror into the refectory.

He began murmuring, holding the parchment to a candelabra on the table in order to see it better. "Boy says abducted by the nun . . . not recognizable in law . . . *hmm*." He put one of the rushes he was holding down beside the light. Absently, he said, "Splendid broth, Prior."

"Thank you, my lord."

"The nun's knowledge and use of the river"—another rush was laid beside the first—"An opiate . . ." This time, the rush was put across the top of the other two. "All-night vigils with an anchorite . . ." He looked up. "Has the anchorite been called to witness? Oh, no, I forgot—this is not a trial."

Adelia's legs became weaker, this time with a hope so tenuous she hardly dared entertain it. Henry Plantagenet's rushes, neatly crisscrossed as if he were going to play spillikin with them, were multiplying with each piece of evidence she'd brought against Veronica.

"Simon of Naples . . . drowned whilst in possession of tallies . . . the river again . . . a Jew, of course, well, what can you expect . . ." Henry shook his head at the carelessness of Jews and read on.

"The laywoman's suspicions . . . Wand-le-bury Hill . . . maintains she was thrown down a pit . . . didn't see who . . . tussles . . . laywoman and nun . . . both injured . . . child rescued . . . local knight responsible . . ."

He looked up, then down at the pile of rushes, then at the judges.

The Bishop of Norwich cleared his throat. "As you see, my lord, all the charges against Sister Veronica are unsubstantiated. Nobody can incriminate her because . . ."

"Except the boy, of course," Henry interrupted, "but we can't give any legal weight to him, can we? No, I agree . . . all circumstantial."

He looked once more at his rushes. "Hell of a lot of circumstance, mind you, but . . ." The king puffed out his cheeks, blew hard, and the rushes scattered. "So what did you decide to do about this slanderous lady . . . what's her name? Adele? Your handwriting is pitiable, Hubert."

"I apologize, my lord. She is called Adelia."

The archdeacon was becoming restive. "It is unpardonable that she should level calumnies such as these against a religious; it cannot be overlooked."

"It certainly can't," Henry agreed. "Should we hang her, do you think?"

The archdeacon battled on. "The woman is a foreigner; she has come from nowhere in company with a Jew and a Saracen. Is she to be allowed to slander Holy Mother Church? By what right? Who sent her and why? To sow discord? I say the devil has put her amongst us."

"It was me, really," the king said.

The room was silenced as if an avalanche of snow had muffled it. From the door behind the judges came the sound of shuffling, splashing feet as Barnwell's canons groped their way through the rain along the cloister to church.

Henry looked at Adelia for the first time and exposed his ferocious little teeth in a grin. "Didn't know that, did you?"

He turned on the judges, who, not having been invited to sit, were still standing. "You see, my lords, children were disappearing in Cambridge and so were my revenues. Jews in the tower. Trouble in the streets. As I said to Aaron of Lincoln—you know him, Bishop; he lent you money for your cathedral—Aaron, I said, something must be done about Cambridge. If the Jews are slaughtering infants for their rituals, we must hang them. If not, somebody else must hang. Which reminds me . . ." He raised his voice. "Come in, Rabbi, I'm told this is not a trial."

The door from the kitchen opened and Rabbi Gotsce entered cautiously, bowing with a frequency that showed he was nervous.

The king took no more notice of him. "Anyway, Aaron went away to consider and, having considered, returned. He said that the man we needed was a certain Simon of Naples—another Jew, I fear, my lords, but an investigator of renown. Aaron also suggested that Simon be asked to bring with him a master in the art of death." Henry bestowed another of his smiles on the judges. "I expect you are asking yourselves: What *is* a master in the art of death? I know I did. A necromancer? A species of refined torturer? But no, it appears there are qualified men who can read corpses and, in this case, might gain from the manner of the Cambridge children's murder an indication as to the perpetrator. Is there any more of this excellent broth?"

The transition was so fast that it was some minutes before Prior Geoffrey roused himself and crossed to the hatch as if a man in a dream. It seemed natural that a woman's hand extend a steaming bowl to him. He took it, walked back, and proffered it to the king on bended knee.

The king had employed the interim in chatting to Prioress Joan. "I hoped to go after boar tonight. Is it too late, do you think? Will they have returned to their lair?"

The prioress was bewildered but charmed. "Not yet, my lord. May I recommend you employ your hounds toward Babraham, where the woods . . ." Her voice trailed away as realization overtook her. "I repeat hearsay, my lord. I have little time for hunting."

"Really, madam?" Henry appeared gently surprised. "I have heard you famed as a regular Diana."

An ambush, Adelia thought. She realized she was watching an exercise that, whether it succeeded or not, raised cunning to the realm of art.

"So," the king said, chewing, "thank you, Prior. So, I asked Aaron, 'Where in hell can I find a master in the art of death?' And he said, 'Not in hell, my lord, in Salerno.' He likes his little quips, does our Aaron. It seems the excellent medical school in Salerno produces men qualified in that recondite science. So, to cut a long story short, I wrote to the King of Sicily." He beamed at the prioress. "He's a friend, you know. I wrote begging the services of Simon of Naples and a death master."

Having swallowed too quickly, the king began to cough and had to be slapped on the back by Hubert Walter.

"Thank you, Hubert." He wiped his eyes. "Well, two things went awry. For one thing, I was out of England putting down the bloody Lusignans when Simon of Naples arrived in this country. For another, it appears that in Salerno they qualify women in medicine—can you believe it, my lords?—and some idiot who couldn't tell Adam from Eve sent not a *master* in the art of death but a *mistress.* There she is."

He looked at Adelia, though nobody else did; they watched the king, always the king. "So I'm afraid, my lords, we can't hang her— much as we want to. She's not our property, you see, she's a subject of the King of Sicily, and friend William will want her returned to him in good condition."

He was down from the table now, walking the floor and picking his teeth as if in deep reflection. "What do you say, my lords? Do you think, in view of the fact that this woman and a Jew, between them, seem to have saved further children from a nasty death at the hands of a gentleman whose head is even now pickling in the castle brine bucket . . ." He drew a puzzled breath, shaking his head. "Can we so much as scourge her?"

Nobody said anything; they weren't meant to.

"In fact, my lords, King William will take it amiss if there is interference with Mistress Adelia, any attempt to charge her with witchcraft or malpractice." The king's voice had become a whip. "And so shall I."

I am your servant all my days. Adelia was limp with gratitude and admiration. *But can you, even you, great Plantagenet, bring the nun to open trial?*

Rowley was in the room now, large, and bowing to the much shorter Henry, handing things to him. "I am sorry to have kept you waiting, my lord." A look passed between them and Rowley nodded. They were in league, he and the king.

He walked up the refectory to stand beside Prior Geoffrey. His cloak was dark with rain and he smelled of fresh air; he *was* fresh air, and she was suddenly overjoyed that her bodice was low and her head bare, like a harlot. She could have stripped for him all over again. *I am your harlot whenever you want, and proud of it.*

He was saying something. The prior was giving instructions to Brother Gilbert, who left the room.

Henry had gone back to his place on the table. He was beckoning to the fattest of the three nuns in the center of the hall. "You, Sister. Yes, you. Come here."

Prioress Joan watched with suspicion as Walburga advanced hesitantly toward the king. Veronica's eyes remained downcast, her hands as still as they had been from the first.

More gently now, but with every word audible, the king said, "Tell me, Sister, what you do at the convent? Speak up. Nothing is going to happen to you, I promise."

It came, breathy at first, but few could resist Henry when he was pleasant, and Walburga wasn't one of them. "I contemplates the Holy

Word, my lord, like the others, and say the prayers. And I pole supplies to the anchorites. . . ." A note of doubt there.

It came to Adelia that Walburga, with her shaky Latin, was so bewildered by the proceedings that she had not attended to most of them.

"And we keep the hours, almost nearly always. . . ."

"Do you eat well? Plenty of meat?"

"Oh, yes, my lord." Walburga was on firm ground and gaining confidence. "Mother Joan do always brings back a buck or two from the
hunt, and my auntie's good with butter and cream. We eat main well."

"What else do you do?"

"I polishes Little Saint Peter's reliquary, and I weaves tokens for
the pilgrims to buy, and I—"

"I'll wager you're the best weaver in the convent." Very jovial.

"Well, I'm pretty with it, my lord, though I do say it as shouldn't,
but maybe Sister Veronica and poor Sister Agnes-as-was run me close."

"I expect you have individual styles?" At Walburga's blink, Henry
rephrased it. "Say I wanted to buy a token from a pile of tokens. Could
you tell me which one was yours and which one Agnes's? Or Veronica's?"

My God. Adelia's skin was prickling. She tried to catch Rowley's eye,
but he would not look at her.

Walburga chuckled. "No need, my lord. I'll do one for you for free."

Henry smiled. "Tut, and I've just sent Sir Rowley to fetch some."
He held out one of the small objects, some figures, some mats that
Rowley had given him. "Did you make this one?"

"Oh, no, that's Sister Odilia's afore she died."

"And this one?"

"That's Magdalene's."

"This?"

"Sister Veronica's."

"Prior." It was a command.

Brother Gilbert was back. Prior Geoffrey was bringing another object for Walburga to look at. "And this, my child? Who made this one?" It lay on his outstretched palm, like a star made of rushes, beautifully and intricately woven into quincuncial shape.

Walburga was enjoying the game. "Why, that's Sister Veronica's, too."

"Are you sure?"

"Sure as sure, my lord. It's her fun. Poor Sister Agnes said as perhaps she shouldn't, them looking heathenlike, but we didn't see no harm."

"No harm," the king said, softly. "Prior?"

Prior Geoffrey faced the judges. "My lords, that is one of the tokens that were lying on the corpses of the Wandlebury children when we found them. This nun has just identified it as being made by the accused sister. Look."

Instead, the judges looked at Sister Veronica.

Adelia held her breath. *It's not conclusive; she can make a hundred excuses. It's clever, but it's not* proof.

It was proof for Prioress Joan; she was staring at her protégée in agony.

It was proof for Veronica. For a moment, she was still. Then she shrieked, raising her head and two shaking hands. "Protect me, my lords. You think he was eaten by dogs, but he's up there. *Up there.*"

Every eye followed hers to the rafters where the gargoyles laughed back at them from the shadows, then down again to Veronica. She had fallen to the floor, squirming. "He'll hurt you. He hurts me when I don't obey him. He hurt when he entered me. *He hurts.* Oh, save me from the devil."

Sixteen

The air in the room heated and became heavy. Men's eyelids half closed, their mouths went slack and their bodies rigid. Veronica gyrated among the rushes on the floor, pulling at her habit, pointing to her vagina, shrieking that the devil had entered her there, *there*.

It was as if the featherweight token had proved a final weight on guilt so heavy and so vast that she assumed it all lay exposed. A door had been broken open and something fetid was coming out of it.

"I prayed to the Mother . . . save me, save me, dear Mary . . . but he speared me with his horn, here, *here*. How it hurt . . . he had antlers . . . I couldn't . . . sweet Son of Mary, he made me watch him do things . . . horrible things, horrible . . . there was blood, such blood. I thirsted for the blood of the Lord, but I was the devil's slave . . . he hurt, he *hurt* . . . he bit my breasts, here, *here,* he stripped me . . . beat me . . . he put his horn in my mouth . . . I prayed for sweet Jesus to come . . . but he is the Prince of Darkness . . . his voice in my ears telling me to do things . . . I was afraid . . . stop him, don't let him . . ."

Prayers, abasement. It went on and on.

But so did your alliance with the beast, Adelia thought. *On and on. Months of it. Child after child procured, its torture observed, and never an attempt to break free. That's not enslavement.*

If she was exposing her soul, Veronica was also exposing her young body: her skirt was above her hocks; her slight breasts showed beneath the rents in her habit.

It's a performance; she's blaming the devil; she killed Simon; she's enjoying it. It's sex, that's what it is.

A glance at the judges showed them enthralled, worse than enthralled: the Bishop of Norwich's hand was on his crutch; the old archdeacon was puffing. Hubert Walter's mouth dribbled. Even Rowley was licking his lips.

In a moment's pause while Veronica gasped for breath, a bishop said, almost reverently, "Demonic possession. As clear a case as I ever saw."

So the demons did it. Another attempt by the Prince of Darkness to undermine Mother Church, a regrettable but understandable incident in the war between sin and sanctity. Only the devil to blame. In despair, Adelia glanced up and into the face of the one man in the room who was looking on with sardonic admiration.

"She killed Simon of Naples," Adelia said.

"I know."

"She helped to kill the children."

"I know," the king said.

Veronica was crawling along the floor now, worming her way to the judges. She clasped the archdeacons' slippers, and her soft, dark hair cascaded over his feet. "Save me, my lord, let him not force me again. I thirst for the Lord; give me back to my Redeemer. Send the devil away." Reasonless, disheveled, the innocence had gone and sexual beauty had taken its place, older and more bruised than what it replaced but beauty nevertheless.

The archdeacon was reaching down to her. "There, there, my child."

The table shook as Henry bounced off it. "Do you keep pigs, my lord Prior?"

Prior Geoffrey dragged his eyes away. "Pigs?"

"Pigs. And somebody get that woman to her feet."

Instructions were given. Hugh left the room. The two men-at-arms raised Veronica so that she hung between them. "Now then, mistress," Henry said to her, "you may help us."

Veronica's eyes as they slid up to his showed a moment's calculation. "Return me to my Redeemer, my lord. Let me wash my sins in the blood of the Lord."

"Redemption is in the truth, and therefore in telling us how the devil killed the children. In what manner. You must show us."

"The Lord wants that? There was blood, so much blood."

"He insists on it." Henry held up a warning hand to the judges, who were on their feet. "She knows. She watched. She shall show us."

Hugh came in with a piglet that he displayed to the king, who nodded. As the hunter carried it past her toward the kitchen, a bewildered Adelia glimpsed a small, rounded, snuffling snout. There was a smell of farmyard.

One of the men-at-arms went by, steering Veronica in the same direction, followed by the other, who held a leaf-shaped knife ceremonially on his outstretched palms, the flint knife, *the* knife.

Is that what he means to happen? God save us, dear God save us all.

The judges, everybody, Walburga blinking, were crowding toward the kitchen. Prioress Joan would have held back, but King Henry grasped her elbow and took her with him.

As Rowley passed her, Adelia said, "Ulf mustn't see this."

"I've sent him home with Gyltha." Then he'd gone, too, and Adelia stood in an empty refectory.

Was it planned? There was more to this than proving Veronica's guilt: Henry was after the Church that had condemned him for Becket.

That, too, was horrible. A trap laid by an artful king, not just for the creature that might or might not fall into it according to how artful *it* was, but to show his greater enemy its own weakness. And however vile the creature it was laid for, a trap was always a trap.

Comings and goings had left the door to the cloister open. Dawn was breaking and the canons were chanting, had been chanting all the time. As she listened to the unison weaving back order and grace, she felt the night air cooling tears on her cheeks that she hadn't known were there.

From the kitchen she heard the king's voice: "Put it on the chopping block. Very well, Sister. Show us what he did."

They were putting the knife in Veronica's hand. . . .

Don't use it, there's no need . . . just tell them.

The nun's voice came clear through the hatch. "I will be redeemed?"

"The truth is redemption." Henry, inexorable. "Show us."

Silence.

The nun's voice again: "He didn't like them to close their eyes, you see." There came the first squeal from the piglet. "And then . . ."

Adelia covered her ears, but her hands couldn't keep out another squeal, then another, shriller now, another . . . and the female voice rising over it: "Like this, and then this. And then . . ."

She's mad. If there was cunning before, it was the cunning of the insane. Even that has left her now. Dear God, what is it like inside that mind?

Laughter? No, it was giggling, a manic sound and growing, sucking life out of the life it was taking, Veronica's human voice turning nonhuman, rising over the dying shrieks of the piglet until it was a bray, a sound that belonged to big, grass-stained teeth and long ears. It went out into the night's normality to fracture it.

It hee-hawed.

———

THE MEN-AT-ARMS brought her back into the refectory and threw her on the floor where the piglet's blood soaking her robe puddled into the rushes. The judges made a wide circle to pass her, the Bishop of Norwich brushing absentmindedly at his splashed gown. Mansur's and Rowley's expressions were fixed. Rabbi Gotsce was white to the lips. Prioress Joan sank onto the bench and buried her head in her arms. Hugh leaned against the doorjamb to stare into space

Adelia hurried to Sister Walburga, who'd staggered and fallen, clawing for air. She knelt, her hand tight round the nun's mouth. "Slowly now. Breathe slowly. Little breaths, shallow."

She heard Henry say, "Well, my lords? It appears she gave the devil every cooperation."

Apart from Walburga's panicking breath, the room was quiet.

After a while, somebody, one of the bishops, spoke: "She will be tried in ecclesiastical court, of course."

"Given benefit of clergy, you mean," the king said.

"She is still ours, my lord."

"And what will you do with her? The Church cannot hang; it can't shed blood. All your court can do is excommunicate her and send her out into the lay world. What happens the next time a killer whistles for her?"

"Plantagenet, beware." It was the archdeacon. "Would you yet wrangle with holy Saint Thomas? Is he to die again at the hands of your knights? Would you dispute his own words? *'The clergy have Christ alone as king and under the King of Heaven; they should be ruled by their own law.'* Bell, book, and candle are the greatest coercion of all; this wretched woman shall lose her soul."

Here was the voice that had echoed through a cathedral with an archbishop's blood on its steps. It echoed through a provincial refectory where the blood of a piglet soaked into the tiles.

"She's already lost her soul. Is England to lose more children?" Here was the other voice, the one that had used secular reason against Becket. It was still reasonable.

Then it wasn't. Henry was taking one of the men-at-arms by the shoulders and shaking him. He moved on to shake the rabbi, then Hugh. "Do you see? *Do you see? This* was the quarrel between Becket and me. Have your courts, I said, but hand the guilty over to mine for punishment." Men were being hurled around the room like rats. "I lost. I lost, d'you see? Murderers and rapists are loose in my land because *I lost.*"

Hubert Walter was clinging to one of his arms, pleading and being dragged along. "My lord, my lord . . . remember, I beg you, remember."

Henry shook him off, stared down at him. "I won't have it, Hubert." He dragged his hand across his mouth to wipe away the spittle. "You hear me, my lords? *I won't have it.*"

He was calmer now, facing the trembling judges. "Try it, condemn it, take its soul away, but I will not have that creature's breath polluting my realm. Send it back to Thuringia, to the far Indies, anywhere, but *I will lose no more children,* and by my soul's salvation, if that thing is still breathing Plantagenet air in two days' time, I shall proclaim to the world what the Church has loosed on it. And you, madam . . ."

It was Prioress Joan's turn. The king pulled her head up from the table by her veil, dislodging the wimple to show wiry, gray hair. "And you . . . If you'd controlled your sisterhood with half the discipline you apply to your hounds . . . She goes, do you understand? She *goes* or I tear down your convent stone by stone with you in it. Now leave this place and take that stinking maggot with you."

IT WAS A RAGGED DEPARTURE. Prior Geoffrey stood at the door, looking old and unwell. Rain had stopped, but the chilly, moist dawn air raised a ground mist and the hooded, cloaked figures mounting their horses or getting into palanquins were difficult to distinguish. Quiet, though, except for the strike of hooves on cobbles and the huff from horses' nostrils and the singing of an early thrush and the crow of a cockerel from a hen run. Nobody spoke. Sleepwalkers, all of them, souls in limbo.

Only the king's departure had been noisy, a rush of boar hounds and riders galloping toward the gates and open country.

Adelia thought she saw two veiled figures being escorted away by men-at-arms. Perhaps the hatted, bowed shape plodding on a solitary course toward the castle was the rabbi. Only Mansur was here beside her, God bless him.

She went and put her arm around Walburga, who had been forgotten. Then she waited for Rowley Picot. And waited.

Either he wasn't coming or he had already gone. *Ah, well . . .*

"It seems we must walk," she said. "Are you well enough?" She was concerned for Walburga; the girl's pulse had been alarming after she'd seen what she should never have seen in the kitchen.

The nun nodded.

Together they ambled through the mist, Mansur striding beside them. Twice Adelia turned to look for the Safeguard; twice she remembered. When she turned for a third time . . . "Oh no, dear God, *no.*"

"What is it?" Mansur asked.

It was Rakshasa walking behind them, his feet hidden in the mist.

Mansur drew his dagger, then half-replaced it. "It's the other. Stay here."

Still gasping with shock, Adelia watched him go forward to speak to Gervase of Coton, whose figure so much resembled that of a dead man, a Gervase who now seemed reduced and oddly diffident. He and the Arab strolled farther along the track and were lost to view. Their voices were a mumble. Mansur's English had improved these last weeks.

He came back alone. The three of them walked on together. "We send him a pot of snakeweed," Mansur said.

"Why?" Then, because everything normal had been cast adrift, Adelia grinned. "He's . . . Mansur, has he got the pox?"

"Other doctors have been of no help to him. The poor man has attempted these many days to consult me. He says he has watched the Jew's house for my return."

"I saw him. He scared the wits from me. I'll give him bloody snake-weed, I'll put pepper in it, I'll teach him to lurk on riverbanks. Him and his pox."

"You will be a doctor," Mansur reproved her. "He is a worried man, frightened of what his wife will say, Allah pity him."

"Then he should have been faithful to her," Adelia said. "Oh, tut, it'll go in time if it's gonorrhea." She was still grinning. "But don't tell him that."

It was lighter when they gained the gates toward the town, and they could see the Great Bridge. A flock of sheep was trotting over it, making for the shambles. Some students were stumbling home after a hard night out.

Puffing, Walburga said suddenly in disbelief, "But she were the best of us, the holiest. I admired her, she were so good."

"She had a madness," Adelia said. "There's no accounting for that."

"Where'd it come from?"

"I don't know." Always there, perhaps. Stifled. Doomed to chastity and obedience at the age of three. A chance meeting with a man who overpowered—Rowley had talked of Rakshasa's attraction for women. *"The Lord only knows why; he doesn't treat them well."* Had that coition of frenzy released the nun's derangement? Maybe, maybe. "I don't know," Adelia said again. "Take shallow breaths. Slowly, now."

A horseman cantered up as they arrived at the foot of the bridge. Sir Rowley Picot looked down at Adelia. "Am I to be given an explanation, mistress?"

"I explained to Prior Geoffrey. I am grateful and honored by your proposal. . . ." *Oh, this was no good.* "Rowley, I would have married you, nobody else, ever, *ever.* But . . ."

"Did I not fuck you nicely this morning?"

He was deliberately speaking English, and Adelia felt the nun beside her flinch at his use of the old Anglo-Saxon word. "You did," she said.

"I rescued you. I saved you from that monster."

"You did that, too."

But it had been the jumble of powers she and Simon of Naples possessed between them that had led to the discovery on Wandlebury Hill, despite her own misjudgment in going there alone.

Those same powers had led to the saving of Ulf. It had liberated the Jews. Though it had been mentioned by none except the king, their investigation had been a craft of logic and cold reason and . . . oh, very well, instinct, but instinct based on knowledge; rare skills in this credulous age, too rare to be drowned as Simon's had been drowned, too valuable to be buried, as hers would be buried in marriage.

All this Adelia had reflected on, in anguish, but the result had been inexorable. Though she had fallen in love, nothing in the rest of the world had changed. Corpses would still cry out. She had a duty to hear them.

"I am not free to marry," she said. "I am a doctor to the dead."

"They're welcome to you."

He spurred his horse and set it at the bridge, leaving her bereft and oddly resentful. He might at least have seen her and Walburga home.

"Hey," she yelled after him, "are you sending Rakshasa's head back east to Hakim?"

His reply floated back: "Yes, I bloody well am."

He could always make her laugh, even when she was crying. "Good," she said.

————

MUCH HAPPENED IN CAMBRIDGE that day.

The judges of the assize listened to and gave their verdict on cases of theft, of coin-clipping, street brawls, a smothered baby, bigamy, land disputes, ale that was too weak, loaves that were short, disputed wills, deodands, vagabondage, begging, shipmasters' quarrels, fisticuffs among neighbors, arson, runaway heiresses, and naughty apprentices.

At midday, there was a hiatus. Drums rolled and trumpets called the crowds in the castle bailey to attend. A herald stood on the platform before the judges to read from a scroll in a voice that reached to the town: "Let it be known that in the sight of God and to the satisfaction of the judges here present the knight yclept Joscelin of Grantchester has been proved vile murderer of Peter of Trumpington; Harold of Saint Mary Parish; Mary, daughter of Bonning the wildfowler, and Ulric of the parish of Saint John, and that the aforesaid Joscelin of Grantchester died during his capture as befitted his crimes, being eaten by dogs.

"Let it also be known that the Jews of Cambridge have been quitted of these killings and all suspicion thereof, whereby they shall be returned to their lawful homes and business without hindrance. Thus, in the name of Henry, King of England, under God."

There was no mention of a nun. The Church was silent on that matter. But Cambridge was full of whispers and, in the course of the afternoon, Agnes, eel seller's wife and mother to Harold, pulled apart the little beehive hut in which she had sat outside the castle gates since the death of her son, hauled its material down the hill, and rebuilt it outside the gates of Saint Radegund's convent.

All this was seen and heard in the open.

Other things were done in secrecy and darkness, though exactly who did them nobody ever knew. Certainly, men high in the ranks of Holy Church met behind closed doors where one of them begged,

"Who will rid us of this shameful woman?" just as Henry II had once cried out to be rid of the turbulent Becket.

What happened next behind those doors is less certain, for no directions were given, though perhaps there were insinuations as light as gnats, so light that it could not be said they had even been made, wishes expressed in a code so byzantine that it could not be translated except by those with the key to it. All this, perhaps, so that the men— and they were not clerics—who went down Castle Hill to Saint Rade-gund's could not be said to be acting on anyone's command to do what they did.

Nor even that they did it.

Possibly Agnes knew, but she never told anybody.

These things, both transparent and shadowed, passed without Adelia's knowledge. On Gyltha's orders, she slept round the clock. When she woke up, it was to find a line of patients winding down Jesus Lane, waiting for Dr. Mansur's attention. She dealt with the severe cases, then called a halt while she consulted Gyltha.

"I should go to the convent and look to Walburga. I've been remiss."

"You been mending."

"Gyltha, I don't want to go to that place."

"Don't then."

"I must; another attack like that could stop her heart."

"Convent gates is closed and nobody answering. So they say. And that, *that* . . ." Gyltha still couldn't bring herself to say the name. "She's gone. So they say."

"Gone? Already?" *Nobody dallies when the king commands,* she thought. *Le roi le veut.* "Where did they send her?"

Gyltha shrugged. "Just gone. So they say."

Adelia felt relief spreading down to her ribs and almost mending them. The Plantagenet had cleansed his kingdom's air so that she could breathe it.

Though, she thought, *in doing so, he has fouled another nation's. What will be done to her there?*

Adelia tried to avoid the image of the nun writhing as she had on the floor of the refectory but this time in filth and darkness and chains—and couldn't. Nor could she avoid concern; she was a doctor, and true doctors made no judgments, only diagnoses. She had treated the wounds and diseases of men and women who'd disgusted her humanity but not her profession. Character repelled; the suffering, needy body did not.

The nun was mad; for society's sake, she must be restrained for as long as she lived. But "the Lord pity her and treat her well," Adelia said.

Gyltha looked at her as if she, too, were a lunatic. "She's been treated like she deserves," she said stolidly. "So they say."

Ulf, for a miracle, was at his books. He was quieter and more grave than he had been. According to Gyltha, he was expressing a wish to become a lawyer. All very pleasing and admirable—nevertheless, Adelia missed the old Ulf.

"The convent gates are locked, apparently," she told him, "yet I need to get in to see Walburga. She's ill."

"What? Sister Fatty?" Ulf was suddenly back on form. "You come along of me; they can't keep me out."

Gyltha and Mansur could be trusted to treat the rest of the patients. Adelia went for her medicine chest; lady's slipper was excellent for hysteria, panic, and fearfulness. And rose oil to soothe.

She set off with Ulf.

On the castle ramparts, a tax collector who was taking a well-earned rest from assize business recognized two slight figures among the many crossing the Great Bridge below—he would have recognized the slightly larger one in the unattractive headgear among millions.

Now was the time, whilst she was out of the way. He called for his horse.

Why Sir Rowley Picot found himself compelled to ask advice for his bruised heart from Gyltha, eel seller and housekeeper, he wasn't sure. It may be because Gyltha was the closest female friend in Cambridge to the love of his life. Maybe because she had helped to nurse him back to life, was a rock of common sense, maybe because of the indiscretions of her past . . . he just did, and to hell.

Miserably, he munched on one of Gyltha's pasties.

"She won't marry me, Gyltha."

"'Course she won't. Be a waste. She's . . ." Gyltha tried to think of an analogy to some fabled creature, could only come up with "unicorn," and settled for "She's special."

"*I'm* special."

Gyltha reached up to pat Sir Rowley's head. "You're a fine lad and you'll go far, but she's . . ." Again, comparison failed her. "The good Lord broke the mold after He made her. Us needs her, all of us, not just you."

"And I'm not going to damn well get her, am I?"

"Not in marriage, maybe, but there's other ways of skinning a cat." Gyltha had long ago decided that the cat under discussion, special though it was, could do with a good, healthy, and continual skinning. A woman might keep her independence, just as she had herself, and could still have memories to warm the winter nights.

"Good God, woman, are you suggesting . . . ? My intentions toward Mistress Adelia are . . . were . . . *honorable*."

Gyltha, who had never considered honor a requisite for a man and a maid in springtime, sighed. "That's pretty. Won't get you nowhere, though, will it?"

He leaned forward and said, "Very well. How?" And the longing in his face would have melted a flintier heart than Gyltha's.

"Lord, for a clever man, you'm a right booby. She's a doctor, ain't she?"

"Yes, Gyltha." He was trying to be patient. "That, I would point out, is why she won't accept me."

"And what is it doctors do?"

"They tend their patients."

"So they do, and I reckon there's one doctor as might be tenderer than most to a patient, always supposing that patient was taken poorly and always supposing she was fond of un."

"Gyltha," Sir Rowley said earnestly, "if I wasn't suddenly feeling so damn ill, I'd ask *you* to marry me."

THEY SAW THE CROWD at the convent gates when they'd crossed the bridge and cleared the willows on the bank. "Oh, dear," Adelia said, "word has got around." Agnes and her little hut were there, like a marker to murder.

It was to be expected, she supposed; the town's anger had been transferred, and a mob was gathering against the nuns just as it had against the Jews.

It wasn't a mob, though. The crowd was big enough, artisans and market traders mainly, and there *was* anger, but it was suppressed and mixed with . . . what? Excitement? She couldn't tell.

Why weren't these people more enraged, as they had been against the Jews? Ashamed, perhaps. The killers had turned out to be not a despised group, but two of their own, one respected, one a trusted friend they waved to nearly every day. True, the nun had been sent away to where they couldn't lynch her, but they must surely blame Prioress Joan for her laxity in allowing a madwoman the terrible freedom she'd had for so long.

Ulf was talking with the thatcher whose foot Adelia had saved, both of them using the dialect in which Cambridge people spoke to each other and that Adelia still found almost incomprehensible. The young thatcher was avoiding her eye; usually, he greeted her with warmth.

Ulf, too, when he came back, wouldn't look at her. "Don't you go in there," he said.

"I must. Walburga is my patient."

"Well, I ain't coming." The boy's face had narrowed, as it did when he was upset.

"I understand." She shouldn't have brought him; for him, the convent had been home to a hag.

The wicket in the solid wooden gates was opening, and two dusty workmen were clambering out; Adelia saw her chance and, with an "excuse me," stepped in before they could close it. She shut it behind her.

The strangeness was immediate, as was the silence. Somebody, presumably the workmen, had nailed planks of wood diagonally across the church door that had once opened for pilgrims crowding to pray before the reliquary of Little Saint Peter of Trumpington.

How curious, Adelia thought, that the boy's putative status as a saint would be lost now that he'd been sacrificed not by Jews but Christians.

Curious, too, that the weedy untidiness ignored by an uncaring prioress should so quickly put on the appearance of decay.

Taking the path toward the convent building, Adelia had to prevent herself from thinking that the birds had stopped singing. They hadn't, but—she shivered—their note was different. Such was the imagination.

Prioress Joan's stable and mews were deserted. Doors hung open on empty horse boxes.

The sisters' compound was still. At the entrance to the cloister, Adelia found herself reluctant to go on. In the unseasonable grayness of the day, the pillars round the open grass were a pale remembrance of a night when she'd seen a horned and malevolent shadow in their center, as if the obscene desire of the nun had summoned it.

For heaven's sake, he's dead and she's gone. There's nothing here.

There was. A veiled shape was praying in the south walk as still as the stones it knelt on.

"Prioress?"

It didn't move.

Adelia went up to her and touched her arm. "Prioress." She helped her up.

The woman had aged overnight, her big, plain face etched deep and deformed into a gargoyle's. Slowly, her head turned. "What?"

"I've come to . . ." Adelia raised her voice; it was like talking to the deaf. "I've brought some medicines for Sister Walburga." She had to repeat it; she didn't think Joan knew who she was.

"Walburga?"

"She was ill."

"Was she?" The prioress turned her eyes away. "She's gone. They've all gone."

So the Church had stepped in.

"I'm sorry," Adelia said. And she was; there was something terrible in seeing a human being so deteriorated. Not just that, something terrible in the dying convent as if it were sagging; she had the impression that the cloister was tilting sideways. There was a different smell to it, another shape.

And an almost imperceptible sound, like the buzzing of an insect trapped in a jar, only higher.

"Where has Walburga gone?"

"What?"

"Sister Walburga. Where is she?"

"Oh." An attempt at concentration. "To her aunt's, I think."

There was nothing to do here, then; she could get away from this place. But Adelia lingered. "Is there anything I can do for you, Prioress?"

"What? Go away. Leave me alone."

"You're ill, let me help you. Is there anyone else here? Lord's sake, what is that *sound*?" Feeble as it was, it irritated the ear like tinnitus. "Don't you hear it? A sort of vibration?"

"It is a ghost," the gargoyle said. "It is my punishment to listen to it until it stops. Now go. Leave me to listen to the screams of the dead. Even you cannot help a ghost."

Adelia backed away. "I'll send somebody," she said, and for the first time in her life, she ran from the sick.

Prior Geoffrey. He'd be able to do something, take her away, though the ghosts haunting Joan would follow her wherever she went.

They followed Adelia as she ran, and she almost fell through the wicket in her hurry to get out.

Righting herself, she came face-to-face with the mother of Harold and couldn't look away. The woman was staring at her as if they shared a secret of supreme power.

Weakly, Adelia said, "She's gone, Agnes. They've sent her away. They've all gone; there's only the prioress. . . ."

It wasn't enough; a son had died. Agnes's terrible eyes said there was more; she knew it, they both knew it.

Then she did. All its parts fused into the one knowledge. The smell—so out of context she hadn't recognized the sour odor of fresh mortar for what it was. *God, God,* please. She'd seen it, a corner of her eye noting with dissatisfaction an imbalance that was the asymmetry of the nuns' pigeonholes which should have been ten on top of ten and had been ten on top of nine—a blank wall where the lower tenth cell should have been.

She understood. The silence with its vibration . . . like the buzzing of an insect trapped in a jar, *"the screams of the dead."*

Blind, Adelia stumbled through the crowd and vomited.

Somebody was tugging at her sleeve, saying something. "The king . . ."

The prior. He could stop it. She must find Prior Geoffrey.

The tugging became insistent. "The king commands your attendance, mistress."

In the name of Christ, how could they in Christ's name?

"The king, mistress . . ." Some liveried fellow.

"To hell with the king," she said. "I have to find the prior."

She was gripped by the waist and swung up onto a horse. It was trotting, the royal messenger loping alongside with its reins in his hands. "Better you don't send kings to hell, mistress," he said amiably. "They usually been there."

They were over the bridge, up the hill, through the castle gates, across the bailey. She was lifted off the horse.

In the sheriff's family garden, in which Simon of Naples lay buried, Henry II, who'd been to hell and returned, was sitting cross-legged on the same grass bank where she had sat and listened to Rowley Picot tell of his crusade. He was mending a hunting glove with needle and twine as he dictated to Hubert Walter, who knelt by his side, a portable writing table round his neck.

"Ah, mistress . . ."

Adelia flung herself at his feet. After all, a king might do. "They've walled her up, my lord. I beg you, stop it."

"Who's walled up? What am I to stop?"

"The nun. Veronica. Please, my lord, please. *They've walled her up alive.*"

Henry regarded his boots, which were being clutched at. "They told me they'd sent her to Norway. I thought that was odd. Did you know this, Hubert?"

"No, my lord."

"You've got to let her out, it's obscene, an abomination. Oh my God, my God, I can't live with this. She's mad. It's her madness that's evil." In her agony, Adelia's hands thumped the ground.

Hubert Walter lifted the little desk from his neck and then Adelia to sitting position on the bank, speaking gently as if to a horse, "Quietly, mistress. Steady. There, there, calmly now."

He passed her an inky handkerchief. Adelia, fighting for control, blew her nose on it. "My lord . . . my lord. They have walled up her cell in the convent with her inside. I heard her screaming. Whatever she did, this cannot . . . *cannot* be allowed. It is a crime against heaven."

"Seems a bit harsh, I must say," Henry said. "That's the Church for you. I'd have just hanged her."

"Well, *stop it*," Adelia shouted at him. "If she's without water . . . without water the human body can still survive three or four days, the *suffering*."

Henry was interested. "I didn't know that. Did you know that, Hubert?" He took the handkerchief from Adelia's fist and wiped her face with it, very sober now. "You realize I can't do anything, don't you?"

"No, I don't. The king is the king."

"And the Church is the Church. Were you listening last night? Then listen to me now, mistress." He slapped her hand as she turned her head away, then took it in his own. "*Listen* to me." He raised both their hands so that they pointed in the direction of the town. "Down there is a crazed tatterdemalion they call Roger of Acton. A few days ago, the wretch incited a mob to attack this castle, this royal castle, *my* castle, in the course of which your friend and my friend, Rowley Picot, was injured. And I can do nothing. Why? Because the wretch wears a tonsure on his head and can spout a paternoster, thus making him a clerk of the Church and entitled to benefit of clergy. Can I punish him, Hubert?"

"You kicked his arse for him, my lord."

"I kicked his arse for him, and even for that, the Church takes me to task."

Adelia's arm bobbed up and down as the king made his point with it. "After those damned knights interpreted my anger as instruction and rode to kill Becket, I had to submit to scourging by every member of Canterbury Cathedral's chapter. Humiliation, baring my back to their whips, was the only way to prevent the Pope laying all England under interdict. Every bloody monk—and believe me, those bastards can lay it on." He sighed and dropped Adelia's hand. "One day this country will be rid of papal rule, God willing. But not yet. And not through me."

Adelia had stopped listening, absorbing the gist perhaps but not the words. Now she got up and began to walk down the garden path toward the place where they'd buried Simon of Naples.

Hubert Walter, shocked by such lèse-majesté, would have gone after her but was restrained. He said, "You take great pains over that rude and recalcitrant female, my lord."

"I have a use for the useful, Hubert. Phenomena like her don't fall into my lap every day."

May was becoming itself at last, and the sun had emerged to enliven a garden refreshed by rain. Lady Baldwin's tansy had taken, bees were busy among the cowslips.

A robin that was perched on the grave hopped away at her approach, though not far. Stooping, Adelia used Hubert Walter's handkerchief to brush off its droppings.

We are among barbarians, Simon.

The wooden board had been replaced by a handsome slab of marble incised with his name and the words: *May his soul be bound up in the bond of life eternal.*

Kindly barbarians, Simon said to her now. *Fighting their own barbarity. Think of Gyltha, Prior Geoffrey, Rowley, that strange king . . .*

Nevertheless, Adelia told him, *I cannot bear it.*

She turned and, collected now, walked back up the path. Henry had returned to mending his glove and looked up at Adelia's approach. "Well?"

Bowing, Adelia said, "I thank you for your indulgence, my lord, but I can stay here no longer. I must return to Salerno."

He bit off the thread with his strong little teeth. "No."

"I beg your pardon?"

"I said no." The glove was put on, and Henry waggled his fingers, admiring the mending. "By the Lord, I'm clever. Must get it from the tanner's daughter. Did you know I had a tanner in my ancestry, mistress?" He smiled up at her. "I said no, you can't go. I have a need for your particular talents, Doctor. There are plenty of dead in my realm that I would wish to be listened to, by God there are, and I want to know what they say."

She stared at him. "You can't keep me here."

"Hubert?"

"I think you will find that he can, mistress," Hubert Walter said apologetically. "*Le roi le veut.* Even now on my lord's instructions, I am penning a letter to the King of Sicily, asking if we may borrow you a while longer."

"I'm not an object," Adelia shouted. "You can't borrow me, I'm a human being."

"And I'm a king," the king said. "I may not be able to control the Church, but, by my soul's salvation, I control every bloody port in this country. If I say you stay, you stay."

His face as he looked at her had a kindly disinterest, even in its pretended anger, and she saw that his amiability, the frankness so charming, was a mere tool helping him rule an empire and that, to him, she was nothing more than a gadget that might one day come in useful.

"I also am to be walled up, then," she said.

He raised his eyebrows. "I suppose you are, though I hope you will find your confines somewhat larger and more pleasing than . . . well, we won't talk of it."

Nobody will talk of it, she thought. *The insect will buzz in its bottle until it falls silent. And I shall have to live with the sound for the rest of my life.*

"I'd let her out if I could, you know," Henry said.

"Yes. I know."

"In any case, mistress, you owe me your services."

How long will I have to buzz before you let me *out?* she wondered. *The fact that this particular bottle has become beloved to me is neither here nor there.*

Though it was.

She was recovering now and able to think; she took time to do it. The king waited her out—an indication, she thought, of her value to him. *Very well, then, let me capitalize on it.* She said, "I refuse to stay in a country so backward that its Jews are afforded only the one burial ground in London."

He was taken aback. "God's teeth, aren't there any others?"

"You must know there are not."

"I didn't, actually," he said. "We kings have a great deal to concern ourselves with." He snapped his fingers. "Write it down, Hubert. The Jews to have burial grounds." And to Adelia: "There you are. It is done. *Le roi le veut.*"

"Thank you." She returned to the matter in hand. "As a matter of interest, Henry, in what way am I in your debt?"

"You owe me a bishop, mistress. I had hopes of Sir Rowley taking my fight into the Church, but he has turned me down to be free to marry. You, I gather, are the object of his marital affections."

"No object at all," she said wearily. "I, too, have turned him down. I am a doctor, not a wife."

"Really?" Henry brightened and then assumed a look of mourning. "Ah, but I fear neither of us will have him now. The poor man is dying."

"What?"

"Hubert?"

"So we understand, mistress," Hubert Walter said, "the wound he received in the attack on the castle has reopened, and a medical man from the town reports that—"

He found himself addressing empty air; lèse majesté again. Adelia had gone.

The king watched the gate slam. "Nevertheless, she's a woman of her word and, happily for me, she won't marry him." He stood up. "I believe, Hubert, that we may yet install Sir Rowley Picot as Bishop of Saint Albans."

"He will be gratified, my lord."

"I think he's going to be—any moment now, lucky devil."

THREE DAYS AFTER THESE EVENTS, the insect stopped buzzing. Agnes, mother of Harold, dismantled her beehive hut for the last time and went home to her husband.

Adelia didn't hear the silence. Not until later. At the time, she was in bed with the bishop-elect of Saint Albans.

THERE THEY GO, the justices in eyre, taking the Roman road from Cambridge toward the next town to be assized. Trumpets sound, bailiffs kick out at excited children and barking dogs to clear the way for the caparisoned horses and palanquins, servants urge on mules laden with boxes of closely written vellum, clerks still scribble on their slates, hounds respond to the crack of their masters' whip.

They've gone. The road is empty, except for steaming piles of manure. A swept and garnished Cambridge breathes a sigh of relief. At the castle, Sheriff Baldwin retires to bed with a wet cloth over his head while, in his bailey, corpses on the gallows move in a May breeze that flutters blossoms over them like a benison.

We have been too busied with our own events to watch the assize in action, but, if we had, we should have witnessed a new thing, a wonderful thing, a moment when English law leaped high, high, out of darkness and superstition into light.

For, during the course of the assize, nobody has been thrown into a pond to see if they are innocent or guilty of the crime of which they stand accused. (Innocence is to sink, guilt to float.) No woman has had molten iron placed in her hand to prove whether or not she has committed theft, murder, et cetera. (If the burn heals within a certain number of days, she is acquitted. If not, let her be punished.)

Nor has any dispute over land been settled by the God of Battles. (Champions representing each disputant fight until one or other is killed or cries "craven" and throws down his sword in surrender.)

No. The God of Battles, of water, of hot iron, has not been asked for His opinion as He always has before. Henry Plantagenet does not believe in Him.

Instead, evidence of crime or quarrel has been considered by twelve men who then tell the judge whether or not, in their opinion, the case is proved.

These men are called a jury. They are a new thing.

Something else is new. Instead of the ancient, jumbled inheritance of laws whereby each baron or lord of the manor can pronounce sentence on his malefactors, hanging or not according to his powers, Henry II has given his English a system that is orderly and all of a piece and applies throughout his kingdom. It will be called Common Law.

And where is he, this cunning king who has moved civilization forward?

He has left his judges to proceed about their business and has gone hunting. We can hear his hounds baying over the hills.

Perhaps he knows, as we know, that he will be remembered in popular memory only for the murder of Thomas à Becket.

Perhaps his Jews know—for we know—that, though they have been locally absolved, they still carry the stigma of ritual child murder and will be punished for it through the ages.

It is the way of things.

May God bless us all.

AUTHOR'S NOTE

It is almost impossible to write a comprehensible story set in the twelfth century without being anachronistic, in part at least. To avoid confusion, I've used modern names and terms. For instance, Cambridge was called Grentebridge or Grantebridge until the fourteenth century, well after the university had been founded. Also, the title of doctor was not given to medical men at that time, only to teachers of logic.

However, the operation described in chapter two is not an anachronism. The idea of using reeds as catheters to relieve a bladder that is under pressure from the prostate may make one wince, but I am assured by an eminent professor of urology that such a procedure has been performed throughout the ages—pictures illustrating it can be found in ancient Egyptian wall paintings.

The use of opium as an anesthetic is not described in medical manuscripts of that time as far as I know, probably because it would have caused an outcry by the Church, which believed in suffering as a form of salvation. But opium was available in England, especially the fenland, very early on, and it is unlikely that less pious and more caring doctors wouldn't have employed it in the same way that some ship's surgeons eventually did. (See *Rough Medicine* by Joan Druett; Routledge, 2000.)

Although I have added fictional missing children and located it in Cambridge, my story of Little Saint Peter of Trumpington is more or less a straight lift from the real-life mystery surrounding eight-year-old William of Norwich, whose death in 1144 began the accusation of ritual murder against the Jews of England.

Though there is no record of a sword belonging to Henry II's first-born being taken to the Holy Land, the sword of his next son, another Henry, known as the Young King, was carried there after his death by William the Marshal, thereby making him a posthumous crusader.

It was under Henry II that the Jews of England were first allowed to have their own local cemeteries—a grant made in 1177.

It is unlikely that there are mines in the chalk of Wandlebury hill-fort, but who knows? Neolithic miners digging out flint for knives and axes filled their pits with rubble once they'd exhausted them, leaving mere depressions in the grass to show where they had once been. Since Wandlebury became privately owned racing stables in the eighteenth century (it now belongs to the Cambridge Preservations Society), even these would then have been obliterated to make the land smooth for the horses.

So, for the sake of the story, I felt justified in transferring to Cambridgeshire one of the four hundred or so shafts discovered at Grime's Graves near Thetford in Norfolk. Even these amazing workings—the public is allowed to descend the thirty-foot ladder leading down into one of them—were not recognized for what they were until late in the nineteenth century, the depressions in the ground giving rise to the belief that they were burials, hence the name.

Last, the episcopal sees of twelfth-century England were fewer in number than today, and enormous. For a while, for instance, Cambridge came under the diocesan control of Dorchester in faraway Dorset. Therefore, the bishopric of Saint Albans is fictional.

ACKNOWLEDGMENTS

I have been particularly fortunate in the three fine editors who have guided the manuscript through to publication: Rachel Kahan of Penguin Group USA, Francesca Liversidge of Transworld UK, and David Davadar of Penguin Canada. My gratitude to them all.

As for my agent, Helen Heller, bless her, she knows how deeply indebted I am to her.

ABOUT THE AUTHOR

Ariana Franklin, a former journalist, is a biographer and author of the novel *City of Shadows.* She lives in England.